# BITTER HEAT

## (Heat of Love, Book 3)

## LETA BLAKE

An Original Publication from Leta Blake Books

Bitter Heat (Heat of Love #3)
Written and published by Leta Blake
Cover by Dar Albert
Formatted by BB eBooks

First Edition, 2019
Print Edition

ISBN: 979-8-88841-005-9

# Other Books by Leta Blake

Any Given Lifetime
Mr. Frosty Pants
The River Leith
Smoky Mountain Dreams
Angel Undone
Raise Up Heart
The Difference Between
Heat for Sale
Omega Mine: Search for a Soulmate
Bring on Forever

**The Training Season Series**
Training Season
Training Complex

**Heat of Love Series**
Slow Heat
Slow Birth
Alpha Heat
Bitter Heat
Winter's Heart
Winter's Truth

**Stay Lucky Universe**
Stay Lucky
Stay Sexy

**'90s Coming of Age Series**
Pictures of You
You Are Not Me

**Co-Authored with Indra Vaughn**
Vespertine
Cowboy Seeks Husband

**Co-Authored with Alice Griffiths**
The Wake Up Married serial
Will & Patrick's Endless Honeymoon

**Gay Fairy Tales**
**Co-Authored with Keira Andrews**
Flight
Levity
Rise

**Audiobooks**
Leta Blake at Audible

**Free Read**
Stalking Dreams

**Discover more about the author online:**
Leta Blake
letablake.com

## Gay Romance Newsletter

Leta's newsletter will keep you up to date on her latest releases and news from the world of M/M romance. Join the mailing list today. letablake.com

## Leta Blake on Patreon

Become part of Leta Blake's Patreon community in order to access exclusive content, deleted scenes, extras, bonus stories, rewards, prizes, interviews, and more.
www.patreon.com/letablake

# Acknowledgements

Thank you to the following:

West Virginia

Mom & Dad

Brian & Cecily

Kim V for her friendship and understanding.

All the wonderful members of my Patreon who inspire, support, and advise me.

Keira Andrews and Elizah Davis for their generous friendship and handholding on the regular.

Thank you to Devon Vesper for the thorough edits and passionate cheerleading.

Catherine Marshall and her book *Christy*, which inspired me in one way as a child and now in a different way as an adult. Amanda Palmer and her song "Voicemail for Jill," which helped inform how I handled aspects of this story.

A.M. Arthur for loving the *Heat of Love* universe so much that she made up her own Omegaverse books. Look for *Breaking Free*!

And thank you to my readers who make all the blood, sweat, and tears of writing worthwhile.

You all have my heart!

**A pregnant omega trapped in a desperate situation. An unattached alpha with a lot to prove. And an unexpected fall into love that could save them both.**

Kerry Monkburn is contracted to a violent alpha in prison for brutal crimes. Now pregnant with the alpha's child, he lives high in the mountains, far above the city that once lured him in with promises of a better life. Enduring bitterness and fear, Kerry flirts with putting an end to his life of darkness, but fate intervenes.

Janus Heelies has made mistakes in the past. In an effort to redeem himself, integrity has become the watchword for his future. Training as a nurse under the only doctor willing to take him on, Janus is resolute in his intentions: he will live cleanly in the mountains and avoid all inappropriate affairs. But he doesn't anticipate the pull that Kerry exercises on his heart and mind.

As the question of Kerry's future health and safety comes to an explosive head, only the intervention of fate will see these desperate men through to a happy ending.

This gay romance novel by Leta Blake is the third in the Heat of Love universe, which began with Slow Heat. It's 111,000 words, with **a strong happy ending** and a well-crafted, **non-shifter Omegaverse**. It features alphas, betas, omegas, male pregnancy, **heat**, and **knotting**. Content warning for a violent and oppressive society regarding reproductive rights.

*For Marsha,*
*I love and miss you.*
*Wish you were here to read this one.*

CONTENT WARNING: This novel deals with sexual and reproductive issues in an oppressive society with the resulting issues of violation and unwanted pregnancy. There may be content within that could stir feelings related to sexual violation, pregnancy loss, or abortion. Proceed with care.

# PROLOGUE

THE PRISON SMELLED like piss and fear.

The scent had soaked into Kerry's clothes and hair during the days he'd spent locked inside. It choked him even as guards led him away from the prison's black iron gates and barbed-wire-covered walls. The bruises all over his body from his alpha's rough treatment made the guards' manhandling difficult to bear, but he didn't have the energy to protest or the strength to cry out.

The guard on his right, the one who spoke with a deep, sub-Calitan accent, placed a hand on top of his head to prevent hitting it against the roof of the waiting, chauffeured car as the guard on his left maneuvered him inside. As if that small gesture was going to cushion him from injury—too little, too late.

"He's clear," the guard said, his accent thick, before ducking down to regard Kerry with carefully tempered sympathy in his eyes. Kerry thought he might be the same guard who'd cared for him after the heat had ended last time, too. "Have a safe trip home, all right?"

Kerry didn't acknowledge him. He was too dazed to speak after his long ordeal. Aching all over from head to hole and down to his toes and back again, he wanted to cry, but tears didn't come. His legs quaked, too exhausted from days of enforced heat spent with his imprisoned, contracted alpha, only sustained throughout by disgusting prison food and the primal urges he wished he could snuff out.

Almost as much as he wished *he* could be snuffed out.

Safe in the backseat of a plush, Monhundy-owned car, driven by a man hired by his wealthy in-laws and entrusted with Kerry's well-being, he smoothed his now-wrinkled silk shirt with shaking hands. He didn't understand why his in-laws always insisted he dress nicely when he came for these visits. No one saw him in his clothes but guards and prison officials. He was naked by the time they led him to Wilbet. But the Monhundys would never approve of Kerry appearing in "public" looking anything but well-heeled.

Outside, the sun poured down—the heat of summer already in full blaze in the arid county around the prison. The air fairly shimmered with heat, and he longed for the cool shadows of his beloved mountains, the wetness of the lake, and his pater's comforting embrace.

Kerry pressed the tips of his fingers to his eyelids, blocking out the light, as gorge rose in his throat. This was the third heat his in-laws forced him to endure since Wilbet went to prison for the rape of Calitan district prostitutes, and each was more humiliating and violent than the last. There had been times leading up to this heat when he'd considered taking matters into his own hands. A knife, a gun, a rope—it didn't matter what he used. All that mattered was stopping the trauma before it started again.

But he couldn't do that to his pater. The Monhundys and their heartless desire for an heir of their son's flesh and blood could be wolf-goddamned as far as Kerry was concerned. But his pater needed him. It'd tear a hole in his heart too large to ever heal if Kerry acted on his urges to end things.

After Kerry had settled in the backseat, the driver pulled the car away from the prison, jostling over the potholes lining the road in front of it. Pain shot through Kerry's core, and he caught a whiff of Wilbet's semen still lodged inside, left over from the last knot they'd shared. It now slipped free. Just like the first two heats after Wilbet's conviction, the prison guards, armed with guns to keep

Wilbet's violent impulses in check, had ignored any non-lethal abuse Wilbet wanted to pile on. They'd only pulled Kerry away from his alpha and out of the heat room when the last wave had finally, completely passed. Like always, they'd had a doctor examine him for any serious injury, watched him dress with shaking limbs, and finally sent him away without a shower or a bath.

Like always.

The prison scent lingered, yes, but as far as Kerry was concerned, Wilbet's scent was far worse. His contracted mate was anathema to him now, and yet Kerry was still legally bound to him so long as the Monhundy family refused to dissolve their side of the agreement. In fact, his in-laws now legally held the reins on Kerry's life choices, finances, and heats since Wilbet's incarceration. It was a side notation in the contract that Kerry had never thought to question, never imagining it would come to fruition. He'd been more concerned about the dissolution of the contract in the event of Wilbet's untimely death—and *that* had been negotiated in his favor. He'd failed to take into account other contingency clauses.

Another slip of semen led his stomach to rebel hard. Kerry managed to alert the driver to his predicament, and the car pulled over to the side of the road with a quick jerk. Kerry shoved the heavy door open, leaned out, and vomited onto the road. The rancid foulness heaved up from deep inside like poison from his soul.

"Reckon it took, then?" the driver said when Kerry wiped his mouth with a crumpled handkerchief and sat back in his seat. Kerry pulled the car door closed again with a weak slam. "Going to be a pater, you think?"

Kerry swallowed back another heave and said nothing, staring out the window. Tears welled in his eyes as they drove away from the behemoth of a prison. It stood—a solid, dark brick building full of shiver-inducing cruelty—backlit by a white sun and a hot, blank sky. As blank as Kerry's future, and just as empty.

Smoothing a hand over his shirt again, and wishing he had a jacket to stop his chills, Kerry closed his eyes to pray to wolf-god that there would be no child. He prayed for a solution. A way out of his wretched life. Most of all, he prayed for freedom.

Because he'd never dare pray for love again.

# PART ONE

## Late Spring

# CHAPTER ONE

THE TWO-STORY, WHITE boarding house was tucked into the mountains five hours southeast of the city and an hour and a half from the nearest supply town. The ride up from the train station in the rickety wagon had left Janus tired and aching all over. After paying the waggoneer—a beta with a grizzled, brown beard and a lot of missing teeth—Janus sent him away, choosing to handle his two medium-sized suitcases himself. Behind him, the afternoon sun set in a ridge of the mountains, lighting a fire in the windows of the house and reflecting the orange radiance of the sky.

He gazed up at the place he'd chosen to be his home for the next year. The steep, angled roofline high above the second story and sparkling clean windows beneath the eaves indicated a well-tended attic space. The stone path going to the porch and around the side of the house was meticulously cared for and weeded. The house had been newly painted sometime in the last few years. There were several storage buildings at the edge of the lawn cleared away from the encroaching mountainside, and they stood in good order, as well. All this was clear evidence of the boarding house being owned by a proud and decent man.

It was also evidence that this new home would share none of the opulence of any of the numerous Heelies-funded apartments and mansions Janus had lived in throughout his life. He had no doubt that with time, these new circumstances would put his resolve to be independent to the test for sure. Yet, there was nothing he could find from a thorough study of the boarding house's exterior to note as a real complaint. It was the kind of place many less entitled men would find quite nice, if not grand. Only the very spoiled, like himself, would ever turn up their noses at the earnest modesty of it all.

Janus hefted his luggage, making his way from the driveway to the bottom of the steps leading up to a wide, wraparound porch. There he paused, taking it all in again, searching for doubts inside, half-expecting to find them easily. And yet, he uncovered nothing of the kind.

After spending too much of his life at the tit of his uncle Doxan Heelies' fortune, Janus had determined to make his own way for better or worse. Even in the face of a clapboard house with little more than running water and apparent cleanliness to recommend it, he remained determined. It was both a matter of pride *and* part of his likely fruitless attempt to improve himself as a person.

*Be careful*, he warned himself sternly as he gazed up at the blue shutters and the sturdy roofline. He shouldn't write the experiment off as a failure before he truly began. No matter how doomed his cousin Xan seemed to think his personal reform might be, he had Caleb's encouraging words to cling to even if he *had* lost the beautiful omega himself. Janus sighed as a familiar sadness washed over his heart.

Now *there* was the regret he'd been looking for. He'd committed far too many mistakes in his past—errors of vanity, egoism, and hubris—but hurting Caleb was the worst of them. He'd let the brilliant, handsome man down, and all because of his ego and his selfish focus on prurient needs.

Janus shook those thoughts away. Caleb was happy now. He'd embraced the most unlikely of lives and found joy in it. For his part, Janus had accepted that he'd lost any chance with Caleb years ago, and he hoped he'd find a way to embrace life and joy, as well. With any luck, this new path would help him. Wolf-god knew his old ways of coping hadn't brought those virtues to him.

Mounting the four stairs up to the wooden porch, he dropped one of his bags long enough to press the ringer beside the blue front door. A trill came from deep in the house, like a fast-repeating hammer on a brass bell. While he waited, he sat the other bag down to brush his hands over his wavy, stylishly overlong, brown hair. It wasn't quite chin-length, but it was far from the tightly shorn buzz he'd worn during the worst of the illnesses he'd endured the last several winters.

Then he double-checked his clothing. His tailored, brown traveling suit was a bit dusty and wrinkled from the road and didn't quite fit him as well as it had before his last bout of pneumonia. He slapped at the dirt near the bottom of his trousers and jerked at the hem of his suit coat, trying to get it to lay a bit nicer.

He supposed the owner of the boarding house would accept him whether he looked a mess or not, especially since he was likely paying enough to keep the place in coal and electricity through the winter on his rent alone. Still, it didn't hurt to show some respect. He'd come to that understanding a bit late in life, but he'd learned it well.

He wondered what was keeping the innkeeper from answering. The beta who owned the place had been eager enough in their correspondence. So, surely, Janus was expected.

A rustle came from around the corner of the house along with a deep creak of the porch floorboards. And then another.

Janus stepped away from the front door, plastering a friendly smile on his face. "Hello?" he called toward the obscuring corner. "Anyone home?"

The rustle came again, along with a screech—the sound of wood rubbing on wood as though someone dragged a chair from one location to another. Janus wiped his still-sweaty hands on his pantlegs. He frowned and squinted back toward the driveway, long empty since the waggoneer had driven away. He searched the grounds for signs of the owner with the falling sun blinding his eyes. He turned to the door again, standing on tiptoe to try to get a look through the glass panes at the top. The shadowed hallway showed no one coming to greet him.

Finally, after ringing the bell once more to no avail, Janus left his bags by the doorway to investigate the noises that had come from the side of the house. Perhaps the owner was outside doing some necessary labor—in the garden, for example—and hadn't heard the bell ring or his call of greeting. Betas were known for being hard workers, and the man probably hadn't wanted to sit around waiting for Janus's arrival.

Peeking his head around the corner, he caught a glimpse of a plain, wooden rocking chair, and a figure ensconced in it. The man had a cozy-looking, gray blanket over him, and his long, dark, wavy hair flew in the breeze, dancing in loose, snaky tendrils. The swirling wind drifted up from the next interesting sight to catch Janus's eye—a spotless sparkle of the wide, green-blue lake. Hud's Basin was known for its soul-repairing loveliness and had been touted as one of the more appealing features of this particular boarding house. Though, being the only boarding house in the area, Janus couldn't claim that had been the true deciding factor.

Still, it was a beautiful lake. Hud's Basin stretched away between the evergreen trees, separated from the house by a patch of thick woods. His mouth watered just looking at the brilliant, enticing circle of water, and Janus could just imagine the pleasure of diving into it on a hot summer's day. Dusty and sweaty from travel, the thought appealed to him even now.

A scent like summer-ripe berries drifted to Janus on the breeze, along with a shocking, raw musk. That was an omega in the rocking chair, then. His pheromones were strong and seemed to shimmer in the air between them. A shiver shot up Janus's spine, and he leaned into the scent, inhaling again. A sudden hooking sensation hit him in his gut, and an arousing tingle began throughout his body as though every cell was responding to this man. It was nearly strong enough to make him groan. The chair rocked again, and the creak of wood-on-wood sounded plaintive.

Janus cleared his throat to form a greeting but was interrupted before he could.

"Can I help you?" The sharp voice came from behind him, and Janus jerked around again. His heart was beating extraordinarily fast, as though he'd been caught doing something wrong. His tongue felt frozen, and he blinked in confusion.

The formerly unforthcoming front door was now open wide, and a gray-haired beta who could only be the boarding house's owner stood at the threshold.

"Ah, hello!" Janus said, gathering his wits with a wide smile. He turned his back on the mysterious figure in the rocking chair, and hastily stepped toward the front entrance. The kind-looking man before him wore common brown pants, and a clean, if plain, white button-up shirt. He held a broom in one hand and wore a flour-dusted, brown apron.

Putting out his hand, Janus began the introductions, "I'm Janus Heelies and—"

"And you'll be staying with us a spell," the beta interrupted with a wide grin, gray eyes crinkling at the sides. He put the broom aside and held the front door open a bit wider. "Yes, we've been expecting you.

He smiled at Janus, ushering him forward. "Well, let's grab your things. I'll get you up to the room we've readied. I'm sure you're tired."

As they entered the house together, Janus assessed the physical state of his host. The beta had gray hair, yes, but he wasn't elderly so much as solidly middle-aged. He was thin, pale, and didn't appear in the best health, but didn't seem actively ill either. He had a bustling energy about him that spoke to a kind of determined personality that Janus admired in any man, but particularly in betas. If he was a little pale, and a bit worn around the edges, then so be it.

Given the recent bout of pneumonia Janus was recovering from, he didn't have any room to be particularly proud of his own health or looks. His appearance had taken quite the beating with each successive winter of sickness, and he was only just gaining weight back. He hoped that Hud's Basin's distance from the cesspool of germs in the city would give him some reprieve from being infected again with the worst of the wintertime maladies.

Regardless, he was hardly the outrageously handsome young man he'd once been. He'd flashed his hazel eyes and charming smile at plenty of omegas over the years—and some betas, too—and ended up in some terribly scandalous situations. But after the toll of his sicknesses, he'd scarcely be able to attract a scandalous affair, even if he still wanted to partake in any.

"I take it you're the proprietor?" Janus asked, clutching his bags as the man removed his floury apron and hung it on a rack by the door.

"Yes, indeed. Apologies." The beta wiped his hands off on the front of his soft, brown pants, and then put out a hand. "Zeke Monkburn. Welcome to Monk's House at Hud's Basin. We're glad to have you."

Zeke took one of Janus's bags off his hands, and the two of them muscled past the furniture crowding the downstairs entry-way—a sideboard, the coatrack, three chairs, and a full bookshelf—and past a living room on the right. They passed three closed-off boarding rooms on the left and then headed up the dark, wooden stairs to the second story.

"I'll give you the house tour whenever you'd like," Zeke said with a smile over his shoulder. "But the kitchen is easy to suss out, and the livin' room, too. Feel free to use both at your discretion. What brings you up to Hud's Basin?"

Janus shifted his bag from one arm to the other, feeling annoyingly out of breath after only a few of the oddly steep steps. He wished Zeke would move faster so that he didn't have to keep carrying the luggage. His arm muscles already ached. "Dr. Crescent mainly. I'll be studying under him."

"Ah. I'd wondered why you'd taken on a place boarding here for such a long spell. Most of our patrons come up for a season at most." As he reached the top of the stairs, Zeke looked over his shoulder, down to Janus still trudging up. "You plan to be a doctor?"

"A nurse for now." Janus smiled, hefting his bag a bit higher. "I've had some health scares in recent years, and they've taught me the value of good medical care. I'd like to share that forward." And he hoped to make something good of his life now that it'd been saved again. Too many had died in the recent flu epidemics. He owed it to those who'd lost their lives not to waste his in gambling, fighting, and pushing the boundaries by sleeping with contracted omegas. Or so Caleb had insisted when they'd last talked. And Janus had reluctantly believed him because he was too tired to believe anything else. "I'm looking forward to working with Dr. Crescent and learning all he has to teach me, but I'm also eager for a chance to live a slower life up here in the mountains."

"Slower, eh? Well, I guess that depends on how you look at it. Still in need of some recuperating?" Zeke asked as Janus met him on the second-floor landing.

Together, they started down the hall. The wooden planks looked freshly swept and polished, gleaming in the light from the window at the end of the hall.

Paper that must be as old as Janus himself covered the walls, decorated all over by images of happy-looking stags, evergreen trees, and the occasional fawn. The paper was old-fashioned, out of date, but somehow homey in a way Janus wanted to crawl into. It made him dream of becoming a boy again and traipsing among those copses of painted trees.

"Been sick of late, have you?" Zeke asked again.

Shaking free of fanciful thoughts that were more common than ever after his various illnesses, he replied, "Yes. I've had a rough time of it these last few years."

"The flu, I imagine." Zeke shook his head, side-stepping a narrow table pressed up against the wall along the length of the hall.

"Indeed. I just recently recovered from a third bout resulting in pneumonia. My lungs haven't been the same since I nearly died during the epidemic four years ago."

Zeke tutted gently. "Each winter now we get a goodly number of folks in from the city trying to avoid being infected. Last year's epidemic was almost as bad as that big one four years back." Zeke paused outside a thick, dark bedroom door and put Janus's bag on the floor, turning to him with his hands on his hips. "I was sick myself for that one. Quite sick." His eyes took on a distant look for a moment, but then he went on. "At the first sign of contagion these days, those who can afford it hightail it out of the city, and many of them come up to these mountains as fast as their wallets can carry them." A comfortable mountain accent and phrasing marked Zeke's speech.

Janus found it charming, and that pleased him. The old Janus would have given into ingrained snobbery and decided the man lacked brains along with any semblance of education. The new Janus was done with that ego-driven, us-versus-them mindset. Zeke was clearly an intelligent, kind man with much to offer—including, hopefully, some sort of tea soon—and the new Janus would be happy to learn a thing or two from him.

Yes, the new Janus wanted to learn and to help however he

could.

Zeke opened the door with a key from his pocket. He went on, "We have three rooms for boarders downstairs, and four of the six upstairs are for boarders, too. We can host up to fourteen men in the house if they all share beds. But we just lost the last of our lingering boarders from this past winter's influx. They packed up and moved on last week."

"It'll be just me in the house then?" Janus asked as Zeke led him into a well-appointed bedroom facing out over the back of the house.

Janus stopped in the doorway, arrested by the view out the window of the shimmering lake, and the shadowy rise of mountains beyond. The sashes were open, and the breeze sailed into the room, offering fresh, cool air. Again, he detected the delicious scent of ripe berries and musk coming from the omega in the rocking chair. The porch where the omega sat must be just beneath his window.

"Yes. Well, no…" Zeke frowned, a slump rounding his shoulders. "My son is staying for some time, as well. He is…" Zeke seemed confused about how to describe the situation. He smiled distractedly and finished with, "Also on the mend."

"Your son?" Janus cocked his head, confused. Betas couldn't have children. He thought of the dark-haired figure he'd scented on the side porch and fought an irrational shiver.

"My nephew technically," Zeke clarified. "But I've raised him since his pater died trying to birth a brother for 'im. So, he's mine as much as anyone's, I suppose."

It would be complicated sharing space with Zeke's son. He'd smelled … unique. Not like Janus's *Érosgápe* mate would smell (not that he even knew what that scent would be, having never found the mate promised by wolf-god to alphas), but he had an intriguingly distinct scent.

"He calls me pater, and I call him son. There's naught but love between us."

Janus smiled, stepping deeper into the well-furnished if somewhat modest room. It held a bed with thick layers of quilts and two big pillows, a wooden writing desk by the window, a chest of drawers, a nightstand, and a cream-colored rug next to the bed. On the walls were four common-looking landscape paintings showing the mountains in each season. "Family is based on love. I understand. My uncle also had a hand in raising me."

Zeke threw open the closet and bathroom doors. "You'll find everything in good order—a closet for your things, a bathroom dedicated to your sole use. The fireplace won't be wanted this summer, but it'll be a comfort in the winter months. And there's a view more pleasant than any other in the house if I do say so myself." Zeke gave a wide smile as he gestured toward the windows. "I opened the sashes earlier to air out any musty scent from where the room's been closed off, but you can close them back up or keep them open as you see fit."

"The view is spectacular," Janus agreed. He put the bag he carried down on the soft, quilt-covered bed as his gaze drifted back to the scene outside. As he traced the lines of mountains and the curve of the lake, he wondered briefly about Zeke's sudden turn away from discussion of family. If his "son's" pater had died, where was the alpha father in the scheme of things? Had he been too heartbroken at the loss of his omega to care for the child? Or had there even been a contract at all?

Things were different in the mountains. Everyone knew that. In the city, an unbonded and uncontracted omega finding himself pregnant was looked down on in ways that he wouldn't be here. The more puritanical dictates of the Holy Book of Wolf were often scorned here in the mountains in favor of more traditional ways. Old styles of breeding—including the occasional alpha free-for-all over a single omega in heat—were still permitted. Much to the horror of city tourists when they stumbled upon the villagers in the throes of such brutish behavior.

For all he knew, this son could be born of those old traditions. He wondered why he cared about the omega's pedigree. It wasn't as though he was going to pursue the man. He was done with that sort of business.

The lake wavered with the breeze, and the tossing waters reflected the sky, blue as a robin's egg, and the verdant green of the trees. The lake became a shimmering mirror of the immediate world around them, not a single brutal thing about it. The scent of berry and musk only added to the loveliness. Janus's shoulders relaxed. He could almost feel the peace of the view seeping into him, healing the places that still hurt, body and soul. He smiled softly.

"Yes, this will do," he murmured loudly enough that Zeke must have heard because when he turned around again the man was grinning.

"Glad to hear it. One last thing, the candles are in the drawer by the bed along with matches to light them. We have electricity in the house during the summer months until nine at night, but then it's out until the dawn."

"Why's that?" Janus asked. He knew a lot of places in the mountains had no electricity at all, and he'd half expected to suffer the use of candles exclusively, but why would they have electricity only part of the time?

"Expensive to run," Zeke said with the smallest of bristles. "There's one charging station on the mountain and the alpha who owns it has a love of profit. We pay him monthly, and he gives us our allotment according to his rules. So, we're shut off after nine. We used to have a few battery-powered lamps, but the batteries ran out faster than we liked and are more expensive to replace than candles. Most boarders don't mind any."

"I don't mind either," Janus said, surprised. He wondered if he could ask Caleb to send him a battery-powered lamp or two from the city, and some extra batteries, too. Then he thought better of that. "Provided there are plenty of candles."

Zeke gave him a long look. "You'll be up late often, you reckon?"

"I might. I'll have studying to do."

"That you may, but I expect Doc would rather have you rested once you begin the rounds with him."

"I expect so," Janus equivocated, subconsciously mimicking the man's mountain phrasing. "Is it the same with the water?" Janus asked. "Limited amounts or times for use? Any need for special heating when it comes to a bath or shower?"

"No, we've got plenty of running water from the creeks that feed the lake, and the newest tanks to warm it, too. Our guests never have to worry about bathing." Zeke sounded proud of that. "How about I put together some nice warm tea and cake to break your traveling fast? The weather is cool enough to warrant hot tea, don't you agree? Or do you prefer it cold?"

The breeze up from the lake coming through the window held a nice chill that felt good after the dusty, hot travel, but it could indicate a cold night ahead. "Hot," Janus said, nodding at the man. "Hot tea would be perfect."

"Yes, I agree." He winked. "Until it gets around midsummer, and then it's got to be cool tea."

Janus tilted his head and queried, "I understand the true heat of summer isn't for another month or so?"

"Indeed. If we get much heat at all." The man motioned toward the hills behind the lake. "The mountains protect us a might, and we've been known to wear light sweaters even into the thick of the summer season. It's hotter down in the city, I hear—no place for the air to escape. Not enough trees to help it breathe. Trees are wolf-god's lungs, you see. And through them, he exhales life into all of us."

Such statements were to be expected in these parts. The mountain people were different from city folk. They held old-fashioned beliefs that even the Holy Church of Wolf hadn't been able to stamp out—ideas about the inherent magic of the earth, trees, sun, sky, and water. They believed that each natural element lived in essential harmony with wolf-god's children. The mountain folk scorned science as much as the conservative beliefs of the old Church. They had their own ways of being, living, healing, and birthing. These were beliefs Janus wanted to learn more about, if only so he could help the mountain people embrace the scientific discoveries of modern health care.

"Now, unless you have questions, I'll leave you to settle in. There'll be tea ready for you in a jiffy. Just pop down. And dinner tonight will be pot pies at six, which isn't long from now. The sun's almost gone, isn't it? Anyway, I expect we'll have more to plan as far as a meal routine goes, especially once you're deeper into your work with Dr. Crescent. But for now, you should settle in and relax."

"I will. Thank you."

It didn't take long to unpack his things. He hadn't brought much. Janus chuckled under his breath remembering his personal beta servant, Wallace, begging him to please take another bag. "Surely, you'll need your tuxedo, Mr. Heelies? And a good hunting jacket?"

He'd told him that he didn't imagine he'd require a tuxedo ever again with his new station in life. Nor would he be hunting much more than squirrel out this way, but even a more organized hunt for deer or wild turkeys wouldn't be formal. No, in the mountains, they'd be more likely to wear threadbare dungarees and shirts that had long seen better days. Not that he'd been able to bring himself to actually buy dungarees despite knowing the mountains would undoubtedly ruin his current wardrobe in no time flat.

Poor Wallace had looked near tears about Janus's refusal to take the clothing, but Janus hadn't given in, not even for the sweet old man. Wallace had been hired by his cousin Ray to handle him during his last round of illness, and the beta servant was an old-fashioned sort of man.

Janus sighed, remembering the circumstances that had led to Wallace joining his household in the city. Upon realizing he was incredibly sick yet again, Janus had been tempted to request respite back at Xan's house under Caleb's care once more. He loved Caleb's way with him, the sound of his voice reading a book to keep his mind off the illness, and his long, pale fingers combing through his hair with a cool, soothing touch. But that would have been unkind to everyone—not to mention dangerous to Caleb's children. Luckily, Ray had seen that selfish idea put to rest when he'd hired Wallace.

And Wallace had been a good servant and a kind man, reading aloud to Janus when he'd been at his most restless, and helping him in the most intimate of ways. They'd grown quite close. It'd been hard to leave him behind, but Janus wouldn't indulge in extravagances he couldn't afford on his own. And servants were a definite extravagance.

He hung his suits and other clothes up in the closet, dusting them off, and seeing them almost as much to rights as Wallace would have done. Then he laid out his shaving supplies and toothbrush in the attached bathroom. He checked, and yes, hot water was at the ready in the old-fashioned, deep tub—no shower, apparently. That was fine. He'd have to fold himself in some contortions to fit in the small bathtub, but he'd keep clean. The towels were a bit worn, but not entirely threadbare. They'd do, along with the soft blankets on the bed that had seen better days...or years. This was reality as it fit his current and future income, and he found it didn't trouble him nearly as much as he'd thought it would.

Coming out of the bathroom after putting all his things away, he found a tray with tea and cake on the writing desk near the window. He sat down to enjoy it and write in his journal as he admired the view. After recording his thoughts, he attempted a drawing of the lake and other doodles until nearly six, long after the tea went cold.

Smelling food downstairs, he left his room and started down the hallway, noting the closed doors on the opposite side of the hall, two rooms empty of boarders for the moment, and a third that might be Zeke's son's room. On Janus's side of the hall, there were also three doors. The one immediately next to him was also shut off, but the one right at the top of the stairs stood nearly two-thirds open. Janus heard a movement from within and wondered if that was, perhaps, Zeke's room. He stepped up to the threshold to ask if dinner was ready downstairs.

But it wasn't Zeke's room.

Inside was a space of stark simplicity—white sheets over a serviceable bed, a rocking chair similar to the one on the back porch, a table with a lamp, and a slim chest of drawers. There were two used candles by the bedside on a small nightstand, and one new one ready for use in a holder.

There was also a birdcage. An ornate, gilded birdcage that looked to be worth more than the value of the entire contents of the room.

At the open window, perched on the wide windowsill, a man sat basking in the final rays of the dying sunlight. His white, long-sleeved shirt was open halfway down, billowing in the air currents, and his dark pants were tailored to fit his slim, well-formed legs. His long, wavy, dark-brown hair was loose, as it had been when Janus caught a glimpse of him on the porch, and it, too, moved in the breeze from the open window.

*This* was the omega he'd scented. Janus took a deep breath, catching the berries and musk again.

The omega cooed inaudibly to the small, brilliant blue and green bird that sat in his open palm. The round O of his pale lips the only indication of noise at all, that and the cock of the bird's head as it listened intently.

His lean muscles were visible in the sunset glow through the pale white shirt, strong lines that were stark but not bulky, and as he lifted the bird higher, the odd shape of his chest—a bit concave if Janus's eyes didn't deceive—was revealed.

The man went very still. The room seemed to hold its breath, and Janus did too until the man slowly, very slowly turned his head to meet Janus's gaze. A jolt went through Janus, and he sucked in a sharp breath. The man's eyes were the color of tinted, backlit, amber-colored pharmacy glass and full of wary hostility. The moment caught and hung. Janus blinked and opened his mouth, but no words came out. Likewise, the man said nothing, only sitting motionless on the sill with the bird now trotting about on his palm and lifting its bright wings as though to take flight.

"Hello," Janus finally managed, his throat strangely dry. "Pardon me. I didn't mean to intrude."

Nothing.

"I was looking for Zeke."

Nothing again.

Janus forced a smile, trying for a hint of his old, charming, arrogant self. Surely the asshole was still in there somewhere. "I'm Janus. I'll be boarding here. You must be…" Here he floundered realizing that Zeke hadn't told him his son's name.

"Pater is in the kitchen," the omega said, not looking away as though Janus were a predator, and he or his bird, the prey. "Downstairs."

Janus shivered. The omega's voice was unlike anything Janus

had ever heard before. It was dark and rough, and yet barely louder than a whisper. The man stared at him in silence, offering nothing more. Not even his name.

"Right. I'll just…" Janus jerked his thumb behind him toward the stairs. "Forgive me."

The man went on staring at him. A wisp of ripe berry scent and musk, coupled with evergreen from the trees, came to Janus on the next draft from the window.

How he wished to be the old Janus then. The one who'd had no sense of when to stop and didn't much care if he offended. The one who'd sweet-talked and finagled his way into many an omega's bed, if not their actual affections—and contracted omegas at that!

Not that he wanted in this man's bed or affections. But the old Janus would have known how to make him smile. Make him offer his name. Make him shake hands like a sensible human being with manners.

But the old Janus was dead, burned up in a series of fevers and one great disappointment. Now he was too skinny, too tired, and definitely too out of his depths to try to charm a man who didn't care to indulge in any social graces at all.

He backed away and then turned to go downstairs to the kitchen, his heart hammering wildly. He licked his lips, trying to find a taste of that tantalizing scent.

Anxiety raced through him as if he'd encountered a ghost, instead of just a young man with a pretty pet bird.

# CHAPTER TWO

TRYING TO IGNORE the strange alpha's pheromones that had flooded into his bedroom and lingered, Kerry stroked Kiwi, so named in honor of the tropical fruit he'd first tasted during his bonding-moon trip with Wilbet. He kissed the bird's head and sighed, memories creeping to the surface of his mind.

Not all couples took bonding-moon journeys after contracting, but Wilbet had insisted, and Kerry hadn't argued. He'd always wanted to see the world, and he'd been eager to start. The fact that he'd landed an alpha with the means to provide the wild extravagance of traveling for a whole month to exotic destinations he'd only ever seen in pictures had puffed him with pride and exaltation. When he'd first left Hud's Basin to attend Mont Juror in the city, he'd dreamed of leaving his mountain-bound life behind, and during the first few weeks of his bonding-moon trip with Wilbet, he'd been so proud of how very much he'd succeeded at that.

They'd sailed south toward the islands on the Monhundys' fancy yacht, fucking and cuddling, eating and drinking, reading and napping before they docked at Saturnalie Island. The warmth of the southern sun and the blue of the vast sea had filled him with relaxation and awe. Upon seeing the green, leafy island surrounded by lacy waves and stunning views, he'd turned to Wilbet, excited and so happy that he'd counted himself almost in love. Kissing him, Kerry had said, "Thank you, Wilbet. Wolf-god, I never want to forget how I feel right now. So grateful. So full of joy."

Wilbet had kissed him back, then taken his hand and led him

onto the beach.

A few sun-soaked, happy hours later, he bought Kiwi as a gift from a local man in a hut by the edge of the sea. Again, Kerry had never been so happy. He felt sure that he'd learn to love Wilbet truly if given enough time.

It'd only been a week later when Wilbet had hurt him for the first time.

Kerry supposed, given everything that followed, Kiwi should be an awful reminder of all that he'd endured and lost, but he wasn't. Colorful, inquisitive, and sweet, Kiwi could never be anything but pure and perfect. Kerry loved his sweet little face, and how he danced around with innocent pleasure, chirruping cheerfully, and shivering his wings. All utterly unknowing of the predicament they were in. Kerry put his hand on his still-flat stomach. The predicament all three of them were in.

Gazing out the window and looking down toward the lake with the water glittering pink and coral with the setting sun, Kerry considered the future. His pater had said nothing as the evidence mounted over the prior three weeks, indicating that the last forced visit to the prison had produced the anticipated end result.

Kerry didn't know if Pater was in denial or if it was his infinite patience that kept him quiet. There were four more months to get through. So much could go wrong with any pregnancy for any omega; everyone knew that.

But Kerry's inherited deformity—the same one that his birth pater, Ranz, had been born with—didn't make the odds of a safe and healthy delivery any better. There was some speculation that the deformity was in part why Ranz hadn't survived the delivery of Kerry's brother. Stroking Kiwi's feathers, he thought about the only photo he had of himself with his birth-pater. In it, he was just a bare-kneed toddler, leaning against Ranz's side, one hand on his swelling belly. The baby hadn't lived either, born too early. Pater had named him Jack and put him in the grave with Ranz.

Kerry shuddered and closed his eyes. That's when his father had left, too. Off to find another omega to make a family with, happily leaving Kerry behind. According to the argument Kerry had overheard, his father had no use for an omega son. Truth be told, if his parents hadn't met when an unmatched Ranz was on the verge of being heat-struck and made Kerry in the aftermath, he wasn't sure his parents would have even been friends. Such had been the sorry state of their relationship. Anger, yelling, the occasional punch thrown from both sides. That had been his earliest impression of the alpha and omega dynamics, which was perhaps why he hadn't seen the red flags waving all over the place before contracting with Wilbet.

He touched his sunken chest. Had it really played a part in Jack coming early and Ranz's death? Pater thought so, but who knew for sure? Those were all issues Pater had brought up before they signed the breeding contracts with Wilbet. Pater had given all his warnings in advance, and now, wolf-god bless him, he seemed ready to accept whatever came next. Just like he'd already accepted everything else—Kerry as his adopted son, Kerry's rejection of Hud's Basin, and his move to the city. And then Kerry's contract with the Monhundys, Wilbet's arrest, and Kerry's shameful return home. And now…this. His fingers caressed his stomach again.

Kerry chewed on his bottom lip, letting Kiwi prance from his palm to his forearm, then over his bicep to his shoulder. The setting sun burst between a ridge and mountain, making the lake shine like a flashlight, stunning Kerry's eyes. He squinted them shut, purple and blue dots dancing on the black beneath his lids.

No matter what happened, his pater was always there with open arms, never uttering so much as a single "I told you so" or word of disapproval. Kerry didn't know if he'd personally be able to hold back the same way if his child made so many mistakes. He clenched his fist against his stomach, nausea welling up as a shudder of loathing wracked him. If this child was his chance to see how unconditionally he could love someone, he had already failed. He couldn't even forgive this baby for being of Wilbet Monhundy's seed. Loving him seemed an impossibility.

The fact was, if he lost this child or his own life in the process of delivering him, Kerry wouldn't mind as much as he should. His deformity and fears about what it might mean for his chances had made him less than discriminating when courted at Philia soirees, but it could still be his salvation now.

The scent of pot pie drifted up the stairs, hearty and filling. The delicious, creamy scent reminded Kerry of the winter months just past. The boarding house had hosted two *Érosgápe* sets of wealthy city dwellers trying to outrun the latest flu epidemic. Zeke had put them in the upstairs rooms with adjoining baths. Single betas—cousins vacationing together—had occupied the three downstairs rooms and shared the bath on the hall. Monk's House hadn't reached its capacity, but they'd been busy enough, and Kerry hadn't minded it. The work had kept his mind off his then-impending heat, and he'd enjoyed the readings and performances put on by two of the beta boarders for everyone's post-supper entertainment.

Summer, though, loomed ahead with no guest booked at all. Aside from this annoying alpha who smelled like sweet roses and lemon with a hint of pine. The lack of boarders was likely his pater's subtle way of acknowledging the upcoming months of rapid physical expansion, along with the frustrating arousal and vulnerability that often came along with it.

Not to mention the inevitable birth due at the end of the summer. If it was Pater's way of giving Kerry the peace and quiet to accept and cope with his fate, it was lucky that Wilbet's parents, the Monhundys, made sure there was plenty of money to make ends meet whenever Kerry stayed at Hud's Basin. Additional boarders weren't necessary for their survival. It was one of the only good things Kerry still found in his contract.

Kerry's only unselfish motivation when leaving Hud's Basin for "something better," had been the hope of contracting with an alpha of enough wealth to back his pater's future. He'd been arrogant and young enough at the time to think that escape was his only option for a good life. He hadn't wanted to end up tied to any of the local young alphas, rutting out of desperation when his heats began, and forced into a hard life on the mountainside, bearing children from a young age and never having more than a pot to piss in.

So, he'd gone to the city, started heat suppressants, and attended Mont Juror. It was only after failing to match with an *Érosgápe* mate that he'd gone on to the Philia soirees, determined to contract with an alpha of means to further distance himself from the life he was ashamed of in his backwoods home. He'd met Wilbet at one such party.

Wolf-god, Kerry felt humiliated looking back now. He'd been so easy to flatter. Even easier to woo. He shuddered, pressing another kiss to Kiwi's beak, needing his return nuzzle more than she ever truly needed his affection.

Another waft of the savory pot pie made Kerry salivate. He breathed it in. His pater used parsnips, and it gave the pie a holiday taste even though they were months away from the Autumn Nights feast days.

His stomach growled, and he gave in to his hunger, placing Kiwi on the perch in his cage. Kiwi chirruped sweetly, and Kerry murmured, "It's nearly bedtime. But I'll fly you soon, darling."

The bird danced merrily and then turned to admire himself in the small mirror Kerry had rigged in the cage. Kiwi loved to look at himself, obviously finding his own feathers glorious. Kerry had once been the same, flattered and puffed up by Wilbet's admiration, but he couldn't stand his own reflection these days.

*Speaking of…*

He smoothed a brush through his long, curly hair so that his pater wouldn't be embarrassed. He tied the mess of it back, then quietly descended the stairs. He paused outside the oven-warm kitchen and pressed himself against the soft, crumbling wallpaper just outside it long enough to listen.

Alphas tended to be overbearing at times, and Kerry didn't want to deal with that. Not tonight. He'd rather go hungry. He wondered what his pater had thought when he agreed to book this alpha here for the year. A pregnant omega and an unmatched alpha living together without the omega's alpha between them as a buffer could become quite awkward. Kerry swallowed hard as some clarity dawned.

*Wolf-god, Pater, what are you thinking?*

"Shouldn't we wait for him?" he heard the alpha ask.

"No, go on. Dig in. He'll come on his own if he comes at all." There was a brief silence. "So, you met Kerry, then?" Plates clattered, and a spoon clanged against a pot.

"Kerry? Is that your son?" The alpha's voice was higher pitched than Kerry's, but it was a nice, bright tenor. This man was probably a fine singer. What was his name again?

Ah, *Janus*, yes.

That was what the alpha had said as he'd stood there in Kerry's doorway looking far too handsome and way too worldly for his own good. It'd irritated Kerry that after everything he'd come to understand about life and alphas in particular, his body would still respond to one against his will. That roses, lemon, and hint of pine had lingered on so enticingly. Surely it was too soon for the pregnancy hormones to already be affecting him?

Regardless, it had affected him.

Janus went on, "Yes, I met him briefly, but I didn't get his name."

"Kerry it is," Pater said, clanging a bit more. He was never a quiet chef. "And his little bird is Kiwi. I expect if you saw Kerry upstairs, he had the bird in hand."

"Yes." Janus was quiet a moment and then said awkwardly, "Such a pretty thing."

Kerry moved to stand in the space just behind the kitchen door, pressing in so that he could look through the crack to observe the scene at the small table. The delicate scent of the new alpha reached him even over that of the savory pot pie, and he fought the urge to breathe it in and taste it. He narrowed his attention on the scene and watched carefully.

Pater seemed in good spirits and had put in a bit of effort with his appearance, his gray hair smoothed down neatly. Janus was also looking well, with a pleasant flush to his skin, likely from the oven's heat. He wore a nice, stylish shirt that somehow came across as only slightly wrinkled after his long trip. Plus, *oh, wolf-god, help*, his strong jaw, big eyes, and loose, curly hair that fell over his forehead were all beyond dashing. This man had undoubtedly brought many omegas to their knees.

Kerry gritted his teeth. Yes, Janus certainly played the part of a dream alpha—handsome, well-built, and likely from a good family. Though Kerry had learned well enough that appearances could deceive, and coming from a "good family" was no guarantee of good character at all.

Suddenly, Janus flushed deeper and cleared his throat. "The bird, I mean. The *bird* is a pretty thing. All the, ah, colors."

Kerry's lips betrayed him, quirking into a small smile.

So, Janus had thought *he* was pretty, too, then. Annoying as it was, Kerry's starving ego took sustenance in knowing that he was still attractive to alphas, even if he truly didn't want to be. Even if it felt dangerous.

He bit into his lower lip and watched Janus carefully, looking for signs of trouble or temper. Anything to tell him what to expect for the next many months, or to give him a reason to insist his pater dismiss the man outright. On the surface, he could find nothing.

"Very pretty," Janus said again, almost desperately.

"That he is. The bird, I mean," Pater said, putting Janus out of his misery.

Janus's relief was so great and obvious that Kerry let out a small huff that, in the past, he'd have loosed as a deep laugh. But true laughter was in short supply for Kerry these days.

"A male of the species," Pater explained, starting in on his pot pie. "As is evidenced by the coloring. The females, from what Kerry tells me, are gray. Can you imagine?"

Janus grunted softly, smearing a hunk of butter onto his bread. Kerry raised a brow. It was definitely going to cut into their budget if their boarder planned to consume butter at such a rate regularly. The Monhundys were generous, but even they had a limit as to how much they'd spare for Pater. He was, in their estimation, a nuisance.

"He was…quiet," Janus offered.

Pater poked at his pie and sighed. "He didn't used to be. He used to sing a lot."

"Oh, I meant your son, not the bird."

"I meant Kerry, too, lad." Pater smiled widely. "He was always singing when he was younger, had a voice that sent shivers up your spine. Gravelly and deep, but earnest. And he could hit low notes you wouldn't imagine possible with his limited lung capacity."

Janus's face flashed with something like interest and then a sudden understanding. He must have noticed Kerry's chest then. Kerry rubbed at the deep indent between his pectoral muscles. He'd been shy about it for a long time, but Wilbet had reassured him that he had plenty of other wiles with which to attract an alpha. Now that he knew the real reason Wilbet had targeted him, he often felt self-conscious of the deformation again.

"Kerry wasn't much for the high end of the range, but oh, the low end! Astounding. Soulful." Pater shook his head grimly. "Alas, he doesn't sing anymore."

"Earlier you said he's on the mend. Did he injure his voice?"

"No, Mr. Heelies. I'm afraid he contracted with an alpha, and it ruined his life."

Kerry rolled his eyes and coughed before entering the kitchen. He was now unwelcomely certain of his pater's reason for taking on an alpha boarder as they faced this particular crisis in their lives. "I doubt our boarder wants to hear our tales of domestic woe, Pater." He took a cup from the cupboard and sat down to a dinner he both did and didn't want. But even with his fluctuating appetite, eating with Janus was better than letting his pater spill their private business to a complete stranger.

A stranger with the last name of Heelies.

From the city.

Kerry knew that bunch plenty well now, didn't he? No one had educated Kerry about the Monhundy business, and he hadn't been granted much information about their dealings while he and Wilbet lived together, but he knew the Heelies and Monhundy families ran in the same circles. He'd even met the old man, Doxan Heelies, and his *Érosgápe* once or twice at parties. And now, with that knowledge in mind, he wasn't even sure he wanted this relative of theirs knowing the name of his contracted alpha.

*Oh, Pater, what have you done?*

"That's all in our past now, anyway," Kerry said in a firm tone, indicating that the subject of his alpha and his ruined life was officially a closed topic.

Janus nodded grimly but said nothing.

Pater shot him a look as though he'd lost his mind. As if *he* wasn't the one who'd gone mad boarding Janus here. Did he really think Kerry wouldn't catch on to what he was up to? Did he think

Kerry would want this?

Stroking a hand over his belly again, he could feel the hardness that hadn't been there just a week before, though he hadn't started to show yet. Kerry smeared a much less generous amount of butter on his bread and then poured tea into his cup. The scent of the heaping portion of pie in his bowl filled his nostrils and made his stomach growl again.

"What brings you to Hud's Basin?" he asked after silence dragged on too long. His false politeness was obvious, but he didn't care. This Janus was probably here for the same things all wealthy alphas came for—relaxation, a misguided idea about a business opportunity, or to wait out a scandal. There was no way it meant anything good for Hud's Basin or for them. So, his pater could take his plans and shove them.

"To study with Dr. Crescent," Pater answered for Janus. "Mr. Heelies here wants to be a nurse." He gave Kerry a significant look, but Kerry chose to ignore it.

As if one's profession said anything about one's character or trustworthiness. How many dentists had Kerry met in the city who were clearly sadists? Just one, but that had been one too many. Being in a helping field didn't mean a man was actually a helper. He chose to focus on the other surprising aspect of his pater's statement.

"Dr. Crescent is taking on students?"

"Yes," Janus said. "I was lucky to get him to accept me."

"Why's that?" Kerry asked, taking a bite and letting his eyes fall closed as the delicious, creamy vegetables and meat spread across his tongue. He opened his eyes to see Janus watching him carefully.

"I don't have all the requirements in line quite yet. After my illness last year caused me to miss a few practicals and seminars, I'm behind. That's why I'll be studying at night," Janus said to Pater. "If you need extra rent for my use of candles, let me know. I'll…" He frowned. "I'll have to cut back somewhere else to pay for them."

Kerry's brow went up again. Why didn't Janus get his rich relations to pay for more candles? Or to send him battery-operated lamps? That's what Wilbet would have done.

No, Wilbet would have accessed his bank accounts and bought enough candles to meet the needs of a dozen late-night students like he'd done that first visit before they'd contracted. Back when he was still wooing Kerry, he'd paid for Pater's entire boarding house's new paint job, the installation of new water heaters, and the full reshingling of the roof. And that had been just the start.

Now Wilbet's accounts were confiscated and the proceeds divided between the prostitutes who'd come forward about Wilbet's rape and abuse. Kerry didn't mind. He wanted nothing to do with anything of Wilbet's now. Not his money, not his house, and not his child in Kerry's belly. Which, should he be an alpha, stood to inherit the whole of the damned Monhundy fortune. Kerry hated the very thought. Nothing but bad luck would ever come from that family. He wanted nothing to do with them. He'd been wrong to run from Hud's Basin. He should never have left the safety of the mountains. But alas, he couldn't turn back time.

Regardless, if Janus wanted to use a ridiculous number of candles or buy a dozen battery lamps, he should be able to get his family to pay for them quite easily. That's what those kinds of families *did*. But Janus acted like that might be a problem. Was there a scandal he was trying to outrun? And was it so big that his family had cut him off then? Was it Wilbet-sized even?

Kerry pushed the plate with the pot pie away as a rush of nausea turned the creamy scent overwhelming. He raised his napkin to his mouth and nose, breathing in and out slowly. Thoughts of Wilbet often did this to him.

"Are you all right?" Janus asked, true concern lacing his voice. "Is he all right, Zeke?"

Kerry wanted to snarl at Janus for daring to use his pater's first name like he was just a common beta, especially when Pater had been so respectful as to call Janus by the name Mr. Heelies. But nausea swelled again, and he swallowed back a taste of vomit.

"He's a bit poorly at times," Pater said gently. "But it's nothing catching. Do you need a cold rag for your neck, love?"

Kerry shook his head. The nausea was already passing. He just needed to keep his mind off the inevitable a bit longer. He wanted to go out on the back porch. Rock in his favorite chair. Stare at the lake again. Feel the breeze in his hair. Ignore the small, fluttering movements he'd just noticed earlier that day beneath his navel.

"Pardon," he said, lowering the napkin. "Pater is right. I'm not feeling like myself. But I'm fine now. Please, go on about how you came to Hud's Basin to work with Dr. Crescent. I'm surprised you'd call yourself lucky. He's a crotchety bastard."

"He's the only doctor who agreed to take me on," Janus said, with a hint of pink in his high cheekbones. "As I said, I'm short of some requirements. Most doctors wanted me to wait another year, but I was impatient to begin. I feel as though, in some ways, I've been waiting forever. I need to prove myself."

Kerry narrowed his gaze on Janus. He doubted Janus had any idea at all of what true waiting really meant. He didn't push it, though, and instead said, "Many men from a certain background would simply ask their fathers or uncles to pay a suitable price to, uh, 'procure' the necessary requirements."

Janus's expression darkened. "There was a time I might have done just that. But I've turned over a new leaf, and I'm a better man for it. I live by my own means and merits now."

Pater said, "I'm sure your father—"

"Uncle," Janus corrected.

"Uncle, then. I'm sure he's proud of you for that."

"He's enraged, actually." Janus chuckled, but it sounded like it cost him. "But my cousins Xan and Ray are pleased, and I suppose, given the fact that I'll be dealing with them for much longer than I'll have to deal with their father, I'd rather be on their good side. Besides, a man needs to stand on his own two feet, doesn't he? If he's ever going to be proud of himself?"

"Omegas do find that attractive," Pater said, sliding a glance to Kerry.

Kerry glared at him.

"Or so I've been led to understand, but I've been wrong before." Pater smiled at Janus a bit too warmly.

Kerry changed the subject back to something safer. "Dr. Crescent probably didn't care because he doesn't even have a medical degree himself."

Janus startled and put down his teacup. "Excuse me?"

Maybe not that much safer.

"It's true," Pater said. "He started doctoring ages ago, before there were laws up this way about who could do the doctoring and who couldn't. He just kept right on at it. No one's ever convinced him to quit. And I'm not rightly sure what Hud's Basin would do if he did."

Janus sputtered. "I'd think the local police might have some power of persuasion over him."

Kerry shook his head. The idea of Sheriff Tintson moving against Dr. Crescent, the man who'd helped his omega give birth to five strapping alphas, was absurd. "Dr. Crescent is beloved in Hud's Basin."

"And Dr. Crescent is a favorite with the local Holy Wolf congregation, too," Pater added. "Always giving them extra tithe at the end of the year to make up for lack of attendance. That might have something to do with why Sheriff Tintson doesn't see fit to charge him with malpractice. Well, that and he's a damn good doctor."

"Not by the city standard," Kerry murmured, knowing that

saying such a thing would rile his pater up. Pater had warned Kerry that if he contracted with Wilbet, he'd be "citified" and changed forever. Well, he'd certainly been right about the latter part, if not entirely the former.

"Dash 'city standard' to wolf-god's own hell. What has 'city standard' ever gotten us mountain folk? Some electricity, sure. Some science, all right. But has it fed our babies and clothed them? Has it pleased wolf-god enough to spare us poverty and keep our omegas from suffering?" Pater jabbed the table with his index finger. "No. City standard has not! I'll take our mountain ways any day."

"The rate of paternal death during childbirth is down significantly in the cities," Kerry said. "Only two percent last year versus the twelve percent we saw."

Janus's eyes went wide at the words "twelve percent" though he kept eating the pot pie like it was the finest meal he'd had in ages. Oh well, let him get his surprise over with. It was best if he knew what he was getting into early on.

"Maybe! But at what cost?" Pater asked, and then shook his head. "Wolf-god gave us our ways and saved us from the finality of destruction when the human females all went with the Great Death. No, keep the city standard, and I'll keep wolf-god's blessings on my tongue."

"It doesn't have to be either-or," Janus said, putting his fork down for a moment. "You could have both. As I used to say to some rather handsome, contracted omegas of my acquaintance: a little bit of both worlds never hurt a soul."

"I'd beg to differ," Pater said softly.

Kerry sighed. "City ways aren't the same, Pater."

"Of course not. I know that." Pater relaxed again and eyed Janus playfully. "So, a playboy, were ya?" Pater snorted. "Why am I not surprised by that? Look at him, Kerry. Handsome, friendly, and with that dimple in his cheek. Wolf-god save us! And did you get a look at his shoes? So fancy. Omegas must just swoon over ya."

Kerry met Janus's blinking, embarrassed gaze and asked baldly, "Well, do they? Swoon over you?"

Janus sputtered a bit, before wiping his mouth with his napkin to regain his composure. "I've had my share of love affairs, but I'm putting *that* behind me, as well."

"Turning over yet another new leaf?" Pater asked, laughing. "New leaf for money. A new leaf for love. Oh, wolf-god's blessings on your heart, lad. Don't get me wrong. I hope it works out for you."

"And when it comes to seductions of contracted omegas," Kerry went on pointedly, shooting a quelling look at his pater, "I do hope you're being honest about that staying in the past. The alphas around here don't truck with city alphas messing with their omegas. They've got guns out this way, and they're not afraid to use them."

Pater groaned softly and shook his head at Kerry but otherwise kept his thoughts to himself. For now.

Janus cleared his throat and settled his earnest, gleaming eyes on Kerry. "The only objective I have for any omegas here in Hud's Basin is to assist Dr. Crescent in whatever way he deems correct to increase their chances of a positive outcome during labor and birth. And, of course, to assist them through any other illness. Nothing more or less."

Janus sounded like such a prig talking like that. As if he had any idea what a mountain labor and birth was like in most cases! As if he had any clue about Hud's Basin at all! Kerry almost couldn't wait until he'd been on his first set of rounds with Crescent. This confident, bordering on arrogant, alpha would have his eyes opened then.

"Just remember things are different here," Pater said with a darkness in his tone that Kerry recognized from the days when he'd discouraged Kerry from signing the Monhundys' contract.

"It sounds like you're trying to scare me away from Hud's Basin," Janus answered a bit haughtily. "But I won't be frightened off. I'm determined to see this through. I will learn all I can from Dr. Crescent, and if all goes to plan, eventually bring my own services to the people of the area."

"All right, little priesty," Pater said with a grin. "May wolf-god be with you and sanctify your aims."

"Priesty?" Janus asked.

"You remind me of the city priests who come through here eager to spread the enlightened word of wolf," Pater said. "So sure they can bring the 'city standard' to the country poor. Never mind that maybe the country poor don't have a wolf-god's damned bit of interest in something new. Not when it comes to their faith. Not when it comes to their way of life." He patted Janus's hand like he was an adorable child with dirty cheeks and a dream. "You go right on, priesty. I'll be here with dinner ready whenever it is you come home at night."

Janus stared at Kerry's pater a moment and then pulled his hand away, took up his bread and butter in one hand and his fork in the other, and returned to eating. He looked tired like the road had worn on him, and while he *was* handsome—even devastatingly so—he was too thin for his frame. Kerry wondered whether that was natural or due sickness.

"What are your plans for tonight then?" Pater asked, motioning toward the darkening windows. The sun had set, leaving the lingering twilight along with the chirrup of cicadas and frogs. "We often read in the living room until bed. You're welcome to join us."

"I thought I'd walk a bit."

"In the darkness?" Pater asked, his brow wrinkling in concern.

"Is it not safe?"

"If the moon is bright, it's plenty safe, but if it's not…" he trailed off. "You're a grown man. Choose as you see fit." He glanced to Kerry with mischief in his eyes. "Unless you'd like to go with him, son? You'd know your way around this property in the light or dark better than anyone."

"Or we could give him a flashlight and be done with it," Kerry said lightly. His throat ached as he considered walking the property after dark. The last time he'd done that, he'd been considering suicide, and now that he was at least temporarily past that impulse, he didn't want reminders of it.

"Do we have the batteries to spare?" Pater said.

"Wolf-god above, Pater, if not, we have the gas lanterns, don't we?" Kerry managed a few bites of his bread and butter and a sip of his tea. "I'm going upstairs. Call for me if you need help with the flashlights or lanterns." He turned to Janus. "But I'm sure Mr. Heelies will be able to figure them out."

"Call me Janus, please," Janus said, softly. "If you don't mind? Mr. Heelies is so formal. It reminds me of…things I'd rather forget."

Kerry noted that there was a story there. Something Janus was ashamed of, perhaps. But he didn't have it in him to care about that now. Kerry found that lately, curiosity was rare for him along with hope.

"All right. Janus, you can call me Kerry." He glanced at Pater. "Shall my pater call you Janus as well?" It was a challenge and issued as such, but Janus acted like it wasn't.

"Of course! I wouldn't have it any other way."

"I'm sure you wouldn't."

Janus rose from the table and put out his hand. "I hope you have a good rest and I'll see you in the morning."

Kerry took Janus's fingers, unsurprised to find them without callouses aside from those acquired by holding a pen. At least it seemed he was a dedicated student. Perhaps he wouldn't be as lazy and entitled as the rest of the boys Wilbet had brought around to the house in the city.

"When you leave on your walk, stay on the path to the right," Kerry advised. "It takes you to the lake. The stars on the water are magical. Or so I used to say when I was a boy." He pulled his hand away, feeling a tingle where Janus's fingers had touched.

"Until morning, then?" Janus said again with a tone of pleading that Kerry didn't want to consider too closely. He wasn't an omega to be conquered by a handsome visiting alpha. He was barely standing on his own feet after having fought his way up to them. Janus and his imploring smile were complications he didn't need.

"Perhaps." Kerry wasn't going to act as though he cared for Janus's company. "Oh, and avoid the path toward the left. It leads to the caves. Wild cats sleep there. Late spring is their birthing season, and early summer is when their cubs grow adventurous. They've been known to tear out a man's throat if they believe their cubs are threatened."

Janus sucked in a breath and pride surged in Kerry to have knocked the confidence out of him.

As Kerry took the stairs back up to his room and Kiwi, he noted a small, stubborn flare of new curiosity in his chest. What was the measure of this alpha?

With Kiwi in his palm again, Kerry sat on the windowsill to watch and wait. He wondered if Janus would still dare to go on his walk at all.

When Janus exited the side of the house bearing a handheld flashlight and heading down the right-handed path, Kerry stroked Kiwi's feathers and whispered, "Well, then."

A dart of satisfaction pierced his numb hide.

# CHAPTER THREE

J ANUS USED TO wrestle alphas twice his size for great sums of cash, but these days he didn't trust his strength to wrestle a small omega, much less a wild cat. He stayed on the dark path Kerry had suggested and didn't place a foot off it.

He didn't know why he'd been so determined to go on a walk, alone in the dark on unfamiliar property. He just knew that reading in the—admittedly quite comfortable looking—living room wasn't something he could stand to do after enduring the weird tension over dinner. Besides, his whole body ached after the long day spent first on the train and then in a hot, rickety wagon. Returning to his rented bedroom to pore over his books in an anxious attempt to jam as much into his brain as possible before meeting with Dr. Crescent in the morning sounded far too stressful. He needed to stretch his legs a bit.

The night was cool, and the moon rose brighter than the flashlight he waved ahead of him on the trail. Shaking off wariness, he strode with satisfaction, claiming this land as his to roam for the duration of his stay. His eyes and ears absorbed the sights and sounds of the world around him, so different from the city. All of nature wrapped up in shadowy wonder.

The forest chattered with the croak of frogs, the night rustles of birds and the constant rhythmic chant of the cicadas. As he walked, the fresh air cleared his thoughts, and he relaxed. Images bloomed across his mind's eye, all fresh memories—the breeze tugging through Kerry's long hair, first on the porch and then by the window. It'd been a sight to see, the way Kerry's hair had moved in the air currents like it'd had a life of its own. And then there'd been his scent…

Janus's blood quickened.

There was no doubt Kerry was pretty. Almost as pretty as his bird.

But Janus shook that observation off. Handsome or not, Janus was trying to avoid entanglements, not dive headfirst into one. He focused his thoughts instead on the mountain community he'd glimpsed while the wagon jostled him as it climbed the rugged dirt roads. The mountains were alive with humanity tucked into the road's hairpin turns and hollows.

Hud's Basin was like stepping back in time. That was the only way Janus could think to describe it, and he decided to do just that in his first letter to Caleb. Additionally, there was no phone at Monk's House. He'd ascertained that earlier when he'd come downstairs, found dinner not quite ready, and so had thought to place a quick call to let his uncle know he'd arrived safely.

"The mail comes every second day," Zeke had said with a vague air of apology as he'd checked the pot pie's crust. "Mayhap a letter will do just as well?"

"No bother. I'll just call from Dr. Crescent's tomorrow."

"I doubt that," Zeke said with amusement in his tone.

"He has a phone, surely?"

"Why would ya think that?"

"Well, to receive calls from patients requiring his help."

Zeke *had* laughed at him then. Not unkindly, just the tender-hearted snicker of an older man looking at a young fool. "And what phones are those sick patients going to use to call Dr. Crescent with, I wonder? The ones tucked up in the birds' nests all around the forest? No, Mr. Heelies. We don't have phone lines up this way. No one wants to pay to run them, you see."

Janus knew he should have been offended by Zeke making fun of him, but really, how could he be? He was spoiled, and it was a shame. This was the way the world worked for most people—alphas, omegas, and betas alike—and the fact that it seemed foreign to him was both a gift and a burden.

So, he'd write letters to his uncle and Caleb tomorrow. He'd tell them both about the beautiful but horribly bumpy ride up the mountain, and the state of the boarding house. But he'd only tell Caleb about the omega he'd met and the strange draw that tugged at him while simultaneously pushing him away. Of course, he'd assure Caleb he had no intention of seducing the man. None whatsoever.

He only wondered what it was that made Kerry seem so angry. And afraid. And vulnerable. And lovely. Kerry was a beautiful man posing as a mystery to be solved. Who didn't love a mystery?

Janus came to the end of the path and stepped onto the sandy beach by the side of the lake. It wasn't quite full dark yet, and the moon reflected in the water beautifully. The star beside the moon—wolf-god's own dimple—glinted in the reflection, too.

The water lapped at the edge of the land, making small, wet sounds of invitation. Janus stretched his arms up, rolling his shoulders around. It was a cool enough night, but he was sticky from his travels. The wagon he'd ridden in had left him dusty. He'd washed his hands and face before dinner, but nothing else. So, he was gummy now and, frankly, prickly from the small embarrassments he'd endured under the watchful eyes of Kerry and Zeke. Oh, these mountain people. They'd put him in his place yet. He had no doubt.

Yes. A swim would do him good.

He toed off his shoes, the very ones that Zeke had found so noteworthy, and shucked his shirt. His pants and underwear came off easily, and he strode to the empty, open, welcoming lake with a quiver of joy. It was a homecoming, slipping naked into the water. Not too frigid after a day in the sun, but the chill was still a balm on his hot skin. He pushed out far enough that his feet no longer touched. Then he floated on his back. The sky above opened to him—stars winking on one-by-one like a string of electric lights in the city.

Perhaps he'd been an idiot to be surprised that Dr. Crescent wasn't a licensed physician. Perhaps he should care about that more than he did. No doubt Caleb's Urho would have words to say—and unflattering ones at that, rule-abiding alpha that he was. But Janus didn't really care. If Dr. Crescent had the trust of the mountain people, then that was what mattered most. If Urho came up to Hud's Basin, he'd scare everyone away with his glower. But this Dr. Crescent had convinced these men to trust him and let him stay. Janus would learn his tricks and teach him some things, too. Together they'd make changes around here. Slow ones, but good ones. They'd get that paternal death rate down for one thing, and then they'd both be hailed as heroes.

He smirked.

Funny how the idea of being called a hero fell flat these days. It used to be a dream of his—for people to see him as the salvation of Heelies Enterprises. He'd more than once drunkenly gloated that he'd save them all from Xan's incompetence and perversions. But that inebriated dream was unbearably disgusting in hindsight, and Xan was…

Well, Xan was annoying, no doubt. But, so what? He was also a good man. A deserving man. At least Caleb swore it was true. He said that Janus had been the villain of the piece the whole time. That he'd been wrong to try to steal what rightfully belonged to Xan—both inheritance and omega. Caleb was usually right.

The stars twinkled their agreement.

From now on, Janus would make do with what rightfully belonged to him and him alone—which was essentially nothing. He had a small monthly income—a payout from their grandfather's will—but after walking away from any pretense of work at Heelies Enterprises, he'd been cut off from that veritable fount of money.

Not that his uncle had been cruel about it. He'd made it plain that if Janus came to his senses and returned to the city and a job there, he'd hook him back up to the firehose of cash. But that wasn't what Janus wanted anymore.

Funny how once a man had seen through the delusions of power and money, it became almost impossible to crave them again. And there were few experiences like being on death's door three damned times to do just that.

The water caressed him, seeming to agree. He buoyed up, lighter than before, and then dropped down lower again. Examining his current motives to see if he was a good man yet, he still came up short.

Being here, now, in Hud's Basin…was that what *he* truly wanted? Or was this an endeavor he thought Caleb would find attractive? That was a question he found he didn't know the answer to anymore. He wasn't sure he cared. Somewhere in the darkness of lingering between life and death too many times, he'd stopped thinking that motivations mattered half as much as outcomes.

In the past, his motivations had always been bad. And even if they were bad now, it didn't matter. So long as the outcomes he produced didn't hurt anyone else. No more seducing contracted omegas for fun. No more drinking, or partying, or making outrageous bets simply because he could.

He could live a good life without believing in anything, including wolf-god, and without being loved by anyone, especially Caleb. He believed this. Because if he didn't, then he should just stop floating now and let the water take him down.

He rose up then, shaking off those morbid thoughts. Two of the boarding house's windows, visible from where he trod water, shone with electric light. On until nine, he remembered and wondered what time it was now. He swam to the shore and shivered in the cooling night air, naked and without a towel. His alpha cock shriveled with cold, and he dripped from every extremity, even his nose. He laughed under his breath, stretching his arms wide, closing his eyes to breathe in deeply—

—And scented the hint of ripe berries and musk.

"Are you always such an exhibitionist?" Kerry's smoky, deep voice drifted softly from somewhere not far away. "Or is this just for me?"

Janus gripped his crotch as his eyes flew open.

Kerry stood nearby with a large, green towel open wide, and his head turned demurely to the side as if he hadn't just gotten a great big gander of exactly what Janus had to offer. All shriveled up at that. Janus felt the urge to tell the man that the cold water had the usual effect and that he was actually quite notably sized. He held off, though. He didn't need to impress this omega with his cock's length and girth. He didn't need to impress him at all.

Wolf-god, he struggled against the urge anyway.

Kerry murmured, "I thought if you went swimming, then you might forget a towel, and it looks like I was right."

"You..." Janus struggled to form a sentence that didn't defend the size of his dick. "I thought you were going to bed."

"As I said, a little bird told me that our city standard friend wouldn't think ahead about a towel, so..." Kerry shrugged and shook the towel at him again, his face still turned away.

"That little bird was Kiwi?" Janus asked, taking the towel and wrapping it around his waist in a hurry.

"He's chatty if you know his language."

"And you know it?"

"Obviously."

"I see." Though he didn't, but he wanted to. Janus suddenly wanted Kerry to teach him how to speak to birds and how to look *that* beautiful in the starlight with wind-whipped hair.

No! He didn't want any such thing. He was here to learn to be a nurse, not fraternize and flirt. "Well, thank you for walking all the way down here. That was thoughtful."

"It was," Kerry agreed with a small chuckle that burned right up Janus's spine. He coughed slightly, hoping to forestall any reaction beneath the towel. Wolf-god help him. This attraction was unexpected. And unwelcome.

The moon shone in Kerry's eyes, making them seem otherworldly. His long hair was free again, lifted by the breeze from the water. He stood with an effortless, sexy grace that Janus had noted by the table, and yet it was evident he was holding back from true relaxation. Even his overture of friendship with the towel felt reserved and apart, as though he'd passed it over to Janus through a hole in an invisible wall.

"I'll let you get dressed," Kerry said, turning his back. "I trust you can find your way back up?"

"Wait!" Janus hadn't meant to sound so urgent. He cleared his throat and said more calmly, "Do you mind walking with me?"

"Afraid of the wild cats?"

Janus's tummy fluttered at the tease in Kerry's voice. He smiled. "Yes."

It was true, even. A vulnerability he never would have owned up to before his near-death experiences, and Janus owed that willingness now to Caleb and the lessons he'd taught him. "I am very scared of the wild cats."

The confession obviously startled Kerry. He turned back around before Janus had his pants up, and then he quickly covered his eyes with his hands. "Sorry."

"No worries, friend. I get the impression you've seen it all before."

Kerry stiffened slightly.

Realizing how that sounded, Janus jumped to clarify. "I mean, I did just stand there in a full-on display a moment ago, didn't I?"

"You didn't know I was watching. That's different."

Oh? Had Kerry been purposefully spying? The idea sent a thrill of dirty delight whipping through Janus's veins, but he held it back, stifling the flirty comments the old Janus might have made. "No, but there's no sense in me being shy now."

Kerry lowered his hand but kept his eyes on the water. "The lake is my favorite place to be in Hud's Basin. When I was younger, I spent all my free time here."

"It's beautiful."

"And peaceful," Kerry added. "The water can wash away anything. Or so I believed as a youngster. There are limits, I find, now that I'm an adult. But it still serves to wash away most things." He flushed, his complexion darkening in the low light from the moon.

"A healing balm," Janus said, unwilling to let the man be embarrassed, though Kerry and his pater had certainly taken the piss out of him a few times that evening. "I felt it while I was floating out there."

"It gets into you," Kerry said. "Everything about Hud's Basin does. The water, the lake, the air…it gets into who you are. Heals you. Makes you whole again."

The poetic intensity was more than Janus knew what to do with. He waited for a moment to see if Kerry backed away from it, but he didn't. Instead, Kerry said by way of explanation, "It's mountain ways. This kind of talk. You'll get used to it."

"Wolf-god approves of such heretical ideas as healing lakes?"

"Wolf-god made it for us, didn't he?" Kerry asked with a raised brow. "I imagine he's glad we don't think ourselves too good for what he's blessed."

Janus rarely heard spiritual discourse like this in the city, and if he did, he'd have written the person off as a religious lunatic. But here, with the stars above and the lake water still drying on his skin, it felt right. Kerry felt right. Which was unfortunate, wasn't it?

Because that was when it hit him.

The scent of Kerry, the layered berries and musk that was so different from anything he'd ever scented before, making him question everything he'd ever known about the smell of an omega?

It was because Kerry was *pregnant.*

Janus let his eyes drift closed as ice and fire chased his blood around his body. As he let the realization sink in, he clenched his fists in unwarranted disappointment, wondering where Kerry's alpha was—the father of this quickly growing blessing from wolf-god—and simultaneously wondering why he cared.

When Janus opened his eyes again, he found that Kerry still studied the lake, moonlight on his face. So pretty. Much prettier than his bird.

Janus released his clenched fists and took a slow breath. "Let's go," he said, indicating the trail. "I'm dressed now."

Kerry turned away without hesitation and took the lead.

KERRY HAD WATCHED from his window as Janus's borrowed flashlight bobbed down to the lake. Then he'd taken out his binoculars. Another gift from Wilbet in the early days of their relationship, intended for bird watching and as an apology for some rough sex that had made Kerry cry. But tonight, Kerry had employed them with a different purpose. One for which Wilbet would in no way approve.

Janus had wasted little time stripping down to his skin and nothing else. Kerry focused the binoculars for a better look at the man's body, aware that he was intruding and not caring half as much as he should.

Muscle definition was lacking, yes, but there was proof it had been there previously. He could tell in the way Janus's body moved and the remaining lean flesh that spoke of the body's own desire for regular use. Janus had been an athlete of some kind and been lain low by his illness. His naked flesh carried the indisputable truth like the dark lines on the face of the moon spoke of its battery and bruising from wolf's unseen claws. Legend had it that even wolf was a rough lover. Though Kerry thought that was only an excuse for alphas to be brutal.

But naked Janus hadn't looked brutal. He'd looked vulnerable. And like he'd forgotten a towel.

Now, walking up the trail slightly ahead of Janus, Kerry thought about every line of Janus's body. He would have imagined that he'd already gotten more than his fill when Janus had come out of the water and stood there, naked as new life, and spread his arms with such carefree joy, but he would have been wrong. Janus's pose had brought a lump to Kerry's throat, and a sadness spiked with envy because there had been a time when he'd have walked out of the water just like that, too. Open and proud, ready for anything…and now? He could barely stand to be naked for longer than it took to wash off. His body housed the enemy, and he hated himself for it.

"You're quiet," Janus said. "Did I say something to offend?"

Kerry shook his head.

"I see. Are you sure?"

Kerry shrugged.

Janus's footsteps fell heavily in the path behind him. "So…it's just you and your father living here?"

Kerry nodded.

"No one else? Maybe a regular friend who comes over?"

Kerry narrowed his eyes. It was obvious that Janus was trying to ask about the alpha who should be living here with them *given the circumstances*. He must have finally scented Kerry's state. It sometimes took a stranger longer exposure to recognize that a pregnant omega's scent was not his alone. Kerry didn't answer the question and waited for Janus to push again.

But Janus did no such thing. Instead, he said, "Your pater said you used to sing."

Kerry continued to walk ahead silently.

"I'm sorry. Am I being too forward?"

"I'm not interested in chit-chat," Kerry said, pitching his voice loud enough to be heard over the lively forest sounds, and firm enough to hopefully shut down Janus's efforts to befriend him.

"You were chatty on the beach."

"A mistake."

"Clearly." Janus sounded injured, and who could blame him?

What had possessed Kerry to bring the towel down? He should have let this strange alpha's tender bits freeze off. Wolf-god alone knew what Janus might have done with them in the past, what harm he may have committed. City alphas weren't to be trusted. If only younger Kerry had known and believed that, he wouldn't be in this predicament now. Compared to what he'd lived through, pairing off with one of the sweeter local alphas would have been a better choice by far.

Janus said nothing the rest of the walk back to the house. Kerry held the front door open for him, allowing him to pass into the furniture-crowded front hallway. The brush of Janus's arm against Kerry's chest as he passed was accidental, but it sent a small shock through Kerry's whole body. He both wanted to rub the touch away and press it deeper into his flesh. He frowned, annoyed.

"Goodnight, Mr. Heelies," he said, sweeping past Janus to mount the stairs.

"I thought we agreed to Janus and Kerry?"

"Perhaps we were presumptuous," Kerry said.

"I don't think so. You've seen me in my bare skin. I insist on Janus."

Kerry stopped halfway up the flight, feeling the fairness of Janus's words. Eventually, he continued up, and it was only when he was shutting his bedroom door, and he heard Janus's feet on the landing, that he gave in. "Goodnight, Janus. May wolf-god bless your dreams."

He was met by silence and then a confused, "And yours, Kerry." He waited a bit longer, heard Janus shut his bedroom door, and then locked his own.

He supposed he deserved worse. Janus had behaved admirably all evening while Kerry had been a confusing, unfriendly brat. Kerry might have judged the man too harshly.

Kiwi slept soundly with his head beneath his wing. Kerry went to the window and sat on the sill again, staring down to the lake. He pressed a hand to his stomach and pondered the possibility of sleep. Would it come to him, or would he see the dawn again? Or worse, would he wake in the night sweating from terrible dreams?

He lingered on the windowsill, pushing against his stomach.

Only time would tell.

# CHAPTER FOUR

D R. CRESCENT'S OFFICE wasn't an office at all.

It was a re-purposed, open-air stable used when the weather was nice. Or so Janus hoped. Surely the doctor didn't make sick patients wait outside when it rained or snowed? But Janus didn't have a chance to ask.

He arrived, panting and on foot, after a steeper-than-he'd-like hike up the mountain from Monk's House, to find a line of patients waiting to see the doctors already wrapping around the stable beside the one-story cabin that must be Dr. Crescent's home.

The line was a varied one but commonly marked with misery. There were a couple of green-around-the-gills and ill-dressed betas holding a vomit bucket between them, an alpha wearing a ratty shirt and gripping a bloody rag around his opposite hand, a terrified pater grasping a baby who kept turning purple with a violent cough, and a skinny, wailing omega supported by his *Érosgápe* while blood soaked through his pants. These were only a few of the patients Janus glimpsed as he came off the forest path.

At first, he didn't know what to do, stunned by this sudden and grotesque demonstration of humanity's suffering, but then he lifted his shoulders, pushed on, and entered the stable in search of Dr. Crescent. And he found him straight away. A bear of a man with huge hands, a long beard, and a craggy face, he was working on setting a teenage boy's broken leg. With barely a glance at Janus, he barked out, "Well, get to it. Do what you can. These folks don't have all day, and I've only got this one pair of hands."

Introductions were apparently unnecessary. Janus washed his hands in hot water kept over a wood-burning stove set up in a former horse stall, and then he did as ordered. He turned to the first man in line, wondering if he should go in order, or by need—worrying especially for the bleeding omega. But there was no time to ask because suddenly a patient was before him, an alpha—tall, impatient, and brutish—thrusting his injured hand out for help.

Janus cleaned out and then stitched up the alpha's finger, though he'd only ever read about the technique in books before. The tug of the thread through skin unnerved him, but he pressed on, and the big man gritted his teeth, not letting out even a peep of pain. Eventually, he closed the cut, and Dr. Crescent flicked an approving glance Janus's way before yelling at the patient, "Keep it slathered in honey, you hear me? If it gets infected, come back."

Then the alpha, who's name Janus had never even gathered, shoved a handful of nuts at him as payment. Janus accepted them and put them in his own pants pocket, unsure what else he might be supposed to do with them. Then he listened helplessly to the next man in line: a scrawny, young omega with bright yellow hair—the boy couldn't have been more than eighteen—with a sick newborn baby. The man looked near tears as he described the onset of the infant's illness.

"It was sudden-like, and all. My alpha said to bring 'im to doc. I'm scared." His voice wobbled. "He's so hot, and he won't chestfeed, and…" He broke down in tears.

Dr. Crescent jerked his patient's broken leg again, apparently having trouble getting the bone just right. Everyone shuddered as the teenager wailed. Then Dr. Crescent, having waited out the scream, called over his shoulder to Janus, "Elderberry syrup and willow tablet. In the stall by the end. You'll recognize the bottle and tin?"

Janus nodded.

Dr. Crescent then flicked his eyes toward the young omega and said, "Charlie, chew the tablet for the babe, and spit the goo in his mouth. Careful he don't choke on it. Brings the fever down. Syrup three times during daylight hours and two in the night. Sleep him sitting up. Keeps the mucus from his lungs. Rough few nights ahead for you and Dax, but hopefully, little Ellis here'll live, and that's what matters."

Then he'd turned his attention back to setting and binding the broken leg with wooden splints and bandages, his movements deft and sure, while the teenage boy—probably a beta, since he hadn't presented yet—whimpered, his young, blotchy face wet with tears.

The young omega, Charlie, looked to Janus with wide, dark eyes, his cheeks a bit hollow like he wasn't getting quite enough food so he wouldn't drain his own stores of nutrition while chestfeeding the baby. "Is that true, Doc? Ellis'll live?"

Janus cleared his throat, about to deny that he was a doctor and to refuse any guarantees, when Dr. Crescent said, "Tell 'im it's a good chance, Dr. Heelies."

"I'm not a doc—"

"You work with me? You're a doctor."

Janus swallowed back further protest and smiled reassuringly at Charlie. He touched the baby's soft, wet cheek, feeling the fever burn his hand, and said, "Dr. Crescent is confident that, if you follow his prescription, your son will come through this illness. Now let me round up the medicine for you."

Charlie actually paid Janus with coin, and as soon as the young man took his still-squalling babe away, Dr. Crescent nodded toward a jar on a long table covered in gruesome-looking, though thankfully clean, doctoring tools. The jar had a few coins at the bottom. "Add it in there. Then get your next patient, son. The bleeding omega, please, in case he's hemorrhaging. And watch that you don't offend his alpha during the exam. You know how we can be."

Janus blinked at Dr. Crescent. "Alone?"

"There's a curtained off table there. Make sure no one sees his omega's body 'cept you. Get on with it, Doctor. This isn't a game. These people need help."

Shaking with fear, Janus motioned both the bleeding omega and his huge alpha back behind the curtain where he did his level best to help without doing anything that would cause the alpha to beat him to bits.

Eventually determining that the miscarriage was complete, no lingering fragments to cause hemorrhaging, he gave the omega a small dose of a new clotting agent he was surprised to see Dr. Crescent had on hand. He delivered the sad news to neither of their surprise and prescribed rest and pampering until the bleeding had stopped. The alpha, obviously in love with his omega, seemed eager to comply, and so Janus decided to lean into it. Noting how weak the omega was, he suggested the alpha carry him home if no other means of transport was available. And after paying Janus with a handful of beans, the man proceeded to do just that.

Unsure what to do with them, Janus put the beans in the jar with the coins, dug the nuts from the first patient out of his pocket to add to the jar, and went on to the next patient.

By lunch, Janus was exhausted and confused. He'd never seen so many sick and hurt people, never imagined that so many folks populated the mountains. "Is it always this way?" he asked as Dr. Crescent led him toward his cabin set far enough away from the stables to provide some privacy, even though there were still a good number of less critical patients waiting for Janus or Dr. Crescent to see them after they finished eating.

"Only in the springtime," Crescent said. "Plenty of folk have been holed up in their cabins waiting for the snow to go away, nursing sickness or injuries in their stubborn way. Pride keeps 'em from coming right at first, but they make it down eventually.

Doesn't hurt that I sent out a notice that I'd have a new doctor working with me starting today. Curiosity drew part of this crowd."

Inside, Dr. Crescent's cabin was neat and tidy. Janus was surprised, though he didn't know why, when a small, black-haired omega turned from the old-fashioned wood stove wearing nice-fitting pants, a fresh, white shirt, black apron, and an assessing expression.

"Fan, this is that city boy I was telling you about. Janus Heelies, this is my Fan. Fan Dunigo."

They were *Érosgápe*, Janus guessed, based on the looks that passed between them, and the shiver of pleasure that jolted through Fan at the doctor's possessive declaration.

Quickly, Fan stepped forward, a steady, small hand reaching out to Janus. "I'm grateful you've come to help my Crow. He's needed it for a long time now, but help is hard to come by."

"He's not helping me, dumplin'," Dr. Crescent said with a tenderness he'd lacked with even the most suffering of patients. "I'm helping him, remember?"

Fan's smile was nearly a smirk, but he ducked his head submissively, and said, "Oh, yes—my mistake. We're happy to help you, Janus. Aren't we, Crow?"

Dr. Crescent shrugged. "I could take 'im or leave 'im. What's for lunch?"

Fan rolled his eyes and shot Janus a funny little grin, but then he turned to the stove and lifted the lid on a heavy, copper pot resting on top. A delicious meaty scent wafted through the room, and Dr. Crescent groaned. "My favorite? You're determined I'm going to like this lad, aren't you?"

Fan shrugged, a diminutive version of the one Dr. Crescent had made, and said, "I had some mutton left over, and I figured a hearty lunch would keep you in a good temper through the rest of the afternoon. We wouldn't want to make a bad first impression."

Janus blinked at that, realizing that he hadn't had time to even consider his true impression of Dr. Crescent, the stables, the patients, or his new position. He'd simply gone to work and tried to stem the flow, like staunching the blood from an injury.

Two place settings at the table held sturdy, blue-flecked crockery, and Fan declined to join them, saying that he'd already eaten. He kissed the top of Dr. Crescent's bushy head, whispered something in his ear, and then nodded to Janus. "We'll have plenty of time to get to know each other, I hope. I'm sure you have questions for Crow. I'll leave you to it." Then he vanished into a back room and shut the door.

"He'll read his romance books and take a nap," Dr. Crescent said with a fond scowl. "It's quite the life of leisure he has." Then he grinned. "But I'm the one who gets the pleasure of letting him live that way."

Janus nodded politely. *Érosgápe* were an unreasonable bunch. Biologically determined mates who bonded instantly at a level most others could barely begin to comprehend, and who loved unconditionally, unreservedly, and irrationally. They often took pride in the very aspects of their mates that other men might complain about. Though, if the worst Fan did was read novels and nap, Janus could hardly imagine finding room to complain about that. He'd spent plenty of his time over the years doing much less reputable and much more harmful things. Besides, the man made a mean mutton stew. Or maybe Janus was just starving after the rush of working all morning.

"I reckon he's right and you've got questions," Dr. Crescent said, his thick, gray-black brows raising. "Never seen anything quite like that lineup before, have you?"

"No, I can't say that I have. I'd been on a few observational rounds as part of my class curriculum last year, but I was sick during the months of hands-on work. I thought I'd made that clear in our correspondence."

"So, you did." Dr. Crescent shrugged. "I figured, with a city man like you, this would go one of two ways: either your balls were as big as they seemed, what with writing me for a position without the requirements for it in hand, and so you'd be fine. Or you were an egotist and an idiot, and in that case, one lineup like today's would send you right back home to the city." He eyed Janus carefully.

Janus took another spoonful of soup and said nothing.

"You're not going anywhere, are you, son? You liked that bustle and chaos."

Janus shrugged, considering. "I did. I felt useful."

Dr. Crescent studied him a long, slow moment, and then he nodded. "You need the work as much as they need help. Well, that's good enough for me. I hope when you've done your healing—" here he tapped his head and then his chest, right over his heart, making Janus feel exposed "—you don't just take your learning and run off. I'm going to need someone to take over most of the doctoring around here eventually. I promised Fan a romantic decade or two of retirement. And, wolf-god, I'm not getting any younger."

"Healing? I've been sick, it's true," Janus said, deliberately misinterpreting Dr. Crescent's comment. "But I'm hoping this mountain air will strengthen my lungs."

"I didn't mean that kind of healing, and you damn well know it." But Dr. Crescent's tone didn't hold any real bite, just an old man's scolding. He rubbed at his eyes and then said, "Now that's settled. Let's talk about your pay: very little. And your hours: extensive. And your skills: need more of 'em. Don't worry, *Doctor* Heelies. We'll work it out."

Janus didn't argue the title even though the lack of earning it sat like a bur on his hide. He didn't think Caleb would approve. He considered asking just what he could expect in terms of payment but thinking about the coin jar that was now more full of beans, bruised apples, and nuts than money, he didn't think he wanted to know.

"Got any other questions?" Dr. Crescent asked.

"Where do we see patients in the snow and rain?"

"I got some tarps to throw over the open sides of the stable. Keeps it warm enough to work."

"Oh."

Dr. Crescent cocked his head. "If you've got the funds to build us a nice clinic up here, son, you go right 'head."

"No. I…" Janus cleared his throat. "Your solution seems reasonable."

"Anything else?"

Janus considered asking the doctor about Kerry. Would it be too nosy to request information on the pregnant omega at the boarding house? He wanted to know about Kerry's alpha and what the situation was there. Was the alpha missing, dead, or what?

But he got the impression that, of the two men, he needed to have that kind of talk with Fan. Dr. Crescent seemed like he would be of no use in the gossip department. So, Janus shook his head, and Dr. Crescent looked pleased to be done with the business part of their conversation.

After Janus finished his stew, he cleaned the bowl in the sink and waited for Dr. Crescent to use the bathroom. When he emerged, wiping his hands on a fresh towel, he jerked his head toward the front door. "Back at it, Dr. Heelies. Once we get through this lot, we'll be done for the day. But tomorrow we'll start bright and early on rounds to check those who can't make it down to my office."

Janus followed Dr. Crescent out the front door, astonished to see that at least six more people had shown up for consultations. As they neared the stable, Dr. Crescent nodded toward the small, rocky pasture where three horses stood eating grass and watching the day turn. "How are you on a horse?"

Before Janus could answer, the clamoring for attention began, and an omega swept him up into a discussion about his alpha's diarrhea—so bad that the man hadn't been able to leave home to come for himself. He raided the dispensary in the stable for more tablets, this time of homeopathic amounts of *cuprum arsenicosum*. Janus got paid in coin for a change, and then he was on to his next patient.

By the end of the day, Janus had stocked up his bag with a few commonly used medicinal herbs and tablets to keep on hand as a new doctor in the area. "You never know when a patient might turn up at your door," Dr. Crescent said with a stern glare. "Best be prepared." And he no longer blinked when addressed as Doc, either. But he was still determined to earn the title as soon as possible.

# CHAPTER FIVE

ERRY WATCHED FROM his windowsill perch as Janus set out
for his second day under Dr. Crescent's tutelage. Janus's
strong shoulders sagged under the weight of the bag he'd slung
across his back, and yet he strode with purpose, apparently
undaunted by whatever horrors he'd faced yesterday.

And Kerry knew he'd faced *something* outside of his citified
expectations. The distant, stunned expression in his eyes when he'd
returned home last night, as well as his stilted conversation at the
dinner table, told Kerry that much was true.

And just like the first night, when Janus had gone out into the
dark and down to the lake despite Kerry's warnings about wild cats,
he couldn't help but feel a little impressed as he watched Janus
leave. Not every man was brave enough to return for a second
helping of hell. Not when they had a choice about it.

He rubbed his abdomen, feeling the taut skin beneath his shirt.
Overnight it seemed, he'd developed a rounding beneath his belly
button and above his pubic bone. The baby would only grow faster
and faster now.

It had been a month since his visit to the prison.

If he was going to end this torment, it had to be today. And
while Dr. Crescent didn't advertise his services in this regard, rumor
had it that he provided them. Or rather his omega, Fan, provided
them without Dr. Crescent's supervision or permission, in a secret
room in the back of their house. But Fan only intervened early on
in a pregnancy and only if there were no counterindications.

Kerry didn't know what those might be, and he hoped his chest deformity didn't count as one of them. If anything, it should count in favor of ending the affair before it proceeded any further. He rose carefully, put Kiwi back in his cage, and dressed in old clothes. If there was much bleeding, he didn't want to risk ruining his best pants. Then he put his hair up without looking at himself in the mirror.

In the kitchen, Pater washed the morning's dishes. He turned from the sink when Kerry entered, and his cheery, red-cheeked smile faded as he looked Kerry up and down. "Today?" he asked.

Kerry nodded.

"Are you certain?"

Kerry shook his head and then shrugged. His pater came to him, hands still wet, and horror all over his face. "Pater, don't. What else am I supposed to do?"

"You could have him, Kerry. We can deal with this together."

Kerry shook his head, wiping a hand over his sweaty upper lip. His stomach flipped over. "My chest…"

"It's not ideal, but you're strong. I believe you can survive it."

Pater's hope was touching, but no guarantee. Besides… "If I have him, they'll want him."

Pater touched his cheek. "If you don't, they'll make you try again. This could be your way out. If the little one is born with the potential to be an alpha—"

Kerry shook his head. "Stop. We've been over this."

Pater gave him a scolding look. "We've done no such thing. We've never talked even the first time about this little 'un inside."

"Well, *I've* been over it. In my head. Over and over and over. What do you think I've been thinking of all these days and weeks?"

"How to love him?"

Kerry scoffed and then crossed his arms over his chest, blinking up at the ceiling with his eyes stinging. "Pater, I can't love him. I can't find it in me. I've searched."

"But the child is blameless."

"I know." Kerry shook off his Pater's touch and turned away from the offered breakfast on the table. "I'd best not eat anything. I don't know what the procedure entails." He moved as though to leave.

Pater grabbed his arm. "Let me come with you."

"No. This is something I have to do alone."

"Why?"

"Because I can't stand to have you see it, or me. I won't be able to go through with this at all if you're there looking at me like that."

Kerry kissed his pater on the head, and then turned away, refusing to hear any more or look into his pater's sad eyes for another moment. He gathered his black cardigan sweater from the coat rack by the door and pulled it on before setting out along the same path Janus had taken. He just hoped that he could handle this and endure whatever happened after without his pater needing to deal with any aspect of it, or this alpha, Janus, finding out.

Miscarriages came on naturally enough. If Janus believed that Kerry lost his child through no fault of his own, then he'd at least continue to respect him, maybe even pity him, which wouldn't be a bad thing. A pitying alpha was often a care-taking alpha, and even though Kerry didn't want to engage the man in friendship or more, having him be solicitous and careful around him wouldn't be terrible either.

The path up to Dr. Crescent's house was steep, and by the time Kerry broke through to the clearing, he was winded. Pausing to catch his breath, hands on his knees, he cast his gaze toward the stables and saw no waiting patients. Two horses were gone, and the doctor and Janus were nowhere to be seen. They must be out on rounds.

A pang of disappointment preceded the wave of relief. Kerry

hadn't realized that some part of him had wanted to see Janus at work to assess his competence, and maybe to laugh at his lack thereof. But no matter. It was better this way, and he was happy that the man wasn't there to guess at Kerry's personal business.

Fan *was* home, though, as always.

Kerry had never seen him outside of the clearing around the stable and house and had at times wondered if that was Dr. Crescent's doing or not. His pater, though, said it had nothing to do with Dr. Crescent and that Fan was a peculiar man with a strange, unreasonable fear of leaving his homestead—a kind of phobia. Kerry knocked on the door, thinking he could almost relate to what it would be like to be afraid to leave home. He'd been in such a hurry to get away from Hud's Basin, but nothing good had waited for him out there in the wide world. Now he never wanted to leave Hud's Basin again if he could keep from it.

The door swung open, revealing Fan in all his handsome glory. The little omega was a good foot shorter than Kerry and dressed nicely in neatly tailored clothes, as always. His nearly black hair swept over his forehead, and he looked younger than he was with rounded cheeks and sparkling black eyes. Fan took one long look at Kerry and then swung the door open wider with a sweeping gesture that invited Kerry in.

Kerry didn't hesitate, stepping into the cozy room—part living area, part kitchen—that he'd visited off and on for social calls with his pater over the years, but never for so serious a reason as this. Fan guided him to a comfortable seat by the fire before serving tea and some delicious little finger cookies that Kerry couldn't resist even though he wasn't sure he should be eating. Fan took up the seat next to him and ate several cookies, too.

"You want to be rid of it, then?" Fan asked gently after the usual exchange of pleasantries descended into an uncomfortable silence. The fire popped and crackled, the flames blue, orange, and red. The heat coming from it was nearly oppressive, but Kerry didn't ask to move somewhere cooler.

"How did you know?"

"That's the only reason young, uncontracted omegas come to me when Crow isn't home. They hear the rumors. About the sorts of things I'm willing to help with that he's not." He took a dainty sip of his tea and then smiled at Kerry.

"I'm not uncontracted."

Fan frowned. "No, I guess you're not."

"And speaking of rumors, I'm sure you've heard the ones about me as well? About my alpha?"

Fan nodded, his eyelashes brushing his high cheekbones, not meeting Kerry's eye.

Kerry swallowed hard and felt his face warm with humiliation. Everyone knew, and yet it was still so degrading.

Fan cleared his throat softly, put down his teacup, and turned back to Kerry before asking, "How many weeks are you now?"

"Four."

Fan tsked and frowned, scratching behind his ear irritably. "Getting on a bit late with this endeavor, aren't you, little one?"

Kerry nodded and tried not to let himself chuckle at the irony of such a small man calling *him* "little one." "I didn't know if I wanted to do this or not." He chewed on his bottom lip and picked at the crumbs on the cookie plate.

"And now you know?"

Kerry shook his head. "It still feels wrong. Against all I've ever believed or been taught. In the mountains, life is so fragile. We see it all as sacred. From the trees to the fish, to the birds in the sky."

"Yes. And the most sacred of all is a newborn human baby."

Kerry bowed his head.

"You aren't alone in feeling uncertain. Most men, when they come to me, are in some way uncertain. But circumstances don't always allow for certainty when it comes to something that needs to be timed so particularly. I'd say you have, at most, three more days before the babe has fastened so completely that only an intervention much more intensive than what I am able to provide will dislodge him." Fan touched Kerry's arm and squeezed. "And to be quite frank, it's possible that it's already too late."

"I can't love this child," Kerry confessed. "And so, I have to end him. Do you see?"

"Others might love it," Fan said. "Me, for example. Childless as I am, I'd be willing to take him."

Kerry swallowed the questions he was dying to ask at that statement. Long had the rumors swirled about Fan's childless state. Some said he used his own methods on himself to keep free of the burden and risk of birth, but still others said barrenness was wolf god's punishment for his part in terminating the pregnancies of other omegas.

"My alpha's family would never allow that. They'd want him for themselves."

Fan nodded. "So, they know?"

"Not yet. But they would find out when my next heat was due and found me pregnant." Kerry shuddered.

"I see." Fan sipped his tea again. "I offer the same thing every time," he murmured. "To take the baby and raise it as my own. No one has ever taken me up on it yet." He sighed heavily. "Each man has his reasons. Some are better than others. But it's not my place to judge, you see. That's wolf-god's domain." He put his tea aside. "Your pater knows you're here?"

"Yes."

Another few moments of silence passed as the fire leapt in the grate. "Do you have questions? Or should we begin?"

Kerry closed his eyes, sent up a prayer begging for forgiveness, and then put his tea aside, too. "I'm ready if you are."

"Follow me."

Kerry braced himself and did as instructed.

For the procedure itself, Fan led him to a quiet back room with pleasant floral wallpaper and a half-sized bed pushed up against the side wall. He handed Kerry a robe made of soft, white material and said kindly, "I'll be in there gathering what I need." He motioned toward a door that seemed to lead into a large closet with an electric bulb hanging down. "You change into the robe, the opening in the back, and make your peace with this. I'll be back shortly."

Then Fan went into the closet and shut the door, giving Kerry privacy.

He looked around the room again, taking in the tasteful, framed drawings of flowers, frogs, and oddly, seashells. He swept his gaze over the clean floor, writing table, and bedding. It was suitable enough for what they were going to do, he supposed. Nicer than he deserved, but it was Fan's home. So, of course, it was nice.

Kerry stripped out of his clothes and folded them neatly on the chair next to the writing table, and then put on the robe backward as Fan had instructed.

His heart hammered, and the cookies and tea started to climb up his throat. He closed his eyes, dropped to his knees, and placed his elbows on the bed, hands raising to his forehead in the prayer position. "Please forgive me. It's for the best. I never wanted this, wolf-god. I only ever wanted to bear blessed sons for you. But…not this way. Please understand."

There came a tapping sound from behind the closed closet door, like stone against stone, and Kerry jolted anxiously, getting up to sit on the bed and wait. The window was open, and the fresh scent of pine and earth drifted in. He closed his eyes again and tried not to cry. His chin wobbled, and his legs shook.

"Knock, knock," Fan's voice came gently. "Are you ready?"

"Yes." But his answer came out so hoarsely that Kerry had to repeat himself to be sure Fan had heard.

When Fan entered, he carried a small dish in one hand and a tin in the other. He set these down on the bedside table and then took a seat on the bed beside Kerry. He turned to him with a calm expression. "This paste is made from a compound of pennyroyal, false unicorn root, and red raspberry leaf. I'll put it on the opening to your womb. The paste will cause it to ripen and, gradually, open. These," he indicated the tin of pills, "are made of sepia and sabina. Strong natural abortifacients. They will cause your womb to contract hard enough to expel the child through the opened entrance to your womb. That part of the process will be very painful. It can take a long time, several hours at a minimum. During this stage, you'll see blood and, if it's working properly, pieces of tissue—perhaps even the whole form of the child, but quite small."

Kerry swallowed thickly, his throat aching. "All right."

"You can stay here through it, or you can wait and take the pills at home where your pater can care for you. Even if he wasn't already aware of what's happening, which you've indicated he is, everything about this will still look like an ordinary miscarriage, even to Crow or another doctor unless you tell them. It's up to you."

Kerry stared at the tin. He looked around the room, imagined sweating and moaning here, imagined the relief-tinged pain of losing the child he'd been forced to make with Wilbet, and the grief that would come after. All while Fan held his hand and pressed cold towels to his head. He squeezed his eyes shut.

"Can I decide after the paste is applied?"

Fan smiled softly, putting the tin aside. "Of course. You can think on it." He stood and then patted the bed. "This is intimate and a bit embarrassing, but since you've endured a heat with that violent alpha you're contracted with, this will likely be nothing compared to the humiliation of that."

Kerry felt the heat in his face again, and he stared at the floor. Fan was often a sweet man, but sometimes he could be cutting. Kerry cleared his throat, trying to dislodge the lump, and then moved as Fan indicated, so that his stomach was against the mattress, his knees on the floor, and his ass sticking up in the air through the opening in the back of the robe.

Fan took up the paste, and then put a firm hand on his hip. "It will be easiest if you assume the lordosis position like when you're in heat."

Kerry pushed his ass up higher, arching his back.

"That's better. It opens you up for better access. Now, I'm going to scoop the paste onto my fingers and press it into you. My whole hand will need to fit inside so that I can reach the mouth of your womb. Because of that, I'll start by massaging your omega glands for slick. Do you understand?"

Kerry nodded.

"All right. Expect the usual twinge and stretch for this portion. When I insert my hand, it will feel a lot like taking a knot."

Kerry held his breath as Fan positioned himself on the floor behind him. He grimaced as Fan pressed against his anus with one slick finger, groaning when the finger slipped inside and mashed hard against the omega glands positioned near the beginning of his passage. The sensation was objectively pleasurable, but the situation was not, and so while his body released slick in copious gushes, it didn't bring him any joy. Fan withdrew his finger, humming a pleased little noise, and then he placed the plate holding the paste— a generous amount now missing—on the mattress beside Kerry. "Take a deep breath in."

Kerry stared at the floral wallpaper. The petals went in and out of focus. Blue and green dots appeared before Kerry's eyes, obscuring his vision. He sucked in a small breath.

"Let it out now," Fan said encouragingly. "And in again."

Kerry took a second, deep, shaking breath, holding it until Fan whispered, "Breathe out."

Kerry let it go in a gush, and at the same time Fan's four slim fingers and his thumb all sank into Kerry's asshole, along with a good portion of his knuckles, but there his hand stuck. Kerry clenched up tight, squirming in discomfort. The floor under his knees dug in hard, and the bedclothes beneath his stomach suddenly felt rough. He flushed hot all over. He remembered Wilbet's hands on his hips, gripping and bruising as he knotted him.

"Shh," Fan said, using his free hand to gently stroke Kerry's flank. "Let's take some long, deep breaths."

Kerry tried, but his breathing was ragged, and suddenly, the scent of pine and earth was gone. All he could smell was the prison's permeating scent of piss and fear.

Fan continued to speak calmly. "Close your eyes and imagine you're standing next to Hud's Basin. Can you see the lake? How it reflects the evergreens?"

Kerry whimpered.

Fan went on, "The sky above is a deep, cloudless blue. The sun is warm. The waters are smooth and lovely. It's summer." His voice was like a lullaby. Calm and tender. "You're floating in the water. The sky above, the lake below, supporting you gently. Breathe in and out. In and out."

Kerry gave into the suggestions issued in Fan's serene voice and visualized his beloved lake. Slowly, his breathing calmed, and his memories of Wilbet faded. His muscles relaxed, including his anus, allowing Fan to move deeper inside.

Fan's hand was small for a man's, but once lodged in Kerry's passage, it did feel quite a bit like a small, squirming knot. Kerry kept breathing, refusing to admit memories of Wilbet's much larger knot to his consciousness. He knew he'd tense again, so he kept his mind firmly on the twinkling, shifting water of his imagined lake. Fan's fingers, as he unfurled them inside, tickled and Kerry made a soft noise, almost a laugh, at the unexpected sensation. Taking that as a sign to move ahead, Fan shoved deeper and pressed his paste-covered fingers against the entrance to Kerry's womb.

Kerry stilled. The sensation was good, like an alpha's cock pressing for entrance during heat, and yet terrifying.

"There," Fan said, after rubbing in circles around the puckered, tightly closed entrance. "Normally, this part of you will only open during heat to admit the crown of your alpha's cock, and, of course, during childbirth. But this paste will trick it into opening now. It'll start to work right away to ripen you, and shortly, minor cramps will begin. Many describe the initial cramps as a burning sensation." Fan gently tugged his hand free, and a wet, slurping sound came from Kerry's ass as he exited.

The familiar gape-and-grip sensation followed, and Kerry shuddered through it, still fervently refusing to think of Wilbet and the way his alpha cock had left Kerry stretched open like this. Shortly, his anus ostensibly returned to normal. It still felt tender, though, stretched too quickly and without any sexual gratification attached.

An urge to sob grabbed Kerry, but he fought it back, and he buried his face in his hands, praying.

"I'll be right back, little one. I need to wash up."

Kerry nodded into the blankets, his buttocks and legs trembling, and his chin wobbling, too. As water ran in the sink from the attached bathroom, he took the time to compose himself. Then, the sound of water came again, from farther away in the small house, perhaps the kitchen area.

When Fan returned, Kerry was still on his knees, face in the mattress, feeling odd and fragile. His anus ached from the invasion. His heart felt burdened with what he'd chosen. And his womb burned with whatever Fan had pressed into him. He rose up onto the bed at Fan's behest, his legs shaking and his hands trembling too hard to hold the glass of water Fan had brought for him.

Finally, after a few sips, assisted by Fan, he was able to calm down enough to take the glass and hold it for himself.

"Do you feel the womb entrance opening?" Fan asked.

Kerry nodded.

"It's uncomfortable, I know, but you can endure it." He put an arm around Kerry's shoulder and hugged. Then he let go, reaching for the tin. "Now, these pills… They'll need to be taken very soon, before the womb's entrance closes again. You can take them now, here with me, and I will guide you through it."

"But if Dr. Crescent comes home…? And the new doctor?" Kerry's mind went to Janus, imagining the alpha seeing him sweating through a miscarriage. He felt sick at the idea.

Fan, misunderstanding, waved his concern away. "Even if Crow returns home earlier than expected, he'll think I'm helping you through a typical miscarriage. Nothing new. Or, if you prefer privacy and home, as I said earlier, you can take the pills with you to miscarry under your pater's care."

"And if there are complications?"

Fan frowned. "Then your pater must call for Crow, of course. Don't bother holding back the truth from Crow if necessary. Crow pretends not to hear anything that has to do with me. But he may need to know what medicines you've taken to treat any complications properly. Hopefully, this will be a smooth expulsion. Well, as smooth as something this painful can be." Fan held up the tin for Kerry to take.

Kerry looked around the cozy room. As kind as Fan was being, and as comfortable as his home seemed to be, Kerry wanted to escape it. He didn't want to be with anyone when he did what he must. He wanted to be out under the sky with the pine needles of the forest beneath his hands and knees, crying out to wolf-god in the temple of his creation as he finally ended this current nightmare of Wilbet's cruel and selfish making.

"I'll take them at home." It disturbed Kerry how easily he lied now. Another thing he'd learned from a life with Wilbet.

Fan seemed to sense something amiss. He cocked his head and examined Kerry closely. "With your pater? At home?" he confirmed.

Kerry smiled tightly in response.

Fan went on, "The pills will take ten to fifteen minutes to take effect."

Kerry nodded.

Fan passed the tin of tablets into Kerry's palm but still seemed reluctant about it. "All right. I'll have Crow call around tomorrow afternoon to check on you—"

"Please don't. I'll be fine."

Fan frowned, his delicate brow creasing. "My gut is telling me to have him look in, little one."

"The new doc is living with us," Kerry reminded him. "Janus will be there if there's a problem this evening."

Fan's expression brightened a little at that reminder. "I suppose he will. Crow trusts this Heelies man. And therefore, so do I."

With that, the post-procedure interview seemed to be over. Fan bustled out of the room and back toward the main living area, leaving Kerry to dress on his own.

Putting his clothes back on felt weird, like he'd just committed a crime and was covering up the evidence with pants and shirt, which is exactly what he'd done in a way. Ending a pregnancy was a hanging crime. Everyone knew that.

Though he hadn't taken the pills yet. He could still change his mind.

As Fan led him to the front door of the house, Kerry shook free of his own, self-centered thoughts to ask a question of Fan. "How did you know what the lake looked like? I thought you never left this land?"

Holding the door open and gazing wistfully out into the clearing, Fan smiled. "I wasn't always bound here. I used to move more freely."

"What happened?"

Fan handed Kerry the cardigan he'd taken off when he first entered. "I lost our fifth son, and I made a promise to wolf-god that I wouldn't leave this clearing until I become a pater." Pain raced over Fan's face, but he hid it quickly. "He has never seen fit to bless me, and so I remain bound by my oath. Now be on your way, little one, and wolf-god bless you. I have lunch to make before my alpha and his partner return from their work up-mountain. They'll be wanting food."

Kerry didn't linger, though the burning of his cramping womb was harsher now. Fan shut the door on his retreating back with a finality that echoed around the hollow. Kerry looked down at the tin in his hands.

He was on his own with his choices now.

KERRY HAD NEVER endured anything so painful in his life. Not even his hours at the mercy of Wilbet's cruel hands could compare to this anguish. He thought he might die.

How was it possible that this pain came from the cramping of his own body? It felt alien and other, like a gripping hand ripping through his lower abdomen, leaving him yelling and gasping on his hands and knees.

Naked and alone, he endured the agony, his mind wiped clean of the reason for it and only understanding the gasping need to breathe between harsh bouts of pain.

He'd chosen a clearing deep in the forest, close to the lake, but far enough from the hollows and houses that he'd felt safe to disrobe and wait. The lake would wash him clean when the pain ceased. And if the worst happened—if there were complications, he'd let wolf-god's earth have his body. It would only be right.

But Kerry hadn't anticipated this kind of pain. Despite Fan's warnings, he was unprepared for the misery. It was beyond the telling of it.

The forest cradled Kerry in its palm as he agonized and suffered. The soft, brown pine needles beneath his palms and bare knees held him. The swaying trees stretching high into the sky rocked him. He grabbed fistfuls of needles in his hands as blood slipped down his thighs and dripped from his swinging balls. He cried out as another cramp wrenched him.

Time passed, and he collapsed to the forest floor, groaning and sobbing, nerves and heart inflamed. The earth was there for him, and perhaps wolf-god, too, and yet he had never felt so alone.

# CHAPTER SIX

T HE COOL WATER of the lake was exactly what Janus needed after a long day in the saddle going up and down the mountainside with Dr. Crescent. He slipped into it naked and aching all over. Groaning as he swam out into the waters, he quickly slipped beneath to wet his hair and then resurfaced to float on his back.

He'd had another eventful day with Dr. Crescent. They'd visited house after house—or hovel after hovel, depending on how one viewed the dilapidated buildings in which many of the mountain families lived. They'd dealt with the decrepit-ness of very old age, they'd done womb-checks for pregnant omegas and performed check-ups on healthy children, among handling all kinds of ailments and injuries. The variety of families he'd witnessed had astounded him—old, young, some with many children, and others with just one or two. He'd met betas, alphas, omegas, and every combination thereof living together as adults, and Janus had seen more ragged-looking children than he knew how to count.

There had even been one shocking household with two young omegas both contracted to one alpha. Janus wasn't positive that was legal. In fact, he was rather sure it wasn't. And worse, both omegas appeared to have born the alpha multiple children. Astonishing! And yet they all lived within the same compound of connected buildings, seemingly without any dispute between them. The omegas seemed to be good friends, despite one being the *Érosgápe* of the alpha, and the other...not. It was utterly deranged as far as Janus could tell. What *Érosgápe* allowed his alpha to knot and reproduce with another omega if they, themselves, were not infertile or sick? He'd never heard of such a thing.

When he'd asked Dr. Crescent about it all afterward, the doctor told him that the family was a member of a small but growing religious sect that believed wolf-god wanted each alpha to reproduce as many times as possible, even if that meant taking on more than one omega. There was apparently another family living over the ridge in which the alpha had contracted with four omegas, and reproduced with three of them. Scandalous.

The family Janus had met, though, all shared the surname Whitehoul—another anomaly since city omegas usually preferred to keep their surname—as well as seven whelps between the two omegas. And the darker of the two, the one who was not the alpha's *Érosgápe*, had been pregnant with an eighth.

Manders—the second-youngest child in the family and a dark little thing with nearly black eyes—had been the reason for their visit. He'd lost his foot in a crushing accident involving a runaway cart earlier in the year. The family had been hauling lumber to add to their ramshackle, sprawling home when the axle broke and the cart ran over Manders's foot. A difficult situation, to be sure, but they all seemed determined to face it together as a family.

After greeting the parents and being taken to where Manders sat inside by the fireplace peeling apples for a pie, Dr. Crescent had checked the way the stump was healing. Finding it scab-free and not in the least inflamed or swollen, he turned to Janus, "Dr. Heelies, what d'ya recommend now?"

Janus had accepted the challenge. He suggested that a specialized, fitted boot for the lower half of the boy's leg, complete with a wooden foot carved to the correct size, might be ordered from the city. The alpha and his two omegas had all shot each other wide-eyed looks until Janus realized that there was no way this family could afford such an expensive prosthesis—especially for a growing boy who would have to replace it within a year. He'd quickly shut his mouth.

"That's a mighty kind suggestion, Dr. Heelies." Dr. Crescent had been generous with him. "Something to aim for in the future, mayhap, when Manders is grown. But, for now, I think a sturdy crutch at his current height with a cushion under the arm might be the less expensive course."

Janus had readily agreed, hot shame at his own ignorance making him sweat.

Now, in the lake, he washed away that sticky residue. He ducked under the cold lake water, swimming with his head beneath and his eyes closed, willing the frustration and helplessness away. He might not be able to help Manders now, not with his limited funds, but Caleb was a resourceful and soft-hearted man. Maybe he could be persuaded to put on a charity auction of his artwork in the city with the benefits going to the mountain people's healthcare, especially to help those like the boy he'd seen today.

Bursting to the surface with a harsh gasp for breath, he shook the water from his ears and eyes. Feeling strong and yet tired, he began to tread water. The lowering sun sparkled on the water and shone in the sky. As the days lengthened into summer, he would be able to stay out in or by the lake longer and use fewer candles as well. Not that he'd even used his first candle yet. He'd been far too tired after his first day with Dr. Crescent to study.

A cry rent the air, human and pained.

Janus searched the land to his right, twisting about in the water, trying to discover from where the sound had come. The echo of the cry bounced on the water, off the cliffs on the east side of the lake, and through the mountain's hills and valleys, obscuring its source. The sound faded out, and Janus anxiously waited for so long that he finally assumed he'd imagined it, or that perhaps it was the cry of one of the wildcats.

It came again.

This time Janus was able to pinpoint its origin as coming from the land to his right. He treaded water a bit longer, heart pounding, listening for confirmation that he was right about where the pained cries were coming from. He nodded sharply, certain when a third scream split over the water. He started to swim.

The space between where he was and the area of the forest where the hair-raising screams sliced through the sky was no easy distance to cover, and yet he dragged himself onward through the lake water. The cries stopped and didn't start up again for a long time. Janus paused in his swimming to listen and, as the silence lingered, he glanced back the way he'd come, considering the stretch of beach along the woods below the boarding house. He could go back, ask Zeke about the screams, and they could go together on land to check out the problem. But just as he'd decided on that course of action, another horribly human cry rose up.

Someone needed help. There might not be time to get Zeke. So, he continued on.

His strong strokes began to fade to weaker ones as he strained toward the narrow, pebbled beach along the western strip of the lake's edge. He'd started to grow scared for himself, and his strength had nearly given out, just as he reached the shallows and his feet touched bottom. Flopping forward, he heaved himself ahead on his hands and knees, trying to catch his breath and listen for the cries again. Pausing for a moment, lake water dripping from his nose and chin, he listened, his eyes scanning the forest's edge. Just as he was about to stand and begin to search the woods, a man crawled from the tree line onto the beach. Naked.

Janus stood up in the thigh-high water, hands on his hips, mouth open in astonishment and fear. The scent that drifted to him on the breeze was instantly familiar. The man crawling on the ground was Kerry. Janus recognized the berries and musk that had gotten under his skin from his first glimpse of the man on the porch. He gawked, trying to grasp what he was seeing.

Kerry dragged himself—stark naked, dirty, and streaked with blood from the waist down—toward the water. His long, bedraggled hair was full of pine needles, bark, and leaves. He was suffering and in distress.

Janus leapt forward, running through the shallows. Water droplets kicked into the air, sparkled, and cracked into rainbows in the sun. By the time Janus broke free of the water, Kerry had collapsed, stomach and face down, into the pebbles. He twisted in pain and groaned in a harsh, low tone, like a foot crunching in gravel.

As Janus fell to his knees next to him, water lapping at their flesh, Kerry began to heave and shake with sobs.

"Kerry? It's me, Janus. What's happened to you? Has someone hurt you?"

Kerry moaned, deep and rough. He shook his head, saying nothing.

Janus scanned Kerry's body, noting the bloody legs and genitals, and his stomach sank. Rape? Or, more likely, miscarriage. He whispered, "Kerry? I'm here. I'm going to help you."

Kerry moaned and shuddered. In his left hand, he gripped a small pill tin. Janus tilted his head, recognizing the imprint on the side. His heart clenched. Those pills were intended for use when a pregnancy had already gone awry, to help when a babe wasn't expelling properly, and as a last resort to save the omega's life. Had something gone wrong with Kerry's pregnancy?

"Kerry, did you lose the baby? Kerry…can you talk to me?"

Kerry shivered and groaned. "I don't know. Did it work? Is he gone?" he rasped, his eyes bleary and lost, his body clenching in agony again.

Janus pressed his lips together, his blood running cold. If he understood correctly, Kerry had committed a hanging crime today with the aid of the pills. He closed his eyes, trying to clear his thoughts. Opening them again, the decision made, he acted before he could change his mind.

Gently, he pried the tin from Kerry's hand and then threw it into the lake. Right or wrong, he wasn't going to let Kerry hold on to evidence like that, and now, with the pills beneath the water, he could forget that he'd ever seen them at all. Quickly, he took inventory of Kerry's state: no fever (thank wolf-god), harsh womb cramps, as evidenced by the tight ball of muscle beneath his navel, and bleeding.

Janus leaned forward and breathed in: berry and musk. That strange blend that was neither right nor wrong but meant Kerry was still pregnant. No hint of death or rot. So far, the baby was holding on. Whatever Kerry's intentions might have been, and no matter how much he'd suffered, Janus didn't think he'd been successful in his plans.

"You shouldn't be here," Kerry croaked, his lips dry and cracked, the corner of his mouth bleeding. "I'm doing this…" He groaned and squirmed as though he wanted out of his body. "Alone."

"Not now, you're not." Janus rolled Kerry onto his side and lifted his head into his lap, trying to make him comfortable. The fact that they were *both* naked only struck him when Kerry's filthy, long hair brushed against his dick. He stroked calming fingers through Kerry's curls, cleaning out the worst of the small sticks and leaves, willing Kerry's pain to calm enough for Janus to be able to examine him.

"Kerry?"

The sudden stillness of Kerry's body was his only acknowledgment that he heard him.

Janus asked, "Have you seen any tissue? Or just blood?"

"Blood. But it hurts so much. The cramps are so strong."

"They're very painful?"

"Yes." Kerry's voice cracked, and he writhed against Janus's leg, but he pushed on, trying to talk to Janus. "He can't possibly withstand them. *I* can barely stand them," Kerry gritted out. He cried out as another spasm hit.

They weren't in the clear just yet.

"I need to have a look to see." Janus wished they were near hot water so that he could wash his hands, but they were where they were, and there was no way he was abandoning Kerry now to seek out additional help. It would be utterly impossible to get Kerry across the water or through the hills to the boarding house in this state. He'd have to hope for the best.

"It's fine. I'm all right," Kerry said, going pale and starting to shake. "I'm just fi—" He screamed again, his body arching, and his legs twisting up. Blood spurted from his anus, and Janus didn't wait any longer.

"I have to check you now. Do you understand? You could be hemorrhaging. I need to see so I can decide what to do."

Kerry nodded, sobbing, as another rush of blood leaked from him.

He positioned Kerry on his side and then bent low, pressing two fingers in to milk the omega glands for additional slick, but the blood was enough that he was able to move on to pressing his hand into Kerry without much effort. Kerry froze, cried out, and then went incredibly, almost horribly still.

"It's all right," Janus said as soothingly as he possibly could. He tried to summon memories of his sweet Caleb's calm tone during the worst of his illnesses. "I have you. It's just a moment of discomfort now. No sudden movements, please, even if it hurts. I just need to check—"

Kerry shuddered and screamed again, and the clamp around Janus's wrist was breathtaking. He knew it had to hurt Kerry as well, so he wasn't surprised when Kerry broke down in panicked sobs as soon as the cramp passed.

"Shh," Janus soothed, pressing as deeply as he could without hurting Kerry more. The mouth to Kerry's womb was soft, no doubt about that, and tacky. Someone had applied ripening paste…but who? Who would leave Kerry alone to suffer like this? Janus had only known Zeke a day or two, but he already knew that was something Kerry's pater would never do.

At least there didn't seem to be anything caught in the opening and no sign of a puncture. He had to hope for the best. Once the pills wore off, the cramping would stop, and hopefully the blood as well.

Removing his hand slowly, he was grateful for the proximity of the water. He washed in the lake, and then came to pull Kerry's head into his lap again. He was still crying, but the cramps seemed to have slowed a bit. Janus swept soothing hands through Kerry's hair, down his neck, and over his shoulders. Kerry didn't protest, but he didn't entirely relax either.

"The womb is still closed," Janus finally said, softly. "The blood is from the harsh contractions causing leaking of lining, and possibly some internal tearing of your inner walls, though I didn't feel a puncture, which would be…" He didn't finish that thought. "There could still be damage to the child from the strength of the contractions. You could still go on to have a miscarriage, but at this point, your womb has held him in."

Kerry curled inward, his head shifting in toward Janus's stomach, his breath rushing against Janus's genitals and lower abdomen. Then he began to cry—wet, harsh sobs that shook his shoulders— but they were different from his sobs of pain before. These were sobs of grief, lost hope, and utter sorrow.

Janus didn't know what to say, so he continued to stroke and comfort. The sun lowered in the sky. He knew there was no way

Kerry could swim home, and he wasn't the man of strength he used to be. Carrying someone of Kerry's lanky frame and size over that great of a distance would be impossible. All he could think to do was to wait it out.

Once the cramps fully stopped, Kerry was able to wash off in the lake water. His dark eyes remained haunted and empty. He slid them away at every turn, avoiding Janus's gaze and ignoring his offers of reassurance.

"We'll have to support each other," Janus finally said, helping Kerry rise unsteadily to his feet. "Do you know the way?"

Kerry blinked, the lost gaze of a man on the verge of saying that Janus should just leave him behind. Janus was about to protest that unspoken sentiment when Kerry raised a shaking hand and pointed toward a path leading into the forest. "It runs the edge of the lake. That way is home."

Janus nodded and hefted Kerry's limp arm over his shoulders. "Come on then. You'll need a hot bath, tea, and a bed. Then I'll need to examine your womb and passage again to make sure everything is working as it should for elimination, which could be problematic for a few days. But we'll make sure that you're going to be all right."

"I will never be all right," Kerry whispered, his legs quivering as he struggled to stay upright.

But they took a step forward together onto the path Kerry indicated. And as the limbs of the trees closed over their heads, Janus heard the sorrowful call of a bird announcing that the sun had finally set.

THEY FLOUNDERED HOME in the gloaming, one man exhausted and broken, and the other still recovering from sickness, a hard day, and a long swim. As they approached the final rise leading up to the boarding house, Zeke met them bearing a flashlight and a worried expression.

"Wolf-god, what's happened?" Zeke exclaimed, seeing them staggering together, naked, dirty, and both beyond exhausted.

"Pater..." Kerry muttered, falling from Janus's embrace into Zeke's arms. The old man could barely hold Kerry up, though, and the flashlight fell to the ground. The forest around them chirped, croaked, and groaned with life—insect, bird, frog, and tree.

"Sweet boy," Zeke whispered, clutching Kerry close. "Oh, what have you done? What have you *done?*"

Kerry began to cry again, and Janus stood by helplessly, his hands dangling at his sides, and his nakedness feeling suddenly important, despite his previous obliviousness.

Zeke caught his eye, taking his measure, and found him trustworthy in some way. He clenched Kerry closer to him and sighed. "Sweet boy, let's—"

The sound of a hiss and growl made them all freeze. Wildcats? Janus didn't know, but Zeke's spine stiffened right up, so whatever it was, it couldn't be good.

"Let's get up to the house now," Zeke murmured, tugging Kerry against his side and wrapping his arm around Kerry's lower back. "The cats smell blood, I think."

Exhausted, Janus picked up the flashlight and followed, glancing behind him into the darkness and fully expecting to see yellow cat eyes gazing back at him. Nothing moved, and no wildcats or glowing eyes appeared. Though, as they moved slowly up the incline to the yard, then up the back porch stairs and into the warmth of the kitchen, Janus couldn't shake the prickle of fear up his back.

They moved on through the kitchen, past the table Zeke had set for dinner, pressing onward for the stairs. Getting Kerry up them was a group effort, and they all gasped with relief when they finally maneuvered him down the hall to his bedroom and let him down gently onto his mattress. From his golden cage, Kiwi squawked in distress, and the room required more light than was afforded by the gloaming out the window. Zeke lit several candles and then collapsed on the bed next to his son. Janus wished for battery-powered lamps now.

"What happened?" Zeke demanded, pushing the long hair out of Kerry's face. "How could Fan have let this happen to you?"

*Fan? Dr. Crescent's omega? Interesting.*

Janus knew that all omegas were a little squirrelly about birth and reproduction, and most, if pressed, would admit to being, at the very least, open to helping those who didn't want to go through the rigors of pregnancy and labor for whatever reason. If such an omega, like Fan, had access to abortifacients...well, there was no telling what he'd do with them. Janus wondered if Dr. Crescent knew what Fan was up to.

Janus had heard plenty from Caleb over the years about the reproductive rights of omegas, and the unjust legal lack thereof, especially back when they'd been true friends in the early days of their youth. Most of him agreed with Caleb. Still, as an alpha, he'd always thought termination of a pregnancy for any reason outside of saving the life of the omega was abhorrent. An alpha's offspring was meant to be a sacred thing, a gift from wolf-god, a blessing not to be taken for granted—if one was a religious sort anyway. And if one wasn't, well, the human population was still in danger. They needed every life they could save, especially after the flu epidemics of the prior years.

And yet, Janus couldn't help but feel scared for, and oddly soft toward, Kerry. Despite not understanding the man's choices or knowing his reasons, he found himself not nearly as judgmental or hard toward Kerry and his actions as he knew he should be.

Surely there was an explanation that made sense. And even if there wasn't—

Kerry was human. Fallible as any other.

And right now, he smelled so vulnerable and scared, and just a touch sad. His scent and tantalizing omega pheromones were strong after his ordeal, making Janus want to protect him, even more now that he also smelled like hurt and pain. His inner alpha wanted to cover him, keep him safe.

"Fan didn't 'let this happen,' " Kerry said. His voice, usually so smoky and low, sounded scraped to a rough whisper. "I lied to him. I told him I'd take the pills at home with you to care for me. Don't blame him."

Zeke sat back, his cheeks going red like he'd been slapped. He stared at his son. "You didn't trust me to care for you? I know that I disagreed with your choice, and told you so this morning, but I would never—"

"Pater, no," Kerry choked out, his eyes filling with tears again. "No. Of course, you'd care for me. I wanted…no, I *needed* to handle it alone. I didn't know it would be so…" He trailed off, his eyes going blank again. He turned onto his side. His back was dirty, as were his buttocks, hips, and thighs. The dark brown of dried blood looked gruesome on his skin and matted into his leg hair.

"Is the cramping over?" Janus asked, kindly.

Kerry nodded.

"I know you're tired, but it would be good to bathe you, change these sheets now that they're dirty, and then, once you're fresh, let me have another look."

Kerry didn't move, but he nodded again, slowly, almost as if he wasn't entirely there.

Zeke turned to Janus then, eyes wide, taking him in with one up and down sweep of his eyes. "You need a bath as well, priesty. I'll handle my Kerry. You go wash off and, well," he blushed a little, "put on some clothes."

Janus looked down at his own naked form. He'd completely forgotten again that he was nude, which seemed so unlike him. He had fixed his entire attention and focus on Kerry and how he smelled so vulnerable. Now here he was, naked as a newborn, his cock waving about like he had no shame. "I went for a swim and…" He trailed off, not sure how to explain how he'd come to find Kerry, and why he was naked, too.

Zeke didn't look offended, though, just eager to set things right and get his son cared for properly. "Please, Janus, get on with it. By the time I put new sheets on his bed, and he's cleaned up all nice-like, you will be long done with your own bath. After that, you'll check on 'im again? Make sure his insides are intact?"

Janus nodded, not bothering to explain that Kerry's insides were just fine, for the most part. Some tears within notwithstanding. It was the child who might be damaged now. So, they might have to go through it all again in a few days, with possibly different results.

As Janus turned to go, Zeke sat on the bed beside Kerry, saying, "I see there's been a lot of bleeding. Is the child gone, then, son?"

Kerry shook his head against the pillow, his body twitching but holding back the sob that ground deep in his throat. Janus wondered at his willpower to keep it all in now. It must be because he was with his pater—no doubt trying to be brave for his sake. Kerry had sobbed freely enough in front of Janus by the lake.

"I still scent the child," Janus whispered.

Zeke's shoulders slumped.

Janus touched his arm and said quietly, "I'll go clean up and get dressed as you asked."

"Thank you," Zeke said, already standing to head into Kerry's attached bathroom. He gripped Janus's arm before he could go. "I still don't know how you came to be with him, or what happened, but thank you for helping my boy."

Janus nodded and took off to his room to wash. Afterward, he'd need to check Kerry's anus, passage, and womb again. His gut churned with hunger, exhaustion, and confusion, but he couldn't stop thinking about Kerry's broken form, crawling from the forest, or the way he'd cried when he'd realized he'd suffered it all in vain.

Why did Janus want to soothe him and take it all away? He should be angry with the man for violating their human need for more life, and wolf-god's gift to him. He should be threatening to call the authorities. Instead, he wanted to cradle Kerry close, breathe in his strange, pregnant-ripe scent, and hope his strength could supplement where Kerry's had failed. He wanted to take his pain away.

As he contorted himself to fit into the bathtub and scrubbed himself with the pine-scented soap he'd brought from the city, he tried and failed to understand his urges. Caleb, with his keen mind, would probably have something to say about it all. He'd have to write and ask him for his opinion.

Janus dreaded to know what Caleb might say.

# CHAPTER SEVEN

KIWI WAS A comfort at least.

Kerry lay on his side in his bed, his entire abdomen aching like a very strong man had punched him repeatedly, and his thighs quaking in exhaustion. He should be asleep, but he couldn't seem to slip down into it. After gingerly tossing around for a while, he'd crept from his bed, retrieved Kiwi, and then climbed back beneath the covers. The bird now hopped between his headboard, his head and his shoulders, sometimes fluttering and taking flight around the candlelit room.

Eventually, he went back into his cage on his own, tired out. Kiwi tucked his head beneath his wing and went to sleep. And still, Kerry couldn't follow him down. He didn't know if he was afraid to dream, or if he just wanted to hear more of Janus and Pater's conversation drifting up from the living room downstairs.

With his door left open so he could call down if necessary, every syllable was audible, all echo-y and disembodied, but still clear. He didn't know if the other two men knew he was listening, but he didn't have the desire—or voice—left to tell them.

"He helps omegas lose their babies?" Janus said again. Teacups rattled, and there was a crunch of someone biting into a cookie. Kerry's stomach growled, but he didn't want to eat, didn't want to breathe either, but he couldn't control that.

"Most omegas on this mountain agree that Fan is an agent of good, or rather, he readily accepts that death is a necessity at times," Pater said grimly. "He's inconsolably childless, and some say that in his bitterness he takes a mite too much pleasure in helping others losing their sons, too. But that's a cruel lie. Truly, he takes on the burden of this work because he knows that if he doesn't, someone else will, and they might not take such care. I'm astonished that he believed Kerry would come home to me."

"Does Kerry make a habit of lying?"

Kerry winced. Was that what Janus thought of him now?

"Of course not!" Ah, Pater to the rescue of his tattered reputation. Never mind that it was as good as ruined to Janus now.

Janus cleared his throat. "Then I understand why he'd let Kerry go. He assumed he was honest and had no reason to believe differently. Plus, Fan knew I was staying here. I'm sure he thought if there was going to be any real trouble, I could handle it."

That's exactly right, Kerry thought. And Janus *had* handled it, hadn't he? No thanks to Kerry's insane scheme to miscarry in the forest, though.

At the time, when he'd made his decision, it'd seemed right—natural. A wolf goes into heat; a wolf gives birth in the woods. Not that he was a wolf, of course. He was as human as anyone else. But wolf-god had made humans in his image, and at his bidding, they had become alpha and omega and reproduced. Kerry had imagined wolf-god would comfort him there amongst the trees and dirt. He'd thought he'd feel safe and in the palm of wolf-god's hand there.

And truthfully, he *had* been comforted. At first. Until the pain had grown so great that he'd passed out and then woken to it again. Until he'd screamed in agony, higher-pitched than he'd known he could achieve. Until he'd sobbed in Janus's lap like an abandoned child.

Wolf-god, what had he been thinking?

Kerry was lucky Janus had found him. He'd have never made it home on his own, and lying in his blood in the forest, even down by the lake with the cats and their cubs about, would have been foolish beyond the telling of it. Food for the predators. Wilbet was right. He *was* an utter idiot.

Downstairs, Janus cleared his throat again, this time proudly. "And I *did* handle it."

Oh, great. Alpha posturing. Kerry would roll his eyes if he didn't find Janus's puffed up comment comforting in a way. He couldn't help but remember how firm Janus's hands had been on his body—both by the lake and in his room—and how kind, too. Many alphas would have been enraged by what he'd done. But Janus, despite his citified ways, had taken it in stride and held strong and steady. Like an alpha should. Like Wilbet never had.

Kerry closed his eyes, listening more closely for Janus's tenor voice, noting a curious, warm sensation inside. A kind of calm heaven that seemed to wash over him with each syllable Janus spoke. Though perhaps that was only the poppy-based tablet that Janus had given to calm him finally kicking in.

Janus went on, "Does Dr. Crescent know? About Fan's side business?"

"It's not a business," Pater hastened to clarify to the chorus of their teacups rattling in saucers. "He takes no money for it. He considers it a grim duty, a harsh kindness. And yes, Dr. Crescent knows, but he pretends not to. It's safer for everyone that way. He even attended a few that went awry, and despite being told Fan had given the omega abortifacient pills, he acted as though it was just any other miscarriage. Some of our local alphas don't like it, but Dr. Crescent is strong enough to keep them in check."

"I see."

"I wouldn't bring this up to 'im," Pater warned. "You're like as not to get a cuff to the ear as any kind of response you'd actually like. He won't have you endangering his omega."

"Of course not." Janus was silent a moment. "And Fan? If I talked to him?"

"He might play coy," Pater assessed. "He's more open with betas and omegas than with alphas. But he knows you a bit and trusts you. Or so I'm assuming since he hasn't advised Crow to kick ya back yonder to the city. If you don't come across as threatenin', Fan might talk to you about it some. But then again, he might not. It is Kerry's private business, after all."

There was a long silence, and not even the sound of teacups in saucers interrupted it. Finally, Janus asked, "This may be presumptuous to ask, but I need to know. Why? Why would Kerry take this course of action when life is so precious and necessary?"

"That's a tale for Kerry to relate, priesty. But he has his reasons. Dark and painful ones, to be sure. While I didn't approve of his choice today, I understood."

"How?"

Pater sighed heavily. "Like I said the other morn, he's contracted to an alpha. And well, lad, he's a mean 'un. Rotten to the core. There's not much else to say about it that I'd feel right comfortable telling. It's Kerry's story to gift to ya if he ever trusts ya enough. Not mine."

Janus seemed to take that well enough, not pressing for more. Kerry listened harder, trying to catch any movements. His eyelids dragged down, heavy and tired, and he finally rested them, letting the world fall black. He still reached with his ears though, and now, too, with his nose, seeking something, though he didn't know quite what.

Then he found it: roses, lemon, and pine—Janus's scent.

Kerry sorted it through carefully, impressed with himself that he'd found it from all the way upstairs. He'd never truly enjoyed Wilbet's scent, and therefore never tested the limits of an omega's wolf-god-given gift of scenting another man. But finding Janus wasn't even hard. There was a new, different, slightly damp smell about him, too. Maybe lingering water from the lake or his bath.

Perhaps both.

He smelled like home and safety. Kerry had never scented anything like it before. He remembered the delicious musk of his groin, too, as he'd sobbed into his lap. He'd been dazed, in pain, but even then, the rarity of an alpha's intimate scents pleasing him had registered.

Kerry sighed as the poppy's liquid warmth spread over and in him, like the most pleasant warm blanket. Protecting and holding him. He was safe to explore Janus's scents drifting up to him along with his voice. It didn't matter anymore what he was saying, only that he was still there, talking, being in their house—keeping his pater company and keeping them both safe.

He put his hand on his stomach and felt the child's flutters again. He was still moving. Still alive. Janus would be pleased. Poppy-warmed sleep stole Kerry away, just as the sound of chairs moving back and the clatter of plates below indicated that Pater and Janus were finished talking.

Breathing in Janus's safe-smelling scent, Kerry was fully gone before he ever heard either man's first footfall upon the stairs.

JANUS COULDN'T SLEEP.

The burden of the afternoon and evening felt too great to bear on his own, so he rose from his bed, sat down at the small writing desk, and decided to light his first candle.

Janus pulled one from a box of them nestled inside the drawer in the desk and scratched a match to light it. He found a small, primitive-looking metal candle holder in the drawer as well and stuffed the glowing stick into the hole. Holding it aloft by the curved, metal handle, he placed it on the desk. Then rose, pulled on his robe over his pajamas, and sat down again.

Taking out a smooth, creamy sheet of paper and a new pen, he stared at the flickering flame for a long time before finally writing:

*Dear Caleb,*

*I hope this letter finds you and all of yours well. I especially hope the children are healthy and strong. Please send some of your illustrations or prints of them if you see fit. I have always loved your art and felt honored when you shared it with me. At this point in my life, I can no longer offer a fair price for any of your pieces, however, so I understand if you don't want to give away anything priceless. I'm eternally your admirer, either way.*

*This probably will not surprise you, but I find myself quite out of my depths here in Hud's Basin. I knew I would be, of course. I'm not an utter fool. Well, I'm trying not to be anymore. But it is far stranger here, and more upsetting, than I had imagined. Can you believe that? I'm sure you can. I can just hear you now, "Janus, that simply shows your failure of imagination more than anything else." And you'd be right, I suppose.*

*Look at that, dear friend, your arrogant Janus has admitted to the likelihood of a failure. Are you proud of me yet?*

Janus stopped and considered the paragraphs he'd already written and thought about inking through the last few lines, or possibly wadding up the whole letter and starting over. He didn't want Caleb to think he was flirting with him.

His body thrummed with wiry exhaustion. He was too tired and wound too tightly to rewrite anything, so he carried on.

*Don't answer that. I know I should be striving to be proud of myself. And yet...*

*I hardly know where to begin tonight and feel that anywhere I choose as a starting point will leave out important background information that further informs the situation. Whether that be the utter poverty of so many of the people here, or the curious way they live their lives, or the difficult position I found myself in tonight with my host's omega son, who is also staying in the boarding house. Not that kind of position, Caleb! Do keep your mind out of the gutter! I've turned over a new leaf!*

He started to ink through that last bit and again held off. So what if he was flirting a little? Caleb could handle it. They both knew where they stood.

*No, this was a position that puts the morals I've agreed to uphold as a nurse and doctor in a fight against my moral fiber as a human being. (They insist I call myself a doctor here, though I'm hardly competent to do so! Another strain on my newly developing sense of right and wrong! And such an oddity!) I don't even know all the details of the situation at hand, and I certainly can't share very much without violating the trust of a man who has, as of tonight, very dramatically become my patient. And yet I feel I must bare my soul and share my confusion with someone safe. As much as we both may not like it, that someone for me, Caleb, is you. Must be you. Have I told you lately how grateful I am for your forgiveness and friendship? Because I am.*

*I ramble on and say nothing. My nerves are twisted up violently, and my heart is racing with the memories of the events of earlier this evening. I shall call the young omega in question by the initial K, to maintain his privacy, and because it is his first initial.*

*Tonight, while swimming in the lake near the boarding house—I believe I mentioned it in my first letter to you, as yet unsent—I heard a cry of pain. Upon searching out the source, I*

*found K in agony, suffering from what appeared to be a miscar-
riage. That in itself may not seem so strange, given your Urho's
experiences with his doctor practice, and omega birth statistics
being generally so poor. But I found a tin in K's hand, and I
recognized it immediately as a very commonly obtained abortifacient and knew what he had done.*

*And yet, though I can see no reason for his choice, beyond
his oddly shaped chest and a missing (and rumored ill-chosen)
alpha, I do not feel anything but pity for him and his desperation. Worse—(worse? it is shocking that I'd put it that way!)—
he did not manage to dislodge the babe. So, he suffered it all in
vain.*

*In vain? IN VAIN? Do you see what I'm saying, Caleb? I
haven't been here a full week, and my morals are twisted all
around, and my feelings for a young man I've barely met super-
sede the law in my heart. I even discarded the evidence of the
herbs he used, hiding the tin where no one would ever find it,
and with that one action sealed my own thoughts and feelings
regarding him. He's my priority now. Not the babe. Not yet,
anyway.*

*What does all this mean? I'm at such a loss.*

*And all of this begs me to remind you, my dear Caleb, to
stay safe in your pregnancies. You are held dear by too many to
risk yourself too often. Insist on precautions during heats. Excuse
my impudence, but I'm far too invested in your health not to
speak up.*

*Wolf-god, I haven't even told you about my home visit to
an alpha contracted with two omegas! And their shared children! Nor have I shared the abject misery of so many of the
people here, all of whom work so hard for so little! Nor did I
explain about the doctor, and his Érosgápe bound omega (who
is, from what I understand, the local abortionist!) and so much*

*more! I'm so undone that I've taken to using exclamation points with abandon. Shameful.*

*Caleb, perhaps I should burn this letter and not send it. The candle is flickering here at my side quite temptingly. I could just shift the page up and set it alight, and yet I yearn to hear from you and know your thoughts. I know you will soothe me even from afar, even if I do not deserve it. Tell me what to think and how to feel. I know you will be just and kind. You always are.*

*Your eternally undeserving servant,*
*Janus*

Addressing the envelope and adding a stamp to the corner, Janus stood from his desk and stretched. He listened for any noise from the hallway, but Zeke had long ago gone to bed, and his patient was tucked up, hopefully asleep as well.

However, Janus decided he should check that Kerry hadn't spiked a fever before he tried to defeat his insomnia again. Though the child seemed to have clung on, it was possible he could lose the baby even yet, and if that were the case, he might develop an infection from decaying, unpassed tissue. It was hard to know when the danger would be fully over, but if Kerry continued to grow round, then they should be able to discern the child's heartbeat by the end of the week at the latest if the timing of conception was as Zeke had led Janus to believe.

He walked down the hallway as quietly as possible, not wanting to wake Zeke or worry him. The door to Kerry's room was cracked, left open by Zeke in case his son needed him in the night. Janus pressed it wider and was relieved to see Kerry sleeping heavily in his bed. The moonlight dropped in against the floor and shafted over the bedspread, lighting Kerry's face, showing off his ample lips and smooth forehead. His eyelashes gleamed darkly against his cheekbones, and his hair spilled everywhere, unbound and beautiful as it dried on the pillows.

The gleaming birdcage stood to Janus's right as he tiptoed in, and he breathed a sigh of relief that Kiwi remained asleep, head tucked beneath his wing. Janus stepped close to Kerry's bed and reached out, tempted to run his fingers through Kerry's beautiful tumble of hair, but then pulled his hand back. It wasn't his place. Kerry wasn't his omega, or even friend, to touch affectionately like that. To touch as a doctor, yes, but not as anything more.

Kerry didn't appear feverish, but Janus allowed himself a soft touch to his forehead to check. If anything, Kerry felt a bit chilled. So, Janus turned away from the bed to close the windows that Zeke had left open and then turned to go.

"Thank you." The whisper came from the bed. Kerry lay there in the moonlight, oddly beautiful in a way that tugged at Janus. He wanted to smooth away the wrinkles in his blankets, touch his cheek again, and declare him safe now, in his care. Janus shook off the weird and possessive feeling. Inappropriate at best and disturbed at worst. Kerry had just tried to abort his child! What was wrong with Janus that all these strange, unwanted alpha urges were kicking in?

Janus whispered to himself, "It's my duty to feel this way. I'm a nurse now." That had to be it, right? Intense emotions surrounding an intense situation. Nothing more. "I only want to help you. It's my job to do what it takes to keep you safe." His voice felt rough, and he swallowed thickly. His job. It was his *job* to feel this way. That was all. That *had* to be all.

Janus turned from the bed, easing back toward the door. He'd almost made it when he heard Kerry say, "You'll make a good doctor."

Janus didn't look around, afraid that if he did, he might say or do something he couldn't take back. As for Kerry, he said nothing else and didn't try to stop Janus from leaving.

Janus left the door cracked on his way out and went back to his own bed. With a confusing mix of feelings, he climbed in and stared at the ceiling for a long time. When he finally fell asleep, it was to dream of dark, curly hair spilling out over a crisp, white pillow, and a smoky voice whispering darkly into his ear. The words were sensual, but not sexual, and he shivered when he woke, trying to recall them.

He failed.

# CHAPTER EIGHT

"*I NEVER WANTED to hurt you,*" *Wilbet said softly, reaching out with his big, strong hand to stroke along Kerry's face. He gripped Kerry's chin hard, and Kerry winced. "But you make it so hard…"*

Kerry jerked awake, his heart pounding, and covers kicked to the floor. At least he'd woken before the nightmare went on to its usual conclusion. He put a hand to his stomach and felt the rigidity there. He squeezed his eyes shut. What kind of person was growing in there? Another monster?

Kerry rolled to his feet and dashed to the bathroom, puking for the first time since the earliest week. He washed his face in the sink, and then returned to climb back into bed. The morning sun poured in sloppily like it didn't care at all what it touched, or how the object of its affection might feel about it.

It'd been three days since he'd tried to abort the child, and he still hadn't left his room. Not because he wasn't capable, but because he was ashamed. Pater brought him food and water, cared for Kiwi, and read books aloud by Kerry's bed at night, poems usually, nothing that required sustained attention by either of them.

Janus, for his part, carried on with his duties and his life as if nothing untoward had happened. Not that he didn't check on Kerry often, because he did. Three times a day: once in the morning, again when he returned from his work with Dr. Crescent in the afternoon, and once more before bed. There wasn't much conversation between them, though, and their interactions were perfunctory and professional. Kerry didn't know what to make of it, but he got the impression that the problem wasn't that Janus didn't care about him or his situation, but rather that he cared too much, and that he had questions he wanted to put to Kerry, but perhaps, didn't feel they were appropriate.

Kerry lay in bed, wondering why Janus hadn't come to him yet this morning; the sun was already far up in the sky. Normally, Janus came just after dawn. Kerry liked the way Janus smelled in the morning—fresh from washing, he was a mishmash of roses and lemon with a good base of pine-scent, too. Kerry wondered if he used pine-scented soap or hair cream, or if he just naturally smelled of the evergreen. He wanted to know the answer, though it was a dangerous question to even harbor.

He didn't mind Janus's scent in the afternoon, either. The sweat and warmth of the day radiated from his skin and clothes, and Kerry could well imagine he'd earned every bit of tiredness that also bled into that odor, like a sour note to all that gorgeous citrus and rose.

And at night...oh, at night, Janus smelled of the lake: damp and green. He swam every evening after dinner. Pater had mentioned it casually, but Kerry wouldn't have needed to be told. The way it altered his scent was undeniable. Kerry had been tempted to get out of his bed of shame, sit on the sill, and use his binoculars to watch Janus again. But he hadn't.

Self-pity was a powerful enemy of any action.

A soft knock came at his door, and Kerry rolled over, eager, curious as to why Janus was off to such a late start. Only to find Pater standing there waiting for Kerry to wave him in. Kerry beckoned him forward, disappointment like a stone in his gut.

"Janus left before dawn to begin his work with Crow," Pater said as if he could read Kerry's mind. "He believes you're past any danger now. Though, he instructed me to check you this morning for fever, cramping, or other unusual pains." Pater sighed, his tired eyes fixed on Kerry with the same hurt they'd held for days.

Kerry said nothing, gazing back at his pater with his heart in his throat. He wanted somehow to turn back time, to bring the pills home and take them with Pater there to care for him—to do it all the "right way." Moreover, he wanted the pills to work this time, for the child he was now stuck with to be gone, and for Janus to be none the wiser. But time was cruelly one-directional. What's done was done, and the outcome undeniable. He'd have to learn to accept it. But how was he ever going to erase the look of betrayal from Pater's eyes?

"How do you feel this morning?" Pater asked after the silence drew out awkwardly.

"I'm fine." Kerry gritted out. His pater raised a brow, and he amended, "Physically, I'm fine. The rest of me…" He shrugged.

Pater nodded, and his shoulders slumped. "Wolf-god help me, I don't know if that there's good news or bad."

"What do you mean?"

Pater let out a long breath. "I need to talk to you, son, in a serious way. Get dressed and meet me downstairs. I sliced berries and cheese for you to eat."

Kerry nodded, his gut knotting up in anticipation. He watched his pater leave before doing as he was told. Taking a little time to let Kiwi out to fly around the room while he dressed, he wondered about his pater's wariness. There was no way to know for sure what Pater needed to tell him, what he had to get off his chest that was this kind of serious, but Kerry reckoned he deserved it. He kissed the bird's beak before replacing him in his cage in front of the tiny mirror.

Tempted to drag his feet as he walked down the stairs, Kerry was aware with every step of the still-strained muscles from the cramps, but he forced himself to a normal pace.

The teapot on the stove was still rattling with heat, and the kitchen was overly warm as the morning sun streamed in the windows. Kerry sat down to the simple breakfast his father had plated for him, eating it slowly as his pater cleaned up from Janus's breakfast earlier. After he put the dishes away, Pater joined Kerry at the table.

"Kerry," he began as soon as Kerry finished with his berries and cheese, "I know you've had a difficult time of it, and I understand why."

"I just—"

"Shh. Don't give me excuses that I don't wanna hear. I do understand your pain. That's why it grieves me to tell you this…"

Kerry bowed his head low, waiting for the excoriation to begin.

"Son, you've had a message."

Kerry's blood ran cold. He jerked his head up to meet his pater's eyes. A message for him meant only one thing.

Pater nodded, his jowls wobbling a bit. "Yes. I know."

"Fuck."

Pater didn't scold him for cursing. "Rodes brought it up from the bottom of the mountain as soon as the sun came up. I met him at the door on Janus's way out."

"A message. For me." Kerry repeated the words, trying to accept what they meant.

"Yes."

Kerry cursed softly again and covered his face with his hands.

"They're at the hotel in Blumzound." His pater's voice had gone all raspy.

Kerry knotted his hands together in his lap. "I see."

"And they're waitin' to see ya, son."

Kerry let out a shaky breath and met his Pater's eye pleadingly. How had they known? There was no sign of his pregnancy yet, no reason for any word to get back to them about his state, even if they'd hired spies around these parts—which Kerry wouldn't put past them—no one knew what he'd done. But, of course, they didn't need any word, did they? Kerry's heat had been a month ago. If a babe had caught in his womb, now would be the time to ascertain that.

In the past, though, they hadn't bothered to come in person. But that was because Kerry had sent a forestalling letter telling them there'd been no luck. He hadn't done that this time. Like with the attempt to rid himself of the child, he'd waited too long, letting uncertainty keep him from acting, and thus sealed his fate.

Pater went on, "They expect you there by noon. The note made it clear. They want ya to join them for lunch. You know how they are. Impatient." He pushed the folded notecard on fine stationery, embossed with a bright, red M, across the table to Kerry.

Kerry took the note with shaking hands and read his pater-in-law's loopy, concisely worded script. Monte, Wilbet's pater, had taken on the surname Monhundy after he'd contracted with Lukas, Wilbet's father. When he asked Wilbet about this curious choice, he informed Kerry that Monte's father and pater had been so embarrassingly poor that Monte had been more than eager to escape any association with them. Despite wanting to escape Hud's Basin back then, Kerry had never felt the same kind of loathing for his mountain heritage, so he'd kept his last name and his pride. That difference alone had been enough to make Monte Monhundy harbor a poorly hidden dislike of him right from the start. Kerry, despite being awestruck and eager, had failed in this one important way to be the easy-to-mold son-in-law Monte had wanted.

"I don't think I can do this," Kerry said, his voice a whisper.

"Fine by me," his pater said, breathing a sigh of relief. "We'll send a return note, tell them that, yes, you're pregnant, but might miscarry. It's true enough. Janus said a few days ago there was a goodly risk, given the beating the baby took from the contractions. And, even though he thinks you're past all that now, it's a good excuse. They'll never know the difference."

Kerry shook his head, rubbing his fingers over his sweaty top lip. "If we tell them that, they'll send a city doctor to examine me, and when they find me sound, they'll insist I come back with them for the duration." He squeezed his eyes shut, trying to think. "No, I have to make them believe I'm fine to gestate and deliver here." Aside from not being certain if he planned to rid himself of the child, another reason he hadn't wanted to alert his in-laws to his expectant state was his fear they'd summon him back to the city and away from Hud's Basin. Another horror to layer on top of all the others.

Pater winced. Neither of them wanted to be separated during Kerry's pregnancy and delivery, and while Kerry was "always welcome" at the Monhundy home in the city, Pater was decidedly not. They had even written it into his contract with Wilbet that Zeke was never to visit the Monhundys' residences, and all family visitations would require Kerry to come up the mountain to *him*.

At the time, it'd seemed like an offensive but understandable request. His pater was appallingly countrified and didn't have any desire to come to the city anyway. Wilbet was generous and had given so many gifts and made so many improvements to Monk's House that Kerry hadn't thought twice about it or considered it more than just generally insulting. But at that juncture, he'd been desperate to improve himself and had wanted the Monhundys and their ilk to accept him so badly, he'd been intentionally oblivious to the true nastiness of it. Even now, he liked to blame simple greed, and claim that it alone had blinded him so thoroughly that he'd signed such an abusive contract, but the truth was, he'd been naïve and blinkered by unearned veneration for the fancy folk in the city, too. It disgusted him to look back on it now. Such a stupid child he'd been.

Pater asked, "Is there another way out of this meeting?"

They both stewed in silence, turning over and rejecting options with heavy sighs between them. Finally, Pater leaned forward and said, "There must be some way to refuse them. Just say ya won't come down. What will they do? Come up here? You know they'd rather die than step foot on my property, and I have a gun that'll teach 'em."

"No." Kerry chewed his lower lip, feeling sick. "That's no solution. They have the law on their side, and we have…" He glanced toward the clock. He'd slept in late, but not that late. His father must have come up to his room almost immediately after Janus had left and once he'd read the note. "But we do have time, perhaps. If I'm lucky."

Speaking of time, they couldn't afford to wait any longer if he was going to make it down the mountain by noon. He rose and lifted his chin, putting on a brave face. "There's nothing we can do right now, Pater. I have to go meet with them."

"We'll need to take the car," Pater said, not fighting him anymore.

The car had been another gift from Wilbet. At the time, Kerry remembered Pater had considered the car a useless waste of money and fuel. But in the end, he'd had to admit that he found it easier than hiring a wagon to go up and down the mountainside for supplies. The closest town of any size being Blumzound, a good hour and a half drive away; a car was faster and more reliable than a wagon. Plus, he could go whenever he wanted without having to owe favors or spend money—fuel being less expensive than a waggoneer, once he took the driver's tip and time into account. Kerry had once glowed to be the reason his father had such a coveted extravagance as a car. Now it too was a reminder of what they'd sacrificed for it.

"I can drive myself."

"Don't be a turnip-head, son." Pater put his hands flat on the table. "I'll drive."

"No. I'll go alone." Kerry shivered and wrapped his arms around his body.

If the Monhundys even saw Pater in the hotel lobby, their irritation at being reminded of Kerry's connection to the mountains could sway the direction of their lunch conversation in ways that would leave Kerry at a strategic disadvantage for the coming months.

"Now look here, son." Pater's cheeks flared with blood, heat in his voice. "You made your choices the other day all on your own, and look at how that went. Today, you'll let me drive. Whether you like it or not." He hammered a fist on the table.

"Don't get upset," Kerry said, trying to soothe him. "I just don't want you to abandon your responsibilities. Who will be here when Janus comes home? He'll need dinner."

Pater shrugged that off. "We should be back long before the priesty returns."

Kerry couldn't argue. Janus's days with Dr. Crescent usually went quite late into the afternoon. If they hurried, and if Kerry managed to achieve his objectives in a quick lunch with the Monhundys, they'd be home before Janus. Pater could serve him cold cuts if necessary.

Kerry closed his eyes. If only this day was already safely behind him, like all the trying days of his past, and he was seated at their cozy table ready for dinner with his pater and a handsome alpha who didn't terrify him quite the way he should. Kerry knew he was foolish to feel safe with Janus already, and yet he couldn't deny that he did. Janus had such gentle hands, and he hadn't even scolded him for what he'd done. At least not yet.

"Time's a'wastin'," Pater said, glancing toward the clock over the stove. "We need to leave now if we plan to make it there by lunch."

Kerry read the note from his in-laws over again. The message truly was an order, not a request. While the Monhundys would never stoop to putting their threats in writing, they always managed to phrase things so that Kerry remembered everything he had to lose if he disobeyed. The most important thing he could lose—the right to remain here in the mountains with his pater away from the city and the memories—being the largest weapon in their arsenal. Holding things over each other was how things worked in that family.

Wilbet had been good at reminding Kerry of everything he'd given him, and all that he could take away, too. Though not quite as good with subtle threats as his parents. He'd been too thick-headed to play it smart, always so reckless and clumsy in his abuse. Kerry supposed that was how the police had caught Wilbet in the end. Cruelty combined with stupidity was destined to be uncovered. If only Kerry hadn't been so quick to look the other way at first, to excuse and accept excuses for both Wilbet and his parents' spitefulness, he could have avoided his current predicament.

Not that there hadn't been warnings aplenty, even from the other omegas at the Philia soirees. Other omegas had pulled him aside at more than one of those splendid parties and warned of Wilbet's nastiness. But champagne had buzzed in his veins, near enough to love, and the thrill of a future laced up with brilliant, untold opportunities had bogged up his wits. Wilbet, after all, had treated him so gently and grandly, at first. Gifts, and compliments, and nuzzles in dark corners. They had gone for wild car rides at night, romantic kisses under the moon, and sex that had been pleasant if not mind-blowing.

Kerry picked through these memories like shiny river rocks. Finding that once picked up, green slime covered the underside. Then he pushed them all aside. He had to keep his wits about him now.

Retrieving the small, green car from where they stored it in an outbuilding near the edge of the garden—along with the tiller, clippers, and household tools—Kerry tried to think of other ways to keep Pater from going all the way down the mountain with him. But in the end, he gave up. After what he'd done with Fan's pills, the risk he'd taken on his own, there was no way out of Pater's escort. He wouldn't trust Kerry to drive down to the town alone. Too many appealing dropoffs, perhaps.

Convincing his pater that he didn't want to hurt himself, that he was past *that* at least, was pointless right now. He'd been reckless. This overprotective companionship was the price they would both pay for his poor choice. Now he needed to focus his mind on how to make sure he paid the price today only, and that he wouldn't be forced to pay even more by spending his pregnancy in the city.

With Pater driving, the bouncing of the car on the rugged roads caused Kerry's bruised body to ache all over. It was a wonder the babe still clung to his womb. He was a determined little thing. Much like Kerry himself, he supposed. Kerry clung to the bar above the door as they jolted along the horrendously bumpy road.

At least the weather was nice.

They kept the windows down, the breeze raking Kerry's hair into a wild bird's nest. But the fresh air pouring in was somewhat calming, even if his hands still shook when they finally drove past the sign announcing they'd entered Blumzound.

It was a tiny town, really, with a small raft of modern houses built in a group after the railway had come through about five years back. Trade had picked up, improving the lives up-mountain to a degree with more easily obtained goods and services. But for the most part, Blumzound was still just a blip on the surface of the world.

The town's houses and main street were tucked around the

eastern base of the mountain, crouched between the slope and the curve of a dark, gray river called the Blum. The hotel stood at the opposite side of town, near the railway station.

"Drop me off here," Kerry said, as they pulled up to the front of the four-story structure. The tallest building in Blumzound. "Park around back, Pater. I'll meet you there when it's all over."

"Oh, no. I'm coming in with you."

Kerry turned to him then. "Please, Pater. You'll make it worse." He hated to be so blunt. His pater liked people to consider him likable and, in the past, had striven quite hard to make a good impression on the Monhundys in hopes of altering their feelings toward him. His failure to do so was something that caused them both pain.

"I see."

Kerry used a mirror and a brush they kept in a compartment between the seats to straighten out his hair. The tangles hurt, but he didn't let himself wince, angrily tearing the brush through, trying to gather his rage into a shield. "Aren't there errands you could run?" He began to tick some off. "Refuel the car. You could buy some more tea and sugar. Stock up on candles." He tied his hair back and hesitated before adding, "Purchase some soft material for paternity clothes for me? I'll be needing some soon. And other fabric to make clothes for the baby." He touched his stomach, his throat going tight.

Pater leaned over then and pushed a stray lock of hair behind Kerry's ear. With shiny eyes, he examined him up and down, and finally nodded his head. "All right, son. I'll let you handle this on your own. I suppose I don't have a choice about it, much as I'd like to go in there to protect you from them. Legally, I have no legs. And they don't respect me much, anyhow."

Kerry squeezed his pater's hand. "I'm sorry."

Pater pulled away, shooing Kerry's apology off. "Don't sign or agree to anything you don't want to do."

"I won't."

"Promise me."

"I do. I promise." He kissed his pater's cheek. "And don't worry, I'll make sure I get to stay in the mountains for the delivery. I know just what to say."

Pater looked skeptical, and for good reason because Kerry wasn't sure how to get what he wanted at all. But Pater nodded anyway and put the car into gear again. "See that you do." He grunted and huffed. "All right. I'll meet you 'round back here at the hotel by two o'clock. Promise me, or I'm comin' in after ya."

"Yes, two o'clock. Around back." Where no one would see their dusty car or see his pater's work-a-day clothes. Kerry was already worried about what the Monhundys would think of his own outfit. He should have taken more care to pack nice things in case of this eventuality. But when he'd left their city apartments, fresh after reporting in following his last heat, he'd left all his nicest suits in the closet there. He had no use for them in Hud's Basin. For multiple reasons.

Kerry looked down at his soft, comfortable pants, tailored to fit him tightly before he'd lost weight, and before his stomach had started to grow. He ran smoothing fingers over his best white button-up shirt and shot the cuffs of the most fashionable jacket he'd taken with him. It was at least two seasons out of date, but it was clean, so it was simply going to have to do.

It wasn't as if the hoteliers in Blumzound would be offended, so even if Kerry weren't a walking advertisement for their power and wealth, the Monhundys would simply have to suck it up.

The lobby of the hotel had undergone a recent refurbishment. Previously, it had been a barely habitable place by city standards, but the influx of new traffic, and thus cash—after Blumzound installed the train station—had allowed them to redo everything, top to bottom. The formerly plank floor was now a pale, pink marble, and matching molded tin tiles covered the new vaulted ceiling. It wasn't city-levels of glorious, but at least it added a sense of *trying* to the humble mountain valley establishment, if not true class.

Kerry's stomach and thigh muscles still twinging, and his gut roiling with anxiety, he strode across the open space while trying not to exhibit any evident physical or emotional distress. Absently, he noted that the lobby now held cream-colored sofas and settees, along with low coffee tables. If he wanted to convince the Monhundys that Hud's Basin was the place for him and that their grandchild would be safe—no *safest*—growing within him here, then he'd need to appear completely healthy and in good spirits.

Wolf-god, if only he were a better actor.

The middle-aged beta with a tidy uniform standing behind the reception counter directed him toward the dining room of the hotel. "Yes, they're waiting on you, sir," he said, with a hush of awe in his voice. Kerry remembered when he'd felt the same way about the elegant Monhundys. Now he knew the truth of what all that gloss and shine was truly hiding, and any awe he'd once entertained had faded away into dread.

The dining room was half-full of patrons and smelled of butter, jam, and a meaty stew of some sort—rabbit, perhaps—that made Kerry's stomach growl. His appetite had decided to return in full, which was good. He'd be able to make a show of heartily feeding the thing growing inside of him, and he could claim his thinness was a result of now-past pregnancy sickness. So long as no one talked too much of Wilbet and made his stomach turn again, he should be able to pull that off.

Kerry spotted his in-laws at a table by the window. Looking out onto the side garden by the hotel, both had their heads turned in that direction, talking quietly about whatever it was they saw outside. Kerry took in their impeccable gray suits, starched shirts, shiny shoes, and fashionable ties with a gulp. He really was underdressed for attending a meeting with them.

Monte's shining red hair was stick-straight and slicked back with a pomade that Kerry knew smelled like citrus-scented hand soap. He was younger than Kerry's pater by about ten years and quite vain about his looks. Kerry knew he wore special powders on his face to protect him from the sun, both so that his fair skin wouldn't burn, and so that he wouldn't get any more freckles. He was quite paranoid about his freckles. Claimed they looked untidy.

Lukas, Wilbet's father, had sterling silver hair, having started to turn gray in his twenties according to the photographs Kerry had seen of his and Monte's contracting parties and celebrations. His strong, alpha jaw and his broad, muscular chest were the sources of Wilbet's similar structure. Lukas looked like a thug, however, while Wilbet had looked handsome, dreamily so. At first, anyway. It was hard to say just when Kerry's opinion on Wilbet's looks had changed, probably around the first time Wilbet had purposely hurt Kerry while fucking him.

Yes, it was probably right about then.

He shook off that wretched memory and slapped on a cheery smile as he stepped quickly toward his in-laws. Some sight outside the window kept their attention. Kerry approached their table unnoticed and stood beside it unseen for a long, dreadful minute. The scene out the window that held their attention was harmless: bunnies in the garden. Brown bunnies, to be exact, hopping about with fluffy white butts.

Kerry cleared his throat. "Father, Pater," he said softly, employing the terms his in-laws had instructed him to use when addressing them, though they'd always sat wrong on his heart. "I got your note this morning and came right away."

His in-laws turned to him at once, almost in unison, like they were the same person. Kerry held back a shiver of revulsion, schooling his face.

"Darling," Monte breathed, rising quickly, his eyes lighting up and a smile stretching over his fragile features. "You look well."

Kerry held back his trembling as Monte smothered him in kisses, his wet mouth pressing against Kerry's cheeks and forehead, again and again. Kerry remembered when he'd thought this behavior a token of Wilbet's pater's true affection and acceptance, instead of yet another way to violate and control. He'd been such a stupid idiot back then.

"Pater," he said again, taking Monte into a warm hug to stop the kisses at least. "You look well, too."

And the man did. Of course, he did. He spent more money than many men made in a year on beautifying products and procedures. Monte's skin positively glowed in the midmorning light from the window on the garden. Kerry hoped his tan complexion didn't look sallow in comparison, and if it did, that they would think he'd gotten too much sun, not that he'd been recently sick or ill.

A strong arm came around Kerry's shoulders.

Lukas pulled him away from Monte's manhandling to guide him into a chair between both of theirs, giving Kerry the direct view on the garden and putting his back to the dining room at large. It left him feeling vulnerable and exposed.

"Now, now, relax," Lukas said heartily, his thick mouth working the words like a hard to chew steak. "You don't look well at all, my boy. Not at *all*. In fact, I'd say you look a bit grim." His hazel eyes glittered with anticipation, and he lifted a challenging brow at Kerry.

Monte, putting a napkin back into his lap, said, "Darling, don't be rude to our sweet boy. He's likely been ill." His eyes gleamed as well, taking on genuinely fascinated interest. He didn't take his gaze from Kerry as he lifted his glass of sweetened iced tea—a mountain staple—and took a sip before opining, "He looks quite well considering."

Lukas's gaze narrowed on Monte for a moment, an equally fervent glow starting in his eyes, too. Settling back into his seat and throwing his arm over the back of his chair, so that he could more fully twist to take in Kerry's every expression and move, he asked urgently, "Is there good news for us then? Does the sickness have you?"

"Let the boy eat first!" Monte cried, motioning toward a waiter. "You're being extraordinarily rude, love."

"He's kept us hanging for weeks, darling," Lukas objected, but when the waiter came over, he held his tongue long enough for Monte to place an order for Kerry—just as he'd ordered for Wilbet in the past, even when Wilbet was a full-grown man who could make his own decisions.

As soon as the waiter left to comply with the vast number of requests—because apparently Monte was going to rectify Kerry's thinness all in one sitting—Lukas was back in Kerry's face, silent, but still demanding an answer.

Kerry smiled, scooted his chair back slightly for more breathing room, and nodded. He lifted his chin and tried to sound happier than he truly felt. "Yes. I have wonderful news! It's true. I'm pregnant."

A satisfied expression fell over Lukas's face, and he leaned back in his seat, pride oozing from him as if he had been the one to impregnate Kerry himself. He nodded to Monte and said with a barely hidden snide-ness, "I told you. It's a good thing we came."

"Why's that?" Kerry asked, taking the bull by the horns. He may as well allay whatever fears they might have had for his mental well-being, the baby's health, and his plans for the future. No matter how correct they'd have been to have them in the first place, the game now was convincing them of his total stability and his enthusiasm for this pregnancy.

"When you didn't write for so long, we started to wonder," Monte said, taking hold of Kerry's hand and squeezing. His fingers were cold and hurtfully strong. He kept his voice soft and sweet. Too sweet. And his eyes wide. Too wide. "We know things have been hard for you, Kerry...*emotionally*...since Wilbet's wrongful imprisonment—"

Kerry barely held back a snort. Wrongful. Monte would maintain that, wouldn't he? Despite the evidence, testimony, and even photographs taken by an undercover investigator hired by the lover of one of the prostitutes Wilbet had been abusing, and despite Kerry's own whispered, tearful confessions to his in-laws in private of what Wilbet had done to him, Monte still insisted it was all a misunderstanding. He claimed that Wilbet must have thought Kerry wanted the sex to be that way, that they *all* had.

Monte was still going on, "—and so we've allowed you to be here, with your, ahem, uncle." He smiled, but there was a nastier edge this time. "After the weeks went on and we heard nothing from you, suspicions began to arise."

"Did they?" Kerry tried to sound confused.

"Yes. Why didn't you let us know about the child as soon as you suspected?"

"The first five weeks are notoriously tenuous," Kerry said reasonably, affecting a tone of voice that implied Monte, and by association Lukas, were behaving oddly to have expected him to confirm the pregnancy with them at any point sooner than this exact moment. "I wanted to be sure this sweet thing would stick with us before getting your hopes up." Here he touched his stomach affectionately and hoped that he wasn't laying it on too thick.

Monte's eyes glowed hungrily. "But you're sure now? That this pregnancy is going to work out?"

"I feel good about the chances," Kerry said carefully. His stomach chose that moment to growl again, and this evidence of his hunger bought him a few precious moments.

"Where is that waiter?" Monte asked, snapping his fingers in the air and looking around. He caught a harried-looking beta waiter's eye and gave him such a look of irritation that the waiter turned red from the bottom of his neck to the roots of his fair hair.

"Coming right up, sir!" the waiter called, dashing into the kitchen.

"We can't have our grandchild going hungry," Monte said, taking Kerry's hand and squeezing it. "Are you eating well? You look thin. Your uncle is taking care of you, isn't he? Not squandering what we send?"

Kerry bit back an angry response to that and said instead, "I'm finally up to eating my old rations again. There for a few weeks, my stomach was tetchy. I understand that's common."

"Yes, especially when carrying a future alpha," Monte said, practically glowing like the moon was going to burst from his pale skin. He grinned at Lukas. "Did you hear that? He's been sickly." Then he let out a little squeal.

"Don't get your hopes up yet," Lukas said, taking Monte's other hand across the table. "You know as well as I do that we'll all have to wait a good many years after the birth to be sure."

"Unless it's an omega," Monte said with a hint of worry. "Then we'll know right away."

"Yes."

When the dishes began to arrive, Kerry realized that Monte had ordered the *entire* menu. The table grew crowded with bread, jam, stew, eggs, fruit, pancakes, bacon, salad, kippers, and a fat cinnamon bun. Kerry took small, fortifying bites from each dish, except for the kippers, which he didn't care for. He was careful not to overdo it, pacing himself to make it all last as long as possible. He didn't want to have to talk too much if he could keep from it, and the Monhundys had a firm rule that no one could discuss serious business while a person was eating. They believed it caused indigestion, and in some cases, if the conversation was especially difficult, diarrhea.

An old omega's tale, to be sure, along with the belief that intense pregnancy sickness heralded an alpha, but the Monhundys, for all their citified ways, believed in plenty of those old tales. Kerry still remembered when they'd insisted he eat nothing but butter sandwiches for two days before his first heat with Wilbet, claiming it would "ease the way" for his knot. Insanity.

Regardless, they watched Kerry swallow like every bite that went into his mouth was going directly toward the health and well-being of their future grandchild. And when he paused to sip water, they held their breath, as if he were going to give birth any second. It was a strange, powerful feeling. He had them in the palm of his hand in some ways. Now, he just had to stay in control and keep them there.

"I believe the babe is strong," Kerry finally said when he could no longer ignore their intense gazes in favor of food. He sat back in his chair, stuffed, and no longer the least bit hungry. "He seems well-latched." Just how he knew that was not something he'd ever discuss with them.

Monte reached out as if he were going to touch Kerry's stomach, but then, after looking around at the other diners at tables near them, he snatched his hand back, apparently thinking better of a public display of that nature. It proved the fakeness of his kisses earlier all the more—those had been for show. This had been a genuine desire to connect to the child within—much too vulnerable a desire for Monte Monhundy to allow in public.

"And his expected date?" Lukas asked, leaning forward and peering at Kerry's stomach as if he could see the babe inside.

"The end of summer or beginning of fall."

"Of course. Yes." Monte's eyes drifted up to the ceiling, going a bit glassy as he did the mental calculations. "That would be right."

"You'll come back home with us, of course. You've had enough time here with your…uncle." Lukas frowned and sucked his teeth. "No reason to linger in the middle of nowhere a day longer than necessary. He's had his time with you; it's our turn now."

"I'd rather stay, actually," Kerry said with a surety he wasn't certain they'd agree he had a right to, but he was going on bravado from here on out. He just had to pray it worked.

Lukas's thick, dark brows went up to his hairline. "Oh?"

Monte gasped. "Why would you want to do that, honey, when better medical care is available in the city? Everyone knows that delivery is a fragile time for an omega, and especially for one with your…" he gestured at Kerry's chest. "Well, *deformity*, for lack of a better word. We should take no chances."

"There's a new doctor boarding at Pat—" He caught himself. He never understood why they loathed it when he referred to Zeke as his pater, but they did. So, he smiled, faked a small burp, then continued, "A new doctor is staying at my uncle's house."

"And?"

"Well," Kerry gathered all his best lying skills, developed by necessity after contracting with Wilbet. "Uh, this new doctor is a beta, which is unusual, I know." He shrugged in a "what can be done?" sort of way. "But it's happening more and more these days."

"Betas don't always know their place," Lukas agreed.

Oh wolf-god, that was the wrong takeaway. Kerry hurried on deeper into his lies, "In this case, perhaps it's for the best. He's a very well-respected, city-trained physician with actual, real-life experience dealing with omegas with my particular structural issues."

"How unusual," Monte murmured, a skeptical expression marring his features.

With a deep breath, Kerry lied as if his fate depended on it. And, in a way, it did. "Yes. It's quite a stroke of luck, truly. He's delivered two babies alive and well from omegas who have my same deformity."

"Indeed?" Lukas stroked his chin thoughtfully, considering this as a beta waiter came around to begin clearing dishes.

"What's he doing in the mountains if he's this good?" Monte demanded as soon as the waiter had gone.

"He's a religious sort," Kerry said, wrinkling his nose as if to acknowledge how distasteful that was. "Holy Church of Wolf devotee. You know the sort. Prays morning, noon, and night, and believes he owes ten percent of his life to charitable works. He's chosen Hud's Basin as his focus for the next year."

Lukas tutted gently, and Monte stared at Kerry as if trying to find the lie but unable to pin anything he'd said as false.

"We'll pay him, of course," Lukas said with a grimace of offended dignity. "Our grandson won't be part of his charity."

"Of course," Kerry said, careful to use a tone that implied there had never been any question otherwise.

Lukas made a soft noise of assent and then said, "Perhaps wolf-god has chosen to forgive this family and give us some luck after all. This is a great coincidence."

Monte bit back a response, turning to his now watery sweetened tea and taking a sip to keep his silence. Kerry assumed he wanted to protest the family's need for forgiveness. On Wilbet's guilt, Monte and his alpha differed in opinion.

Still, Kerry was shocked that his in-laws seemed to buy into his story, given how unusual his chest was in terms of malformations. He'd never met another like himself.

"I can give you referrals for this doctor," Kerry went on, hoping that this next bit went as smoothly as his last. "His last name is

Heelies." He waited for the name to sink in. It was a risk. This could go either way. If they decided they needed to check on Janus's credentials in person, they'd scent his alpha state immediately. Not to mention the lies would reveal his lack of credentials and experience. Kerry braced himself. "Yes, Dr. Janus Heelies? I believe you know his family. I remember meeting a man with that last name at a few of your parties in the city."

Monte and Lukas exchanged loaded glances, and Monte cleared his throat anxiously. "Heelies, you say?"

"Yes."

"We've been trying to win back their respect, and their business, for the last two years," Lukas said under his breath.

"I'm sure Dr. Heelies could put in a good word with his uncle," Kerry said brightly. "As my doctor, he'll want to help me in any way he can. You know how betas can be. So eager to help."

"Ass-kissers, you mean," Monte said with a laugh.

"Your words, but yes," Kerry said with a tight smile. His tongue felt dry with the lies. He took up his water glass, took a long swallow, and put it down with a slightly shaking hand. He hoped his in-laws didn't notice. "And everyone knows how important it is to keep omegas happy during pregnancy and labor. If he thinks it will please me or make things easier, he won't hesitate."

Lies, lies, lies. He was walking such a thin line between getting what he needed out of this and going too fucking far. He could feel the tug of gravity warning him that he was about to step off that line.

Monte leaned forward eagerly. "Has this Dr. Heelies spoken to you at all about his family's prior business connections to us?" He chewed his lower lip for a moment, trembling a little as he leaned in even closer. "Or, oh dear, has he said anything to you about...*the situation?*"

Kerry knew that "the situation" was Monte's code for Wilbet's imprisonment and the reason for it. At least he didn't have to lie for this part. "No, Dr. Heelies hasn't. He doesn't seem to be aware of *the situation* for now. I get the impression that he wasn't part of the gossip circles during that time." The only way that lie was going to stick would be if Monte wanted to believe it, hopeful that some decent part of society was still unaware of what his son had done. "I believe Dr. Heelies was very sick during that time with the flu. He told my uncle something to that effect, anyway."

"Oh, yes, that was a dark year," Lukas said, his lips turning down. "So many flu deaths and then, of course, well…" He looked toward Monte, sighed, and gritted out, "the situation." Lukas put his hand on Kerry's shoulder reassuringly. "It's best not to think about it too much. There's a bright future ahead for all of us. Especially now with new hope on the way."

Kerry swallowed hard again. "Anyway, I'd like to keep Dr. Heelies in the dark about Wilbet."

Both of his in-laws at the table jolted, their son's name landing like a bomb in the middle of their plates. But Kerry wouldn't shy away from it in front of them today, no matter how much he tried not to think of Wilbet privately. His false bravado on the Wilbet front was one of his few bargaining chips with his in-laws.

They believed him committed to the family, if not to their son. After the Monhundys declined his initial pleas for leniency and protection from heats spent with Wilbet, he'd realized that convincing them of his devotion to their family would be his only shield from being used indefinitely as nothing more than a brutalized baby factory.

"Our private family business is just that. Private." Kerry arched a brow at both of his parents-in-law. "Isn't it?"

Monte and Lukas sat back in relief and exchanged another glance or two, clearly having a conversation with subtle expressions in the way that only *Érosgápe* could. Lukas then leaned forward again to ask with a bare hint of suspicion, "Is this Dr. Heelies, ah…" He smiled sweetly. "How can I put this? Is he overly invested in your well-being?"

"He's dutiful, as all doctors are. I trust him." Kerry said the next words carefully, because if the Monhundys thought he cared for Janus or found him attractive in any way—which of course he didn't—they'd snatch him from his pater's house quickly before yet another type of scandal might arise. "I believe in his skill. As I said, he's successfully delivered healthy sons from men like me before."

"Perhaps we should speak with him," Monte said, his eyes earnest and bright, seeking out agreement from Lukas. "We could take Dr. Rose up-mountain with us, allow him to consult with this Dr. Heelies to ensure that he truly does have the best training available, and then—"

"No," Kerry said, hoping he hadn't voiced his objection too quickly.

Lukas grimaced. "Go up-mountain? To that dirty little boarding house? And stay the night there? Eat a meal with that man?"

Monte frowned, too. "Where are your priorities, love? It's for Kerry's safety! And that of our grandchild, too!"

Kerry interjected again, "I understand how much you care for me and want me to be safe and well. But I'm worried that it would seem like you didn't trust Dr. Heelies or his skills if you brought up a city doctor to evaluate him. You know how doctors are. Arrogant. Prickly. He might not be an alpha, but…" He searched desperately for a believable explanation. "He's arrogant all the same. And a bit touchy about his reputation, you see. Worries that people won't respect him as much as an alpha doctor."

"Well, of course, they won't!" Lukas exclaimed.

"Right. But the problem is he'd be upset. And if we didn't care what the Heelies thought of us, I'd say that it would be worth upsetting him for the sake of caution, but we do care. Plus, I don't want to lose the opportunity to be his patient. No one else has the experience he does. It's riskier to deliver under anyone else but him."

Lukas had bristled at the implication that this beta doctor thought he deserved the same respect as an alpha doctor, but Monte was convinced. He was an omega, after all. He knew pregnancy and its dangers all too well.

"Yes, yes, we wouldn't want to offend him if you're that convinced he's the best doctor for you, Kerry. And especially since he's a Heelies," Monte murmured. "Word might get back to the family. Their acceptance and friendship in society and business again would make a huge difference for us." Monte grimaced and then turned to Lukas. "Don't you agree?"

"If we insist Kerry come home with us now, then it won't be a personal slight on this Heelies beta, so much as us quite reasonably wanting to be close at hand for our grandchild's birth."

Wolf-god, this had gone sideways. Kerry opened his mouth to say something—he didn't know what—when Monte shockingly came to his aid. "Yes, well, as much as I would love to have Kerry nearby, and as much as I loathe to leave him here, Kerry must be allowed to choose where and how he delivers." Monte's eyes glowed earnestly with the light from the window. "You know how important omega comfort is in the outcome of any pregnancy. I wish it weren't, but...it *always* is, everyone knows."

"Yes, but in the mountains? Without emergency services at the ready? How can his whimsical desires outweigh the excess risk?"

Monte sighed. "Darling, there are few risks greater to the outcome of a pregnancy than an unhappy omega, and whether we like it or not, Kerry is attached to his uncle and that ridiculous lake." Here he rolled his eyes as if this affection was insufferable but tolerated for the sake of their grandchild. He whispered, "The mountain people believe there is magic in it. Kerry believes it too, even if he would deny that to our face. Omegas are superstitious around birth. You know how it is."

"And we should condone our son's hillbilly omega's absurd religious beliefs about a *magical lake* even at the risk of his and the child's health?"

Here Kerry did interrupt again. "I know you'd like not just the child, but also for *me* to survive this birth. We all know that there's no telling for at least several years, probably longer, if the child will be an alpha or not. It's better to hedge your bets…" He didn't need to say the rest.

The Monhundys were aware that no omega would ever again contract with Wilbet, their only child, even if Kerry died and Wilbet was set free of their contract. Their only hope at an heir was through Kerry and his continued ability to bear children for Wilbet into the future, even if this one should die or turn out to be a beta or omega.

"I see." Lukas dropped the words like stones.

Kerry swallowed hard. "You know I'm most at home in the mountains with my uncle and the land that I love, and yes, near Hud's Basin itself. But also, I need to be far away from the humiliation and scandal Wilbet brought into my life. The gossip nearly killed me."

It hadn't been the gossip that had nearly killed him, but rather his sheer horror at what the man he'd contracted with had done to other human beings. But Monte would easily believe Kerry's words because the scandal had almost killed *him*. He'd been in bed for weeks after discovering the charges against his son, and again after his imprisonment.

"The rumors are dissipating," Lukas said, touching Kerry's hand gently, a deep empathy in his gaze that left Kerry feeling dirty. "People are eager to move on from it, and we're happy to let them. Please, Kerry, consider coming home with us. What better way to wipe it all from their mind than with the joy of a newborn babe?"

"Then perhaps we should wait until the babe *is* newborn," Kerry said. "Or even older—a toddler perhaps. Don't you agree society would better accept living, healthy evidence of the family's future than a waddling, irritable, upset, and pregnant omega?"

They looked between each other again.

"You *were* terribly difficult when you were pregnant with…" Lukas trailed off, unwilling to say his son's name. Lukas hadn't forgiven his son any more than Kerry had, even if he had a very different way of handling it.

Monte huffed softly, almost as if he would argue, but then he took a long, assessing look at Kerry and said, "Your uncle will, no doubt, cater to your every whim much better than I could. And I'd hate to pay a servant when we already send your uncle so much money as it is. Let him earn it for once."

Kerry swallowed down the flash of rage at that and smiled instead, though it felt like eating glass.

"Yes, let him earn it," Lukas said, nodding with a curtness that Kerry wanted to slap away. "He should see what it's like to work once in a while."

Kerry hastily shoved a piece of chocolate into his mouth from a little plate of desserts he'd barely touched. He let the sweetness glide over his tongue and color his words. "He would be happy to care for me, and it would bring him honor if you felt he'd earned the money you send to him."

Never mind that it was Kerry's money, sent to fulfill the contract they'd made together when he became Wilbet's omega. Never mind that as far as he was concerned, carrying their demon son's spawn and delivering it was more than enough to "earn" that payment and a million years more. He kept his mouth shut and smiled as soon as he'd swallowed another chocolate. "Thank you for letting me stay in Hud's Basin. My home brings me so much peace.

And I know that Dr. Heelies is up to the task of the delivery. As I said, he's been city-trained."

They nodded and looked out the window, again turning their heads simultaneously, as though they had a tether between them. A moment of stiff silence followed before Monte looked back to Kerry saying, "It goes without saying that the child will be raised in our house in the city."

Kerry nodded, clenching his jaw to keep from speaking. He didn't know why he wanted to protest anyway. Sending the child to live with the Monhundys had always been his plan. He wouldn't want to see this son every day, to be tortured by the living, breathing reminder of Wilbet. He didn't want to have the daily burden of hating the child. He wished that he could love it.

"And you will chestfeed him, if you're capable, for the first two years."

Kerry nodded again.

"Do we need a separate contract?" Monte asked. "To ensure we all understand our roles?"

Kerry's fists clenched in the napkin he held in his lap. "That seems unnecessary. We all agree. The child will be raised in the city, but I will give birth to him here...well, at Hud's Basin."

They exchanged glances again, hesitation clear between Kerry's in-laws. They did so loathe to relinquish control. "We'd hate to offend the Heelies by doubting a doctor of their family...." Lukas said again.

"When the time draws near, you'll alert us," Monte said, touching Kerry's arm. "And a few days after the child arrives, you will bring him to us here in town where we'll meet you with a doctor for a full examination."

"If you insist."

"I do."

Kerry agreed and took a long, cool sip of iced water. He wasn't too surprised to hear the ice rattling or to see that his hand shook a little as he put the glass back down. "I agree to your stipulations."

"And if you see any hint of an impending miscarriage, you will alert us right away and accept the doctor we send to tend to you."

"Yes."

They again stared at each other over the table.

"Very well then," Monte said, ducking his glowing red head. "I suppose that is all we can ask of you at this juncture."

Kerry nearly went limp with relief. He knew they were well within their rights to ask so much more. In fact, they could demand that he leave with them right now and go back to the city to deliver whether he wanted to or not. As far as the law was concerned, he was carrying Wilbet's property, and while Wilbet was in prison, all his property not awarded to his victims had become the property of his parents. And that included the child in Kerry's stomach if not exactly Kerry himself.

"You've been so kind and understanding," Kerry said. "I don't know how to thank you."

"Thank us by delivering a healthy son. An alpha preferably, though I suppose you can't control that." Monte sounded bitter as if he wished he could hold Kerry responsible. "And remember that we've given you a lot of leeway, and allowed you many perks and freedoms…" He trailed off, seeming to sense that his words sounded ominous. So, he gave Kerry a sweet smile and a kind pat to his arm. "We're so excited to become grandparents, and we can't thank you enough for doing this for us."

As if he'd had any choice! He'd been forced, and they damn well knew it. Twice he'd petitioned to allow another alpha to service his heats with use of alpha condoms to prevent insemination, and twice they'd refused. They'd wanted a grandchild more than they'd cared about violating his body and soul, and for that he could only hope wolf-god would one day hold them accountable.

Kerry smiled demurely, ate another chocolate, and said nothing. But for now, they had him in their grasp.

THAT SHOULD HAVE been the end of it, but it was not.

As it turned out, Monte and Lukas had brought Dr. Rose, a city doctor in their employ, to examine him in case he denied being pregnant. And, it seemed, despite his confession that he was, indeed, carrying their grandchild, they wanted to confirm the news.

"My uncle is waiting for me in the car," Kerry said softly.

"We have a room reserved for you here. We'll have a driver take you back up the mountain tomorrow morning," Monte said dismissively. "I insist you allow our doctor to examine you, and then you must rest for the afternoon in a decent bed. And, of course, you'll join us for dinner as well. Don't you agree, Lukas? We have so much to catch up on."

Did they? It seemed as though lunch had been hard and awkward enough. How could they truly desire to repeat it? And so soon?

"I prefer to sleep in my own bed." Kerry touched his stomach and played the only card he had. "It's better that I sleep well at night. For the baby."

Monte narrowed his eyes suspiciously but went on as though Kerry had voiced a legitimate concern. "Oh, darling, we'll send you home in the morning. You'll be fine for one night."

Kerry's mind churned, trying to think of another excuse but failing. He glanced toward the clock on the wall, and said, "I told Pater—I mean, I told my uncle that I'd meet him at two o'clock. He'll worry if I don't come home with him."

"Don't be silly. He'll understand that we've missed you. Go tell him that you're staying here with us. Lukas can walk you out to the car and speak to him for you if that would help."

"No," Kerry said quickly. "I can handle it." He stood up, smiling tightly, and agreed to meet his in-laws in the lobby in no less than fifteen minutes after sending his pater back up-mountain.

"Surely it won't take that long to dismiss the man," Monte said irritably, but with a sweet smile to cover it up.

"I just want to make sure he understands what's going on. He worries." But Kerry didn't elaborate more than that. He didn't want to make it plain to them that his pater would be frightened that they were keeping Kerry here against his will, or that they might try to abscond with him back to the city. Kerry would need to convince his pater that he was remaining behind of his own volition or risk him blowing in here and starting a ruckus. No one wanted that.

Parked in the shade of an oak tree with the windows rolled down, his pater napped patiently in the driver's seat. There were shopping bags in the back seat where Pater had indeed run the errands Kerry had requested of him—a bag with material peeking out of the top, a bag with tied up bundles of seeds for the garden, and a collection of candles.

Kerry stepped up to the driver's side window and bent low, whispering, "Pater, wake up. Pater…it's me."

Pater jerked and dropped the newspaper that he'd been holding in his sleep. "Oh! How did it go, son? Everything all right with ya?"

"I'm going to stay here for the night. They've invited me to dinner."

Pater narrowed his eyes. "I see. And why are you really staying?"

Kerry smirked. He might be able to lie like wolf-god's own devil pup to his in-laws, but Pater could always see right through him. "They have a city doctor here with them, and I thought I should take advantage of the situation. I'd like to have him examine me."

Pater's eyebrow popped up skeptically. "You don't trust Janus's assessment?"

"A second opinion never hurts."

Pater's lips twisted, and he looked like he might argue, but then he nodded sharply. "Fine. You're right about that. Even if you're lying about whose idea it was."

Kerry didn't deny it but leaned in to kiss his pater's head. "I'll see you in the morning. It'll likely be early still when their driver drops me off. I'll find a way to get myself out of an awkward breakfast at least, even if I have to suffer through a miserable dinner."

"I'll be eager for you to be home again."

"I know. And oh, Pater, don't tell Janus about any of this. I don't want him to know about Wilbet just yet."

Pater looked like he might argue, but then nodded and took Kerry's hand to squeeze it. "Watch out for yourself, Kerry. Don't sign anything. Promise me."

"They aren't asking me to sign anything, Pater. They just want to have a doctor look me over."

Pater gripped his hand harder. "Don't. Sign. Anything."

"I promise."

Kerry stepped back from the car then and waved his pater off. He waited until the little green car was out of sight before he turned his attention back to the hotel. He forced a fake smile to find his in-laws standing at the back entrance, waiting for him.

# CHAPTER NINE

INDING AN OPPORTUNITY to confront Fan about the situation with Kerry was difficult. Dr. Crescent was incredibly solicitous of his omega, and like most *Érosgápe*, more than a little possessive. Therefore, he didn't give Janus much of an opportunity to talk with Fan alone. Claiming a bathroom break in the house in between patients didn't give Janus enough time for the kind of conversation he wanted to have, either, so for three days he'd bided his time, looking for an opening.

Fan, as it turned out, seemed to want to talk with Janus, too, because just as the last of their afternoon patients rode away with a tin of willow bark tablets in hand, the omega himself stepped out of the house and sauntered down to the stable.

"Dumplin'!" Dr. Crescent called out eagerly, a smile cracking across his grizzled face.

Fan came toward them with a sly smile on his lips, a slow sway to his hips, and his hands behind his back. When he finally reached Dr. Crescent, he pulled his hands around and fanned out a stack of letters. "I'd like them to go out today, Crow," he said with big eyes. "Will you run them to the maildrop before the postal wagon comes back down the mountain?"

Dr. Crescent's face fell slightly, but Fan sidled up next to him, touching him sweetly and looking up at him from beneath his lashes. "You know how my family worries about me up here in the mountains. I need to reassure them that I'm still happy. You don't want my father and pater to visit, do you?"

LETA BLAKE

Dr. Crescent grumbled, his face twisting up in disgust. "They're too old to get up here now. Thank wolf-god."

Fan smiled again. "Are they, though?"

Dr. Crescent grumbled even more, and Fan batted his lashes. It was almost ridiculous, but Janus held back his laughter.

Dr. Crescent rolled his eyes at his omega's machinations, but it didn't take more than another small smile and whispered "please" before Crow was reaching for a hat and shoving Fan's stack of letters into his deep coat pocket. He turned to Janus just as he was about to stalk off toward the horses, and asked, "Don't s'pose you've got anything you wanna send in the post, do ya?"

"As a matter of fact," Janus said, "I do." He reached around for the satchel bag he carried with him between Dr. Crescent's place and Monk's House, and pulled out the two missives he'd written to Caleb—having wavered in uncertainty for days about whether or not he should send them—along with the letter to his uncle he'd drafted that first day. "Would you mind?"

Dr. Crescent shoved Janus's letters in beside Fan's, and then kissed his omega soundly, before climbing up on his favorite mare, Jenny Blue Bells, and leaving the clearing. There was a moment of silence, and then Fan turned to Janus with curious eyes. "How is Kerry doing these last few days?"

Janus washed his hands in the hot water kept over the fire, and then began to put the stable area to rights so that he could call it a day. "He was still in bed when I left at dawn." He gave Fan a long, appraising look. "He didn't lose the babe if that's the information you're after."

Fan's lips pressed together in a taut line, and he leaned against a support beam, frowning at the dirt floor of the stable. Then he suddenly kicked at it hard with the heel of his boot. After a brief moment where he visibly gathered himself, he smoothed his soft-looking black hair away from his forehead and let out a long, sad sigh. "I see."

Janus lifted a brow and went on, "He cramped for hours, bled a lot, passed out, and caused a lot of trouble for his pater and me. But the child clung to its chance at life."

Fan nodded slowly, his expression one of tense neutrality. "He could still lose it."

"Yes, any omega can miscarry at any time. But I think, with regard to the tablets you gave him, the danger is past."

Fan groaned and rubbed at his face, leaning back against the support beam. "Damn."

Janus's irritation flared. Who did this omega think he was, messing with wolf-god's work? "Why would you help him do such a thing? Or any omega? It's not as if his life were at stake!"

Fan straightened up and finally met Janus's gaze. He stepped toward him slowly, with measured, even steps. He removed the tools Janus was cleaning from his grip and set them aside, then he took hold of Janus's chin and pinched hard.

Janus tried to pull away, but Fan was surprisingly strong.

"Listen carefully to what I say, young alpha. You don't get to ask that question. It's not up to me, or even Kerry, to offer you the 'right explanation' to excuse his actions, and it's not your place to demand it of either of us."

"It was wrong."

"By whose definition?"

"Well, the law's for one!"

Fan cocked his head. "Have you never broken the law?"

Janus stared into Fan's dark eyes and gritted his teeth. Of course, he had broken laws, both secular and holy, and for ridiculous reasons. But this was life and death, not a dalliance with a contracted omega, not a joyride in a car that wasn't his own, and not a wrestling match held outside of the clubs for profit and fun. This was *life*, for wolf-god's sake. "It's hardly the same thing."

"Oh, so you're the judge now, are you?" Fan smirked. "Judge, prosecutor, and jury all in one? Interesting, and here I thought you weren't even a doctor. Just a nurse without the full credentials there, either." His dark eyes were cruel with rage, and he clenched Janus's chin so hard it hurt. "Amazing how you suddenly know more than Kerry or I do about what's right and wrong, and what, exactly, constitutes a life being at stake."

"I never said that." Janus jerked his chin free of Fan's grasp. "I just wanted to understand."

Fan's thin black brows jumped to his hairline. "Here's what *you* need to understand: no one ever *understands.*" He spit out the word like poison. "Not me. Not you. Not his pater. Not his alpha, locked up in prison where he belongs. Not Crow. Not even another omega who made the same choice as him. *No one* truly understands, darling, and that's what makes this such a bitter time for any man who's tried it." Fan shook his head, his dark eyes stabbing and sharp as he went on, "To have tried it and *failed?* To have put his soul on the line, and not even have saved himself or the child from whatever fearful horror the future holds for them? I can assure you the last thing Kerry needs right now—or ever—is inquiries, incriminations, and interrogations into his *reasons.*"

Janus gaped at the small omega, so fierce in his fury. Speechless in the face of it, Janus turned back to washing the tools, taking especial care with the surgeon's scalpel and the other sharp objects, like the needles.

"That's right. Do your work and keep your mouth shut. Your job is to doctor him, not judge him. Or me, for that matter." Fan put his hands on his hips, regarding Janus carefully. "But because I like you and Crow needs you, I'm going to say one more thing. Think, Janus Heelies. At *your* worst moment, what saved you?"

Janus blinked at him in confusion, not sure how Fan's sharp focus had landed on him and his own past failures and pain.

"What gift did someone give you, Janus, when you faced the worst part of yourself?" Fan's brows darted up again. "Or have you never had a good long look in the mirror?"

Janus gritted his teeth together. He'd had plenty of deathbed experiences to contemplate his past abuses of affection and trust. He'd seen how close he'd come to becoming a monster and he'd chosen another path. Who was Fan to question him now? He only had one man to prove anything to, one man to convince of his goodness! Caleb's handsome face swam to the surface of Janus's thoughts, his kind voice, and of course, his undeserved forgiveness.

Janus swallowed hard, lifting his gaze to Fan's.

"Ah, yes. That moment. Right there. Consider *that* for a good long while before you go home tonight," Fan went on. "Ask yourself: can you give that kind of gift to Kerry? Wouldn't *that* be a better balm than requiring him to make you understand the unfathomable?"

Fan turned on his heel to stomp back up to the house with his little back held ramrod straight. Janus watched him go, mind whirling, and when he could finally breathe right again, he finished tidying up. He was tired and hungry. He wished he didn't have such a long walk back to the boarding house before he could enjoy whatever supper Zeke had prepared for him that night. And it would be awkward seeing Kerry at the table again after all that had transpired between them.

But so be it.

He was a doctor now—well, a doctor-ish nurse—and seeing people at their worst was his new everyday situation. The fact that he'd seen Kerry at his worst only made things uncomfortable because Janus wanted to protect him. Every alpha instinct in him wanted to bundle up the vulnerable omega and keep him safe, make him his own, and—

*No.*

He almost poked his finger with a needle he was cleaning, and he focused his thoughts on his work instead. Sharp objects and distracting, confusing thoughts about pregnant omegas—or one pregnant omega, in particular—didn't go hand-in-hand. And Janus knew enough about alpha/omega dynamics to know that this pull to protect and care for Kerry would only get stronger as the months passed. But he was a strong, newly principled man...he could resist it.

Finally finished cleaning up, Janus took the steep path back down to Monk's House, Fan's words playing like a loop in his head. He wanted to be outraged by the implications of them, and he tried to hold onto anger at Fan for the position Kerry had been in when he crawled out of the forest to the lake. But Janus found he couldn't maintain it. There was something too real in Fan's rage, and too sharp in his words for Janus to dismiss them as anything other than the truth. Who was he, an alpha, to know what an omega endures? And just like that, he found himself coming back to Kerry's side again and again.

Janus still couldn't bring himself to say that what Kerry had done was right, but regardless, no one owed him an explanation.

As the path narrowed into a piney, rock-strewn tunnel, he spotted branches of white flowers ahead. They reminded him of white lace, the kind worn on the old-fashioned shirts of the Old World, and he approached the branches curiously. He gazed up at the tree, admiring the way its gray limbs stretched out above him, white flowers glowing against the pine bough background. Janus reached up and gripped a thin branch covered with the flowers, tearing it free.

When he'd been at his worst, Caleb had come to him with forgiveness, even though he hadn't deserved it. Caleb had demanded no explanations for his horrible behavior—though Janus had offered them up desperately—and Caleb had requested nothing but

Janus's return to health. His loving lack of cruelty had turned Janus's world upside down and brought him to his current place in life. That was worthy of emulating, wasn't it? Fan seemed to think so.

Janus considered his mission to become a better man. Was offering unconditional acceptance to Kerry part of that? Or was it just a cover for cowardice? It was certainly *easier* to not confront Kerry with demands for a reasonable justification for his actions, but was it right?

He chewed his inner cheek and pondered. The motivation didn't matter. The outcome alone was important. And the outcome must be Kerry's full return to health—emotional and spiritual—for both his own and the babe's benefit.

Kerry needed to be able to trust Janus and Dr. Crescent to get through the months and labor ahead. Raking him over the coals now, demanding that he explain himself or express regret, wouldn't help with any of that.

Janus grabbed another bough of white flowers and headed onward toward the boarding house. He let the chatter of the woods wash over him and picked up his pace, eager to see Kerry again now that he didn't feel obligated to find a suitable time to confront him. He could be a hero and offer Kerry a blank slate between them instead.

But Kerry's room was empty when Janus returned, except for the colorful bird in the cage.

Zeke was down in his garden poking at carrots and beets, and so Janus took a cursory peek around the rest of the house, but Kerry didn't turn up in any of the other rooms either.

When dinner came and Kerry still wasn't home, Janus's pulse thudded with worry. He confronted Zeke about Kerry's absence, hoping he didn't sound too possessive. But Zeke just excused his absence by saying Kerry had other obligations for the evening. Yet if

Janus could read the furrow of his brow correctly, Zeke was anxious, too.

"You saw him today?" Janus demanded to know.

"Yes. Of course."

"You don't think he should be, oh, I don't know, *observed* right now?" Janus asked, pushing around his potatoes and meat without taking a bite. "His emotional state seems fragile. He shouldn't be left alone."

"I agree, but as I said, he had what you city folk call 'an obligation of a personal nature.' He's not alone."

Janus felt the blood drain from his face. "Is he going to try again?"

"No." Zeke patted Janus's arm reassuringly. "He's past that now, truly. He's safe, but I can't tell you much more. Kerry wouldn't like it."

Janus barely kept from gnashing his teeth in frustration. "But you're certain he's not out there somewhere right now, traipsing around with a fever? Or, worse, miscarrying in actuality this time?"

"He's in good care." Zeke's lips tightened.

Janus stared at him. "Does that mean you're certain he has no fever?"

Zeke seemed tense but refused to give in to Janus's worry. "Not the last I saw him. Aside from being a bit sore, both in body and soul, it seems you're right. There's been no real damage done."

Janus harrumphed but didn't ask anything more. He found his tongue harder to hold when his egoistic plans to gift Kerry with the floral boughs and his version of Caleb's unconditional grace had gone awry due to the recipient's unexpected and ill-advised absence. Plus, he wasn't at all certain that Kerry's mental health didn't warrant a suicide watch, much less a watch for other abortifacient behavior.

"He'll be home in the morning," Zeke reassured him with another pat. "I was promised that by one who has every reason to earn my trust right now. Don't worry."

"Morning?"

"Yes." Zeke took a bite of his potatoes but didn't seem to enjoy them much. "By the way, tomorrow being Saturday and wolf-god's regular day of rest, I assume Doc has given you the day off?"

Janus nodded.

"Good. I usually start a bit later as well. Breakfast will be served at nine instead of dawn if that's all right by you."

Janus could only nod again.

Zeke set about eating this time as though he had something to prove, stopping only to put his hand on Janus's shoulder to reiterate, "Don't worry about Kerry. He's in safe hands."

But Janus did worry. He didn't understand why Zeke had let Kerry out of his sight at all, or how he could insist the man was safe when he was nowhere to be seen, or touched, or scented.

The hours wore on, and Kerry's absence gnawed at Janus. The scent of musk and berry began to fade from the air of the house, and Janus missed it.

At bedtime, he tossed and turned beneath his soft quilts until his eyes finally closed. Sleep finally came and stopped his fretting about Kerry, who was, reasonable or not, becoming part and parcel of Janus's newly developing concept of Monk's House as his home.

As Janus drowsed in and out of sleep, the pearly light of dawn peeked in through his windows and bounced around his room. Distantly, as if in the dream he kept falling in and out of, he heard someone singing. It was a low, plaintive song that reached into him and filled his heart with an ache he couldn't ignore. He allowed the vibrations of the song to rumble through him, tugging at his soul, rousing him from his lulling slumber.

When he finally slid his eyelids open to greet the rising morning light, he felt like he could almost see those low, sad notes shimmering in the air around his head like summer heat. It was as if he might reach out his hands and grasp the rough sound, clutch it like a woolen blanket. He listened longer, making sense of the fact that someone was singing, and based on the delicious return of the berry and musk scent, that someone must be Kerry.

Janus relaxed back in his bed, all feeling right with the world now that the pregnant omega of Monk's House was back home where he belonged. The resonant melody of Kerry's song made Janus's eyelids heavy, and he let it carry him back to a half-sleep where he listened with a small smile on his lips, letting dream images play teasingly behind his closed lids.

A sudden thump came from overhead. Janus jerked fully awake. His bedclothes tangled about his body, and he lay trapped in them as he stared up at the ceiling, pondering the noise. The singing continued reassuringly though, only to cut off mid-melody a few seconds later by an ominous thud.

Janus sat up in bed and listened hard. A peculiar sliding sort of sound began, as though something was lightly dragging in an arc over the same space of flooring. Over and over.

*Kerry!*

Janus's heart began to race as he rose from the bed, pulled his robe on over his pajamas, and threw open the door of his bedroom. Down the hall near the stairs, Kerry's bedroom door stood open, and when Janus darted over the wooden planks separating his room from Kerry's and poked his head inside, he found it empty. The bed was undisturbed, clearly unslept in. The bird was gone, too.

Janus cocked his head toward the ceiling and listened again. No sound.

It was obvious that Kerry was the one singing up there. What if he'd done something unspeakable? The thud could have been a chair kicked over, the scratching sound on the floor his toes dragging as he swung...

Janus squeezed his eyes shut.

Raking his hands through his hair, he shoved that image away. Turning on his heel, he rushed across the hall to knock on Zeke's still-shut door. Zeke had been serious about sleeping late on his day of rest. At the last second, though, Janus dropped his hand without knocking. If there was any chance that the worst might have occurred in the attic, well...Zeke didn't need to see that. No parent did.

Gathering his courage, Janus lifted his chin and decided to investigate on his own. He ran to the far end of the hallway, opened the narrow door that hid the attic stairs, and took them up quickly, one by one, trying to hold back the surge of panic in his chest at the thought of what he might find.

As Janus gained the final step, a green and blue bird swooped past his face. Startled, he nearly fell down the stairs again but gripped the banister just in time. The green and blue vision winged by again.

*Kiwi.*

Janus looked up to the rafters, heart in his throat, and took in the creamy morning light spilling in from the high windows and lighting up swirling dust motes all around. His eyes searched every inch of the rafters and found nothing but surprisingly clean wooden beams, and not a cobweb in sight.

Then he saw him.

Kerry.

He was sitting perched in yet another windowsill, alive and well, breathing and vibrant. Janus's heart galloped with relief so strong he bent over to clutch his knees, taking in a sharp breath that almost felt like a sob. He repressed the urge to rush to Kerry, pat him down, and search him over for any sign of hurt or injury. He stood back up, tears in his eyes, as he sucked in that sweet combination of scents he associated only with Kerry.

Finally, gathering his wits again, Janus stepped fully into the attic room and cleared his throat softly.

"I'm sorry, Pater," Kerry murmured, not turning his head from where he stared out the window and over the back of the house. Judging from his position, and Janus's knowledge of the property, he probably had an unobscured view of the lake.

Kerry wore another loose, blowsy white shirt and a pair of pajama bottoms. They hung loosely, too, and yet Janus could see the outline of his body beneath the fabric, all strong muscle and lean limbs except for the swelling around his belly.

"I didn't mean to wake you," Kerry went on, still not bothering to turn his head from the view. "I managed to get out of that miserable breakfast and convinced them to let me catch a ride home this morning. I arrived too early to wake you, but I couldn't sleep, and I felt guilty that Kiwi had been locked up all day and last night, too." He paused and, still without turning his head, gestured toward an overturned trunk. "I accidentally kicked that over trying to get him down from that rafter over there. He was being stubborn. I'll be quieter. I know I shouldn't disturb our good priesty."

"Your priesty has already been disturbed," Janus said quietly.

Kerry jerked around. His dark, tired eyes flew wide in his paler-than-normal face. His loosely tied hair was unkempt, and he looked as though, wherever he'd spent his night, he hadn't slept a wink. Kerry lowered his eyes, apology and embarrassment coming off him in silent waves.

Janus didn't feel the usual pulse of power that had always come over him in the past when he'd caused another man to flinch. No, this time he winced, too, and wished that he'd called up in advance to warn Kerry that it was him on the stairs. Now he stood there, his back to the stairwell, wondering if he should turn around and go right back down since he'd ascertained that Kerry was, indeed, still alive.

But seeing Kerry, scenting him, was such a relief. He took a deep breath of the berries and musk and wallowed it around in his mouth and throat. It was such a good smell, the best he'd ever known. Not *Érosgápe*, but…something strong and visceral all the same. Janus wondered what Kerry smelled like when he wasn't pregnant. Musk alone or perhaps just berries? Or something else entirely? He wanted to know the answer to that question far more than he should.

Kerry broke eye contact, whistled softly, and Kiwi flew to him, landing on his shoulder and nuzzling his ear.

"He's obedient," Janus observed.

Kerry rose stiffly from the windowsill as if his body was still aching from its ordeal by the lake, and he kissed his bird's beak all while watching Janus warily. Finally, he whispered, "I'm sorry for waking you. It's been a long week. You must be tired."

Remembering his anxiety of the night before, and his worry when he heard the heavy thud of the trunk knocking over, Janus found himself asking tersely as if he had the right to know, "Wolf-god, where the hell were you last night?"

Kerry stared at him for a very long time. The silence became heavy and reminded Janus that Kerry didn't owe him an answer. He was about to withdraw the question when Kerry offered the answer anyway.

"Blumzound." Kerry sounded oddly guilty.

"What? The train depot at the bottom of the mountain?"

"Yes."

Janus cocked his head, the question out before he could stop it. "Why?"

"I had a meeting."

Janus studied Kerry's reluctant posture and uncertain eyes. Understanding bloomed in him, and while it hurt, he didn't blame the man. "With a doctor?"

Kerry squirmed slightly. "I saw a doctor while I was there, yes." He put up his chin. "The babe and I are fine."

It stung a bit that Kerry hadn't trusted his judgment on that matter as if Janus had no investment in Kerry and the child's health, as if he wouldn't keep them both safe no matter what or who or—

Janus frowned, confused for a moment.

But then he wrangled his mind and got back on track. Then again, why should Kerry trust him on such an important matter? Janus wasn't a doctor or even a qualified nurse, and Kerry knew that. If Kerry didn't feel comfortable going to Dr. Crescent given the situation with Fan and the abortifacients, then Janus could understand that, too. His own protective feelings were likely due to proximity—an alpha living with a pregnant omega with no contracted alpha or *Érosgápe* as a buffer. The pheromones alone would create a protective bond. Nature kicking in to nurture life.

Janus stepped closer, still needing to be sure. Just knowing the why didn't stop the urge. "No more bleeding? Or swelling? No fever?"

Kerry shook his head. With a small chirrup, the bird left Kerry's shoulder to swoop around the room again. "I'm still sore," Kerry confessed. "As if I've been lifting heavy things, but I'm certain the child is fine." His lips quirked, almost like a smile, but not quite. "The doctor heard a heartbeat." His eyes lowered, and he bit down hard on his bottom lip before he lifted his lashes and whispered, "He made me listen to it, too."

"*Made* you?" Why would the doctor do that? Usually, an omega wanted to hear the proof of life, but if one didn't, then why force him?

Kerry shrugged and turned away.

Janus clenched his fists and released them again, letting go of the bizarre urge to seek out the doctor who'd examined Kerry and rough him up for forcing him to do anything at all, and maybe just for touching him.

He blinked rapidly. Wolf-god, he might need to invest in some alpha quell if he was going to feel this strong of a tug toward Kerry. Meant to stop *Érosgápe* from physically bonding too soon, the drug was also good for helping an alpha keep their head during heats, and when faced with an unattached and unrelated pregnant omega. He'd been around plenty of pregnant men in his life and never felt this way about any of them, though.

He shook his head free of the pheromone-induced cobwebs and managed to offer up a polite blank slate, the way he'd intended. Too bad he didn't have his flower boughs with him, too. "Kerry, don't worry. I'm glad you and the child are well. And I understand that you wanted a second opinion."

Kerry flinched again but then turned back to face Janus. He clenched his fists at his sides, and his shirt rose and fell with the quickness of his breath. "It wasn't that." He sounded almost pleading. "I promise. I trust you." He stepped closer. "I do."

Janus smiled, trying to summon up all his memories of Caleb's goodness, all of his generosity and sweetness, all of his willingness to forgive. Janus would show Kerry that he could be generous to a fault, too. "It's all right if you don't. Trust me, I mean." His entire person rebelled against that statement, but he schooled his expression and hoped he appeared pleasant and open-minded.

"Is it?" Kerry frowned. "Why?"

"You barely know me. Why should you trust me?"

Kerry gazed at him, giving him a long once-over. He remained silent. He crossed his arms over his chest, shoulders hunching vulnerably. He smelled even more divine, almost heavenly with that scowl on his face.

"You were singing," Janus said desperately as the silence drew out, and he was tempted to pull Kerry close to nuzzle his neck and behind his ears. "The song came through the floor, and I woke up to the sound of it. It was beautiful. I couldn't resist coming up to hear more."

It was a fib, but there was no need to put morbid thoughts in Kerry's head or let him think that Janus had ever thought him capable of such a terrible thing as suicide.

Kerry's expression—previously tentatively pleading and set in his desire to reassure Janus that his visit to the town doctor wasn't an intended insult—went blank, and then closed off entirely. "I don't sing."

Janus stepped closer, and Kerry stepped away. "But I heard you."

"You heard wrong."

Janus stared at him. Was Kerry really going to lie to him baldly? After all they'd been through over the last few days? After all he *hadn't* confronted Kerry over or demanded answers concerning his attempted abortion? "I know what I heard."

Kerry shook his head. Took another step back.

Janus held his ground. "Are you suggesting it was the wind? Or a ghost? Or the house creaking?"

"Or a dream." Kerry tilted his chin up defiantly.

"A dream?"

"Yes."

Janus cracked, stepping forward again with hands up and a nearly embarrassing note of beseeching in his voice. Too revealing to anyone who wanted to listen. "Why are you lying?"

Kerry thrust his shoulders back and put his chin up even higher. The position emphasized his concave chest, the slight deformity evident by the fall of his shirt. "Because you should take a hint, Janus. I don't sing for audiences. Not anymore. Not ever again."

Janus tilted his head, trying to figure Kerry out. He scented him in the air again, tasting his anxiety and his fear, and settled on ignoring Kerry's rudeness. That's what Caleb would do. Probably. Maybe. It didn't matter. It's what Janus was going to do. He crossed his arms over his chest and said nothing.

After a few tense moments, Kerry rolled his eyes, and with a sweet exhale of held breath, relaxed his stance. Janus's chest felt cracked open with the victory of it, and satisfaction poured out of him so strong it felt like a light shining in the shadows of the attic. Kiwi flew back to Kerry and nosed at strands of his long hair.

"Hint taken," Janus finally said. "But just so you understand, I know exactly what I heard, even if you hadn't meant it for me."

Kerry wiped a hand over his top lip, and then he spoke again, with more care in his voice than Janus knew what to do with, "It's still early, Janus. You should be asleep. I'm truly sorry for waking you." He smiled a little like maybe he was giving in to something he'd been resisting, even though Janus didn't know what that might be. "The start of the workweek will be here before you know it, and Dr. Crescent always travels over to Stumbling Rock on the first of the month. It's an ordeal, and there will be plenty of sick men to treat when you get there." Kerry stepped forward again, reaching out his hand as if he wanted to touch Janus and steer him back down the stairs. "You'll need your rest. Why don't you go back to bed? Pater won't be up for another few hours. I promise, Kiwi and I won't bother you again."

"I wasn't bothered." Janus noted the way the shadows played in the room, sliding as the sun rose. He was tempted to step forward, too, and touch Kerry, run his fingers into his hair, tip his chin up and… What? There was no place for that in this situation. He cleared his throat. "Yes, all right. I'll go back to my room as you've asked. But, Kerry, please let me say this one thing."

Kerry stiffened as if he expected something horrible. Maybe

those recriminations that Fan had warned Janus against.

"You have a lovely voice, and it was a pleasure to hear you sing."

Kerry relaxed again but said nothing, keeping his eyes on Janus as he made his way back downstairs. Even once Janus was below eye level, he could feel the intensity of Kerry's energy boring into his back, almost forcing him to down the stairs and to his room.

Finally, just as he reached the bottom of the attic stairwell, Kerry's deep voice floated down to him. "Thank you. For the compliments."

Janus paused, almost turned around and went back up, but instead replied, "You're welcome."

He carefully closed the door to the attic behind him and leaned against it, suddenly realizing he was shivering. It was probably because he was wearing nothing but his pajamas and robe in the cool air of the morning. Or maybe it was because Kerry was such a confusing knot of contradictions.

One Janus wanted to unravel.

KERRY HAD KNOWN better than to go up into the attic, but some part of him had wanted to be heard singing. And by Janus at that.

He'd spent the night before in comparative luxury at the hotel in Blumzound's finest suite, but he hadn't felt safe there at all. Every sound in the hallway had startled him awake. Every sigh the building released as it settled with the descending night had left him wishing for his lumpy bed at home in Hud's Basin. Every cough or whisper of his in-laws he'd overheard through the walls left him longing for the safety of his pater and the strangely comforting scent of the alpha boarder he'd only just started to trust.

In that jittery restlessness of the long night, he'd let his mind move away from worries and fears regarding his pregnancy, and dwell for the first time on Janus. He'd wallowed in the safe feeling of the man and alpha, and he'd fantasized about Janus in ways he'd never allowed himself before. Not when they'd been in such close quarters. Janus was undeniably handsome, but the events around Kerry's attempt to abort the child had also proven him to be caring, competent, and kind. He had never interrogated Kerry or demanded answers. He'd treated him entirely professionally, and maybe *that* had stung a bit more than Kerry wanted to admit, but at the same time, it was a comfort. It was safety. There was nothing threatening about a respectful and attentive alpha. Nothing scary. It was enough to wonder what kind of man Janus might be when he truly cared for someone…

The strange yearning and curiosity had followed Kerry home in the pre-dawn darkness as he'd bumped along in the backseat of the hired car. It tugged at his heart as he'd let Kiwi out of his cage and filled his senses as he'd taken deep breaths of Janus-scented air permeating the boarding house. The longing had held fast as he'd climbed the attic stairs.

So maybe he'd tipped over that trunk on purpose. Maybe he'd sung a song it pleased him to imagine Janus hearing. *Maybe*, in the pearly dawn hours, he'd felt strangely romantic for the first time in a bitterly long time. So, *maybe*, he'd staged a meeting with a strong, handsome alpha in a remote area of the house where, had he been a different man, in a different place, and not nearly so afraid, something might have happened between them. Maybe he'd pretended to think Janus was his pater initially to save face and to play out his fantasy of being discovered and seduced.

But that absurd dreaminess had finally dissolved as soon as he'd turned to see Janus's physical form there at the top of the steps. Yes, Janus was still skinny for the size of his frame, but he was large. Not that much taller than Kerry, but broader by far, and his muscles were already returning after just a few swims in the lake. Janus could easily overpower Kerry. Hurt him. Force him.

And that sudden realization had killed the wistful, romantic staging Kerry had set up. The physicality of Janus's person had sucked the air out of the room for a few crucial seconds, and by the time Kerry got his head around it, it was too late.

Besides who did Kerry think he was? A single omega ripe for seduction? He was a contracted, pregnant omega with an alpha in prison for rape. He was in the least romantic situation imaginable. No amount of sweet singing and mysterious bird-flying behaviors in an attic would change that. Janus might feel for him as any alpha would feel toward a pregnant omega alone, but that was due to pheromones, not true desire or respect. Not what Kerry ached down to his bones to experience, even if he didn't dare hope for it.

And why would Janus ever respect Kerry? Underneath, Janus was probably like all those city people Kerry had met while living with Wilbet—snotty and snobby, and disinterested in omega rights or feelings, so long as there was plenty of money to go around. And even if Janus wasn't like those city people...it didn't matter. Nothing mattered. Kerry was on a crash course to an unavoidable collision with more pain and misery. He would birth a child he loathed, and there would be no reprieve or salvation for him. Why was it taking him so long to understand that? Why was he letting himself want someone he could never have?

Climbing back up into the windowsill, Kerry pressed his hand against his stomach and felt it again: the fluttering kick of the child inside. Kerry moved his hand away. He knew what that sensation meant. Despite the tea, the blood, and the cramps, the child continued to grow and thrive. Dr. Rose had said so, and when Kerry had listened to the child's heartbeat through the stethoscope, it had sounded demanding in its strength. Determined.

His alpha had always been a stubborn bastard. Of course, his son would be, too.

Dr. Rose had been incredibly pleased. So had Monte and Lukas. Kerry shuddered remembering the glee on their faces when they'd listened to the heartbeat, too.

Searching desperately for another thought to overshadow that one, he focused in on the recent memory of Janus declaring Kerry's song lovely. His hazel eyes had shone so earnestly as he'd said it, and for a moment, Kerry had almost started to sing for him again.

But romantic ideas and hopes were what had gotten him into the situation with Wilbet. He'd be worse than a fool to indulge in them ever again. Kiwi chirruped from his perch in the rafters. Kerry stared out to the lake, blue and glistening in the sun. One by one, he banished all his questions about Janus, along with his lingering dreams and fantasies. He swore to never again indulge in a staged encounter like this one. The time for youthful romantic hopes was gone forever. He'd sealed his fate when he signed the contract.

Not even the good opinion of a handsome, gentle alpha doctor could salvage his future now, much less his heart. There was nothing more to be said or done about it.

Pheromones and temptations be damned.

# PART TWO

EARLY SUMMER

# CHAPTER TEN

TWO WEEKS PASSED and yet another holy day of rest was upon them. Despite his curiosity, Janus grew no closer to solving the mystery of Kerry. He'd remained a bundle of contradictory signals. Janus had come to think of their interactions as a dance called "come here and get away from me." The scent of the man continued to intoxicate and intrigue Janus. But Kerry ran warm and cold like a tap. One moment he'd flush prettily when talking with Janus over breakfast, and the next he'd be cold, distant, and withdrawn—his hand over his swelling stomach, and eyes devoid of interest, much less passion.

As the days slid by the pregnancy hormones did their work, too. Janus could easily smell the sweet ripening of Kerry's body, and he felt the call of that scent down to his very cells. He wanted to protect and touch, to soothe and coddle, and yes, to own and fuck. It was frustrating, to say the least. And it seemed absurd to him now that he'd ever been around a pregnant omega and *not* felt this way before. Because it *had* to be Kerry's pheromones and the absence of a buffering alpha that made Janus react so strongly. There was no other explanation for his urges.

Janus sat in his window pondering the sweet scent of slick he'd picked up when he'd passed Kerry in the hallway earlier in the day. Licking his lips, he closed his eyes and reached for it again, hoping the scent still lingered in the air along with Kerry's usual odor. Kerry boasted the most delicious slick Janus had ever scented, and he'd had the opportunity to indulge in the smell and taste of many an omega's slick over his young life. But none had ever left him horny and thunderstruck like Kerry's.

*Yes.*

There it was. The delicate wonder of it made Janus's cock swell and ache, and he massaged himself gently, enjoying the tease of scent and sensation together. He closed his eyes and pictured Kerry in the attic, hair loose and free, and he dared to imagine him on his knees, mouth open, and—

The sound of purposeful feet on the stairs jerked him from his fantasy.

Standing up, he quickly hid the evidence of his arousal and was glad he had when his door swung open after only a perfunctory tap.

"Letter for ya," Zeke said distractedly. He wore an apron and a serious expression. Janus knew from their morning discussion over breakfast that Zeke was making an experimental cake containing rhubarb he'd grown in his garden. He didn't linger. He handed over the letter and then dashed back downstairs to his kitchen.

Eagerly, Janus looked at the handwriting on the envelope, and his heart did a small flip to see that it was Caleb's and not his uncle's. He ripped open Caleb's letter and read it greedily.

*Dear Janus,*

*Accept my sincere apologies for the lateness of my reply. You sent your letter to our house in Virona, where it sat unopened for two weeks. Unfortunately, our servants hadn't been informed to forward on any mail from you, and so assumed it wasn't urgent. We had been in the city, residing in Urho's residence, as we do from time to time to visit Xan's brother and parents before the babe is born (which should be any day—any second really). Imagine my distress to return to Virona and find two missives from you, and one of them asking urgently for advice.*

Janus read over the rest of the letter quickly, and then, getting the gist of it all at once, went back over it more slowly from his perch on the windowsill in his bedroom. He took long breaks from it to consider more fully the implications of Caleb's sentences, drinking in the reassuring sight of the lake reflecting vibrant green leaves as late spring transitioned into summer.

In addition to the incredibly thoughtful and thought-provoking letter, there were two photographs, captured family moments that Xan had taken with one of the new-fangled portable cameras recently available for purchase. Caleb wrote they had multiple copies of each shot and were sending them around to friends and family. Janus studied them both carefully with a longing in his heart that had less to do with the people in the pictures, and more to do with the sense of family captured within them. Would he ever have that?

The first photo was of Caleb dressed all in loose, white clothes and round with child again, sitting with his oldest son, Riki, on the beach, helping him make a sandcastle. The second photo was of Urho holding Caleb and Xan's second child, an alpha or beta (only time would tell), named Levi. Urho swung the child by his fat little arms around in the garden. There was no picture of Xan. He was most likely the one behind the camera.

Janus stared at the photo of Caleb a bit longer, taking in the large mound of his stomach. At this rate, Caleb was having a child nearly every year and a half. It made Janus nervous. He knew Caleb loved being a pater, but he didn't see why he had to risk it so often. Two healthy sons should be enough for anyone, especially if Levi turned out to be an alpha.

Soon Kerry would be round like this, too, and ready to give birth. Janus wondered what that would be like, who would be there when the labor began, and if it would fall to him to deliver the child or not. Kerry would be just as beautiful as Caleb at this size, no doubt about it. Janus could easily imagine the way Kerry would look as he grew heavy with child. The image gave him warm chills. They washed over him easily, a peace descended as he held the image in his mind's eye.

Finally, Janus put Caleb's family photos aside and returned his attention to the most interesting paragraphs at the bottom of the letter. He'd already read them over twice now, and yet he still wanted to wring more understanding from the words.

*In your letters to me, you didn't directly identify the young, pregnant omega living in the boarding house with you. However, I was startled to realize that I know just the man you're describing. Not intimately, but in passing. His first initial, along with the description of his chest gave him away. It isn't your fault. You did well in trying to obscure his identity, but his contracted alpha moved in the same social circles as Xan for quite some time, and I was still attending Philia soirees when unmatched omegas of his year of wolf began.*

*Therefore, know that I'm not sure if what I'm about to propose is even appropriate to offer, but wolf-god must damn propriety in this case! If you see fit, or you think it might help, please tell Kerry that he has friends in Virona. To be explicit: Xan and I would be happy to help him in any way we can. Urho too, of course.*

*We are all far too familiar with the brutality Kerry may have experienced in the past from his contracted alpha, and which he may be facing in some ongoing way. Especially if he is indeed with child from his alpha as you say. We'll happily assist with legal aid, monetary help, or the provision of suitable healthcare for him or the child should he require it. I know that his alpha's family has plenty of money, but we would never trust them to use it fairly. Lastly, don't hesitate to ask for help on his behalf if you think he's too prideful to ask for it on his own. We desire to make sure he is safe.*

*As for all your concerns and your moral compunctions, my friend, that is the way of life. Take a deep breath and follow your gut. Be true to your heart. Choose to act with love. Those are the only guidelines I can give you.*

*And dear Janus, if I detected a note of interest in Kerry that goes beyond that of pure friendship, please do understand that he may have been exposed to abuses of a horrific nature. I can't reveal more regarding how or what I know about all that, but I can't emphasize it enough. Be gentle with him. Give him nothing but kindness. I trust that you will.*

*Wolf-god be with you,*
*Caleb*

Janus stared at the signature for a long moment. Then he moved from the windowsill to his writing desk to pen a letter in reply. With dinner still hours away, he took his time, first addressing the subject of his initial shock upon arriving in Hud's Basin, and how that had, over the prior two weeks, transformed into an urgent desire to help.

*There are alphas, omegas, betas, and children here who require more of a life than they are currently able to eke out. Our patients rarely pay us at all, and when they do, it is often by barter. I don't know where Dr. Crescent gets his funds to live on, frankly. Perhaps his Érosgápe has family money that came into the good doctor's hands when they contracted? I would ask because I admit to a great curiosity on the subject, but the man is gruff and sometimes rude, and his omega frightens me, if I'm honest. I know they never go hungry and yet the money clients give us is not enough to buy what they need to live.*

*Alas, my portion of our shared wages will not be enough to cover my room and board here at Monk's House once my pre-paid year runs out. I've sent word to my man Warren to begin selling my things. But don't worry about me. I don't need the clothing or the collectibles up this way, and should I ever decide to return and practice in the city, it will all be sorely out of fashion by then. I'd rather have the money now to help here as I see fit.*

He sat back and chewed on the end of the pen and then started writing again. After a few more sentences, assuring Caleb that he would be all right and find a way to make ends meet, his eyes slid back over to the window and the view there. He wondered what Kerry was doing on this warm weekend. The sun had finally started heating Hud's Basin enough during the day that Janus no longer wore a jacket or coat when he left the house. Like the other men on the mountain, he went around in his shirtsleeves or even a T-shirt, sweating through the material during the midday.

At night, the water in the lake had grown warm enough to swim quite comfortably. He'd noticed that since the water had warmed, there wasn't as much shrinkage down below. There had been a few occasions when the effect of Kerry's pheromones floating around the house had inflamed him so much that he'd hoped Kerry might come down to join him so that he might see Janus's true size for himself.

Janus sat back and thought about the last time he'd seen Kerry.

Kerry's stomach had grown much larger over the last few weeks, the child inside entering the most rapid growth of its development. In fact, the skin over Kerry's stomach looked stretched and taut now. At least it had the one time they *had* passed each other at the lake—Janus still clothed and on his way in, and Kerry, entirely naked, coming out. They never seemed to go for a swim at the same time, and Janus was starting to take it personally.

Around the house, Janus had noticed Kerry moved more slowly now, too, but not with the waddle of an omega close to birth. He had weeks to go yet before he reached that state. Instead, he moved with more care, like his balance had been affected by the sudden change in his core, and therefore, his surety of movement had lessened. He also groused a lot about intense growth pains as his ligaments and bones adjusted to make space for the baby. He didn't complain to Janus directly, of course, but the house was small, and his grumbles to his pater carried up the stairs quite often.

Janus found Kerry's presence, whenever he managed to be in it, heady. He sampled Kerry's scent as often as possible, loving most the evenings when Kerry succumbed to his pater's insistence that they all sit and read together in the living room after dinner.

Janus would close his eyes, pretend to drowse over his book, and instead wallow in the delicious scent. He'd often tried to decide whether it was the musk or the berries that was Kerry's alone, and which belonged to the child. But Janus couldn't tease it out. He just knew that he reveled in it all.

Two nights before, he'd opened his eyes to find Kerry watching him with a measuring expression as if trying to determine something about Janus's soul by the way his body rested in the chair. When their eyes met, Kerry had jerked his gaze away and pretended to be fascinated by the page he held open in his book of patterns for baby clothes. Janus didn't look away, though, watching as Kerry sat in his armchair, flipping through the pages. Kerry kept his expression impassive as he folded over the edges of patterns he planned to try.

Constant curiosity had long burned in Janus about Kerry's contracted alpha. From the beginning, he'd wanted to know why he was absent from Kerry's life, and then, when Fan had disclosed that he was in prison, Janus had wanted to know what, exactly, had put him there. Caleb's letter only made his curiosity burn hotter. For Caleb to write about Kerry's alpha in such a harsh manner, and with such empathy for Kerry, left Janus certain that his least desirable guess had been right: Kerry's alpha must be very violent, or cruel.

But if that was the case, how had Kerry ever contracted with him? While Kerry was a bitter man, he wasn't a hateful one. Any alpha who was wouldn't have drawn him either. So, how had he ended up in a cruel man's clutches? That was a story no one seemed interested in telling him.

Janus had hinted at some questions regarding Kerry's situation to Dr. Crescent, but the man ignored him. Gossip wasn't one of Dr. Crescent's pastimes. And Janus hadn't spoken one-on-one with Fan since the feisty omega had told him off for daring to question Kerry's choice. And Zeke, when prodded, maintained that he couldn't say much more than he already had, because it was Kerry's story to share.

And Kerry...

Well, Kerry grew daily in so many ways. He grew stronger, more handsome, rounder, and even more distant. Ever since the morning Janus had called him out on singing in the attic, Kerry had seemed to slip deeper into himself, an inward turn that many pregnant omegas took as their pregnancy progressed. And yet Janus wanted to know more about him by the day. It was an itch that he couldn't reach, and Janus's chances of getting Kerry to share anything about himself seemed slimmer and slimmer.

Pulling himself from those thoughts, Janus returned to penning his letter to Caleb:

> *There's a boy in the mountains who has lost his foot due to a crushing accident. When helping Dr. Crescent treat him, I was put in mind of the new prosthetics available for such inju-*

*ries in the city. But there's no way this young man's family could afford to buy one for him now, much less replace it as he grows. It struck me as the sort of issue that, while endemic in this area, you might find especially compelling. It's overstepping, I know, (but when haven't I overstepped with you?) but I must ask anyway. For this boy's sake, not my own. Would you consider holding a charity auction for this young one, so that he and his family might come to the city to see what his options are at this time? I know that as Xan's omega you're expected to do charitable things such as this from time to time, and I can personally vouch as to the value and need. Please consider it. He's an omega as well if that makes any difference to you.*

He finished up his letter by describing some more details of his day-to-day life, and what he was learning about medicine. Then he wrapped it up quickly by thanking Caleb and Xan for their willingness to help Kerry should there ever be a need. And then he went on:

*As for the alpha in question, I've heard little to nothing of him except that he was a bad match. Kerry and his pater are both reluctant to describe more. I don't ask you to illuminate the situation, because I know you are, for the most part, above gossip and tale-telling. But if there is more you think I should know, as the young man's cohabitant and sometimes medical care provider, I will be ever so grateful. He keeps his business to himself, and I have yet to break through his reserve.*

He considered telling Caleb how distracting he found Kerry's scent, and asking Caleb if he'd had any trouble while pregnant with some alphas being more than usually attracted to him but decided that would be outside the bounds of their current relationship. Bounds he'd already pushed quite far enough with his last letters and with his requests in this one. So, he wrapped everything up with compliments on Caleb's healthy sons, wishes for Caleb's happiness, and a renewed plea for his safe delivery.

Then he put the letter in an envelope, sealed and stamped it, and dropped it into the bag he'd take with him when he left to work with Dr. Crescent again.

Stretching, he gazed out his window at the blue, glistening water, and he made up his mind to go for a swim. There were still several hours before dinner, and he was eager to work out some of his worries with physical activity.

# CHAPTER ELEVEN

J ANUS GRABBED A towel from his bathroom, something he never failed to do after the embarrassment of Kerry seeing him in the nude that first night, and headed out of the quiet house into the sunshine. Zeke was in the garden, apparently finished with his cake, digging around and singing to himself. He had a decent voice, a tenor like Janus, but nothing like Kerry's deep, rumbling tone that had, on occasion, vibrated through the floorboards from the attic. Janus had never dared go up and confront Kerry again, though. Kerry had made it clear that any singing he did wasn't meant for Janus's ears.

"Heading down to swim?" Zeke asked, sitting back on his heels in the dirt. His cheek had a swipe of mud on it, and his eyes glistened with early summer energy.

"Thought I'd take the opportunity."

"Enjoy it!" He started to say something else, but then shook his head and waved Janus on. Zeke broke into song again, going back to his work.

Janus hesitated, wondering if he should offer to help, but decided that Zeke had it well in hand. He was used to working alone, and while Janus might make it all go a bit faster, Zeke seemed content to be in the fresh air and sunshine. It was healthy for him.

The path down to the water didn't seem as long now that Janus had taken it enough times to be familiar with its curves and dips. The green leaves swayed above, and dappled light fell to the brown earth, lighting his way through until he came out the other side at the sandy beach by the lake. The sun was bright on the water, and he had to shade his eyes to look out onto it.

Not far out from the shallows, Kerry floated on his back. He wore nothing whatsoever as far as Janus could tell. From Janus's position slightly above the water, he could see Kerry's cock and balls, his thighs, and his strangely made chest, rising and falling in the water. His rounding stomach lifted above the water most of all, and his hair spilled out across and under the surface. His closed eyes fanned dark lashes on sun-golden cheekbones, and he drifted in a state of relaxation Janus had never witnessed on him before.

Janus scented the air. He couldn't make it out clearly, but he believed that underneath the strong pine scent of the surrounding trees, and the scent of the lake water, he could just barely whiff that luscious berry and musk.

He hesitated on the sand, arousal stirring in him. Then he disrobed quickly and waded out toward where Kerry floated, splashing a lot as he went, in hopes of not frightening him.

It must have worked, because as Janus finally left the shallows, and started to swim out, Kerry righted himself from floating and began to tread water, wary eyes on Janus's approach.

"The lake's been nice lately. Not too warm and not too cold," Janus said as he advanced. The strain of keeping afloat making him sound breathless. Kerry's scent came stronger now, and he felt a stirring in his dick that he tried to ignore. "Are you enjoying yourself?"

Kerry cleared his throat and his voice, always so deep and rumbling, made Janus's dick even harder. "The water relaxes me. It takes the pains away."

"Pains?" Janus tilted his head, immediately concerned and any arousal flickering out. "New pain? Different from before?"

"No," Kerry said. "Just the growth pains. The water lightens the weight on my hips. It helps."

Janus could have suggested swimming would help had Kerry ever given him a chance to give his input on the pains, but he supposed all that mattered was Kerry had found out for himself. "Glad to hear it." Janus flopped to float on his back, his breath coming a bit harder than he wanted, and he hoped his dick continued to behave. "I've been coming out here most evenings. I enjoy it. You know you don't have to leave when I get here?"

"I know," Kerry said, his voice sounding far away as the water lapped in and out of Janus's ears.

"Then why do you go?"

Kerry shrugged. "It doesn't matter now. Besides, I'm hurting too much today to want to go back to the house just because you decided to swim, too."

Janus righted himself again, shaking the water from his ears. Kerry held up his hands as a shield and then ducked under the surface, clearly preferring submersion over a shower. When he popped back up, he smoothed his long hair back from his face and wiped the water from his shining brown eyes.

Janus asked, "I've been meaning to ask: do I have more to apologize for?"

"I'm sorry?" Kerry asked, tilting his head in confusion. Water dripped from the end of his nose, and he wiped it away. "Apologize?"

"It's just that you've been avoiding me. I must have done something else that warrants my apologies. If so, tell me what it is, and I'll own up to it." He raised a brow and grinned cockily. "I used to be terrible at apologies, but I find that, like most things in my life, I get better at it with regular practice."

The water slapped and licked around them, keeping them bobbing up and down slightly as Janus waited for an answer. Finally, Kerry chuckled, rolling his eyes. "I think I'm probably the one who owes the apology."

"You don't owe me anything. Not an apology and not an explanation." Janus lifted his chin, hoping his magnanimity was as great a gift to Kerry as Caleb's had once been to him. All right, so maybe not "as great a gift," but at least something worthy of admiration. He truly wanted Kerry to, at the very least, admire him. What alpha wouldn't want that? "You did what you did, and I don't need to understand why."

Kerry's face clouded slightly. "I meant I owe you an apology for when I was rude to you in the attic."

"Oh. Well, of course. I mean, you don't—" Janus stumbled. "I accept your apology. I want to be your friend, Kerry. I think you might need one."

Kerry ducked under the water again, and when he resurfaced he wiped the water from his eyes and then pointed toward the shoreline. "Care to join me in the shallows?"

Janus hadn't quite gotten his fill of swimming yet. He usually swam to the side of the lake where he'd found Kerry crawling from the forest, and then back to the beach again, but if Kerry wanted his company in the shallows, then exercise could wait.

He followed Kerry to where the water was only thigh-deep, and then they both sat down in a cross-legged style. The water came up to their chests, covering their nipples, but leaving their shoulders exposed. The clay beneath his ass was mushy, and fish darted between and around the men, but the lake water was clean and clear, and Janus could see straight to the brown, muddy bottom.

Which meant he could also see Kerry's dick, balls, and hairy treasure trail making a stripe down his expanding stomach. Quickly, Janus averted his gaze, feeling a rush of blood throughout his body. Forcing himself to breathe normally, and gazing at the jagged line of green, spikey treetops delineated against the blue sky, Janus resisted the urge to have a second look until he couldn't resist any longer. He hoped Kerry didn't notice when he stole a long glance at Kerry's cock again, taking in the entirely omega-appropriate length and heft of it. Certainly, it was nothing to sneeze at, but the size was nothing shocking either. Janus decided Kerry had a very nice package with a sweet set of balls beneath. He found Kerry's dick kissable, and yes, given enough drink and an open mind, rideable. Plus, who could withstand the intrigue of that lush tangle of dark pubic hair, and the fragile fold where Kerry's inner thigh met his groin?

Kerry cleared his throat, and Janus darted his eyes up. Had he been caught? Luckily, it didn't seem so. Kerry was busy staring toward the house, just visible through the trees. "I think you should know a few things about me."

"I would love that," Janus said, and then almost bit his tongue, embarrassed to sound overeager. His brain had still been working on the image of cock and balls, and his proximity to Kerry, bringing in regular, nearly intoxicating traces of his delicious scent, made him feel reckless. But again, Kerry didn't seem to notice.

With a bitter tone, Kerry said, "I don't have many friends."

"Why not?" Janus asked, trying to get his head out of the gutter. He genuinely did want to know Kerry so much better, and letting his arousal get in the way would mess everything up. "I'd think you'd have a lot of friends. You grew up here, didn't you?"

"Yes, but—and you can laugh at this if you want—I wasn't considered properly 'purebred.' I'm not 'true mountain folk.'"

"How is that possible? I don't understand?"

Kerry's lips tweaked into a small, bitter smile. "Because my father wasn't from here."

"And that's a problem? Why?"

"Isn't it a problem in the city, too?" Kerry asked. His well-formed brow lifted, and his tone told Janus that they both knew it was. "Outsiders aren't welcomed with open arms. Not even *Érosgápe*. Class matters."

"And it matters out here, too?"

"Of course. *You'll* never be from Hud's Basin, no matter how long you live here," Kerry said, pushing a hank of wet hair off his shoulder. The divot where his shoulder muscle attached to his collarbone was fascinating. Janus felt an urge to lick the lake water away and leave Kerry's collarbone glistening with Janus's saliva instead.

He gritted his teeth, holding back. What was wrong with him? Wolf-god, he needed help. He'd never felt this kind of sexual draw before, and it wasn't likely to be well-received if he acted on it or even let on that he felt it. He focused back on what Kerry had said, though it was hard to pull his thoughts away from how Kerry's skin might taste. "Right." Wow, he sounded breathless. "I'll never be a native here. But surely you are?"

"No. My father was from Sandhouzen near the city, and I was born there."

"A nice suburb," Janus said. He'd fucked an omega or two out that way during one of his less sober periods. He rubbed at his forehead, appalled to realize that he didn't even remember their names.

"I wouldn't know. I was only two when pater brought me here."

"That's not good enough for the Hud's Basin crowd?" Janus asked with a small bump against Kerry's shoulder.

Kerry smiled at that. Light glinting against his shiny white teeth. Janus smiled, too. "No. Not good enough at all."

"I'm ignorant of the ways here, but why not?"

"Well, for starters, I grew up here in the boarding house," Kerry said, gesturing toward the house. The white clapboard was visible through the trees, as well as the attic windows. At night, the downstairs lights were visible, too. "Which is, by city-standards, pretty slummy, I know, but by mountain-standards, this house is incredibly fancy."

"I can attest to that."

"At this point, I'm sure you can. You've seen how the majority of us live up here."

"You said 'us.' So even though they don't consider you to be one of them, you consider yourself part of their group?"

"Now, yes. Back when I should have? No. Part of living here in the boarding house, growing up here, was that I saw a lot of people, and all of those people told me one thing: get out of here when you can because Hud's Basin is good for a visit, a respite, or retreat, but it's no place to live."

Janus frowned. He knew there were a lot of things about Hud's Basin that he hoped to see improved and changed, and he was only just coming up with some ideas on how to do that, but the mountain and the lake had their charms. The people were friendly and glad to see him whenever he came to call, and there was an earnest sense of community that Janus had never experienced before. He might always be on the outside looking in, but he saw no reason to encourage any of the Hud's Basin people to leave their home.

Janus nodded his head slightly, hungry for words from Kerry's mouth, but afraid if he spoke in reply, Kerry might shut up tight like he had been for weeks now.

"So, I left Hud's Basin as soon as I could. Because I'd bought into the ridiculous idea that I wasn't really part of this place or its people. And wolf-god's own truth is that I thought I could do better." Kerry guffawed, but it sounded even more bitter than all that had gone before. "Better. Ha. I thought I'd do *better*." He squeezed his eyes shut. Janus was tempted to put an arm around his shoulder, but instead he held still and waited.

When Kerry opened his eyes again, he continued calmly, "The folks around here haven't ever forgiven me for that. They claim they have. But I know better."

"Maybe you haven't forgiven yourself," Janus offered cautiously.

He knew what that was like. All he had to do was think of his behavior after he ruined his relationship with Caleb, walked away and started acting like a heartless tough, and later, the way he'd treated and talked to Xan. The things he'd threatened. The nastiness he'd harbored in his heart. He'd been horrible. Somewhere deep inside, he worried that he must still be that kind of man. And that man was undeserving of love or kindness. That man shouldn't sit here with a wounded soul like Kerry.

And yet he couldn't bring himself to get up and walk away. Not now. Not when Kerry smelled so vulnerable, real, and raw. Not when Janus felt like he would do anything to be allowed to cover this man with his body, shield him from the outside, to keep him safe from whatever was tearing him apart inside. "Forgiving yourself is the hardest part."

"Maybe," Kerry admitted. "And maybe I'm embarrassed. To have been so wrong. To have made such a mess of it all."

They sat in silence, weaving their hands around in the water, watching the darting fish. Letting the sun beat on their shoulders and the tops of their heads. The words they'd shared drifting on the air around them. Finally, when enough time had passed, and the silence felt safe again, Janus dared to interrupt it with a question, "When did you leave? How old were you?"

Kerry didn't hesitate to answer. "When I was fifteen. I knew it was time. If I stayed much longer, I'd go into heat, and that meant I'd have to choose an alpha to handle it for me. Here in the mountains, we don't have ready access to heat suppressants before the onset. That's why so many of us contract young. And part of why our birth survival rates are so low."

Janus nodded. He was well aware of that. He'd checked on a pregnant seventeen-year-old omega the other day. It was something unheard of amongst the middle and upper classes in the city. There, the heat suppressants were administered to young omegas while they attended Mont Juror. They were then weaned off after meeting their *Érosgápe* or making a contract. First heats after years of suppressants were terrible, he understood, but better than beginning the paternity path at such a young age.

"I didn't want to become a pater that young. And there were no young alphas on the mountain who appealed to me. I wanted to get to the city, be educated, and then find my *Érosgápe*. I believed he was out there. That I'd find him. I knew it deep in my soul. I belonged to someone." Here, Kerry's voice trailed off, and the yearning in it reminded Janus of the first night they'd met and his words about the lake not being able to heal everything.

"I thought I'd find mine as well," Janus offered quietly. "When I didn't…" He shook his head. "I turned my back on a man I cared about—and who cared about me—for incredibly selfish reasons, and then went on to make some very poor choices with my life."

"How poor?"

"Let's just say I decided if life wasn't going to give me what I thought I deserved, then I'd ruin what I couldn't have. I drank. I gambled. I fought. That kind of poor."

Kerry turned to him, a small smile playing on his lips. "I didn't take your path, but poor choices are something we have in common at least."

Janus wanted to protest that they'd always had plenty in common, but he didn't know what that might be. Sharing a home, not to mention half-carrying Kerry through the woods—both of them naked and Kerry bleeding and in agony—seemed like enough to start a friendship to Janus, but it clearly wasn't for someone as wary as Kerry. "Oh?" Janus asked, hoping the neutral question would open Kerry up again.

"I made so many poor choices," Kerry said, slapping at the water with one hand. "Not at first, mind you. I mean, not willfully." His brows furrowed and a thickness filled his voice like he was holding back a strong emotion. "Not on *purpose.*"

Kerry scooped water up and let it drain from his hands, leaving a sparkle of sandiness in his palm. He dunked his hand under and washed it away. "Anyway, so I left Hud's Basin when I was fifteen. I got on the heat suppressants and went to Mont Juror. I was young to attend, I know. I tested in, and they accepted me despite my age. And I did well enough in my classes. I'm not the brightest student, but I made it worth the scholarship they awarded me."

"If you had a scholarship, then you are plenty intelligent."

He shook his head. "I got the scholarship due to my deformity. It was an Omega Medical Scholarship, so while I was at Mont Juror, I had to submit to tests and allow research into my…" He trailed off and waved at his sunken chest. Water ran between his pecs. Janus's eyes drifted down to his bulging stomach again, and the urge to touch it filled him. But he held back.

Kerry sighed, tucking his chin down to look at his chest. Shrugging, he met Janus's eyes again. "I didn't like having to let them do all of that to me, knowing that I was going to be in medical books as an oddity, but it paid for my schooling."

"What kinds of exams did you have to submit to?"

Kerry raised a brow again. "All kinds. For example, one doctor told me that based on the location of my womb, which is lower than the average omega, I should be safe to birth a child. Probably." He frowned. "Other doctors have been less sure."

The nurse and now pseudo-doctor in Janus leapt on this new information about Kerry's chances. He needed to know more so that he could prepare for any eventuality, and he felt vaguely ashamed that it wasn't until this conversation that he'd realized he should even ask. He'd been too busy worrying about the reasons why Kerry didn't want the child to consider the safest way of delivering him of it when the time came. "Was there any indication that if the child grows too large, labor should be brought on early by a doctor?"

Kerry shrugged. "I don't remember them talking about that, no. But if the child grows very big, I suppose, it could get dangerous. But the Mont Juror doctors said my womb was low, nearly down between my hips, so…" He shrugged. It went without saying that his hips were quite slender and, therefore, a very big child would pose a danger there as well. "Is that right? It's still low, isn't it?"

Janus nodded. He'd noticed that in his examination, too. All omegas were different, but most had their wombs located a bit higher up. When their womb dropped and opened during heat, only an alpha's long cock could reach inside. Kerry's womb was low enough that Janus wondered if a very large beta's cock might breach him. Of course, that was a test that no one would be performing.

Janus ran a hand over his face, trying to dispel thoughts of *any* cocks breaching Kerry's womb. It both aroused and upset him, especially imagining another alpha's cock. He needed to be careful. The urge of an alpha to protect a vulnerable, pregnant omega was well documented, but his feelings were so laced with eroticism and possessiveness that he was in danger of forgetting that Kerry could never belong to him.

"Anyway, after Mont Juror, I didn't meet my *Érosgápe*," Kerry said softly, the disappointment still in his voice. "Obviously." He picked up a rock from the muddy bottom and tossed it, making rings in the surface of the water. "I moved into a small apartment with my friend Reyman. He was a beta and had some extra space. He'd come from Blumzound, so he knew what I was trying to escape."

"Escape…" Janus frowned. "I understand that you felt like an outsider, but I thought you loved it here."

Kerry splashed his face, and Janus admired the copper-colored freckles appearing on his nose and cheekbones. So pretty. "I do. But before…" Kerry grimaced. "Before *everything*, I believed that the world was better *out there*. Anywhere out there. The boarders here had convinced me that city alphas were more cultured and brighter, that they all had fantastic jobs and wealth. I dreamed of a future that wasn't about scraping by and hoping for the best, and working my fingers to the bone."

Janus had seen enough of that in the last few weeks that Kerry wasn't far from the mark. Had he stayed in Hud's Basin, he'd have several children and be working himself into exhaustion most likely.

Kerry went on, "Monk's House is nice now, but six years ago it was falling apart." Kerry twitched and darted a shy glance at Janus. "My alpha paid to have it fixed up. A courting gift to me. One of many. Too many, I see now." Kerry's shoulders drooped. "I wasn't worth all that."

Janus bit his tongue, wanting to argue, but something about the distant look in Kerry's eyes and the careful set to his face told Janus they'd reached a fork in the road. A single word from Janus could end this now.

It reminded Janus of the nights when he'd courted Caleb at the Philia soirees. Sometimes, he'd sensed that Caleb wanted to confess something important to him, and not wanting to hear it, knowing it would change everything, he'd purposely cut Caleb off, redirected the conversation, and dragged the charade of their potential future out for so much longer than it'd needed to go. Hurting them both in the process.

This time, he kept his mouth shut and let Kerry say whatever he needed to say. They weren't courting. They were just trying to be friends. Or housemates. Or doctor and patient. Janus didn't know anymore, but he wanted Kerry's truth out in the open, so they could both move past it.

Kerry caught Janus's eye and said, steadily, "When I met him, I was nothing and no one. He didn't have to work that hard to win me. I'd have gone with him for *so much less*."

Janus's chest tightened at the sorrow in Kerry's voice.

"I might as well tell you his name," Kerry said, lowering his gaze again. "Then, you'll understand."

Janus waited patiently, trying to remember the way Caleb had given him long moments of quiet while he was recovering, so that he could talk in his own time and when he'd needed it most.

Kerry whispered, "Are you aware of the Monhundy family?"

Janus blinked, staring at Kerry as horror and sudden understanding rushed into him. "You—you mean to tell me…" He almost couldn't voice the words. "You're contracted to Wilbet Monhundy?"

The alpha had been found guilty of raping Calitan prostitutes—not just of raping them, but of *brutalizing* them.

Kerry's long lashes pressed hard against his cheekbones, a tear slipped from under them and ran down his freckled cheek, as he ducked his chin and nodded.

"Wolf-god." Janus didn't know what else to say. His throat clenched tight, and sickness roiled within him.

# CHAPTER TWELVE

"WILBET WASN'T A nice man."

"No. He was not."

"Still isn't."

"No."

Caleb hadn't been exaggerating in his letter. Though why Xan and Caleb felt they owed Kerry any more care than another abused omega was still beyond Janus.

It didn't matter.

Janus tried to clear his head of the anger, disgust, and revulsion that filled it at the idea of Kerry in the hands of a man like that. He struggled to come up with the right thing to say. He had questions, a lot of questions, but he didn't think he should ask any of them. He thought back to Fan's insistence that no one could ever really understand an omega's choice to abort their child, and that the best anyone could offer was unquestioning acceptance. He thought back to his first recuperation, the time that Caleb had cared for him. Remembered the long, open silences. This seemed a similar situation, best handled very carefully, and with as few words as possible.

Janus said nothing but didn't break his gaze or shift away from Kerry.

"What if he's like his father?" Kerry whispered, finally disrupting the silence. He touched his stomach with his long, beautiful fingers, sliding them gently over the naked bulge beneath the clear water, and then quickly pulled away as if the skin there burned him.

"How will I ever love him?"

The time for words had come. Janus hoped he didn't say the wrong ones.

"What if he's like you?" Janus touched Kerry's chin lightly, feeling the bite of unshaven stubble on his fingertips. "He's made of you, too, and carried in your womb, and he'll be fed and nurtured at your chest."

Kerry blinked at him.

Janus went on. "You're a strong man, Kerry. So much stronger than an alpha who can't curb his desires. Your child will be more like you than—"

Kerry jerked his chin away.

"Did I say something wrong?"

"No." Kerry swiped at his chin with a wet hand as though wiping away Janus's touch. "But I don't want you touching me."

Janus swallowed the hurt. "Apologies. My friends have always been free with each other, and I thought we were becoming friends."

"Not all friends are affectionate," Kerry said. "But yes, I'm your friend, or I'd like to be. I think. I don't know. I just..." He trailed off, shame and despair making his rasp sound like ashes again. "I can't be touched like that right now. Understand?"

"Oh." Janus took a slow breath, straining not to reach out again, a new kind of understanding landing hard, like an unexpected slap across the face. "He hurt you."

"He hurt a lot of people."

"I know, but..." Janus choked, and he could barely force out the rest. "But he hurt you. Physically."

"Yes."

"And more."

"Sexually," Kerry admitted. "He liked it to hurt."

Janus didn't know if he was going to throw up or roar in rage.

The world around them blinked in and out with each beat of his heart. He wanted to beat someone or something, but there was nothing and no one.

Kerry took a deep breath and slowly reached out his hand, touching Janus's cheek with his wet fingers. "It's all right," he said, with a roughness that made Janus doubt that. "He didn't hurt me as much as he could have." His fingers trailed, cool and smooth, over Janus's hot face.

"I thought you didn't want me to touch you," Janus gritted out, his feelings shifting erratically between anger, sorrow, sympathy, and a possessive flare of want.

Kerry whispered, "I don't. But let me touch you instead."

Janus held still and let Kerry's fingers drift along his jawline. Tears rose to Janus's eyes, surprising him, and he tilted his head into Kerry's palm. "I'm so sorry he hurt you, Kerry," he whispered.

"Me too." Kerry's fingernails scratched softly against Janus's stubble, almost like he scratched into Kiwi's feathers. "But I'm not broken. He didn't break me."

Janus nodded his agreement. Kerry was strong. Stronger than Janus could ever imagine being. Maybe all omegas were like that. Caleb was. Now Kerry. How had he never understood before the inner strength omegas harbored? He'd been blind.

Janus didn't bother insisting that he was trustworthy, or that he would never hurt Kerry. Those weren't the kind of promises a man like Kerry, a man who'd endured what he had at the hands of his contracted alpha, would ever believe simply because another alpha swore them to be true. No, Janus would have to prove his trustworthiness.

So, he sat perfectly still and let Kerry's fingers run over his face and down his throat. He let him explore his collarbones and his chest, let him touch his nipples without reacting except beneath the water where he had no control. His cock grew hard and throbbed.

Still, Janus didn't move. *He* wasn't a slave to his urges. He could control his desires. He would show Kerry that he was a trustworthy friend.

Reaching out, Kerry threaded the fingers of his free hand with Janus's and then, after a slow intake of a breath that felt more like an influx of new courage, he lifted Janus's hand to press it against his own cheek. Janus didn't move a muscle on his own. He let Kerry do the stroking, seared to the bone by the roughness of Kerry's stubble and the softness of his skin. When tears slipped out of Kerry's eyes, Janus had to hold back from wiping them away.

"Your hands are soft," Kerry said at last, releasing Janus's hand and pulling his own back from Janus's cheek.

"Thank you."

"Wilbet was the first man I'd ever met with soft hands. I was so amazed."

Janus wanted to defile his hands until they were rough and nothing like this monster Wilbet's.

"But now his hands are rough. Like the rest of him." Kerry choked softly. "Inside, he was always rough."

"I'm sorry," Janus said. He wanted Kerry to take hold of his hands again, to guide them over more of his body so that he could soothe Kerry's pain and show him gentleness. "You deserved better."

Kerry jerked back, as though woken from a dream he'd glided into as they'd touched. "Did I? I thought I did back then, but wolf-god alone knows my true heart. *Wolf-god* knew all the ways I'd thought I was better than this place, so much better than these rough mountain alphas deserved." He sneered. "I guess wolf-god showed me 'rough,' didn't he?"

"Oh, Kerry."

"It's blasphemous, I know. Pater would be appalled."

"No, it isn't that...it's that no one deserves that, and wolf-god didn't want that for you."

"Maybe. Who knows wolf-god's mind?"

"Kerry—"

"Wilbet said I was beautiful," Kerry said, cutting Janus off and looking up at him with a curious expression that Janus couldn't quite place. "He was the first alpha to ever say that to me, and I believed it. I'd always thought I was passable, but the alphas around here had always made it plain that, because of my chest, I wasn't much more than that. But Wilbet said I was beautiful, his dream come true." Kerry drifted a little away from Janus, and Janus had to resist the urge to tug him back. Instead, he let the lake's current drift him closer again. "Wilbet always liked to lay it on thick. And I, being stupid and young, bought it."

"But you *are*—" Janus bit off his words, not sure what to say.

Kerry lifted his gaze slowly. The sun sparkled on his freckles maddeningly. "I am... what?" A coy smile bloomed unexpectedly on his mouth. "Pretty? Like Kiwi?"

Janus's heart raced, confused by the turn of conversation. Taking the opportunity to splash water on his face and shoulders, he tried to shake free of the way that smile worked on him, filling him with hot and cold pinpricks that urged him to do something, to act, to own, to possess—and no. *No.*

The water was cold against his sun-reddened skin. The sun was coming down hot and hard, no doubt burning them both, but he wasn't about to suggest they move. Kerry might stop talking to him again, and for who knew how long? Days maybe. Months. Forever.

"Well?" Kerry persisted. "I'm what?"

"Pretty," Janus said gruffly. "Very pretty. Monhundy wasn't a good man, but he didn't lie about that. You *are* beautiful."

Kerry bit into his lip, his lashes dropping to touch his cheekbones again. Janus wanted to pull Kerry's lip free, kiss it and suck it into his own mouth, and...*stop.*

"I wish I didn't like hearing that so much," Kerry whispered. "But I do. Especially from you."

Janus's heart thudded, and he felt as if he'd been sniffing Caleb's printing chemicals—lightheaded, a bit dizzy, and in a dream. A nightmare? A dream? A green and blue bubble of intimacy that he didn't want to break.

Kerry put his hand down on his stomach beneath the water. Janus's eyes followed it, noting Kerry's floating cock and balls again, so delicious, but then he dragged his gaze back up to Kerry's long fingers splayed at the largest part of his stomach. "I like that you think I'm pretty. But you won't think it for long. I'll be as big as a pig with a litter in its belly soon enough."

"I don't think you bringing life into this world could possibly make you any less pretty," Janus whispered, trying to keep from reaching out to cover Kerry's hand with his own. "If anything, you'll be more beautiful." The urge to protect Kerry and the child, to make Kerry smile, to make him laugh, and groan and orgasm like Kerry was his very own, burned right up his spine. Janus tried not to moan as his cock suddenly filled and grew completely hard, helmet exposed as the foreskin drew back. "Sorry," he whispered.

"Why?" Kerry's eyes dropped, and he spotted the problem. Janus went hot all over, inside and out, and he wanted to apologize again, but no words came. "Oh," Kerry gasped. "That's...you're...oh."

In the face of Kerry's mild distress, Janus found the will to form words, grunting out, "I'm sorry. I assure you I'm in control and have no intention to act on the..." He blinked, trying to think of the word, but his mind had gone blank, and his cock was hardening even more under Kerry's persistent gaze. "It's rude. Forgive me."

Kerry bit into his bottom lip, and, to Janus's amazement, beneath his swollen belly, his cock grew hard, too. "Oh, wow. It's been a long time."

Janus moaned softly as Kerry closed his eyes and shuddered, a motion made by many omegas as slick released from their glands. "It's the pregnancy pheromones," Kerry whispered. "Affects alphas."

"Yes," Janus agreed, though he felt in his bones that it was something more than that.

"I'm an omega alone, and you'll want to…help me."

Janus whimpered, holding back from touching and helping. Holding back from owning and fucking.

"And the hormones, in me, they, ohhh," Kerry groaned darkly. "Affect pregnant omegas. Make us want."

Janus nodded. Yes, but like this? He wasn't sure anymore. It seemed unbelievable that he, a medical student and nurse, wouldn't fully understand the implications of a pregnant omega alone. Of course, he knew that pregnant omegas were easily aroused, often considered slutty by many standards and that a healthy omega had a quite strong sexual drive throughout a pregnancy. He'd witnessed it, seen it for himself. He recalled Xan's friend, Vale, getting rammed regularly by his alpha, Jason, for the whole time he was staying at the Virona house before he gave birth. They'd been quite loud and indiscreet, screwing all over the gardens and less-public rooms.

But they'd been *Érosgápe*. And this kind of draw…

Was it natural? Just because there was no alpha to buffer them, to care for Kerry's needs? It felt like so much more than that. It felt like a tide held back by a flimsy dam, and it was about to break.

He restrained himself, though, mindful of Kerry's trauma and history, and not wanting to presume or terrorize him more.

But Kerry broke first, diving toward Janus. He cupped his hand behind Janus's head and dragged him in for a kiss. His tongue was eager and bold, moving against Janus's stroke for stroke, and his lips and teeth were ferocious, sucking on Janus's lips, nipping at his jaw, and crying out softly into Janus's ear when Janus finally gave in to his need, too. He jerked Kerry into his lap, stirring up mud in the clear shallows.

Kerry clung to him, heart pounding like a terrified bird. Janus felt it against his chest as Kerry buried his face against Janus's neck and panted, rigid with terror and need all at once.

Janus hushed him, rubbing wet, soothing hands up and down Kerry's overheated back, and groaning as Kerry shifted to press his cock flush against Janus's own, circling his hips and rubbing them together. The friction and water made Janus's need to hold back as frustrating as it was necessary.

"Don't," Kerry whispered. "Please, don't."

"Calm down now," Janus said, though it took everything he had. He released his grip on Kerry's back, letting his arms drift out to his side. "I'm not going to hurt you. You don't have to do this, Kerry. You can let go. I won't come after you."

Kerry moaned, and shook his head, gripping onto Janus tighter. "It's been so long," Kerry grunted. "You're so nice to me. No alpha's ever been so nice to me. Not really. Not like this." He pushed against Janus again, his breath hitching and his heart beating madly, making his whole body shake with each heartbeat.

Janus didn't want this to be a thank you. He wanted it to be so much more than that. But reasonably, he knew he shouldn't have this at all. Not with Kerry half-sobbing like Janus might do something terrible to him and holding on like Janus might let him go.

"Please," Kerry moaned. "Please."

"Kerry, if you keep moving, I'm going to come," Janus said, his breath emerging in sharp huffs and his dick aching with each hunching circle of Kerry's hips. The musk and berries scent overwhelmed him, and he wanted to drown himself in it. He wanted to be out of the water, somewhere he could get fingers into Kerry's ass to press that delicious odor out of his omega glands and then rub it all over them both.

*Fuck.* He had to get Kerry to stop, or it wasn't going to end with anything but an orgasm for them both. And very soon at that. "Kerry, if you don't want this, please stop."

Kerry shook his head, refusing to let go, and licked the shell of Janus's ear. His voice shaking, he whispered, "Just do this, Janus. Get it over with. *Please.* For wolf-god's sake. *Please help me.*"

It was like a thunderbolt. His cock was harder than it'd been in years. The sweet note of pleading, the desperate clinging, and the words that every alpha ached for, usually during heat, but anytime would do—*please help me.* Oh, wolf-god, Janus wanted to be in control, wanted to be the kind of alpha who would walk away from inappropriate sexual encounters with contracted omegas, but—

"Fuck," he whispered.

"Please, yes," Kerry said. "Get it over with. Help me. Fuck me."

Janus wanted to protest the rush, to take them both off to a place where they could talk clearly without the mind-muddle of all this lust and need, where they could figure this out together and make sure they both wanted to pursue this, given what it all meant.

And yet what he did was lift Kerry by the hips, spread his ass cheeks, and position him so that gravity would help Kerry slide down onto Janus's cock, the wetness of the lake and the slick from his glands easing the way.

And, eye to eye, nose to nose, breath to breath, that's what Kerry did.

Janus let Kerry choose how far down to go, how deep he allowed Janus to go. And, wolf-god, he took him in completely, his head falling back, his eyes dropping closed, and tears spilling down his cheeks as a cry of sheer pleasure ripped out of his throat. Janus roared in response, clutching Kerry close, holding him tight, as they both shuddered and exploded in gratification together. He felt his cock push against the opening of Kerry's womb, and he imagined during heat how he would push inside, fill him with his seed, and—

He cried out again, his body shattering with orgasm. His cum pumped up into Kerry's passage, and just like that Kerry was coming, too. Between them, Kerry's cock throbbed and spurted into the cool water. Jizz floating between them as Kerry squirmed and writhed, his face cast up to the sky, and his hands gripping Janus's shoulders tight. But it wasn't over…

Janus's mind cleared slightly after the first orgasm, but with his cock still throbbing inside Kerry's clenching body, he had only two clear thoughts, one obvious and the other irrational: *Wolf-god, he's tight,* and, *Fuck, he needs to be mine.*

"Yes," Kerry moaned, his head dropping as his orgasm faded. He ducked down to press his face against Janus's neck, breathing him in deeply, scenting him again and again. "You smell so…fuck, so perfect."

Janus kissed Kerry's shoulders, licking his neck, and tasting him. He was delicious, and Janus agreed—his scent was divine. So close to the most perfect scent imaginable. So close. So very close.

A thread tugged at Janus's mind, a whisper, but then Kerry moaned again, clenching around Janus's cock more tightly. He rose up until his asshole tugged against the ridge of Janus's cock's crown, and then he pushed back down again. Janus clutched Kerry's hips, not sure if he should or could stop what was happening. He trembled as Kerry rose up and dropped down again.

"Yes," Kerry hissed as though Janus thoroughly scratched an itch that had been out of reach for years. "You're so big. It's, ah, oh fuck, Janus. You're perfect."

*Perfect.* Janus sat stunned as Kerry impaled himself on Janus's dick again and again, riding him with slow, liquid movements that sloshed the water around him. Sex had never felt so complete. So right. The fit so delicious, the friction so keen. The scent of Kerry's neck, the taste of his mouth when they kissed, and the urgency of Janus's need was beyond flawless.

So whole. So good. Wolf-god, he was fucked.

Kerry cried out, whimpering and clenching, an anal orgasm rocking him softly. "More," Kerry begged, even as it held him in its grip. "Please give me more. I need it."

Janus gathered him close, kissing his chest and nipples, licking his way up and down Kerry's neck, noting when Kerry shuddered in pleasure, and when he tensed in fear. Janus didn't grip too tightly, letting Kerry choose how to ride. Kerry's pleasure mounted again and again, and his chest and cheeks flushed red as anal orgasms rushed over him, making him twitch and shake, making him cry out and beg for another.

Janus let him do the work, allowing Kerry to find the way to his own pleasure. Janus shook with desire, too—his cock rock hard and his balls surging with the need to come. Every nerve felt alive, every touch an ecstasy. As Kerry's wide-eyed pleasure gripped him again, Janus couldn't hold back any longer, either. He grunted as a second orgasm pumped through him, and he bit down on Kerry's shoulder accidentally as he came, shooting his essence into Kerry's body. Planted it deep. The sharp pleasure finally released him, and Janus let his head rest on Kerry's now bruised shoulder, his breath coming in heaving gasps.

"This is why I've been avoiding you, why I didn't want you to touch me," Kerry whispered into the aftermath. "I didn't want this to happen."

Janus jerked as if slapped. He stared into Kerry's dark eyes in a panic that his accidental bite had ruined everything. "I'm sorry. I didn't mean to hurt you." He put his finger over the bite mark. "I didn't want to, it wasn't—please forgive me. I wouldn't ever—"

Kerry shook his head. "No, no, shh. It's not that." He glanced down toward his shoulder, surprise glinting in his eyes. "I didn't even feel that." He pulled Janus's hand away from it and then kissed his fingertips. "You're forgiven."

"I am?"

"Yes."

"Then, why? I'm sorry, I just shot my brains out of my dick twice and, well, I'm confused."

Kerry's lips twisted slightly with a bitter but amused smile. He kissed Janus's nose, and then pulled back, a strange expression flying over his features. "I didn't want to put us in this position." He motioned down below the water where Janus was still shoved deep within him. "It complicates things."

Janus gasped at a strange sensation: a movement against his cock from deep inside Kerry. A kick from the babe inside Kerry's womb. The other alpha's babe. He growled softly.

Immediately a sense of protection reared up inside him for Kerry and the baby as an extension of Kerry. He wanted to be the alpha to protect them both. No cruelty could ever be allowed to touch Kerry or this babe again. Never.

"Complications," Janus whispered in agreement.

Kerry swallowed hard, looking shy. "Yes. But I knew if you wanted me, I'd give in to this."

"Why?"

Kerry shuddered, and the movement squeezed Janus's still half-hard cock. "Because I need it. And there's something about you."

"What about me?" Janus asked, needing to hear it, needing to know he wasn't going insane alone.

Kerry shrugged, but he sounded vulnerable as he answered, "You're safe. You'll take care of me."

Janus felt like he might burst into tears, or scream, or grab Kerry into a hug that would collapse them into each other's bodies. Take care of him? Take *care* of him? Wolf-god, what he felt was so much more than that. "Yes," he said, breathless with confusion and fear. "I'll take care of you."

"I know. I knew it when you helped me. And I was scared."

"You're scared of me?" Janus asked.

Kerry shrugged, and Janus felt the movement around his cock, still buried deep in Kerry's body. "I don't think you'll like the answer to that."

Janus frowned, confused how Kerry could be so contradictory. He was safe but scary? He was perfect but not what Kerry wanted? He felt his cock jerk inside Kerry, sending another shot of possessive pleasure up into him, sharp and angry, not sweet at all. Kerry gasped and then pressed his forehead against Janus's shoulder. He shuddered and shook, a small orgasm wracking him, too.

"Wolf-god," Kerry murmured. "This feels so good. I didn't know. I never...it was never..." He shuddered, and his cock jerked between them with another small orgasm, cum drifting around them in the water as he again came down from the heights.

Janus pressed a kiss to the slight bruise on Kerry's shoulder and tried to order his mind. He found that he couldn't. He was entirely out of his depths here in the shallows.

# CHAPTER THIRTEEN

F INALLY, IN THE silence that followed their surprise resurgence of pleasure, Kerry slowly lifted off Janus's still-hard dick. The slow slide of Janus's fingers on Kerry's hips as he rose was his only protest of this movement, but the loss of Kerry's clenching heat around his cock and the coolness of the lake made him whimper.

Kerry seemed to feel it, too, his head falling back as he knelt in the water, his fingers reaching between his thighs to explore where Janus's cock had just been. Ridiculously, Janus suddenly hated the water as it washed away his cum and all evidence of their coupling.

Separated, Janus wanted nothing more than to find a way back inside Kerry, and the ache in his chest told him that he meant that in ways that had nothing to do with his dick. With a weird sense of unreality, Janus asked, "What just happened? Why did we do that?"

Kerry winced but then moved away, making that ache in Janus's chest grow until he felt it in his whole body. When Kerry was a good three feet away, kneeling in the mud, his half-hard cock bobbing in the water and his nipples raised in the breeze, he pronounced it, "Pheromone delirium."

"That's between *Érosgápe*," Janus said, frowning, and that new itch began in his head again, something that wanted to be understood.

"Usually. But it's fair to say we want each other because of this," Kerry waved at his beautiful stomach. Janus wanted to hold it. He hadn't done that while they were fucking, and now he wished he had. Kerry seemed to sense that, though, and shifted another half-foot back. "Biologically we find it hard to resist, I suppose. I'm a pregnant omega alone. It's natural that a single alpha will grow protective and want to satisfy my urges." He looked a bit shame-faced all of a sudden. "I'm sorry. I thought you knew or at least realized by now?"

"What?"

"That my pater accepted you as a boarder partly because he hoped this would happen?"

Janus shook his head. It couldn't be. This was so much more than *that*. Whatever he felt, whatever this was—

"Pregnancy is difficult for omegas without this relief," Kerry said, his voice shaking and his eyes darting around to anywhere but Janus. What did that mean? Why didn't Janus know? He felt like he should *know*. "Pater probably didn't want me to go to a local alpha and cause trouble on the mountain. No one up here has the means to weather any fallout."

Janus growled at the thought of Kerry with one of these moun-tain alphas that, on any other day, at any other time, he felt protective of and wanted to help.

Kerry's lips twitched up like he enjoyed Janus's reaction more than he thought he should, but then Kerry schooled his face again, a veil of imperviousness dropping. "But Pater wouldn't want me yearning for what I need without satisfaction, either. So, when your request for a boarding room came, he realized that I might have two needs met at once. So, he arranged for you to stay here. Alone. Without other boarders around to complicate things."

Janus blinked. Had he been so blind? Of course, part of the attraction he felt for Kerry was the natural draw of a pregnant omega, but there was something else happening here. Something strong and passionate and irritating in a way he wasn't going to be able to ignore. But despite that, he hadn't ever considered the role Zeke might have wanted Janus to play when he accepted his request to board here.

Janus fought the urge to squirm, feeling confused and worse, used. But the certainty that he was missing an important piece of the puzzle, the ongoing after-bliss of orgasm, and the distraction of sunlight sparkling on Kerry's wet skin as he moved farther away in the water distanced him from those feelings.

"And you're handsome," Kerry said, with a flicker of embarrassment and a shy duck of his head. "There's that. It doesn't hurt."

Janus looked down at his own body beneath the clear water as if he'd never seen it before. The muscle he'd lost was making a slow but sure return, and his dick still pointed up angrily, like he hadn't just come twice with Kerry. It hardened still further, refusing to dismiss whatever intensity had happened between them as something related to pregnancy hormones and not…and not…

Janus couldn't put words to what that other reason might be.

"But I didn't want to follow Pater's lead," Kerry went on. Perhaps sex made him chatty, whereas it made Janus brainless because he couldn't figure out what was happening. All he knew was that Kerry's explanations were wolf-god's own bullshit. Still, they came out of Kerry's mouth anyway. "Being a beta, Pater doesn't understand how complicated a situation like this can get. Betas aren't like alphas and omegas."

Janus blinked again. Almost said, "Tell me something I don't know," and then didn't. Because that would hurt Kerry, and he never wanted to do that. Even when the man was being obtuse and lying to them both, because what they'd done? That wasn't fucking. It was more than that.

"They don't know how the pheromones affect us," Kerry babbled on. "And what feelings they can evoke. *Érosgápe* we might not be—"

Janus gritted his teeth at this downplaying of the bright, intense *something* they'd just shared.

"—but an alpha will eventually want to own any omega he regularly fucks, body and soul." Kerry made this statement like it was a given, and Janus wanted to tell him how wrong he was, how many omegas he'd fucked for weeks, months even, and never wanted to own body or soul. Not like he yearned to have Kerry.

But then Kerry went to the crux of the problem, a simple truth that made Janus have to work to suck in his next breath. "And I'm contracted to another, and, well, I always will be. I'll give birth to his child, and then his parents will make me try again at my next heat. That's my future. We can't get confused just because of this." He motioned at Janus's still hard cock. How was it still so fucking hard?

Janus's blood ran cold. Wait. How had he not realized? How had he not seen the truth? "He still handles your heats? In *prison?*"

Kerry squeezed his eyes closed, and Janus scented a change in him, a horrible one that was all shame and deep sadness. Janus reached out, wanting to haul Kerry against him, protect him, make that scent never, ever, ever happen again.

But Kerry shook his head, rising to his feet. Janus stared after him in helpless bewilderment for a long moment as Kerry walked away, the water splashing around his legs and his small, tight ass.

Janus rose to follow, aware of his white limbs and ass, feeling exposed and horrified, like a fish flopping unexpectedly onto shore. His cock wasn't hard anymore, either. Just the thought of Kerry sharing a heat with someone else—but especially with someone like Wilbet Monhundy, a man the papers had drawn a clear and ominous portrait of—awakened a dread and proprietary anger in Janus that he didn't know how to contain.

Following Kerry out of the water, it took everything in Janus not to grab him, throw him over his shoulder, and take him up to the house, lock him in his room with his sweet bird, and never let him out to be hurt by his contracted alpha again.

Janus now had no doubt Monhundy hurt Kerry during the heats, even in prison, even with guards keeping watch. One look at Kerry's face, the hunch of his shoulders, the change in his scent had told him that, and Janus wanted to wipe it all away. To cover Kerry with his own scent and cum and displace any right Monhundy had to Kerry's body or life. He wanted to refuse to let that man knot Kerry ever again, to reject his right to stuff Kerry with his seed and grow his child.

But Janus had no rights at all over Kerry in this scenario. And a beautiful, deliriously perfect fuck in the healing waters of Hud's Basin didn't give him any.

"Tell me you have other options," Janus begged, chasing after Kerry's naked form, his throat tight and raw. When he reached Kerry on the shore, he grabbed for his hand and demanded it again. "Tell me there's another way for you."

Kerry tugged away and shrugged, drying off with the towel that Janus had brought down for himself. When he spoke, his voice was rough but steady, and the attempt at nonchalance pierced Janus to his soul. "I petitioned my in-laws to allow me a surrogate for heats, and they refused. They want grandchildren." He put his hand on his belly and gave a horrible, tight smile. "Here's number one."

Janus's stomach ached, and he reached out to pull Kerry in for a hug, but he shrugged Janus off with a fast jerk away and a sharp swat against his outstretched hands.

"Stop," Kerry hissed, angry eyes hitting him like darts. "You don't have any right to pity me. You don't have any rights *at all*."

Janus heard all that Kerry was saying with his broken-hearted words. More than not having any right to pity him, he didn't have the right to comfort either, or to have opinions about Kerry's situation, or to express emotions Kerry himself had to bear in a visceral and real way, not just in the realm of imagined transgressions and horror.

But Janus wasn't able to let go. He'd held Kerry in his arms not ten minutes before and felt his living, beautiful body around his own and watched his soul take flight in pleasure. He'd felt his child kick and flutter. He wasn't going to shrug his shoulders and say that changed nothing. He'd lived at the edge of right and wrong for years, and he'd seen some ugliness, had been that ugliness himself, but this…this was beyond anything he believed an innocent man should be forced to endure. Wolf-god, or faith, or law—none of it could demand the degradation of a beautiful man's soul and the risk of his life over a contract, could it? "There has to be a way. Petition the court for your rights back. Omega freedom groups do it all the time."

"And get nowhere." The wind off the lake picked up, making goosebumps rise along Janus's arms and back, and pebble Kerry's nipples.

Janus shook his head, his mind desperately trying to recall an article he'd seen months ago. "There was an omega last summer. He was contracted to a prisoner, too, but the law granted him the right to be serviced during heat by—"

"He was alone in the world. His alpha's parents were dead. His own were, too. Don't you think I already looked into that?" Kerry bit out, his eyes dark and angry. His wet hair whipped around in the wind off the lake. "Don't you think I've explored every option?"

Janus stepped closer, an instinct unlike any he'd ever felt ordering him to calm his pregnant omega, to soothe him, no matter what it took. He brushed his hand against Kerry's arm.

Kerry jerked away again. "Don't."

"I just want to help you."

"You can't. Because I'm not…" Kerry squeezed his eyes shut again, ducked his chin down. He covered his face with one hand. His long hair hung in wet streaks down his chest. "I want to be angry with you. That's all."

"Then be angry with me. I can handle it." He could. If that's what Kerry needed, he'd take it on.

"No. You don't understand. If you're gentle like that...if you take care of me? I'll want you again."

"Want me again?"

"Yes." Kerry motioned at his own exposed cock, and Janus looked down to find it half-hard again already. "I'm sorry."

"Because you want me?" Janus stepped closer, his dick tingling as it rose slowly with each beat of his heart. "I want you, too. I want you to feel safe. I want you to *be* safe."

Kerry cried out softly, his cock jerking at Janus's words. "Stop. You're making me feel so..."

"Feel so what?"

"So desperate. Like...like..."

He could comfort Kerry, hold him, fuck him, make this moment a good one. It wasn't right or proper, and he'd probably have strong feelings about it later—regretful feelings, even. But right now...

He whispered, "Let me help."

"No," Kerry whispered. "It'll just make it worse. It already has. Every gentle thing you say..." His voice broke, and his eyes filled with tears. "Oh, fuck. It's too late."

"Too late? How?" The scent of slick filled the air between them, copious and insistent.

"I want you again. So much. And if I let you, it won't just be this time. It'll start something we can't finish."

Janus shook his head, reaching out. "I want to help you. Say you want me to help you."

"Please hel..." Kerry bit it off and shook his head. "I can't."

"Please let me be here for you, Kerry. I can take on this burden. I know I can."

"You have no idea."

"I do. I've handled heats, I've fucked a lot of omegas, but never for the right reason." He didn't step forward, but Kerry's body softened and slumped toward Janus a bit more. "Let me do it for the right reason."

"And what's that?"

"You. You're the right reason." Janus didn't know how he knew, but he did. Deep down, something had split open in him, a part that felt soft and needy, perfect and complete when he thought about spreading Kerry open and thrusting into him. He'd never felt this way about an omega before. It was almost as if...

But that wasn't possible. He'd *know*. He'd have known immediately.

Kerry squirmed, his beating pulse visible in his neck, and he chewed on his bottom lip again. Janus wanted to suck it until it turned pink, wanted to swallow the cries of release and pleasure he could bring to Kerry. He wanted to make Kerry melt into his arms, give in to whatever this was, and agree to let Janus help him with the bigger problem of his contract.

But Kerry had other plans.

"Once more," Kerry whispered. "But that's all. Just to get it out of our systems."

"You know that's not how it's going to work. You just said so yourself," Janus said, approaching anyway and taking Kerry into his arms. He pressed his erect cock against Kerry's hip and slipped his hands down to his stomach, rubbing over the roundness there, feeling a wild giddiness when the child moved under his palm. Kerry winced, and moved Janus's hands down and away from his stomach, leading them to his thick erection instead.

"Let me lie to myself," Kerry whispered. "Just this one more time."

Janus took Kerry in hand and slid his loose fist up and down Kerry's hot shaft, softly kissing his mouth, and sucking on that worried lower lip. Kerry shifted so that he was leaning against Janus, letting him hold his weight. He whispered, "Do it, Janus. Hurry. Please, get inside of me. Make me forget again."

Janus wasn't a man to ignore pleas like that from any omega, but he could never refuse Kerry. All berries and musk, sweet and perfect—he nuzzled the hot space behind Kerry's ear before flipping him around and rubbing his cock between the globes of his ass.

Kerry moaned, arching back, presenting himself in as close to lordosis position as he could muster standing up, pregnant, and without anything to keep him steady. Janus desperately looked around, trying to find something steadying for Kerry to grip, and grunted in relief when he saw the fallen log near the edge of the forest. That would do nicely.

He steered Kerry toward it, hands gliding first over the strange indent in Kerry's chest, then over his swollen stomach, and finally down to grip his hips to propel him forward. Once they reached the log, Kerry didn't need any instruction or prompting. He fell to his knees, ass up, chest down on the log, and hard cock tight up against his stomach, already dripping. Slick slipped down his thighs, aromatic with his unbearably good scent, and Janus ached all over, like his entire being wanted to thrust into Kerry and own him, possess him, fuck him blind, and then kiss him all over.

Janus didn't take any time to examine his thoughts and instead dropped down behind Kerry, parting his thighs with his knees, and with a possessive grip on Kerry's shoulders, he shoved in with a long, slick-wet push. Kerry's anus released a pulsing flow of slick, and he moaned pitifully, his hips shuddering and flexing as a first, hard anal orgasm gripped him.

*Easy. Delicious. Yes.* Janus's thoughts were simple as he moved in and out of the wet, tight heat of Kerry's body. *Fuck him until he comes, and then fuck him until he comes again.*

Kerry seemed to have a similar idea because he rode Janus's cock like he was in heat. His body writhing, humping, twisting, desperation in every single muscle until he came again, his cock emptying on the ground beneath them—a scent so poignant it brought tears to Janus's eyes. Then Kerry rode Janus's cock even harder, sweat breaking out over his skin, until he crowed in triumph, his anus squeezing rhythmically with another anal orgasm. Not done yet, Kerry panted and squirmed on Janus's cock, his chest and cheek resting against the wide log, and his body flushing red up his back.

Janus bent low to kiss his shoulders, the back of his neck, and to whisper in his ear. Little nothings that must have meant a lot given Kerry's whimpers of pleasure whenever he spoke: *wanna make you mine, so perfect, oh, sweet Kerry, I've never felt so good.*

Kerry came several more times, in various ways, as Janus worked in and out of him. Anal and penile orgasm gripping him again and again as they succumbed to a previously unknown lust, and a sort of blind madness that left them insensible to time or place, and only able to pursue pleasure together. Finally, Janus leaned down, huffing against Kerry's wet cheek—was he crying?—and roared as he came hard, a ripping sort of pleasure that screamed through him with a near agony of bliss.

Kerry's muscles worked around Janus, slick still slipping from Kerry's asshole and wetting Janus's balls and thighs. The aftershocks of orgasm dragged on, the amount of cum that shot from his tingling balls filled Kerry's insides and slipped out along with the slick. It was a wet, sloshy mess below when Janus pulled out, leaving Kerry gaping open and, if his trembling haunches were any indication, still coming. Janus leaned in and licked the cum and slick around Kerry's hole, gratified by the trembling muscle of his anus and the shocked swearing that burst from Kerry's mouth.

"That's too much," Kerry finally gasped, twisting his hips out of Janus's grip. "Please stop. He never—I've never—" His voice broke off, and tears filled his eyes. He looked like he was going to die or swallow his tongue, or both.

Janus had questions. So many questions. But his mind was an endless roar of satisfaction. He gathered Kerry to him, nuzzled his hair, his neck, and his chest, and then muttered, "Let's get you somewhere safe."

Kerry shivered against him, a cry of release making him go rigid and then soft again. "Stop," he finally huffed, using what seemed to be every ounce of energy he had left to pull free of Janus's embrace. "Stop saying things like that to me. It's not fair. It's not even true. There is nowhere safe for me, Janus." His right cheek was scraped from where he'd pressed it against the bark of the fallen log, and his chest held scrapes, too. Janus wanted to bandage them properly and kiss Kerry after, begging his forgiveness for hurting him, for making their joining rough, but Kerry rasped on, "This was such a bad idea. I can't afford to…" He shook his head, then looked down at his beautiful, round belly. He raised a fist as if he might punch it, injure himself, but Janus leapt up and grabbed it from the air.

"What are you thinking?"

"I'm thinking nothing," Kerry said, uncurling his fist, though Janus still held his forearm in a tight grip. The fire in Kerry's eyes winked out. He was the cold, distant man from Zeke's reading hour in the living room at night. All heat vanished in the blink of an eye. "I think I should wash off and go inside," he said, as if from a great, great distance. "This can't happen again."

Janus stared after him in frustrated perplexity as Kerry walked back to the water on obviously wobbly legs and splashed off his cum- and slick-covered penis, balls, and thighs. He paid special attention to his hole, and Janus wanted to growl, to make him stop washing their combined odor away. He wanted to cover him with his scent again. Immediately.

But Kerry was shaking, and not from the sex they'd had. His

expression was grim and determined, and when Janus rose to follow him up the path, he shook his head and held a hand up to stop him. "Give me space," he whispered. "Please. Let me breathe."

Janus held back, his heart beating like he'd run a marathon and his hands itching to grab Kerry and drag him to his side. But he let him go. The last thing Kerry needed was to be manhandled and hurt by another alpha. Some sneaking thought to that effect kept him silent, too. Kerry had a right to his feelings and fears. Janus needed to respect them. And not feed them. Soothe them and not irritate them.

Kerry took the only towel and so when Janus washed off, too, sorrow at the loss of their combined odor striking deep in him, he had no choice but to dry off in the sun or put on his clothes while still wet.

So, he spread out on a rock near the edge of the lake, laying back to stare up at the sun and clouds above, and tried to make sense of what had happened, what they'd done.

Tried to figure out if it could ever happen again.

# CHAPTER FOURTEEN

"**I**'M NOT GOING to fuck him, Pater."

"But you already did," Pater said, rolling his eyes. They were sitting together in the rocking chairs on the porch, with a pleasant view of the sparkling lake. It was Kerry's preferred place to rest and think.

Janus had left for his work with Dr. Crescent at dawn, and Kerry had watched him go before coming down to the kitchen for his breakfast. The night before had been awkward over dinner, but Kerry had claimed to be too tired to read in the living room, and Janus had claimed the same, so they'd both headed up to their respective bedrooms, alone, rather than sit in discomfort with Zeke.

Kerry hadn't anticipated being able to sleep, but he'd fallen into a deep state of rest as soon as he tucked up in his bed. The swimming and sex caught up with him like a freight train. He'd dreamed of pleasant things for the first time in ages. As if Janus's touch had banished the nightmare of Wilbet for a time.

Dawn had brought with it a fresh sense of optimism that Kerry hadn't felt in years. The sensation wore off, though, as the memories of Janus's kiss, touch, and passion flared up in his mind and made him *want*. He'd been wet with slick all morning, craving more, and wishing he'd never had the first taste. Worse, the baby was restless, too, twisting and turning inside, a constant reminder of how completely tied Kerry was to another alpha and another life.

Determined to focus on the reality of what was to come—a life that couldn't include Janus's passion and care—Kerry rocked back and forth, sewing a baby's sleeping gown from the cloth Pater had bought while he'd met with the Monhundys. Kerry had made a handful of paternity clothes for himself already, including the drawstring pants he had taken to wearing after his stomach had expanded to the point where he could no longer button his pants.

Pater wasn't about to give up his plan easily, though, and so carried on with his argument. "I'm only a beta, so maybe I can't smell 'im on you, but I have eyes. I can see what happened. You're both softer from it, and yet tense at the same time. I know ya took pleasure with 'im."

Kerry groaned, rolling his eyes again.

"What? It's good for ya, son. Wolf-god wants omegas to be pleasured during pregnancy. It makes for an easy birth."

Kerry pricked his thumb with the needle, and he cursed softly before lifting it to his mouth to suck the blood away. There was a small red stain on the cloth where he'd bled on it, and he frowned, holding it up to the light. "I'm contracted to Wilbet."

"No," Pater shook his head. "Mark my words, that'll be broken. It can't last."

"Pater, what madness are you going on about? It *will* last!" Kerry burst out. His thumb throbbed, and he blinked rapidly, trying to keep tears from coming to his eyes. It was just a prick—nothing he couldn't handle. "Stop believing in fairy tales, Pater. The Monhundys want me to make more babies for them. Don't be foolish. They know he'll never win another omega over. No one in their right mind would agree to share a heat with him again. So, they aren't going to let me go. The best I can hope for is…" Kerry trailed off.

He didn't know anymore. He'd thought the best he could hope for would be a life here with his pater in between bouts of complete misery and passing off his sons to be raised by the Monhundys, but he didn't know if that was enough. How many pregnancies would they try to wring out of him before he died? Or went insane? Or decided to kill himself for real this time?

Pater had an answer to the question, though. "The best you can hope for is to attract a powerful alpha who will save you from—"

"Janus is not a powerful alpha. He's poorer than either of us. He can barely afford an extra candle."

"Now you're being an obtuse brat. Janus has influence in a powerful family. The Heelies are wealthy enough that even I've heard of 'em here in ol' Hud's Basin."

"I'm assuming he's lost their support given his situation here. And even if he hasn't, I'm not going to use him like that." Kerry tossed the baby's gown into the sewing kit by the rocker and shoved his thumb back in his mouth. Why wouldn't it stop bleeding? If he couldn't get the stain out, he'd have to waste the material and start another gown from scratch. Even he wasn't morbid enough to dress his child in a blood-stained garment.

"Yes, you are going to use him exactly like that," Pater said, slapping his hand against his knee. "For wolf-god's sake, Kerry, he wants ya to use him."

Kerry shot his pater a droll look. "He's a horny alpha. Nothing more."

"Lies. He aches for you. You should see how he looks at you, son. All that desire writ as plain as day on his face."

Kerry huffed, his eye catching the slink of a wildcat near the forest's edge. "That's pheromone delirium. Nothing more."

"Pheromone delirium is reserved for *Érosgápe*, son." He raised his hand when Kerry started to argue. "Yes, the pheromones of any omega will act on all alphas, that's true. But this with Janus is something more."

"He's an alpha. That's all. Why do you want to make it into something it's not?" Kerry stared at the cat as it hid in the green leafy bushes close to the trail, its eyes on a rabbit chomping innocently on the long grass near Pater's garden. He didn't believe his own words, so why did he hope his pater would?

"Any alpha would be willing to relieve your needs, of course, especially if you spent much time around each other without the buffer of your alpha's presence. And yes, I hoped Janus would follow that instinct. But son, the good news is it's gone beyond that. Janus *wants* you, truly, as only an alpha wants an omega. Haven't you noticed how he samples the air when you walk into the room? There's more between you than a simple case of pheromone-enhanced lust."

"Stop. Don't do this to me, Pater," Kerry said, his throat going tight and his voice husky. He dashed is fingers over his wet eyes. "Don't make me hope. Please. Don't be so cruel."

"I'm trying to save you."

"You can't!" Kerry rose from the rocking chair, leaving the sewing kit behind, and stomped up the stairs to his room, tears standing in his eyes. He shut the door and stood against it, shivering.

Wolf-god, he didn't know what to make of what he'd done with Janus, how it had felt. Sex had never been like that before. Not with anyone. He hadn't been a virgin when Wilbet had first fucked him. He'd screwed his roommate Reyman a few times, but he'd been a beta, and while that was always fun, always pleasant, he'd been unprepared the first time with Wilbet, for the fullness that came from being fucked by an alpha-sized cock. For years, he'd told himself that he hated it. Hated that feeling of being so vulnerably full. And when it was over, he hated being left wrecked, gaping open, and empty.

But after Janus, he remembered it wasn't true that he'd hated being fucked by an alpha. Memories of the first few weeks of his contract with Wilbet had come pouring in throughout the day. At the very first, right after they'd contracted, sex with Wilbet had been good. Exciting. Fun. But after they'd left the island where they'd purchased Kiwi, Kerry had the unpleasant discovery of the way Wilbet really preferred to fuck—violent, painful, and with a punch at the end—and sex had never been the same again.

Until yesterday.

With Janus, there had been genuine lust, excitement, and pleasure. There'd been delicious orgasms of multiple types and duration, and *fuck*, there'd been such sweet feelings, too. Kerry was terrified.

What was he going to do? And Pater urging him to do it again wasn't helpful. What if it kept on feeling good? What if Kerry grew to *need* it? Like all the time? After the pregnancy even? What then? How was he ever going to go back to never feeling cared for and truly full? What if he was never again made to come like all wolf-god's joy was bursting from him? What if all his future held were episodes of Wilbet's rough hands around his throat, choking him as he was forced to come on his enormous cock and endure endless pregnancies from the monster's seed? What if Wilbet killed him next time?

Kerry was losing his mind.

Sliding down to the floor, he felt tears slip from his eyes and slick glide from his hole as he remembered Janus's gentle caretaking the evening before. The sex had been so good. So incredibly, intensely good. Kerry hadn't had any idea that it could be like that. None at all. Even the "good" sex with Wilbet before it'd gone so bad hadn't compared.

Kerry put his hand on his belly and felt the baby somersaulting within. Why would Janus want him? Why would he make him feel good like that? Kerry was full of a monster's child, growing larger by the day, and wolf-god, he wasn't even nice to Janus half the time, terrified by the draw he felt toward him.

And yet, Janus had wanted him, maybe even more than Kerry had wanted Janus. And both times, when Janus had come, his huge cock thudding like a rocket in Kerry's ass, he'd looked starstruck, dazzled, and undone. He'd nearly begged Kerry not to walk away, to let him help him again, and yet…

Janus hadn't come to Kerry's room last night. He hadn't stopped by before leaving this morning. What if he'd rethought his desire for Kerry in the meantime? Kerry was making himself crazy with all his second-guessing and wanting.

Shaking free of the morass, he stood again, forcing himself to his writing desk. He took out a piece of paper and started a letter to his in-laws, ignoring the ongoing release of slick and the sensitive twitching of his needy hole.

# CHAPTER FIFTEEN

N EAR THE STABLE, Dr. Crescent and Fan had arranged outdoor seating made out of logs around a central table on which sat several books and a few tools of the trade including diagrams of pregnant omegas, their womb, and the channel the child inside must exit through.

It was three days after the events by the lake, and Janus was in the crowd rather than assisting because childbirth education was something Fan had long experience with and enjoyed doing. Fan stood by Dr. Crescent, next to the table as he taught the assembled group of omegas and alphas, demonstrating everything they would need to know with the models, diagrams, and occasionally, with his own body by miming the birthing process. This last bit was very dramatic and left many omegas and alphas laughing nervously, but Fan clearly had a flair for the theatrical, and so it went on a bit long.

"Now that we've covered the basics," Dr. Crescent said, pulling his omega up from the examining table which was doubling as a 'birthing bed' for Fan's lesson, "Fan'll go over a few other issues pregnant omegas might face. Darlin'? Go on."

Fan smirked and raised a dark brow. "Let's discuss undue arousal." He sent a considering look around at the crowd, his gaze catching on Janus before trailing around the circle to where Kerry sat alone, his hand on his stomach and his eyes wide with worry. "All pregnant omegas experience strong lust during pregnancy. The increased blood circulation to the womb inflames the genitals as a whole. Slick will be released. Erections will become erratic like during puberty. It's all entirely normal and nothing to be ashamed of."

The other alphas around the circle guffawed, and put their arms around their omegas, shaking them gently, murmurs of "little slut" and "that's my sweet whore" rose up with a jovial, teasing enthusiasm. Janus saw Kerry's face turn red and his gaze fall to the ground. He wrapped his arms more securely around himself, looking small and alone. Janus fought the urge to go to him, slip an arm around his waist and reassure him. But he'd been explicitly warned away and wouldn't violate Kerry's consent and autonomy. He'd court but never press.

"Oh, don't pretend it's all on them," Dr. Crescent interrupted the teasing alphas. "Yeah, they're eager as rabbits on a full moon night, but you're all just as hot and longin' for wolf-god's so-called union o' souls. That's the way of it."

Fan nodded in agreement, lifting a finger. "Now, can anyone tell me why?" His sharp, dark gaze met Janus's. "How about you, Janus?"

Janus coughed. He was there as Dr. Crescent's nurse. He wasn't an alpha with a pregnant omega, so he didn't know why Fan decided to single him out. "Pheromones."

"Right." Fan snapped his fingers. "That's correct. Pheromones are always strongest between *Érosgápe*, undeniable in that case."

Dr. Crescent laughed. "You'll fuck and fuck a lot. Have fun with that." Another round of laughter.

Fan, with a prim little lift to his chin, went on as if his alpha hadn't spoken so crassly. "The next-strongest draw is between bonded and contracted pairs. There may also be a draw between an alpha and a pregnant omega who are friends. Well, if the alpha who impregnated the omega doesn't suitably protect him, that is." Janus noticed that Fan looked at every omega in the group but Kerry now, and that, in itself, seemed pointed and rude. Kerry was nearly disappearing behind his hair. "And then, yes, in extreme situations, even strangers may feel a sexual pull toward one another. If an alpha abandons his omega during his pregnancy, for example."

This last Fan directed toward Kerry. whose eyes went wide before he hid behind a fall of his long, curly hair.

"That's right," Dr. Crescent said, nodding his agreement. "We've all of us felt something similar from time to time, isn't that so?"

The alphas of the group nodded or carefully remained neutral if they had a jealous omega. Janus, for his part, looked at his finger-nails rather than dare a glance toward Kerry.

Fan stepped in front of his alpha, still in small-professor mode. "All alphas will feel the call to protect a pregnant omega. In fact, recent research by Urho Chase and his new team in Virona has illuminated exactly why that is."

*Urho Chase.* Janus rolled his eyes. *Of course.*

"Additionally," Fan said, "they've outlined a few rare cases when a pregnant omega is less receptive to sexual congress than is usual and how to help them through pregnancy as well. If that's a problem for your omega, don't hesitate to come to me, Dr. Crescent, or Dr. Heelies. There is specific advice to follow for a better birthing outcome in that situation."

No alpha sitting around the circle seemed at all worried about their omega not wanting to be fucked enough, and all the omegas except for Kerry seemed shyly pleased to be given medical permission to indulge in their every erotic wish.

"So, that there's the real reason he wants to jump on my dick all the time, Doc?" an alpha named Lowsen asked, laughing when his omega, a tall man named Fray, rolled his eyes and said, "Me? What about you? Always wanting to screw me even when I'm busy napping."

"Busy napping, he says!" Lowsen crowed, and everyone laughed.

Even Kerry peeked out from his shielding veil of hair to flash a small smile at that.

"Napping is serious business for a pregnant omega," Dr. Crescent said with a nod and craggy grin. "Don't be interrupting him when he's sleeping now. Wait until first thing after he wakes up."

Everyone laughed again.

Fan snapped his fingers for attention, and when everyone was quiet again, he asked, "Can anyone guess what else Dr. Chase's studies have told us about the reason *why* alphas find pregnant omegas arousing? And, no, Lowsen, it's not because a pregnant omega is 'just so hot.' Anyone?"

Heads shook.

Rubbing a hand over his sweaty forehead, the morning growing warm enough to make the scent of sweat and arousal rise in the air, Janus watched as Kerry shrank in on himself again. He could still feel the way Kerry had trembled in his arms, had come violently on his cock, and had clung to him as if his life depended on it. He still remembered Kerry's tears. Maybe he'd fooled himself into believing they were tears of joy and satisfaction, but even if they'd been tears of grief, he wanted to be allowed to wipe them away, kiss his cheeks, and protect him from the future, whatever it held.

Clearing his throat, Fan caught Janus's attention, and when he was sure Janus was listening, he went on in an almost scholarly fashion. "There are several reasons, some social, some biological for alphas to be attracted to pregnant omegas, and all of them are evolutionarily beneficial to our human race."

"Get on with it!" an alpha named Tyson yelled. He'd been down to Doctor Crescent's earlier in the week for a tonic to help with virility. "Else I'm gonna hafta drag mine off and fuck him now." Everyone giggled, especially the very pregnant omega next to him.

"Stick around, Tyson. You need this information more than

most." Everyone chuckled again. Then Fan carried on with his lesson. "First, let's talk about the biological function of this attraction—"

A groan went around the group. Fan spoke louder to cover it, "Regular sex keeps the omega's passage loose and ready for birth. Some suggest fisting as a stretching technique if there's concern about there being room for the baby to pass, but generally, a good, alpha-sized cock will do the trick of keeping an omega's passage stretched and ready." He rocked back on his heels, and Dr. Crescent stared down at him raptly, as if wolf-god's divine grace laced every word he said. *Oh,* Érosgápe. *They could be so annoying.*

"Dr. Chase's work shows that regularly penetrated omegas have a lower risk of trouble during delivery. It's speculated that along with the stretching of the passage, the alpha's sperm—long known to reduce inflammation and deaden pain during heats—also softens the ligaments and tissues, again preparing the passageway for the stretch of delivery. There is also a potentially beneficial emotional effect—"

Dr. Crescent interjected, "A well-fucked omega is a well-loved omega."

"Yes, and a well-loved omega is one who can trust in their mate, their future, and the road ahead. Dr. Chase's research shows that regularly penetrated pregnant omegas are more optimistic about birth, and report higher rates of joy and satisfaction, as well as decreased dread and fear. These all bode well for the delivery."

Alphas grunted in gratification all around. There was a rising scent of lust, which wasn't unexpected since everyone was horny and eager in the crowd. Being given permission by the doctor and his little omega to fuck to their heart's delight definitely aroused them all.

"As for why alphas can develop the desire for pregnant omegas, regardless of relationship, that's also evolutionarily beneficial, according to Dr. Chase. The human race was so close to perishing after the Great Death that the prior animalistic response of the Old World humans, negative emotions toward raising a child not his own, was replaced by an attraction to, and a desire to protect, *all* pregnant omegas, regardless of paternity."

Fan's eyes strayed over to Kerry and lingered before coming to rest on Janus for the next part of his speech. "Dr. Chase's study went on to examine the few cases where an omega was left alone without an alpha to satisfy his urges and needs, and the outcomes were less desirable." Janus shifted on his feet, the meaning of Fan's words hitting home. Had *everyone* on the mountain assumed he'd fuck Kerry through his pregnancy? And why did he want to protect Kerry from that assumption? When that was, indeed, exactly what he wanted to do? Fan's brow rose pointedly, and he said, "When an omega was left alone, incidents of omega and infant deaths rose."

Janus's blood ran cold, and he darted a glance toward Kerry who hid behind his hair again. Janus couldn't make out his reaction to this statement at all.

Here, Dr. Crescent interjected, "So follow your instincts. Have plenty of sex. Don't deny yourselves for any reason."

Alphas and omegas around the circle glanced toward Kerry, and then their gaze drifted speculatively toward Janus, but seeing him staring coldly back, quickly skittered away. They were plenty eager to stare into each other's eyes and contemplate fucking as soon as possible instead.

The meeting broke up with everyone lining up to make their next appointments with Dr. Crescent or Janus for checkups. Most of them requested that Janus or the doc visit them on their rounds since they preferred to be in the safety of their own home while the doctors looked them over, especially if any intimate areas needed to be manipulated or checked. Alphas, in general, didn't like their omegas exposed for all and sundry to see, and the privacy of the homestead gave them a bit more peace and security when standing aside to let another alpha, doctor though he may be, touch and prod their beloved.

Janus looked around for Kerry as he said goodbye to the last of the couples who asked him to come by and check on them, eager to walk him home and ask his opinion of the lecture. But he didn't find him anywhere. Disappointment welled.

He started toward the path as well, his bag hitched over his shoulder, when Fan grabbed him by the arm. "Come with me," Fan said, glancing over his shoulder to see that re-doing the dressing of an alpha's injured shoulder while his pregnant omega cooed and watched closely still occupied Dr. Crescent. "We need to talk."

Janus didn't see what they could need to discuss. He'd taken Fan's advice and kept his mouth closed about everything to do with the abortion attempt, and Kerry rewarded him with weeks of silence, followed by confusing intimacy of both the personal and sexual kind, followed by silence again for the last three days. All he wanted to do was find Kerry, and for once make *him* do the listening.

"You have to convince Kerry to let you handle his needs," Fan said as soon as they were clear of the stables enough that Dr. Crescent and his patients wouldn't overhear them. "He's stubborn and afraid to trust anyone, but an omega shouldn't be alone through his pregnancy. He should be cared for and well-tended. You heard what this Dr. Chase has discovered in his studies. Kerry's chances go down the more alone he feels." Fan leaned close and hissed, "You must seduce him. For his own sake. And the babe's. It's your duty."

"As a doctor?"

"As an alpha!" Fan rolled his eyes. "As a doctor, please. No. That's not what doctors do, Janus." He huffed again, glancing toward Crow, where he was still helping the omega learn to change his alpha's bandages. "But alphas must think of the future of our species, and the health of omegas in their midst. Besides, do you want another alpha from the mountain getting it into his mind to help Kerry?"

Janus bristled at that. "He wouldn't allow it."

"Wouldn't he? If he was alone and feeling vulnerable and needy?"

Janus thought back to the lake and the beach, the way Kerry had given in and urged him to 'get it over with' as if he'd needed it—wanted it, maybe—but didn't truly trust in Janus wholeheartedly. Kerry himself had called what they'd done the result of pheromone delirium and made it seem as though Janus's personal volition in the act was less important than their biological draw to fuck and be fucked. Janus rubbed a hand over his face, scratching at the beard that he'd failed to shave that morning in his hurry to make it to the lecture on time. He'd wring the neck of any alpha who touched Kerry. He'd throttle them, and beat them, and rip off their manhood, and—

Wolf-god, what was he thinking?

"I see," Fan said with a hint of smugness. "You've already fucked him. That's good."

Janus growled softly, annoyed that Fan could see through him so easily.

Fan laughed softly. "Ah, protective. That's even better. It means you've also become emotionally attached. But, to be completely frank, that's also a bit problematic. As I'm sure you know, he's contracted to a wealthy and powerful man who's also a brutal criminal."

"They force him to share heats with that monster," Janus croaked out, sweat breaking out on his lower back and nausea filling him. "They give him no choice. Isn't that rape?"

"Consent for heat-sharing is considered a given at the time of the contract," Fan said with a grimace. "Omegas can't change their mind when in heat. You know that. Legally, Kerry must do as his alpha wants when it comes to his heat, criminal or not, so long as the contract is binding. And if not his alpha, then whoever has taken over his alpha's concerns. The parents, most likely."

Birdsong rose from the depths of the green forest. "There has to be a way out of it for him."

Fan tilted his head, deliberating. "Have you considered taking it up with a lawyer? Several omega freedom groups are looking for test cases like this one to push through the court system. Kerry is a good example of people misusing the current system in horrifying ways that abuse omegas and restrict their rights in unfair ways. One could argue this could damage the omega's chances at successful reproduction. You know how the courts feel about that." His eyes flew to somewhere over Janus's shoulder, and he smiled widely, with only a brittle hint of worry. "Crow! C'mere, love, and say goodbye to Janus. He's trying to talk me into making berry pie for next week." He turned to Janus again with a tension in his face that Janus hadn't ever seen there before. He went on with his lie, "I've heard good things about Zeke's cooking, but I know he's never made a decent pie in his life."

Janus turned to Dr. Crescent with a fake chuckle in his throat. He wasn't sure why Fan was hiding their conversation from his alpha, perhaps the mention of omega freedom groups was more liberal than an older, devoted *Érosgápe*-bonded alpha like Dr. Crescent could stand. Or maybe he feared what Fan, still barren, might do if omegas had more rights—*Érosgápe* or not.

"I do love your Fan's pies," Janus said with a shrug, playing it off. "I'm thinking snowberry? The last time he served snowberry tart it was so tasty, I almost cried. And they're ripe all over the hills out there. Surely a pie would be even better." He shifted his gaze back to Fan. "I'd be happy to gather them for you, Fan, if it makes things easier."

"No, I'll do it," Dr. Crescent said possessively, putting his arm around Fan's shoulder and gazing down at him with that sickening *Érosgápe* devotion that made alphas want to be the ones who got the credit for doing every last little thing for their omega, right down to tying their shoes in some cases.

In fact, the father of one of Janus's former lovers had tied his disabled omega's laces every morning as part of some elaborate dressing ritual, because he couldn't bear the thought of beta servants touching his *Érosgápe*. It'd been both devotion and possession, and Janus hadn't known how he felt about it.

Until now.

Thinking of Kerry, if he were in a wheelchair and unable to tie his shoes, Janus would want to be the one to do it. He'd want to kiss each toe and Kerry's slim ankles, too, before slipping on the socks. He'd want to run his hands up Kerry's strong, lightly haired calves and...

*Wolf-god, he was losing his mind.*

Since when had he felt this way about any omega other than Caleb? And even with Caleb he hadn't been willing to sacrifice, had he? That's how he'd lost him in the first place. He'd wanted it all, and at Caleb's expense. And afterward, he'd never allowed himself to ask *anything* from an omega except for the one thing Caleb hadn't been able to give him: sex.

But with Kerry...

Wolf-god, with Kerry, Janus felt like he might sacrifice nearly anything to be allowed to care for the man. That was easy to say, though, given that they'd already fucked, and he knew Kerry had a strong interest in it. Sex was important to Janus or had been until he'd determined to give it up to improve the state of his character. But if Kerry didn't ever want to have sex with him again, then so be it. There were other ways for an alpha to care for a pregnant omega.

No matter what, Janus would find a way to be there for Kerry in those other ways. He'd court him, show him what it meant to be fawned over, appreciated, and revered the way every pregnant omega should be treated. And he'd do more than that, too. He'd contact an attorney. See what their options truly were and if there might be an eager omega freedom group looking for a test case.

Kerry could benefit from having other men on his side, even if he rejected all of Janus's carnal desires going forward. Yes, there had to be something he could do for the quiet, prickly man he'd come to feel the urgent need to protect and soothe.

He cleared his throat, took his leave of Fan and Dr. Crescent, and started back down the hill toward Monk's House, wondering if he should feel irritated or used by the fact that Zeke, and now Fan, were clearly planning to involve him in a situation that was way above his pay grade and complicated beyond measure.

But when he reached the door of the house, opened it to the scent of berries and musk, and the low tones of Kerry singing to Kiwi in the attic, he no longer cared. He just wanted to bottle this feeling of coming *home* and uncork it daily. He needed to find a way to make Kerry his in truth.

If only Kerry would let him.

# CHAPTER SIXTEEN

KERRY STARED AT the peach sitting in the middle of his pillow. It was perfect. Fuzzy and ripe. Golden and pink tones glowed in the light from the window. There was a note there, too. Two words.

*For you.*

Not in Pater's handwriting. So, it must be from Janus. Kerry reached out and picked up the fruit, holding it to his nose to breathe in the sweet, tangy scent, imagining how the freshness would burst over his tongue. He put out his tongue, touching it to the fuzzy skin, but not biting into the peach just yet.

It'd been two days since the pregnancy education meeting by Dr. Crescent's stable, and he'd valiantly avoided Janus's efforts to talk with him ever since. The peach weighed heavily in his palm, an offer of care and sweetness.

Kiwi chirruped from his cage, and Kerry went to let him out. He smiled as the bird danced around and then burst into flight around the room, lighting on the headboard, the night table, and then Kerry's shoulder. Kerry tucked his chin down and let Kiwi rub against his stubbled jaw. Sometimes he thought Kiwi would purr like a cat if he could.

"Back from your swim?" Pater asked from the hallway.

Kerry turned to see him outside the door, as though he'd been passing by and noticed Kerry. "Yes," he said, then held up the fruit. "Do you know what this is about?"

Pater shrugged. "I saw him out by the tree this morning, looking over peach after peach, and in the end he chose this one. Plucked it. Brought it inside. I thought he must have eaten it, but I see he's determined to take care of you."

Kiwi flew to land on the windowsill and chirp at the sights visible through the glass panes. Kerry rubbed the peach to his lips again and then said, "I shouldn't have let you take him as a boarder. I knew your plan."

"Mayhap you did, but you can't say that it was a bad one."

Kerry started to protest, but Pater had already moved on, heading toward the stairs and whatever work he had in the kitchen to prepare for dinner. Kerry lay down on his bed, his hand resting over his swollen stomach, and he picked up the note again. Just the two words, still. Nothing more.

Still, it warmed him to see the firm, strong lines of Janus's letters, and the simplicity of the statement. The peach was a gift for Kerry. Nothing more or less. No demands. No promises.

Kerry took a bite and moaned softly. The sweet, ripe fruit filled his mouth with juice and flesh, and his tongue burst with the flavor. He felt a cool dribble down his chin, and he wiped it away with his fingers. Before he knew it, he'd devoured the whole of it, leaving only the pit and stickiness behind.

He rose to wash his face and hands, and wondered, not for the first time, if there was a way to have what he needed without ruining Janus's life. The sticky sweetness on his hands and face reminded him of his own slick and the way it poured from him when he was aroused, which was nearly constantly since the fucks by the lake. Just scenting Janus in the house was enough to cause his knees to buckle and his asshole to grow wet. He didn't want to complicate anything anymore than they already had, but he was growing less certain that he would refuse again if Janus approached him offering something more than a peach.

He washed his face and hands quickly and then changed into a clean shirt that didn't smell of lake water, reminding him of the fucks they'd already shared, or peaches, reminding him of the potential sweet fucks they could share if only he'd approach Janus and ask for them.

He wanted to ask for them, yearned for that gentleness and passion. If he could only believe that fucking would make things better instead of worse. But in his experience, omegas who allowed themselves emotional entanglements ended up suffering.

He'd had enough of that to last a lifetime.

THAT NIGHT, KERRY trembled as he pushed open the door to Janus's bedroom, slick already running down his legs and making his thighs wet. He promised himself that if Janus was asleep, then he'd leave. He'd keep his need to himself and beat off again in his room, alone, and lonely, and unloved. Unwanted.

But Janus was awake and naked, his body displayed like a beautiful statue spread over the bed, his cock hard and massive, rising into his fist as he pumped and jerked his hips up. His eyes caught Kerry's, but he didn't stop his self-abuse. He kept right on fucking into his own loosely clenched fingers and stared silently at Kerry with hot, boiling need in his eyes.

Kerry shut the door behind him, letting his long nightshirt drop to the floor, gratified by the noise that came from Janus's throat at the sight of Kerry's naked body. He felt the child move within, and it only made him more needful, because he wanted to forget, to feel something that wasn't fear.

Janus rose up from the bed, his cock sticking out violently from his body, and his large balls dangling low. He reached out his hand but still said nothing. His chest heaved with breath, sucked in and out like he was struggling to get enough air, but he waited, sweaty and strong, healthier by the day, and very ready.

Kerry stepped into his arms, burying his face in Janus's warm-scented neck. He gasped in joy as Janus's fingers found his ass cheeks, spread them open, and three fingers plunged inside, finger-fucking him roughly as Kerry clung and shook. He came quickly and hard, his mouth open against Janus's neck, his tongue pushed out to taste him, and his body spasming with pleasure.

"That's my sweet omega," Janus whispered. "Come for me again, Kerry. Show me how good it feels."

Kerry didn't need to be told twice. The pressure on his omega glands and prostate, and the rough friction of Janus's fingers twisting in and out of him, left him strengthless, held up by Janus's strong arm, and writhing in bliss. The next orgasm was even harder, and his anus clenched rhythmically around Janus's fingers. He cried out as the pleasure crested again, and he shot a hot, wet load of omega cum on Janus's belly and thigh.

"Yes," Janus hissed. "That's right." He removed his fingers from Kerry's body, leaving him aching and open, scooped up the cum, and smeared it over his own cock. Then he pushed Kerry toward the bed and laid him flat on his back before dragging Kerry's ass to the edge of the mattress.

Positioned perfectly, Janus held him open and then pushed inside with one hard stroke. "Fuck," Janus whimpered. "Oh, wolf-god, Kerry. It's perfect."

Perfect? No. It was *glorious*. Every bit of Kerry felt so full and satisfied.

Janus touched Kerry's cheek, bent low and nuzzled him. "Let me kiss you," he whispered. "Please."

Kerry growled and quivered, his body convulsing in pleasure. "Yes, please." It was strange to think they had only kissed on that day by the lake. He reached up to drag Janus down, both of them careful of Kerry's belly, and he dissolved into the fierceness of

Janus's kiss. He squirmed and tensed; his cry of ecstasy swallowed by Janus's mouth. His anus squeezed hard, and his cock spurted as he lost himself in a wave of sensual pleasure reminiscent of the orgasms of heat.

Janus fucked him thoroughly. Kerry came again and again, his legs shaking, and his hole gaping when Janus pulled out, cursing and determined to make it last. But nothing could last forever, and so eventually Janus came, too, his cock jolting in Kerry, filling him with cum.

In the aftermath, holding each other in Janus's now wet bed, Kerry finally spoke. "I told you he could have had me for so much less. All it took was a peach, and here I was with my legs spread for you."

"It took more than a peach," Janus whispered. "It took gaining your trust. And that started on that first day, with Kiwi in your palm—and me mesmerized by your beautiful hair in the wind. The hurt in your eyes. The way you smell. I wanted you from the start but didn't understand how to reach you."

"You've got me right now," Kerry whispered. "I'm not sure how long it can last. But for now, I'm all yours."

Janus put his hand on Kerry's stomach. "And his."

Kerry pushed Janus's hand away. "No, not yet. Just yours. Can you let me have that? Please?"

Janus nodded and pulled Kerry closer to him. He nuzzled his neck. "We'll have to talk soon about him, though, and your plans."

Kerry got the sense that Janus had some plans of his own, but he wasn't going to spoil the moment any further by asking about them. Instead, he just shrugged and whispered, "Put your fingers in me? Please? Help me?"

Janus growled softly, and soon Kerry was writhing pleasantly on three fingers pressed into his hole, and then a fourth, and finally there came a scary stretch for Janus's thumb. When Kerry woke that morning, he hadn't imagined his evening ending with Janus's hand inside him. And yet by the time the moon fully rose up above the trees, Janus had him spread wide on his bed, impaled on his fist and caught in a lovely loop of keen ecstasy followed by the even keener release of coming.

Janus, for his part, was clearly enthralled and shoved aside all discussion of the future, the baby, the *plan* in pursuit of pleasure. It was a scary place for Kerry to let himself be. Trusting in Janus was easier than it should be, riding his fist was deliciously easy, too, but forgiving himself enough to let go and enjoy it was hard.

With greedy determination, he carved himself free of the guilt and the fear, allowing himself to wallow in Janus's scent and caretaking. He was safe for now.

It was scary as wolf's own hell to allow any of this ecstasy for even a moment. Terrifying to let down his shields and let himself feel good. But for Janus's sake, for the joy of seeing Janus so entranced, he did it.

No, not for Janus—for *himself.*

# PART THREE

LATE SUMMER

# CHAPTER SEVENTEEN

KERRY HUMMED SOFTLY as his knitting needles clicked a rapid tattoo. His stomach was growing rounder as the days grew longer, and the child was often an active little dancer in his womb. The labor still loomed ahead, as did the scariest and most dangerous part of pregnancy, but he was feeling more like his old self than he had in years.

Janus was going to meet him for a picnic by the shore of the lake once he was through with his work with Dr. Crescent, and they were going to engage in their private pleasures that night in Janus's bed. Over the last few weeks, Kerry had given up fighting their draw to one another, and instead spent most of his days fantasizing about the hours he spent safe and naked by Janus's side. If he had to suffer under the tyranny of Wilbet and the Monhundys' desires, not to mention giving birth to this monstrous child, he'd take what pleasure he could from Janus. He'd hold it tight in both hands for as long as he could manage.

Sex wasn't the only thing happening between them, though. Even Kerry couldn't deny that his attachment to Janus was growing outside the bedroom, too. He enjoyed the small attentions Janus offered, like finding fresh fruit on his pillow every morning after his shower or a handful of sweet-smelling flowers Janus found on his walk to a patient's house. Or the small gifts of pretty rocks Janus collected by the lake during his afternoon swim. Or a copied-out poem written in Janus's firm hand and pinned like a blessing to one of Kerry's shirts hung on the line to dry. Nothing extravagant, nothing that required maintenance from Kerry, or even a response of his own. Just constant little reminders that Janus cared for him. It was intoxicating and addictive.

Along with the little clothes Kerry had resigned himself to making for the baby, he was also knitting a scarf for Janus. It would be warm and ready for him by the time winter descended on the mountain. Kerry wouldn't be there any longer to make sure he wore it, of course, since he'd be in the city chestfeeding the baby by then, but he hoped Janus would feel his gratitude and affection every time he wrapped it around his throat.

A knock sounded on the side of the house, and Kerry jerked, looking up from the small sweater he was knitting for the baby. While he had no doubt the Monhundys would buy the child the most fashionable of baby clothes in the city, he didn't want the little thing naked in the meantime. The babe might be a monster's child, but he'd still be a vulnerable little infant, with fresh new flesh and tender skin. So, the thread Kerry used was exceedingly soft to be gentle against him.

"Just a moment," he called out. "I'll be right with you." Coming to an end of the row, Kerry looked up to find Rodes the postman had come around the corner of the porch with an envelope in his outstretched hand.

"Sorry to disturb ya. Letter for the new doc," Rodes said, meaning Janus. "The seal is broken, Mr. Monkburn, but I swear it t'weren't me that done it. Arrived in my satchel that way."

Kerry motioned Rodes forward and took the creamy, thick envelope from his stubby fingers. "I believe you. There's a peach tart cooling on the counter in the kitchen for payment. Sorry, I don't have coin. My pater has gone down to the bank in Blumzound today, though. I promise we'll have something more for you on your next visit."

Rodes was happy enough with the peach tart, though, because

everyone loved Pater's baking. Whistling, he went on his way. Kerry started to pick up his knitting again, but as he did so, he fumbled the envelope. With the seal broken, the letter came loose, falling to the boards of the porch floor, along with a photograph. Kerry picked the items up, sliding the multi-page note back into the creamy, white envelope, intending to do the same with the picture, but instead, he sat arrested by the image.

It showed an ethereally beautiful man with blond, chin-length hair and features like an angel. He directed his glorious smile toward the infant in the picture with him. Newly born, it was all tiny and wrinkled, and the little thing was screaming with good health. Kerry swallowed hard, a strange feeling settling over him. He put a hand on his swelling stomach and flipped the photograph over.

In fluid handwriting, it read: *Bekhem Riggs Heelies, four hours old.*

Kerry glanced around, a sudden, unexpected curiosity burning in him. He'd told Janus all kinds of things about his life, and it only occurred to him now that he'd asked Janus very little about his. Perhaps Kerry had been so desperate to continue to feel safe with the man that he'd been afraid to do anything to challenge it. If he dug into Janus's past, who knew what he might find?

But now, holding the photo of this gorgeous omega, he itched to know what was in the letter, too. No doubt, it contained a detailed birth announcement for this Bekhem Riggs Heelies, but what if it held more? Some kind of key to Janus that Kerry hadn't ever thought to look for, and didn't know he needed? Or maybe that was just his excuse for violating Janus's privacy and sliding the note back out of the envelope again. He ignored the pangs of guilt as he unfolded it and began to read.

*Dear Janus,*

*I'm pleased to tell you that all your prayers for another safe delivery weren't in vain. Bekhem was born a week and a half ago, and I am doing very well. Oh, Janus, he is such a beautiful boy! I find I'm quite overwhelmed with love for him! Each time I'm pregnant, I think there's no way I can love a new child as much as the ones who came before him, and each time I do. He's a little angel. Though he looks nothing like Xan, nor does he look like me. Thank wolf-god he doesn't look like Urho! The less said about that, the better, obviously. But it isn't as though it wasn't a possibility...*

*Urho says he looks a bit like Xan's pater, but in actuality, I think he looks only like himself.*

*In your last letter, I found much of interest in between all your lines of fretful worry over my health. And all because I hadn't responded quickly enough for your liking to the three missives you'd sent over the course of the week before. Three letters in a week, Janus. Really? It's a bit much, don't you think? Have you heard of this small thing called patience?*

*Regardless, again, I apologize. I'm afraid I was rather busy, oh, giving birth and then being forced into a ridiculously long recovery period by my adoring alpha and overprotective doctor. I felt fine straight away after Bekhem made his appearance, but oh, no, they wouldn't hear of me doing anything they deemed strenuous. Which apparently included reading mail. So, yes, I'm sorry for the delay in my response and for causing you anxiety. My alpha and doctor can be quite annoying, to say the least, but they are both so absurdly protective around births. Especially since I struggled so much to regain my strength after Levi came along. His was a brutal birth, but he was such a sweet, fat baby. Luckily Bekhem was a skinny little breeze to push out, and healthy as can be.*

*Nevertheless, what I meant to say, my dear friend, is that in between your frantic blathering concerns about my health, I sensed a change of some kind has occurred in your relationship with K. Your tone when writing of him has adopted a rather, shall we say, affectionate and protective air. Do be careful. The Monhundys aren't a clan to be trifled with. They're powerful and not above putting their own interests above those of K.*

*Though admittedly they are much less powerful in society than before their son destroyed their family name, but that doesn't change the law regarding their control over their son's omega. Besides, what is more dangerous than a wounded lion? Not that I've ever seen a lion myself, much less a wounded one, but you take my meaning all the same.*

*Otherwise, my only advice to you regarding K remains the same: gentle, gentle, gentle, dearest Janus. He is also a wounded man. Use your nursing skills to their best effect.*

*Now, on to your other concerns: Urho and Xan insist that I continue to "recover myself" (whatever that means for I feel quite well) before I pursue arrangements for the charity auction you asked me to put on for the poor boy with the crushed foot. But have no worry. I will indeed put forth effort toward help-ing your mountain people in their struggles toward a more secure and healthy life. Your mountain people...do you see what I've done there, darling? I've already accepted that we've lost you to the hills for good.*

*The verve and life in your letters might not signify happi-ness, per se, but they do signify commitment and passion. And that, dear friend, I'm grateful to see finally directed somewhere useful. (And if we're forward with one another, which we always are, I'm delighted to see your passion **not** directed at me for a change.)*

*Please write soon. I'm perishing for entertainment. The al-*

*phas in this household won't even let me work in my studio for another week. I have a few pieces to finish up and now a charity auction to organize. But after that, I'm considering some travel. I'm tired of the sea air—all salty, bracing, and fresh. And I'm tired of the city air, too, for that matter. Too much exhaust from cars these days. What do you think, Janus? Do you recommend a sojourn in your beautiful mountains for a change of pace? Is there room to spare at your boarding house?*

*Ah, my handsome alpha is summoning me. It's time for Bekhem's feeding to begin, so I must wrap this letter up quickly.*

*Xan and Urho send their best, the children send their babbling regards, and I, as always, send my love.*

*Your friend,*
*Caleb*


Kerry stared at the signature. His heart squeezed in his chest, and he clenched his jaw tight. Flicking his eyes back to the photograph included in the letter, he gazed at the beautiful man and child again. There was no comparison. At his youngest and most beautiful, Kerry had never shone half as bright as this omega. He slipped the picture and the note back into the envelope and shoved it into his sewing kit to give to Janus when he came back from his day with Dr. Crescent. But as soon as he sat back with his knitting needles again, the temptation to grab the note up and read it again rose up in him even though he'd already burned most of the words into his mind.

Janus and this Caleb shared no ordinary friendship. The letter was written with such candor and teasing, bordering on flirtation, that Kerry couldn't help but wonder at the history between the men. Had they been lovers? Were they lovers now? Was this the scandal that had run Janus out of the city and society? Taking another alpha's omega as a lover was beyond the pale, and yet everyone knew it happened. But taking his cousin's omega as a lover? That would be something society and family wouldn't easily forgive.

Kerry tossed his knitting aside and rubbed a hand over his face. Wolf-god, perhaps that was why Janus had been so easy about taking Kerry on as his lover, despite his contract with Wilbet. Janus must be accustomed to screwing men with commitments elsewhere. Possibly he liked that Kerry could never be his, maybe it was...what did they call it? A kink of some sort.

Kerry felt sick. A ball of rage burned in his gut. He felt as though he might vomit. So, this was how jealousy felt. He'd never truly known. When he'd been with Wilbet, he'd only been grateful when another man attracted Wilbet's attentions. Even though it was humiliating to know Wilbet was cheating on him, it meant it was all that much less likely for Wilbet to come to Kerry's bed to take pleasure in Kerry's pain. He'd never been jealous of those men. Mostly, he pitied them.

As for his sex life before Wilbet, Kerry had never been in love. He'd never even had a close friend to confide in. In fact, there was no one in Kerry's life who he could ever speak with so candidly and with such teasing affection. Not even Pater, and definitely not Janus.

While Kerry trusted Janus as much as he could trust any alpha, at night, sated and curled around Janus's muscled body as he slept, some part of Kerry was still waiting for Janus to betray him. He glanced down at the letter again. Maybe he didn't have to wait. Maybe Janus had been betraying *someone* all along. Caleb, Kerry, other men...who could say?

Kerry strode up and down the length of the side porch and then looped around the house. His hands shook, and his stomach twisted gruesomely. He shoved his hands in his pockets and took them out again. The baby flipped around and around inside him, using his little feet to shove off vital, tender organs. It hurt.

"Wolf-god damn him," Kerry whispered, stomping down from the porch and starting up the path leading up-mountain to Dr. Crescent's house. He didn't know if Janus was working there today or if they would be out on rounds, but if he couldn't confront Janus to his face, he could ask Fan for his advice. Fan would take many an omega's secrets to the grave, and while he wasn't someone Kerry called 'friend' exactly, he already held one of Kerry's secrets close. Perhaps he could handle one more.

When Kerry burst out into the clearing near the former stable where Dr. Crescent met with patients, he was stunned to see a fairly large line of patients waiting for help. A baby wailed from inside the stables and as Kerry approached, he saw Janus holding it against his chest, comforting the small thing, while Dr. Crescent worked on an unconscious, pale omega that Kerry immediately recognized as the sickly young Charlie Myles, while his alpha, Dax Gregg, stood by wringing his hands and moaning.

"Kerry!" Fan's voice called from near the house. He was standing by the vegetable garden wearing a wide-brimmed hat and gloves, but he didn't seem to be doing any work. He motioned Kerry over, and as soon as he approached, Fan wrapped his arms around Kerry and hugged him tight.

Shocked for a moment, he didn't know what to do. But when a harsh cry rose up from Dax, Kerry understood, and he flung his arms around Fan, too, both clinging to each other in mutual omega support. The baby in Kerry's womb didn't comprehend the somberness of the moment, and kicked around, until Fan rested his hand over Kerry's bulge and, as if sensing it from the inside, the babe calmed.

"He's dead?" Kerry whispered.

"Near to it," Fan whispered back. "Dax took him down to the lake twice a day for healing instead of bringing him here."

"Is he breathing?"

"I don't know," Fan said as Dax fell to the ground by the table where Charlie lay motionless, cradling his head in his hands and sobbing. Dr. Crescent continued to work on Charlie, until he yelled, "Janus, pass that babe off. I need your help, lad. We got nothin' to lose." He held up a thick tube attached to a machine of some sort with bellows.

Fan released Kerry and darted toward the stable, shedding his hat and gloves along the way. Taking the baby from Janus quickly, he headed back toward Kerry with a clipped step and wide eyes. Janus didn't look Kerry's way, joining Dr. Crescent over Charlie's form and helping to hold his neck back and mouth open, while Dr. Crescent greased the tube.

"Inside," Fan said, gripping Kerry by the arm. "Let's take this wee one inside. There's nothing we can do here. Dax is enough in the way as it is."

Kerry straggled after Fan, casting worried glances back over his shoulder. Dax sobbed and rocked, and Dr. Crescent fed the tube into Charlie's throat. Shuddering, Kerry stepped into the cool house and took the baby from Fan when he passed him over.

"Ellis is hungry," Fan said, nodding to the baby who was whimpering and crying, chewing on his fist. "It seems Charlie's milk went dry a few days ago." He shook his head. "Why they didn't come here when Charlie caught Ellis's cough, I don't know. Ashamed they can't pay, maybe, but Charlie deserved better than this."

Kerry put his nose to the top of Ellis's head, breathing in that delicious baby scent, always a distilled, perfect sweetness that faded as the babe grew and developed his own, unique odor. The child inside kicked once, twice, and then grew quiet again. Kerry wondered if his own son would smell this good. He probably would. And how strange would that be? To loathe something that smelled like heaven?

"Now here," Fan said, shoving a bottle with a fake nipple into his hand, and thrusting Kerry toward a comfortable chair by the fire. "Feed him."

Fan went to stand by the window, watching what was happening outside for a long moment. "They're using the bellows to push air into his lungs. Dax is standing up. Oh! Oh, no. Janus is pounding on Charlie's poor chest." Fan's voice caught. "Why is life so hard?"

Kerry said nothing, watching the baby's fat lips suck greedily at the fake nipple. After a few strong pulls, though, he pulled off and screamed, rubbing his eyes with small fists.

"Sit him up a little," Fan suggested, coming to Kerry's side. "He misses his pater's scent."

The sentence hung in the air between them, and they met each other's eyes. Kerry's lips trembled, and a horrible sinking sensation went through his gut.

"Now, none of that," Fan said. "This one needs our strength." He slipped his fingers over the baby's glossy, straight hair, barely growing in over his baldness. "Eat, Ellis," he whispered. "Then you can sleep until the worst has passed."

"What will happen to him?" Kerry asked as Ellis accepted the bottle again, his small weight resting against Kerry's belly as he ate.

"It depends on what happens out there."

"They're *Érosgápe*."

Fan nodded, his face pale and grim. "Just feed the baby. That's all we can do right now."

Sitting in the chair next to the one he'd put Kerry in, they were silent for what seemed like ages. The baby fell asleep, and the one in Kerry's belly seemed to do the same. The room was warm, though the summer day outside was still mountain cool.

Finally, the door burst open and Janus ran in, his hair a mess and his eyes wild. He stopped in shock when he saw Kerry but then went on, rushing to the kitchen area and running water in the sink. "We need fresh water. Fresh...um, cold water, yes." He grabbed a glass from the cupboard and, ignoring them both, rushed back out with it, yelling, "Bring more!"

Fan leapt up and grabbed a bucket from the corner and poured water into it from the sink. Kerry felt helpless and trapped with the baby asleep on him, but he didn't want to wake him and add more screaming to the chaos outside because it *was* chaos! He could hear it!

Men's voices raised in shouts, Dr. Crescent's orders, and the wails of Dax, and then Fan burst back into the room. "He's breathing! He was dead, but now he's breathing."

"What?"

"Janus and Crow worked together and, somehow, they may have saved him."

The door opened again, and this time Janus, Dr. Crescent, Dax, and three of the patients who had been waiting their turn for the duration of the dramatic revival appeared, carefully carrying little Charlie through the door and into the living room. Dax was still crying and sending up loud prayers to wolf-god.

"Sorry, dumplin'," Dr. Crescent barked out, leaving the other men to handle Charlie while he went to open the door of Fan's back room. "But we have to use your room for 'im. He'll need to stay the night, probably the week."

"I won't leave him," Dax said, muscling his way through.

"Wouldn't expect you to," Fan said, helping guide the men into the room, past where Kerry remained trapped in the chair by the sleeping weight of the baby, showing them where to lay Charlie on the bed.

Then the door slammed, leaving the other patients, Janus, and Kerry on the outside of it, and Fan, Dr. Crescent, Dax, and Charlie on the inside. Janus ran a hand in his hair and then turned, his attention going immediately to Kerry, not to the men who'd been waiting for hours for a doctor to see them.

"What are you doing here?" he asked, falling to his knees at Kerry's feet, his hand coming up to press his palm to Kerry's forehead. "Are you well? Is it the baby? What's wrong?"

"I'm fine," Kerry said, the burning questions he'd had about the letter from Caleb dying in the face of the urgent worry shining from Janus's eyes. "He's going to live?"

"Who? Charlie?" Janus's hands were continuing their check of him, taking his pulse and finding it sound, sliding around to press against his stomach until he felt the baby inside give a protesting kick. "Yes, maybe. Perhaps. We don't know. But he's breathing."

"Like wolf-god's own kin, he rose from the dead!" a strong omega Kerry recognized as Bryant Mox said, eyes wide and fervent, and staring at Janus like he was the living end. "And you did that. You pounded on his chest until his heart started up. Wolf-god bless you."

Janus had moved on from checking Kerry over to looking over the slumbering babe in Kerry's arms. He felt the baby's pulse, lifted its arms and tugged gently on its little legs. "He needs to eat more. Too small."

Kerry held up the half-finished bottle. "He fell asleep before he finished."

Janus frowned. "I'd say wake him again, but he must be exhausted." Turning to the other men, he said, "Who here has a real emergency? I'll meet you at the stables. The rest of you"—he shooed them off—"can wait. We've got a crisis here and now isn't the time to ask me for tinctures to make your perfectly good sight better so that you're able to shoot more squirrels for stew."

The men laughed, and only one requested Janus examine him in the stables. The others agreed to go, eagerly telling the story of how Dr. Heelies and Dr. Crescent had worked a miracle with the tube, the bellows, and the banging on Charlie's chest. Kerry sat by the fire with the baby alone, listening to the voices behind the closed door to the room where Fan had attended him. He couldn't make out words, but it all sounded very grave and serious. From time to time, Dax still sobbed.

Finally, Fan came out with a sober expression and knelt by Kerry. "I have a very big favor to ask of you."

"Anything."

Fan smiled and touched Kerry's cheek. "Oh, you say that now, but you'll balk once you know what it is."

"What are you asking of him?" Janus's voice cut in. He'd entered nearly silently after handling his patient in the stable. "He's in no condition to do anything strenuous."

Fan rolled his eyes. "Of course not. Charlie will need to stay here for some days, even if he lives. Dax, as *Érosgápe*, won't leave his side, and frankly, is in no frame of mind to care for Ellis here. I will be busy helping Crow, and so…"

Kerry's eyes went wide, knowing what Fan wanted of him. "But I don't know what to do."

Fan raised a brow and glanced pointedly at Kerry's stomach. "It'll be good practice then."

"It's fine," Janus said quietly. "I can help. And your pater. We'll take little Ellis home with us. We'll just need a few bottles with those fake nipples. Do you have another?"

"Of course. I'm a doctor's omega. I have to keep all sorts of things for the unexpected arrival of unexpected patients." Fan rose and gathered together a bundle. "Diapers, bottles, and nipples. A set of clothes that will likely fit him, but it's all right for him to be naked."

"You know a lot about taking care of babies," Kerry murmured, his nose dropping to scent the little one in his arms again. "How?"

"Again. Doctor's omega. I've never been blessed with one my-self, but I've had to care for many temporarily." Fan looked exhausted, and the sun hadn't even started to set. "Now, if you don't mind, I need to get back in that room to hold Crow together so that he can hold Dax together."

"Yes, of course," Janus said. "I've already cleared up things at the stable." He took the sleeping Ellis from Kerry's arms, miracu-lously not waking him, and then helped Kerry up from the chair. "Let's go home, sweetheart. We'll have a strange night ahead."

Kerry's head buzzed strangely. Sweetheart? *Sweetheart.* What did he mean by that? Was it just a slip of the tongue?

"Ready?" Janus asked, taking Kerry by the elbow and directing him toward the door.

"I'll hold the baby," Kerry said, taking hold of Ellis and cud-dling him close. The scent of the infant calming his now pounding heart. "You keep me steady on the walk down."

"I'd never let you fall," Janus said, closing the door to the cabin behind them and leading Kerry toward the path down the moun-tain. "You can depend on me."

# CHAPTER EIGHTEEN

"EAT," JANUS WHISPERED, rubbing the bottle's fake nipple over the baby's mouth with a heavy sigh. He had managed to get the little one to take over half of the last bottle, but the little guy's system couldn't handle much more. He'd need to eat smaller amounts more regularly.

"Here," Kerry said, reaching for the baby. "Let me try."

Janus gave him over to Kerry. "He's a stubborn little thing."

"Misses his pater's scent," Kerry murmured like he was repeating something he'd heard someone else say. His own pater, maybe? Though Zeke, upon returning from his trip to Blumzound and seeing the baby, had set about cooking up a storm, saying that Fan shouldn't have to handle feeding two alphas and a sick man all on his own. Once he'd finished baking and wrapping up several days' worth of meals, he'd gone up to bed, leaving Kerry and Janus to deal with little Ellis.

Settling into the corner of the comfortable sofa in the living room, Kerry rested the baby on the hump of his stomach, and holding him close to his chest, pressed the fake nipple into Ellis's mouth. Ellis closed his eyes and sucked, a little discontentedly, but better than he had before.

"I'm not his pater, but he probably scents the milk coming in," Kerry murmured.

Janus hummed his agreement and blinked hard as a sudden memory of Kerry riding his cock the night before came to mind. Milk had slipped from his nipples to sweeten the air with more than just the usual musk of slick and cum. It'd been a beautiful sight to see and an utter thrill to taste. Kerry hadn't protested, holding Janus's head to his chest and letting him suck for all he was worth. The orgasm Kerry had experienced from stimulation had seemed intensely pleasurable, given the noises Kerry had made. Truly, they should try harder to be quiet because they must surely be disturbing Zeke's sleep at night.

But now wasn't the time for such thoughts. They had a babe to care for and becoming distracted by the memory of how sweet Kerry's milk tasted would not be helpful to anyone.

Janus took the spot on the sofa next to Kerry and then patted his lap.

"What?"

"Put your feet here."

Kerry looked at him a bit suspiciously but then shifted so that his back was on the arm of the couch. He clutched the still eating Ellis against his chest to keep him from falling. Janus took Kerry's socked feet in hand and began to rub. The wool of his socks itched against Janus's palms, and so, without asking, he stripped them off, baring Kerry's fine arches and well-made toes to his examination.

"Wolf-god, what are you doing?" Kerry asked, barely restraining a giggle when Janus lifted his right foot while simultaneously bending low to sniff it.

Janus shrugged and scented the left foot, too, for good measure. Satisfied that Kerry smelled as delicious there as he did everywhere else, Janus began a tentative massage of Kerry's feet.

"Harder," Kerry said, trying not to laugh and disturb the baby. "I'm ticklish. You have to do it harder, or I'll kick you in the face."

Janus chuckled. "Is that a threat?"

"It's a warning."

Janus dug his fingers in harder, and Kerry relaxed, no longer twitching with suppressed laughter. Ellis continued to feed, his long lashes sweeping down over his too thin cheeks. The scent of the child rose up into the room, distracting from Kerry's usual scent. Still, the baby-smell was every human's favorite. It was like the best dessert and sweetest wine all rolled into one. Janus remembered liking the way Xan's insufferable friends' child had smelled, too. The Sabel boy. What had they named him? Virona, or Viro for short, he thought.

Remembering his time in Virona brought Janus's thoughts around to how long it had been since he'd heard from Caleb. He wondered what was keeping him from replying and hoped it wasn't a problem with the pregnancy or his health. He had to believe that Caleb was safe. At least Janus knew he could count on Xan and Urho to watch over Caleb and provide him with all the best, most advanced care. Not every omega was so lucky.

"Charlie should have come to us sooner," Janus said, massaging Kerry's arches firmly.

"I know."

"Why didn't he?" Janus asked, his throat tight. "This baby needs him. Dax adores him. Why would they go to the lake instead? That old omega's tale…"

"The lake is healing," Kerry insisted. "But some things it can't repair. Some illnesses need medicine. I've heard rumors about the two of them. Dax is possessive. He doesn't like anyone touching Charlie. I'm not surprised it took him so long to bring him to you."

Janus snorted, rolling his eyes. "Alphas."

Kerry smiled tenderly. He looked like he wanted to reach out and ruffle Janus's hair but didn't want to disturb Ellis. "*Érosgápe* is more like it. The bond makes them too possessive sometimes."

"No, it's always the alphas," Janus protested. "You don't see omegas refusing to let doctors touch their alphas."

"An alpha with another alpha isn't a risk. There's no attraction."

"You'd be surprised," Janus muttered. "Still, it doesn't matter.

It's down to alpha pride. We're possessive assholes."

"I can't dispute that," Kerry said with a wry smile. "And it makes sense that you'd see that side of alphas more often as a doctor treating their omegas."

"I feel it, too," Janus said irritably. "As an alpha myself."

Kerry tilted his head. "What do you mean?"

"I wouldn't want Dr. Crescent touching you," Janus said quietly, feeling heat rise in his cheeks. He wasn't sure he should be admitting to that, but it was something he'd known was true as soon as Kerry called Dax possessive. He hated the idea of Dr. Crescent touching Kerry in any way. And they weren't even contracted or bonded. "Not that I wouldn't take you to him if I couldn't treat you myself. I'd override my instincts. For you." But if they were *Érosgápe*, he knew it would be even harder to push back his need to be his omega's everything, even possibly to his detriment and danger.

"Dax thought he could treat Charlie himself," Kerry said. "With the lake and his medicine cabinet at home, I'm sure."

"I know. That's what I mean," Janus huffed. "Alphas. We're assholes."

"I don't know. You've been pretty sweet to me." Then Kerry stiffened strangely, his feet tensing under Janus's hands.

"What? Ticklish again?"

Kerry shook his head and removed his feet from Janus's lap before carefully rising with Ellis in his arms. His long hair was down, and it cascaded over his shoulders, clinging to the soft, brown paternity-style shirt he wore.

"What's wrong?" Janus asked.

Kerry bit into his lip and frowned. "I forgot."

"What?"

"That I was angry with you earlier."

Janus's eyes flicked wide open. "Angry with me? What did I

do?"

The baby squirmed in Kerry's arms, and it was time to burp him. Kerry put the nearly finished bottle down and hiked the infant up to his shoulder and began to jostle him while patting his back. Janus had seen plenty of omegas do this over the years, but he wasn't sure Kerry was doing it properly until Ellis let out a belch louder than Janus's own.

Janus's serious expression wobbled, and he chuckled a bit, before sobering again. "Loud little bugger."

"I don't think I had a right to be angry," Kerry said, pacing with the child in front of the sofa where Janus continued to sit. The babe, exhausted and now freshly burped, lulled on his shoulder, long-lashed eyes drooping into slumber. Kerry continued to pace back and forth, oblivious to the fact the baby had fallen asleep on his shoulder. "I was going to confront you, demand answers."

"Then do it."

"I don't know if I have the right," Kerry murmured, his expression distressed.

"I don't have anything to hide from you, Kerry. If I've done something to upset you, I'd like the chance to apologize. I've been told I need all the practice I can get at it."

"Who's Caleb?" Kerry burst out, coming to a dead stop in front of Janus.

Janus stared at him for a moment. "Caleb Riggs is my cousin's omega," he said slowly.

"What else is he to you? Why did he write you a long, flirtatious letter hinting at a past between you and signing it with his love? Is he the reason you left the city? Are you in love with him?"

"No." Janus was as surprised as Kerry looked at the abrupt certainty of his answer. "I was once in love with him, but now I am definitely not."

"Why?"

Janus stood and took Ellis from Kerry. He carefully adjusted the babe's head, so that it rested against his bicep and then he carried him to the makeshift crib they'd made for the little guy out of a packing crate, pillows, and the softest throw blanket in the house. When he had the baby settled inside, tucked in and sleeping with flushed cheeks and a wet, open mouth, he turned back to Kerry, motioning him toward the sofa again.

"Why did I love Caleb once or why don't I love him now?" Janus asked, tugging Kerry by the arm to sit beside him. "What do you really want to know?"

Kerry squirmed, a red flush starting at the base of his throat and going up to brighten his tanned face and neck. "I don't have a right to ask these questions. I'm contracted to another alpha. You're…" He motioned at Janus with a confused expression. "We don't mean anything to each other."

Janus frowned, not liking the sound of that at all. "I listened while you told me of your past once. Why don't you grant me the same favor now? There's a lot about me that you don't know, and Caleb's part of that."

Kerry shifted again like he might stand up and run out of the room, but then he nodded once, sharply. "All right. I'm listening." He crossed his arms over his chest tightly, and his jaw jumped with tension. But he stayed on the sofa and gazed at Janus with wary eyes.

"I met Caleb at a Philia soiree in my early twenties. He was, I admit, the most beautiful man I'd ever seen. Intelligent, funny, and unwilling to commit to any alpha. I pursued him, courted him, and felt certain I would win him. And then he confessed an aspect of himself, a hidden truth, that I hadn't been prepared to hear, much less accept. I was foolish and young, and frankly, arrogant. I thought finding another man I cared for like I'd cared for Caleb would be easy. And when it turned out that it wasn't easy at all, that

I'd broken my own heart, I set about punishing myself and anyone else I could for what I saw as the unfairness of it all. The self-absorption of youth. I couldn't even see that I'd shattered Caleb's heart in his own way, too."

"What was this 'hidden truth' that you found so abhorrent?" Kerry murmured, swallowing with an audible click. "After what you've seen of me, I have to wonder, what must an omega do to disgust you?"

"I wasn't disgusted," Janus said. "I was devastated." He shrugged. "I was young and wanted things from Caleb that he never wanted to give me."

"Children?" Kerry guessed, but then he frowned. "He's had several though, including one just recently."

"That must have been a very informative letter," Janus said, his heart jumping in his chest. "I take it his third son has been born?"

"Yes. I'm sorry. Let me get the letter. It's in my sewing kit in my room."

Janus tugged Kerry back to the sofa. "Never mind. You can give it to me later. All went well with him? And the baby is healthy?"

Kerry nodded. "I didn't mean to read it. The seal was broken, and I dropped the envelope. A photo came out. He was so hand-some, I got...curious." He dropped his eyes, his cheeks glowing even more. Had Kerry been jealous? Janus thought he must have been, though he would never admit it. The thought warmed him all over. "I violated your privacy, and I'm sorry."

"You did, and I don't mind. I should mind, I'm sure, but I don't for some reason. It feels right that you should know every-thing about me. I don't have anything to hide, Kerry." Janus took his hand, relieved that Kerry let him. "Caleb is a man I loved in my youth until I ruined things with him, and then I ruined my own life, too: affairs with contracted omegas, gambling, drinking, illegal wrestling competitions. The worst thing I did was shame my cousin out of jealousy that he'd been smarter than I, securing a contract with Caleb despite his differences."

Kerry tilted his head, clearly wanting to know more about Caleb's disclosure, but Janus had never broken his promise to keep Caleb's confidence in that matter. At least, so far as he recalled. He might have said hurtful things in a drunken state on more than one occasion. It shamed him to consider the likelihood of it.

"He hit me once," Janus said, rubbing his jaw.

Kerry gasped. "And you still like him?"

"I deserved it. He hit me for coming on to him and insulting Xan. My cousin. Caleb's alpha. He hit me for being an ass."

"No one deserves to be hit."

"Oh, sweetheart, you certainly could never deserve it, but I sure as wolf-god's own hell did." Janus sighed. "I wasn't a good man. I've resolved to be better. Caleb inspired me. After he forgave me, he told me I could be a good man if I just put some effort into it. For whatever reason, I believed him." Janus laughed helplessly. "I'd say it was going well, but I find myself having another affair with a contracted omega, so…"

Kerry squeezed his fingers.

Janus squeezed them back. "This affair, though, feels the furthest thing from wrong. Nothing like the contracted men I've been with in the past. Or what I did to Caleb."

Kerry ducked his head. "It sounds like you still have regrets."

"For my behavior and for hurting him, yes. For the years of being an arrogant fool, yes. But I don't yearn for him anymore. I want to be his friend now. Nothing else." Kerry didn't look up, and his posture indicated that he didn't believe Janus. That wouldn't do. "My heart has moved on to someone else."

"If you mean me, then you're still an arrogant fool—not reformed at all," Kerry muttered bitterly. "Caring for me is meaningless. My life is set in a different direction. The law will uphold Wilbet's right to me, so long as he lives." He tugged his hand away. "If you harbor any designs on me aside from a self-described 'affair with a contracted omega,' then you're holding on to yet another self-destructive, and frankly pathetic, dream. Just as pathetic as whatever it is you wanted from this Caleb man that he wouldn't give you." Kerry huffed. "In fact, if you can go back to caring for him, perhaps you should. Despite his contract with your cousin, you'd still have a better chance of happiness with him than with me."

"I can't do that. I don't want to do that," Janus said. "I will always love Caleb as a dear friend and an inspiration—as a reminder of what selfishness lies within me. But I also believe that self-same selfishness might do some good in this situation with you instead of only bad. I'm unwilling to say that we can't have more than a dalliance, Kerry. Unless that's truly all you want?"

"I'm not allowed to want things, Janus."

"You're allowed to want me," he whispered. "You don't have to promise anything. There may be no future in it, as you insist, but there's no man on earth who can force you *not* to want me. Laws may dictate certain things about your life, but they can't control your heart." He took Kerry's hand in his own and pressed it to his chest so Kerry could feel the steadiness of his heartbeat. "You're allowed to want me. And I'm allowed to want you back."

"Acting on it, though, is…"

"*Not* a hangable offense," Janus reminded him. "And we already know you're willing to commit an actual hangable offense for a chance at a better life. Isn't what's happening between us better than what went before?"

"And when I give birth to another alpha's child," Kerry spat out, motioning at his stomach. "And when I'm forced to spend my next heat with him, per the law and my in-laws' demands? And when I give birth to yet another of his children, and another, and *another* for the rest of my childbearing days, you'll feel how? Satisfied? In love with our life together?" Kerry snorted. "I think not."

"Are we talking about a future now? That's an improvement," Janus said, slipping his fingers up Kerry's neck to touch his cheek again. Kerry pulled away. "A few minutes ago, according to you, we were nothing to each other. Now we're talking about the coming years and how I will handle these violations of your—"

"Stop. I shouldn't have put it that way. You're twisting things around. I'm not saying I want a future with you. I'm saying that we can't have any future. It's different."

"We both know what you said," Janus replied. "But the future is hazy. We have only begun to fight this together. You aren't alone against the Monhundys anymore. I refuse to believe that your future is as hopeless as you think. Omega freedom—"

Kerry cut him off. "Janus, omega freedom groups can't help me." He stood up and resumed pacing in front of the sofa again. "You and Pater! You're both so frustrating! Insisting there's hope when there isn't any at all. I can't bear it. I won't. You *can't* make me hope. I refuse to hope." Kerry stopped in front of him, eyes wide and hands out in a pleading gesture. "Can't we just fuck each other until the baby comes and be satisfied with that?"

"No, I don't think we can," Janus said quietly.

Kerry froze. "Why not?"

"Because you wanted to know who Caleb was and whether I was in love with him. We're already beyond fucking and being satisfied with that, sweetheart, and we're only a few weeks in."

"Then we should stop," Kerry gritted out. "It's too complicated already."

Janus rose to touch Kerry's cheek, then he slipped his hand into Kerry's hair and took a handful into a strong grasp. He pulled Kerry toward him, pressing their foreheads together. Kerry's eyes stayed closed, but his panting breath rushed over Janus's lips, and the scent of slick rose between them. Janus didn't move, just held Kerry in place and breathed in the odor of him, the child within, the slick and sweetness of his breath.

Finally, Kerry broke, ducking in to press his lips to Janus's, kissing him desperately. Janus herded Kerry toward the hallway and the stairs up to their rooms. Kerry paused and looked over his shoulder toward the makeshift crib. "Will Ellis be all right?" he whispered, his breath shaky and his hands clenching in Janus's collar.

"He'll be fine," Janus said gruffly. "If he wakes, he'll cry, and we'll hear him."

Kerry kissed Janus again, his tongue delving into his mouth and his teeth nipping Janus's lips. His hips canted forward, his hard cock digging into Janus's leg, and the scent of his slick rising stronger and stronger, making the need to strip him out of his clothes all that much greater before his pants became soaked.

Berries and musk, sweet milk, slick, and saliva. Janus reveled in it, lost to whatever discussion they'd been having before, aching to get Kerry on his bed, so that he could pleasure him for as long as it took to make the man understand that they weren't nothing to each other. They never had been and couldn't be.

They were alpha and omega. The beginning and the end.

The everything.

# CHAPTER NINETEEN

I N THE DAYS following Charlie's near death, Kerry completely forgot to show Janus the letter from Caleb, and Janus forgot to ask for it. They were both far too busy caring for Ellis, keeping up with their usual work with patients or around the boarding house, fucking like desperate creatures at night, and ignoring Pater's knowing looks at meals.

In the chaos of it all and the ringing, buzzing high of being so well and thoroughly pleasured, Kerry forgot about other things, too. As became immediately evident on the morning after Dax had finally come to retrieve Ellis.

By wolf-god's grace, Charlie was sitting up and well enough to demand to see his child. Dax didn't have much, but in his gratitude for their help with Ellis, and for Janus's role in reviving Charlie, he had dragged a fairly new-looking rocking chair up to the porch and offered it with his thanks.

"Is that Charlie's rockin' chair, d'ya think?" Pater asked as Dax walked away with the babe happily cradled against his chest, held there by an ingenious wrap that Kerry thought he might want to copy to take the load off his back when…well, when the inevitable happened.

"I think it is," Kerry said quietly.

"The one he made 'im as an *Érosgápe* gift?" Pater asked.

Kerry nodded, setting the chair rocking with his right hand and his left settling over his stomach.

"Oh, dear. I think we should send it back."

"Alphas have their pride, Pater," Kerry said. "It's best we keep it. He'll no doubt make him another."

No sooner had Dax and Ellis disappeared into the thicket, taking the path up toward Dr. Crescent's house and Charlie's convalescent bed there, than a cleaner-than-average message delivery boy started up the drive. His jaunty cap kept the sun off his face, but the way he held the crisp, white note out like it was a snake told Kerry all he needed to know about who wrote it.

With shaking fingers, Kerry took the note and walked around the corner of the house, dropping into his favorite rocking chair to read the summons, leaving his pater to scrounge up some coin for the delivery.

*Due to a failure to keep up your agreement to inform us weekly of the progress with your state, we have found it necessary to return to Blumzound. Meet us at the hotel this afternoon. You'll be joining us for dinner. Prepare yourself to stay for the night.*

*Your loving parents,*
*Monte & Lukas Monhundy*

Loving parents. Kerry scoffed as he folded the paper and pushed it into his pants pocket. Pater followed him as he went back into the house, anxiety rolling off him in waves.

"What do they want?"

"To meet them in Blumzound this afternoon." Kerry started up the stairs, Pater at his heels.

"Where are you going?"

"To pack a bag."

Pater gasped. "No. That's not going to happen. I'll get Janus."

Kerry stopped halfway up the stairs, turning to face his pater. "Why? What are you saying?"

"They can't take you with them to the city. They agreed you could stay here." Pater's unspoken "with me" was plain as day on his face.

"It's just for an overnight, Pater. They'll let me come back up. They're worried because I forgot to send them an update. It's my own fault."

Pater crossed his arms over his chest. "Janus should go with you."

"Janus definitely cannot go with me," Kerry said as if Pater had gone insane.

"Why? He'll keep you safe at least. I'll feel better with him at your side."

Kerry shook his head. "It's a long story, but if you think letting the alpha who is servicing me—" he felt the heat creeping up his neck at admitting that "—anywhere near Wilbet's parents, you're a lunatic. They'll take me away for sure. And there are other reasons besides."

"What reasons?"

"Pater, just leave me in peace to pack the bag. I'll take the car and be back by tomorrow morning."

Kerry left his pater scowling on the stairs and, once in his room, took a moment to compose himself. He removed Kiwi from the cage, kissing his beak and muttering softly to him. "I've neglected you lately, little one, what with that big, human baby in the house demanding all our attention." He frowned, thinking that it wouldn't be much longer now before the one in his womb would be demanding attention that had formerly gone to Kiwi.

Kerry had grown so large now. There was a definite waddle to his walk, and he found it confusing that Janus seemed to enjoy his body even though he was currently stuffed full with another alpha's son. Janus never shied away from his swollen stomach or leaking nipples during their love—

Kerry's mind lurched. He'd come so close to naming their activities something he shouldn't. Stroking a soothing hand over Kiwi's feathers, he deposited him back in the cage, cringing at the chirrup of protest. "I'll fly you tomorrow, sweet boy."

Then he gathered his things, shoving them into a worn leather bag that he'd taken with him when he'd first left Hud's Basin for the city. He had nicer bags that had been gifted to him over the years—first by Wilbet and then by his parents—but Kerry preferred this one. It was sturdy and a reminder of home. It had once belonged to his biological pater, a gift from his father, and it had survived longer than anything else they'd shared, aside from Kerry.

As he came down the stairs, his heart sank. There were voices in the kitchen, and though they were hushed and the kitchen door closed, Kerry recognized one of them as Janus's tenor.

He tiptoed down the hallway toward the front door.

"Where do you think you're going?"

Kerry froze and turned slowly. He'd never heard that kind of firmness in Janus's voice—almost anger, but maybe fear, too. "I've been summoned. I have to go."

"I'll go with you," Janus said.

Kerry rolled his eyes and dropped his bag. Dust motes rose, and he made a note that he needed to sweep the entryway again already. "No, you won't."

"Your pater thinks it best if I do."

"Then he's a fool," Kerry called out, aiming his voice over Janus's shoulder into the kitchen where he knew his pater was hiding and listening. "A fool without all the information." Kerry crossed his arms over his chest.

"I won't let them take you to the city."

Kerry flung his arms wide. "They aren't going to take me to the city. They just want to exert their control a little and make me do a dance for them. Show them my stomach, let them listen to his heartbeat, have the doctor check my womb. The usual."

Janus bristled. "A doctor checked your womb…"

"Don't."

"I've checked it nightly."

"With your cock?" Kerry asked and then laughed. "Oh, for fuck's sake, Janus, you can't do this to me right now. I have to go. They're waiting. And you can't come."

"Give me one wolf-god blessed reason why I can't!"

"Because they think you're a beta! With experience in delivering babies from omegas with my deformity! Because I told them lies about you to get them to agree to let me stay in Hud's Basin! Because one scent of you will prove me a liar and then they *will* make me go back with them."

Janus blinked at him in confusion. "Why would you—"

"They needed to think I would be in just as good hands, if not better, here in Hud's Basin than back in the city. And hell, maybe they wanted to believe it because lord knows I'm a thorny reminder of difficult times for them. They both want me and don't want me." Kerry rubbed his stomach again. "They *want* the child. A fresh start. They could take me or leave me aside from the fact that I'm the only baby-maker they're going to get their claws into, and they want more from me than this one alone."

Janus stared at him, wide-eyed. "So, you lied to them about me being an alpha?"

"Do you think they'd want me serviced by an alpha? That they'd share my pater's desire for me to find pleasure during my pregnancy and risk me falling in love and causing them more scandal and problems? They probably saw my isolation in Hud's Basin as a way to keep me away from eligible alphas with an itch to fuck an easy, slutty, pregnant hole."

Janus flinched. "Don't talk about yourself like that."

"Why not?"

"Because I said so."

"And who are you to tell me what to do?"

"Your alpha!"

"You sure as wolf-god's own hell are not! Would that you were!" Kerry turned on his heel, grabbing up his bag. "I have to go. I don't have time for this right now."

Janus followed him down the hallway. "I'm coming with you. I won't introduce myself. I won't be in your presence in front of them. But I'm not letting you face them alone."

Kerry ignored him, jerked open the front door, and headed toward the outbuilding where they kept the car. Janus remained on his heels. Kerry said nothing.

As much as he hated to admit it, he wanted Janus with him. He wanted to feel safe, even if he knew it was a lie.

He wanted Janus.

JANUS FOUND THE trip down-mountain by car much faster than his initial wagon ride up. The descent was a confusing one. In his month and a half at Hud's Basin, he'd lost his bearings and nearly forgotten that a world outside truly existed. His mental map had fractured into globs: Hud's Basin, the city, and Virona. They all existed, yes, but as separate things that didn't connect except through the mail.

But no, there was a serviceable town at the bottom of the mountain. Janus hadn't even spent one night there when he first arrived before taking a wagon up. It was surprisingly bustling, and he noted that there seemed to be a whole set of new storefronts that had gone up since he'd last been through the town.

"I'll drop you off here," Kerry said, clutching the wheel of the car, his belly almost touching it, too. "You can't be seen with me.

The hotel is at the end of the block. Please, don't do anything unless they try to take me."

Janus nodded, a lump rising in his throat and a strange resistance in his muscles. He didn't want to leave Kerry in the car, unprotected and pregnant on the streets of this strange town.

But he'd agreed to a plan of action and understood the need for it after their extensive conversation in the car on the ride down. Kerry had his reasons for lying to the Monhundys and had even played the Heelies name as a card in the game. Hopefully, he'd gotten away with it so far. Being caught out would spell doom to his desire to stay at Hud's Basin for the birth.

On the way down, Janus had finally broached a topic of conversation that had plagued him for some time: Kerry's plan for when the baby was finally born. Janus had long had a bad feeling about it and a strange fear that Kerry would leave Hud's Basin with the child. But Kerry had shut down his inquiries roundly, with Kerry saying that it wasn't any of his business and that he wasn't ready to talk about it anyway, which sounded grim.

But given how wildly dark Kerry's eyes were, and how pale his usually golden face had grown as they approached Blumzound, Janus had let it go. Kerry was anxious about meeting with his in-laws despite his attempt at a brave face, and if it upset Kerry to talk about what the plan was for after the birth, then it could wait.

Right now, they had to get through the day and night, make sure they allowed Kerry to return home, and in the meantime, throw off any suspicious concerns of his in-laws. That was enough.

"Janus, you have to get out here," Kerry said more firmly, leaning over him to open the passenger side door. The scent of berries and musk rose out of his wind-tossed hair, a result of the open windows on the ride down, and Janus wanted to grab hold of his head, press it to his chest, and breathe in that scent deeply. But Kerry leaned back once he'd popped the door open and shooed

Janus with his hands. "Go. Please."

Janus got out and leaned in to ask through the open window, "Are you sure they won't force you to go with them immediately?"

"I'm sure. They'll see my stomach and be relieved. They'll want to have tea in the salon of the hotel, make me squirm a bit, and then they'll have me examined up in the hotel room they've reserved. After, we'll have an awkward dinner. I'll spend the night, endure breakfast with them, and we can return by noon."

Janus didn't know how Kerry could be so certain, and he doubted even that he was, given the paleness of his skin.

"Janus, let go of the car," Kerry said rather gently. "Let me go."

Janus gripped the car door a bit harder but then forced himself to release it and to step back onto the sidewalk, where he stood helplessly as Kerry drove on toward the hotel alone.

When he finally shook off the dread balling up in the pit of his stomach, he started walking down the sidewalk toward the hotel. The scent of freshly baked bread and roasted coffee rose up around him, and as he looked around, he took in the quaintness of the town. Horsepower was still the preferred mode of transport, with only a few cars gliding down the wide roads. Clearly, the town's planners had accounted for the boom in automobile manufacturing in other cities and had left plenty of room for them in the future.

The sidewalks were bustling, but not crowded like in the city. There weren't a lot of locals. Most of the men he glimpsed in shop windows or saw on the street had either moved to town to run businesses or were merely passing through on the trains.

On another day, Janus would have liked to sample the pies he saw in the window of the bakery, or visit the tailor for a new set of sturdy pants. But all he could think about was how every last person on the street was in the way of him reaching the hotel to do what he could to supervise Kerry's interaction with his in-laws.

When he finally reached the hotel, he was a little sweaty and appalled to realize that, in his hurry to follow Kerry into the car, he'd left his presentable clothing behind. How was it possible that he'd reached town without realizing that he wore a sweat-stained white button-up shirt and a pair of dingy pants. Luckily, he did have his wallet in his pocket, having taken it that morning up to Dr. Crescent's cabin to receive his "payment," which amounted to a few coins and several pounds of dried deer meat. *That* he'd taken back down-mountain to Zeke where he'd informed Janus of Kerry's situation with the Monhundys.

Janus hesitated at the hotel door, glancing down at his clothes, and then back up the road again to the secondhand clothing shop he'd passed. He didn't want to draw too much attention to himself in the hotel, not if he wanted an opportunity to slide under the Monhundys' radar.

A few coins later, nearly all that he'd earned from his work with Dr. Crescent, he wore a crisp shirt with a stain along the bottom hem that could easily be tucked in. He'd bought a decent-looking suit jacket and pair of matching pants that didn't have a single thing wrong with them as far as Janus could tell, except that someone else owned them previously. He hadn't ever shopped in a store like that before, usually having his clothes tailor-made, but it struck him as economical and smart to do so going forward. It wasn't as if he was going out into society any time soon.

However, he *was* entering the nicest hotel the area had to offer, and he at least looked clean and neat. The clerk allowed him to use the toilet in the secondhand shop where he'd washed his face and hands and smoothed down his rambunctious hair. It startled him to realize how long it'd grown. He determined that perhaps while in Blumzound, he might be able to see a barber. But for now, he'd smoothed it down into curls around his cheekbones until he looked like someone who could afford a night in the hotel, at least.

Stepping into the hotel's lobby, he noted that it was nicer than any building he'd been in since leaving the city, but that it was still rather shabby by his former standards. Everything was gleaming and new, but it all came across as crass in the obvious attempt to cover the hotel's rustic bones with fashionable façades.

The man behind the desk was in a far nicer suit than Janus even though its cut was several seasons out of date from when Janus had left the city a few months back. But the man didn't blink an eye when Janus asked to reserve a room for the night.

"You're in luck that we still have an opening. The latest train came in and dumped a pile of tourists off until the train picks them back up again tomorrow. But we've got one room on the uppermost floor. It'll be quiet because the rest of the suites up there have been taken by a city *Érosgápe* couple and a doctor. They're regulars." The clerk rambled on as he systematically went through the paperwork of checking Janus in and taking payment via direct bank order. "They come to visit their son from time to time. I'm not quite sure what the story is there, but it's not my place to ask."

It wasn't his place to wonder, either, but Janus was grateful for the information and the stroke of luck that had landed him a room on the same floor as Kerry. He hoped he could find a way to work that to his advantage in keeping Kerry safe.

"Speak of wolf-god's own kin," the man muttered, handing over the key to Janus's room and shooting a glance toward the staircase leading up to the rooms above. "I suppose that's wolf-god's way of reminding me that gossip is his enemy."

Janus flicked a look over his shoulder to see Kerry between two tall men. The redhead had his arm slung around Kerry's shoulder, and his other hand rested on Kerry's belly, making each step down the stairs awkward. A small smile lay tense on Kerry's face, false to Janus's eyes, but it seemed believable to the men beside him. They turned at the end of the staircase and steered Kerry toward a room at the back of the hotel.

"What's back there?" Janus asked.

"Ah, the between-meals salon," the clerk said.

"Tea is still being served?" Janus asked, letting his gaze trail Kerry and his in-laws into the room.

"Yes, for another two hours. Then they'll clear up for the day and get the place ready for evening cocktails." Following Janus's gaze, and defying his own observation about gossip, the clerk said, "Their son doesn't look so happy to see them, does he? He never does. It's strange." Clucking his tongue, he went on, "He's a bit pregnant to be traveling up and down the mountain, too, ain't he? I'm surprised his alpha lets him do that."

Janus gritted his teeth, feeling the criticism down to his bones. "I'm sure he didn't want to. Likely he had little choice. You know omegas."

The clerk, a beta, grinned. "I've heard. Opinionated things, aren't they? And alphas just can't resist their methods of persuasion." His tone indicated something filthy, and Janus felt his fist clench in irritation.

But he loosened it, offered a false smile, and said, "You know we alphas are helpless when it comes to the needs of the men we love." It wouldn't do to make a scene in the hotel lobby, and the clerk had been quite helpful.

"Well, I, for one, wish that omega didn't 'need' to meet them here. Something don't sit right about it." Then, realizing he'd lapsed into mountain-speech, and into gossiping to an alpha at that, the clerk flushed and ducked his head. "Apologies, sir. I hope you enjoy your stay."

Eager to get to the salon and find a seat where he could keep an eye on Kerry, Janus smiled and nodded his head. "May wolf-god bless your day," he said, offering up a parting that he heard a lot from the mountain people he treated.

"And yours," the man replied before turning his attention to a well-to-do beta couple approaching the counter with a sheaf of local flyers in their hands and a question about how far up-mountain the famous healing lake was located.

The salon was set up much like the back room of the Philia soiree parties Janus had attended in his youth. Divided into semi-private partitions, each with comfortable sofas with knee-high tables before them, and all with curtains that one could draw partially or all the way closed for privacy.

Janus spotted the Monhundys and a beta waiter guiding Kerry into the nook near the back corner of the room. His walk no longer the strong, graceful stride that Janus had first seen when they'd met, but rather a careful waddle. His middle was large and still had more growth to go. Janus felt a burst of near consuming protectiveness, especially as Kerry nearly toppled over as his in-laws urged him into the center portion of the sofa. It seemed he found the maneuver difficult in his larger form. Janus had to hold himself back from rushing over to ease Kerry into his seat and distracted himself by looking around for an open nook close to the one where the Monhundys had corralled Kerry and pinned him between them.

The one beside Kerry's would be ideal, especially if Janus wanted to eavesdrop on the Monhundys, but it was currently in use, and so Janus took up a casual position against the wall not far from the nook where the Monhundys were now getting settled in, too.

"Can I help you find a seat, sir?" a beta waiter asked, his mustache glistening with a bit too much product.

"No, thank you. I'm waiting on a colleague," Janus said.

"I'd be happy to seat you and then alert your friend to your location when he arrives."

"I'm not sure we plan to stay," Janus said. "He mentioned a few options. I'll just wait here."

"Of course, sir," the servant said, bustling off to collect a tea tray and take it over to a young family positioned near the door.

Janus tilted his head toward the curtain blocking him from being able to see Kerry and listened, but he couldn't make out more than the rise and fall voices. No details of their conversation reached his ears in his current station. Becoming frustrated and worried, he was thrilled when the curtains flung open on the nook he'd originally assessed as the best location for his guardian activities. Two men exited looking decidedly worse for wear, and the omega sported red, chapped lips, along with a love bite on his neck for all to see. A new couple on a bonding-moon trip, then.

Janus darted a glance around. The waiters and servants were all distracted in one way or another, so he slipped into the abandoned nook and shut the curtains back into place. Ignoring the remains of the couple's barely touched cake and tea, he slid over to the side of the nook shared with Kerry's group. He carefully, with as little movement as possible, adjusted the fall of the curtains so that he could see into their booth. And if he held very still, he could finally make out the exchange of words within.

"Darling, you don't have to hide the truth from us," the red-headed omega—Monte, he believed Kerry had called him—was saying. "We understand pregnancy. I went through it myself with…" He trailed off, not saying his son's name. "It's a difficult time without an alpha to service those needs."

Kerry shrugged. "I understand what you're referring to, but I haven't had any trouble with it."

Janus took a surreptitious sniff of the air and found his tense muscles relaxing when the scent of berry and musk reached his nose. He held in a sigh, though, not wanting to alert anyone in the other booth to his eavesdropping.

"None at all?" Lukas, the alpha, sounded suspicious. "Omegas are always randy, everyone knows that, and in pregnancy even more so."

Kerry's jaw clenched, but he put on a smile. Janus wanted to crawl over the back of the booth separating them to throttle Lukas for being so rude. "I've barely felt a twinge."

The Monhundys shared a look, and Janus didn't like it at all. "Well, we have good news all the same."

Kerry shifted the way he did when he was trying to get the baby off his bladder or some other tender organ. "Oh? What's that?"

Lukas said, "Our attorney has convinced the prison warden that, with our support and sponsorship, Wilbet isn't a flight risk."

Monte interrupted him. "And given your needs right now, and your innocence in all that occurred, Wilbet is being given the option to spend the rest of your pregnancy imprisoned in our home. That way, he can help you during your time of need and be present for the birth of his son. Isn't that wonderful news, Kerry? He'll be home, and in your arms again, at last."

Rage began to pulse in Janus's bloodstream. He gripped the side of the sofa where he sat and held his breath. If he moved, he'd make a mess of things, because they were talking about letting that monster touch *his* Kerry. *His* omega. *His* vulnerable and pregnant omega. What if Wilbet hurt the baby? There was no doubt he'd hurt Kerry. Sweat slipped down Janus's back and temple from all the effort to hold still.

Kerry stared at his in-laws, his eyes gone so hollow and dark that they almost looked black. "Why would I ever want that?" he whispered.

"Why would you...? Darling, he's your alpha!" Monte exclaimed, putting a hand on Kerry's shoulder and rubbing it gently. "I know you have much to forgive him for, but you also know that you need him."

"I know no such thing," Kerry bit out. "I've told you what he did to me. I begged you to allow me to let another alpha service my heat—"

"Because you were upset. Jealous that he wasn't faithful. But love, all alphas who aren't *Érosgápe* are like that. Insatiable beasts. Isn't that right, Lukas? If not for our bond, why you'd be fucking every omega you could get your hands on."

"Not so," Lukas said darkly. "Monte, watch your tongue. You'll go too far."

Monte's cheeks flushed, and he looked down at his plate, but then he was back at it, saying, "Darling, what he did was very wrong, and he's serving out a long sentence for it. Doesn't he deserve a reprieve for the few weeks you have left before—"

"No." Kerry's deep, low voice sounded like ash being scraped from a grate. "Absolutely not. You will not take this from me. I don't care how much you want him home; I won't do it. *I won't do it.*"

"We don't have to allow you to stay with your uncle—" Monte started, his eyes narrowing.

"Monte, stop." Lukas sounded almost as cold as Kerry looked, but not half as enraged as Janus felt.

Monte's jaw grew tight, and his eyes blazed, but he stopped talking like his alpha asked. He shifted closer to Kerry, though, clenching his arm and leaning in, taking his air and space.

"Kerry," Lukas said slowly, "I can't feign surprise at your reaction. I didn't think you'd accept this well, and frankly, I can't blame you. We both know my son is an abhorrent monster—"

"No!" Monte cried, but Lukas hushed him with a simple lift of one finger.

"Yes, love, he's a monster. He abused Kerry, and he raped prostitutes and brutalized them. You don't want to believe the truth about him, because he's your only child and you love him. But I've faced the facts long ago."

"If you believe that, then why do you let him continue to rape me?" Kerry gritted out. Janus nearly clawed at the booth between them, wanting to climb over and rip Monte and Lukas apart. "Why did you deny my petition to get a surrogate? Am I that expendable to you?"

Lukas swallowed hard, and while Janus could only see half of his face, it looked as though he was forcing something distasteful down. "In a word: yes." Janus almost didn't hear the rest over the roar of his pulse in his ears. "We need an heir, and you're our only means to that end. But I don't like the idea of torturing you, Kerry. We'll do what we must, but no more. And now that we've seen your reaction to this proposition, I'd like to think my Monte will come to the same conclusion that I have."

Monte hissed slightly, digging his fingers into Kerry's arm hard enough to make him wince, but then he deflated like a balloon, going limp at the table. He let go of Kerry's arm and slumped over, putting his hands over his freckled face. "Wilbet's changed, Kerry. He *promises* me that he's changed."

Kerry just blinked at Monte, an expression of frozen horror on his face.

"If Kerry doesn't want him during this time, it will only endanger the pregnancy to force him," Lukas said softly. "Keep your priorities in line, love."

"Oh, I see," Kerry bit out. "You don't like the idea of torturing me, but if it was somehow better for the baby, then, what? You'd make me?"

"There is recent scholarship that makes it clear that an omega and the baby have better survival rates when they are being serviced throughout their pregnancy by a caring alpha." Lukas lifted a brow with a bitter sneer. "I do believe the word 'caring' is operative. I imagine the outcome of the study would show that an omega being unwillingly serviced by an abusive alpha would be quite grim."

Kerry was shaking, and Janus was, too, but with fury instead of fear.

"I'd planned to put my foot down about this regardless, but I was hoping that if Monte saw your genuine reaction, he'd believe me when I say there is no hope for our son's soul. Our *only* hope lies in your womb and the future fruit thereof." He turned to Monte again. "So, please love, leave Wilbet in the past. Embrace the future. It's right there in front of you." Here he put his hand out to touch Kerry's belly, and Monte, breaking into tears, did as well.

Kerry remained frozen, his dark eyes sunken with disgust and rage, and his skin paler than Janus had ever seen it. He sucked in a long, deep breath, and his eyes suddenly widened. And just like that Kerry's gaze locked on Janus's, tears welling up and sliding down his sharp cheekbones as he stared, wordlessly and helplessly, at him. Janus's throat tightened, his heart pounded, he held back with all he had for Kerry's sake because no matter how he felt, the law was clear.

They held each other's gaze for a long, horrible minute as the Monhundys rubbed Kerry's stomach, leaning close to coo at it, and then to kiss each other over it, a brief but clear indication of Kerry's place in their plans for the future. All too soon they were insisting that Kerry follow them back upstairs for the doctor's examination, and Kerry, looking empty and desolate, meekly followed.

The curtain of Janus's nook twitched, and Janus leapt away from his position to sit awkwardly in front of the prior couple's cake and tea, as a waiter poked his head in, eyes squeezed modestly shut, saying, "Sirs, I believe it's time for you to move on. My manager suggests you may want to take this up to your room?"

Janus cleared his throat then, and the waiter's eyes popped open in surprise. "Oh! Oh, my! I thought you were waiting for a friend. Where did the couple who…oh, never mind. Might I get you tea, sir? Or cake?"

"I'm fine," Janus said, slipping out of the nook and following Kerry and the Monhundys out of the room and into the hotel lobby again. He waited until they had a good head start up the stairs and then he discreetly followed, marking what room they guided Kerry into, and then hastening into his own to wait for a new plan to come to him.

Salvation for Kerry couldn't come too soon.

# CHAPTER TWENTY

K ERRY SAT ALONE in the hotel room. He'd refused to come down to dinner after the examination showed him to be perfectly healthy, with a robust passage that seemed well-stretched and ready for birth. The baby inside had shown off by doing lots of flips and kicks, delighting Monte out of his tearful state. His heartbeat had been strong, and the doctor had remarked that if he had to place a bet, he'd say there was every chance the child was an alpha. "Alphas are said to be more active in the womb," he'd remarked with a toothy grin. "You'll likely find this one is a sporty, active, dominant sort."

Lukas hadn't been quite as handsy as Monte, but he'd done plenty of touching, too, and when all was said and done, Kerry had claimed to be too tired to eat immediately and promised he'd ring for room service later. The doctor had said that was perfectly acceptable and expected given his drive down-mountain from Hud's Basin, the emotional discussion over tea, and the poking and prodding afterward.

Monte had looked ready to argue, but Lukas had put his arm around him, whispered in his ear. Then they'd both been sweet as punch, asking how to make Kerry comfortable and whether or not he needed anything at all from them before they went down to eat and then retired for the night.

"Nothing," Kerry had said, shutting the door and turning the lock on them. "Nothing at all, please. I just need to sleep now."

He couldn't sleep, though. He felt too violated and unsafe, even to close his eyes. Knowing Janus was somewhere there in the hotel did little to alleviate the sense of sick betrayal he'd experienced at Lukas's admission at the table. It was one thing to know a horrible thing was true, quite another to have it confirmed.

And while Dr. Rose was a good doctor, and likely a good man, too, his fingers hadn't had the delicacy and tenderness of Janus's when he'd pushed inside to feel around, testing the resiliency of his passage, the position of his womb, and the fullness of his omega glands. He'd looked a bit surprised by his findings, and his eyes had lingered a bit questioningly on Kerry when he'd said that everything appeared "well-oiled." He'd even dared to ask, "How often are you being serviced?" as part of his examination, and had only blinked once when Kerry had answered, "Never. There's no one."

Kerry closed the curtains in the room, sat on his bed, and stared straight ahead. He took long, deep breaths, trying to find any evidence of Janus in the air, but the hotel was large and well-ventilated with the latest fan system, plus there were all the scented perfumes and products coming from the Monhundys' room. He scented nothing of Janus at all.

The room seemed to cave in on him then. Blackness surrounded him. It reeked of the abandonment and fear he'd been fighting off since the moment Monte had mentioned the warden's agreement to allow Wilbet in-home imprisonment so he could rape Kerry.

He gagged.

*Service* him, rather.

A strange rustling sound came from the hotel room door. He ignored it, but then there came a rap, sharp and singular. He stood up to investigate and found a note slipped beneath the door.

*It's me. Let me in.*

The handwriting was familiar from the notes Janus left around the house for him along with the small gifts, and so Kerry carefully unlocked the door and eased it open. Janus stood in the hallway, his hair a wreck like he'd done little but rub his hands in it for the last two hours since they'd made eye contact in the salon. Kerry stepped back and let Janus through, then locked the door behind him again and leaned back against it. His heart pounded, and his eyes filled with tears as he stared at Janus, who stalked around the hotel room as if checking it for predators.

When Janus turned and strode toward him, Kerry shuddered at the dark expression in his eyes. But when he reached Kerry, he gathered him into his arms so gently that Kerry lost whatever control he'd managed to keep and broke down crying in his arms.

Janus hushed and stroked him, kissing his hair and ears, kissing his jaw and neck. But there was no lust in it, only comfort and protection, and Kerry wallowed in that. He tried to shove it into his cells—a balm against violation—by pressing himself harder against Janus's firm body. The baby was in the way, of course, as always, but Kerry pushed against him harder, wanting to fit more easily in his arms.

Janus kissed his mouth then, licking it open to press his tongue inside. His hands slipped into Kerry's pants, sliding to cup his ass, and then to quest into the crack, touching where Kerry still felt a bit used from the doctor's ministrations.

"Please," Kerry whispered, feeling slick rush from him at the gentle tap of Janus's fingertips. "Make me feel safe again."

Janus didn't need to hear more than that, apparently, because he took Kerry's jaw in both hands, tilted his head up and kissed him with slow, determined moves that washed Kerry's mind clean of anything but how entirely safe he felt in Janus's arms.

The kiss turned passionate, and Janus steered Kerry to the bed, pressing him down on it and quickly removing all their clothes. He started with Kerry's feet, kissing and licking his way up to his thighs, and then he nuzzled Kerry's cock, where it pressed up against the bottom of his bulging stomach. As Janus worked, Kerry sank into a dazed reverie. A compelling need to be as close to Janus as physically possible, to join flesh, filled him. He didn't even let Janus get around to sucking his dick into his mouth before he was urging him up, rolling onto his side, and presenting his ass in the closest thing to lordosis position he could manage with such a big stomach.

"That's what you want?" Janus asked.

"I need it," Kerry whispered, tears pricking at his eyes. "Please, Janus. Don't make me wait."

Janus was always so obedient when Kerry begged, and he wasn't any different now. He positioned himself, and the delicious burn of his cockhead nudging against Kerry's abused hole made Kerry moan. Then his omega glands released slick in a rush and Janus slid in, thick and long, deep enough to butt up against the tightly closed mouth of his womb.

"That's right," Janus muttered in Kerry's ear. "You open up for me. Only me. Understand?"

Kerry shuddered at the possession in Janus's words, tone, and grip on his hip, and when Janus pulled out and thrust back in, he came instantly, his cock spurting over the sheets and painting a stripe against the wall beside it.

"Fuck," Janus whispered. "You like that, don't you? Me owning you."

Kerry twisted on Janus's cock, and his own cock jolted again, a hollow, empty pleasure that was more like an ache. He wished Janus *did* own him, was his alpha, but he wasn't going to let himself think about anything but this moment right now.

Janus rubbed his hands down over the baby's bump and then up again to pluck at Kerry's sensitive nipples. Milk began to leak from them, and the scent rose up, clean and sweet, all around, adding to the mélange of odors they generated separately and together. Janus huffed against Kerry's neck, lifting his long hair up and away, nuzzling behind his ear and kissing the shell.

"You're my omega," Janus whispered. "Mine. From here on out. And no one's going to take you from me."

Kerry squeezed his eyes shut, concentrating on the rapid build of pleasure in his core, and then he shuddered as an anal orgasm quaked through him, and he gasped when Janus's hand covered his mouth, muffling his cries of joy. He didn't care that Janus's declarations were impossible. At the moment, he let himself feel them as true, and the words echoed as bliss in every cell. The orgasm was sweet and wanted, so unlike the brutal, unwanted pleasure of heats, that it felt as healing as his beloved lake.

Rocking on Janus's cock, Kerry let all his walls fall, and for a precious, sanity-saving moment, he *was* Janus's: owned, complete, safe.

WHEN JANUS STOPPED coming, his dick was lodged against the mouth of Kerry's womb, and he felt the sharp punch of the life within. He chuckled, dazed, and then carefully, slowly withdrew from Kerry's still pliant body, proud and happy to have covered up every last wrong scent on his omega with his own.

In fact, the room reeked of sex and coupling now. Milk, slick, sweat, copious cum, their individual pheromones and scents, and Janus loved it. He fell back on the mattress, tugging Kerry close, so that his back lined up against Janus's side, and lay there in a panting, sweating heap, satisfaction oozing from him like honey from a comb.

A sharp knock sounded at the door, and it rattled with intent.

"Kerry, darling, we've brought you some food! You need to eat for the sake of the baby!"

Kerry froze, every languid muscle going tense and hard. Then he rolled onto all fours, his still-gaping hole visible to Janus in the light peeking in from the crack in the curtains, along with Janus's cum slipping down his slick-wet thighs.

"Just—just a moment," Kerry called out, his legs and arms still visibly shaking from the intense sex they'd shared. He looked around, bewildered, his hair a complete wreck, some of it, despite its length, even standing up straight from his head.

The door rattled again. "Kerry? Do we need to get someone from the front desk to let us in?"

"No! I'm just…a moment, please."

Kerry stared at Janus in terror, and Janus, to his shame, stared right back. For all his fucking of contracted omegas, he'd never actually found himself in this exact position. He'd been discovered in his affairs, of course, but not in flagrante delicto as the Old-World Italians had once put it.

All at once, he rose and put on his pants, a plan formulating in his mind. It wasn't a pretty one and Kerry might not like it, but it was the only plan he could think of, and this was, obviously, his own fault for allowing their sexual impulses to take over when danger was so near. His need to comfort Kerry should have followed his need to keep Kerry safe, and yet, in the moment they'd connected and exploded together, they'd seemed the same thing. But right now, with Kerry's in-laws outside the door, he realized they should have talked, discussed their plan for the next morning. They should have figured out how to make sure the Monhundys had entirely let go of the idea of Wilbet's home imprisonment to service Kerry's needs. He hoped what he was about to do didn't endanger that at all.

Tossing Kerry a robe from where it had been hung across the back of a chair, presumably after it'd been used earlier during the examination, Janus strode to open the door despite Kerry's hissing calls of, "What are you doing! You can't!"

Swinging the door wide, he flung his shoulders back and peered into the shocked faces of Monte and Lukas Monhundy. "Who are you?" he demanded in a gruff voice, summoning all his most affronted alpha qualities.

"Who are *you*?" Lukas Monhundy asked, his hands coming up in fists and his nostrils widening in rage.

"I'm Jordan Riggs, and I'm in the middle of servicing a very neglected and very pregnant omega. Who are you to interrupt us?"

"His parents!"

Monte and Lukas blinked rapidly, their noses wrinkling at the scent of sex and pheromones wafting out of the room. They seemed like they might press inside, but at that moment, Kerry stepped up behind Janus and said, "I'm sorry. I went down to the lobby to request some ice not long after you left for dinner, and he was there, and I was there..." Kerry trailed off, wringing his hands anxiously. His belly protruded slightly from the opening in the robe which he hadn't managed to tie closed all the way.

"Pregnant omegas need service," Janus said with a sneer. "Where's this omega's alpha? As his parents, you should be ashamed to have him in such a state. He says he's been abandoned."

Monte and Lukas garbled out a response that somehow includ-ed the edifying information that they were only Kerry's in-laws and hadn't realized. All the while, they both reeked of embarrassment and horror.

"I was overcome," Kerry said shyly. "It's been so long since I've seen an unattached alpha. All the alphas in Hud's Basin are already paired up, and..." He scrunched his nose disgust. "Not my type."

Lukas and Monte stared, open-mouthed, and uncertain.

"If you'll excuse us," Janus barked. "My train leaves in the morning and this omega is sorely in need of pleasure. It's my duty to give it to him."

"But your dinner..." Monte said, holding out a well-wrapped

box with a napkin and silverware balanced on top.

Janus took it. "Thank you. I'll see that he eats it. Now, move along. He's mine tonight."

Shutting the door in Monte and Lukas's face, Janus locked it with a fierce twist, satisfied by the heavy thunk of the tumbler. Kerry slumped against him, and Janus held him tightly, both of them breathing quiet and shallow, listening for noise in the hallway.

"C'mon, Monte," Lukas said, his voice sounding firm and strong, right outside the door still. "It seems the boy can get his needs met on his own without your blasted interference. For all we know he's been coming down here once a week with the car our lunatic son gave him, hitting up travelers for his basic needs."

"He said there's been no one," Monte argued.

"And I saw the doctor's eyes at that response. He didn't believe him. He'd felt him on the inside, said he was well-stretched. Of course, Kerry wouldn't want to admit to having needs when you're trying to bring our son, the man who brutalized him, out of prison to 'service' them."

"But…" Monte sputtered. "How can you be okay with this?"

"So long as it's not the same alpha again and again, it's fine. We can't risk feelings arising from it, but as far as getting his itch scratched, well, no one will blame him even if word gets out back home. Pregnant omegas are horny omegas, and that's just the way of it. Kerry's a resourceful one. He's got pluck. I admire that."

"He's fucking a stranger in that room with our grandchild in the middle of it. There are *diseases*, Lukas! What if he catches something! What if it damages the baby?"

"That alpha's fine, Monte. He doesn't have any sickness. Plus, he's got the right priorities."

"You don't even know him!"

"I scented him. Sometimes that's all the information an alpha needs. He's going to take care of Kerry tonight, and from the smell of things in that room, he was doing a damn good job of it. Don't worry. Our grandbaby will be all the better off for it. Come on, love. Let *me* take care of *you* tonight. You can pretend you're pregnant again, and we can…" His words fell away to whispers.

Monte protested, though. "How can you think about that…when…" There was a thud of a body being pushed up against the wall beside the door. Breathless kissing sounds ensued, and then, "Oh, *oh*…well, all right."

Janus and Kerry stood huddled together by the door until they heard the door of Lukas and Monte's suite open and close down the hall. The baby kicked hard, making Kerry gasp and Janus put his hand down low to settle it. As always, the baby seemed to calm as soon as his palm made contact. No more flutters, kicks, or jabs.

Kerry started to relax again, too, but he still shook, and not with the aftereffects of fantastic sex like before, but with fear.

"Oh, wolf-god, what if they take this as proof that I need Wilbet to—" He convulsed with anxiety and Janus caught him before he fell to the ground. "Monte wants that. He wants his son home. He doesn't care. He doesn't *care*, Janus."

"Lukas does," Janus said, hauling Kerry to his feet again and guiding them both to the wrecked and soaked bed. "If he thinks you're picking up high-class men from the trains, he'll be satisfied."

"But how? That's not necessarily safe. We both know it."

"It's probably just as safe for your baby as letting Wilbet have at you. If anyone is likely to damage the child, it's his father."

Kerry shuddered and squirmed, unable to relax down onto the bed. Janus gathered him from behind, forcing him into the position of the little spoon, and crooned softly in his ear. It was a lullaby his pater had sung to him, and Kerry started to unwind, slowly but surely.

The scent of slick release rose again, and Janus slowly unbuttoned his pants, positioning his cock so that it was resting against

Kerry's hole. He paused his song to say, "It's up to you."

And Kerry shifted one leg forward and his ass back, letting the tip of Janus's cock slide inside his tight, hot hole, and then he whispered, "Fuck me, Janus. Please."

Janus's heart exploded in his chest, like confetti made from shards of glass tearing him up inside. He shoved his cock in deep and hard, holding it steady there, feeling the way Kerry's body thrummed around him.

"I'll fuck you all night," Janus whispered. "Hold tight. You've never felt anything like this, sweetheart."

By the time Kerry passed into sleep five hours later, the moon was shining through the curtains, and Janus had fucked him while he had sobbed his way through so much delicious pleasure that he'd confessed on a broken breath that he didn't know how he was supposed to live without it now.

Janus, his dick still buried deep inside Kerry's sleeping form, felt much the same.

He considered the problem of the Monhundys and Kerry's contract. He'd let himself become so distracted by the sexual congress between them that he hadn't done all he should to engage an attorney on the matter. He knew just who to ask, too, and resolved to place a phone call to his cousin before leaving Blumzound.

# CHAPTER TWENTY-ONE

"THERE ARE SEVERAL attorneys that Heelies Enterprises has relationships with," Ray said, his voice sounding tinny but concerned down the telephone line. "But I think, for these matters, you'll want a beta, someone friendly to the cause and friendly to the family. Have you heard of Xan's friend Yosef Deckel? He's been working off and on with some omega freedom groups, and I spoke to him a few years ago regarding some, well, interest I had in an omega living in a difficult situation. He wasn't as useful as he could have been, but that was the omega's fault, not Yosef's."

Janus wanted to ask more about that, but he was running low on time. Each minute cost money, and he was nearly out of money after the new-to-him clothes, the night in the hotel for a room he didn't even sleep in, and now this phone call to his cousin Ray, the CEO, and brains of Heelies Enterprises.

"I'm afraid I don't have a lot of time, Ray, and I'm running out of coin to continue this call. Is there any way you'd be willing to have this attorney contact me by post? It'll take a little longer, but given the expense of a call like this one, and the current state of my finances, I think it'll be the best we can do for now."

Ray was silent for a moment and then asked, "Are you all right up there, Janus?"

"Getting by just fine." Another tick of the timer had the owner of the phone reaching out a grubby hand for another coin. Janus reluctantly handed one over. He only had a few left, and the meager savings in his bank account needed to go toward board at Monk's

House and, possibly, toward this Yosef for Kerry's attorney. Assuming Kerry and Zeke needed help paying for him.

"All right, well, you know you have my support. I'm not entirely dependent on Father. I have my own savings. If you—"

"I'm all right," Janus said again. "I don't want to be beholden to you or anyone. I'm going to make it on my own."

"Of course you are, but you don't have to suffer until you get there. Your family has your back."

Janus winced. He didn't deserve Ray's loyalty, not after what he'd said and done to his baby brother, but perhaps Xan had kept all that ugliness to himself. If so, that was another thing Janus didn't deserve. "Thank you, cousin. I'm grateful to you. I won't need any help for myself, but maybe for my friend. The omega in question."

"Of course, I'm open to that as well, if he's important to you."

Janus swallowed a strange lump that came up in his throat. "Yes. I think he truly is. Important to me, I mean."

Ray chuckled. "I got that."

The timer was about to tick over again, and so Janus ended the call. He needed to get back to the corner where he and Kerry had agreed to meet once his in-laws finally set him free. Janus thanked the phone controller and wiped his sweaty hands on his newish pants before heading out into the morning sun.

He hoped Kerry was all right and surviving whatever interrogation his in-laws gave him over breakfast. Most of all, he hoped his instincts about Lukas Monhundy were correct and that Kerry was going to be safe from any further interference from them until the baby came.

At that point, once the child arrived, Janus knew all bets were off.

AFTER A NIGHT of untold bliss, breakfast was sheer misery.

Kerry poked at his eggs for a few minutes, until, catching Monte's suspicious gaze, he began to fork them heartily into his mouth. He did the same with the jam and toast, the bacon, and a heaping bowl of oatmeal. By the time he'd finished, there was no way they could say he wasn't eating well or that he showed signs of ill health. In fact, after the fucking he'd had the night before, the mirror across from their table showed that he was positively glowing. With a blush of embarrassment perhaps, but still.

"So," Monte began as soon as Kerry had put down his fork. Of course, now that he was through eating, interrogation was fair game. "Who was that alpha last night? How did you really meet him?"

"In the lobby," Kerry said, wiping his mouth with his napkin and striving for a suitable tone. He wasn't sure if he should be nonchalant, bashful, or defiant. Somehow, he felt like he came across as a mixture of all three. "Just as he said. And I believe he said his name was Jared or Jordith? Well, *something* Riggs. I was a little too busy to catch much more."

Monte turned the color of his hair, and Lukas chuckled under his breath.

"And what does he do for a living?" Monte finally said once he could breathe again.

"I'm afraid I have no idea. What do alphas tend to do? Business things, right? Maybe he owns a business." Kerry frowned, thinking it over. "He did say something about the 'ride' being as smooth as a brand-new motorbike, and I think he meant it as a compliment." Monte almost choked on air at that, but Kerry went on as though he didn't know better. "Perhaps he owns a motorbike company? Maybe the Sabels know him? Why does it matter? He was a single night—a pleasant memory already in my rearview mirror. Nothing more." He thought he sounded convincing.

"Dr. Rose told us this morning that there was a good deal of enthusiasm coming from your room last night. His was next to yours," Monte said with a vicious expression, clearly hoping to embarrass Kerry. And he succeeded, but Kerry wasn't going to let him know that.

"Oh, yes. Mr. Riggs was very good. The best I've had, probably. If he hadn't already left on the train this morning, I'd be tempted to ask him for another night." Kerry shrugged. "Oh well. Isn't that the way of it? I suppose it's for the best. We wouldn't want feelings to develop. I have duties, after all." He smiled at them, and he knew it was an ugly one. He didn't care. Fuck them for doing this to him.

Now that he better understood Lukas, he didn't see any point in faking enthusiasm for being on their team any longer. Let Wilbet's father feel guilty for what he was doing. At least one of the two of them should. Kerry wondered, avoiding direct exposure to Monte's flushed and enraged face as he sipped his coffee, whether Wilbet's lack of conscience came from his pater. It seemed likely.

Lukas came to his rescue, though that seemed a bit too chivalrous a word for it, given everything. "Leave the boy alone, Monte. It isn't his fault things turned out the way that they did. It's Wilbet's."

The name, as always, was like a bomb in the middle of the table. Monte froze, his smile like a knife, and Kerry exercised his complete disregard for it by taking up his thus far untouched glass of orange juice and sipping it like nothing untoward had been said.

"Isn't it partly *his* fault, though?" Monte hissed, his eyes going dark with impotent rage. "If he'd been more suited to Wilbet's tastes, if he'd liked the same things, then maybe Wilbet would never have sought out those prostitutes. It could have been something they enjoyed together."

Lukas stared at his *Érosgápe* with a pale face. "Are you saying, love, that if Kerry had liked Wilbet hurting him, then none of this would have happened?"

"Yes." Monte nodded firmly. "I'm sure he didn't even try to like it."

Lukas blinked rapidly and then rose from the table. "Stand up. Now."

Monte swallowed hard.

Lukas's jaw clenched. "Would you like to test it? See if you can 'try to like' being hurt? Perhaps we should see just what you think about that when we get home."

Monte's chin wobbled and his eyes filled with tears. "Don't be angry, love. Please. I'm sorry. I didn't mean, I just—he's—please, Lukas."

"Does my disgust with what you've said hurt?" Lukas said, balling up his napkin, which he still held in his clenched fists. "Try to like it. Because it's not going to change anytime soon."

Conflict between *Érosgápe* caused intense emotional pain, Kerry knew, but seeing the way Monte crumbled in the face of Lukas's rage was still incredibly satisfying. He sipped his orange juice again and waited.

"I'm sorry," Monte said, panting, as several fat tears fell from his eyes. "I just—"

"I don't want to hear your excuses. Apologize to Kerry, and then we're leaving."

Monte seemed to balk for a moment at that, but then he turned to Kerry with wet eyes and a red nose. He didn't look at him, though. Instead, he stared off over Kerry's shoulder. "I'm sorry. That was a horrible thing to say. It wasn't your fault. It was…Wilbet's." His voice broke. He ducked his head. "It was Wilbet's fault. I'm sorry. I'm so sorry."

Kerry gritted his teeth together. *You're not forgiven*, was right on the tip of his tongue, but he held it back. He wanted them gone more than he wanted to dig the knife in deeper. Still, he couldn't stop himself from saying, "I will petition again to share my next heat with someone else. Will you grant that?"

Lukas and Monte shared a long look, and then Lukas shook his head.

Kerry rose, put his napkin down on the plate, and saying nothing more, left the dining room. Neither Lukas nor Monte tried to stop him. He went upstairs for his bag and the keys to the car, and without hesitation, he left without saying goodbye.

What good was an apology for hurting his feelings when they planned to continue to violate and use his body? No good at all.

Janus waited on the corner, just as they'd discussed, and the sight of him—slim and strong, tall and steady—leaning against the pharmacy's exterior wall kicked Kerry in the chest like a mule. He could barely see through his tears when he pulled the car over, and he buried his head in his hands, hair falling forward like a curtain on either side.

Janus climbed into the passenger seat next to him. "Sweetheart, wolf-god, what's happened? Why are you crying?"

"I'm so happy to see you," Kerry gasped, snot leaking from his nose and a sob catching hard in his throat. "I'm just so happy to see you waiting there."

Janus made a noise of confusion, but he tugged Kerry over the gearshift, careful not to let it dig much into Kerry's protruding stomach and sang that soft song from the night before. The one Kerry wanted to learn by heart and sing right back to him.

Their lullaby love song.

# CHAPTER TWENTY-TWO

THE WEEK FOLLOWING the stressful meeting with the Monhundys in Blumzound was a hectic one. A midsummer storm had led to a flooded mine, which had trapped some miners down below. Once rescued, they required all sorts of doctoring for everything from chills to wounds to panic attacks. Add on the usual patients, the omegas due to give birth, and those who did go into labor (all thankfully came out the other side alive), and it was a stressful, long day. Not to mention the continued medical attention Charlie needed in his convalescence. After everything, Janus was too exhausted to follow up on writing a letter to Yosef Deckel explaining Kerry's situation, and almost didn't have the energy to enjoy Kerry at night.

But finally, the week was over, and the day of rest had begun. With no true emergencies to deal with and Charlie discharged and on his way home, Janus was able to sleep late, take his time over breakfast, and sun himself on a rock by the lake for several hours. And, wolf-god, it all felt so good.

Especially everything with Kerry. It felt perfect.

Janus had noticed Kerry making good progress with his stack of baby clothes, but he'd also been working on some secret knitting project, too, one that he hid whenever Janus was around. Janus assumed it was a gift of some sort, but he didn't want to get his heart set on it only to be disappointed when it turned out to be something for Zeke later. Still, it gave him a lot of pleasure to imagine Kerry working on a gift just for him. Whatever it was, he was certain it would be perfect in every way.

Just like Kerry.

The thought brought him up short. He'd been having more and more of thoughts of that nature lately, undeniable and compulsive, and yet...

Objectively, Kerry was far from a perfect man. But try telling that to whatever part of him wanted Kerry for his own, because that part was willing to start a fight about it.

Kerry was, to him, *perfect*. It was strange. He'd never felt this way about any other omega and hadn't heard other alphas, aside from *Érosgápe*, describe these kinds of feelings. Was it love?

The sun was halfway up the sky, and he decided to douse his worries in cool water before heading inside to write that letter to Yosef. He walked into the lake, feeling the healing balm of its water on his hot skin, and with a sigh, ducked beneath and swam far out. When he surfaced, he flipped onto his back and floated, feeling all his stress, tension, and anxiety slip away. If only Kerry were here with him, then it would be perfect.

There was that word again.

Janus rose up to tread water and, looking back toward the house, wondered what Kerry was up to now. He'd left him helping his Pater with the airing out of the closed, unused boarding rooms, based on a note sent up that morning from Blumzound.

Despite it being the day of rest, apparently the promise of a handsome bonus sum could persuade Zeke to open the closed rooms for some travelers determined to see the miraculous Hud's Basin. Peering through the trees, he caught sight of movement on the trail. It had to be Kerry, freed from his work at last, and coming down to join him in the lake.

Janus ducked under and swam for shore.

When Janus surfaced, his heart giddy with anticipation, he searched the trail and didn't see anyone or anything. Finally reaching the shallows, he stood up and walked to the beach, naked as always, and called out, "Kerry?"

A most unexpected figure emerged from the trail. Janus blinked in confusion and briefly considered that he might be dreaming. But no, when he looked more closely, it had to be real.

There in the sun, emerging from the green tunnel of trees, was Caleb, a wide smile on his face and a baby strapped over his chest. "Janus!" he called out. "I was afraid you'd gone mountain-wild, and it looks like I was right."

Janus strode forward, soaking wet and confused as hell, but he gripped Caleb in a hug, getting his white clothes and the baby all wet. He released him and looked him up and down. "You're here? Why? How?"

"*How* is easy. We came by train. Then we had to wait overnight for a car willing to make the trip up because I wasn't going to risk Bekhem's neck on a wagon. The *why* is also easy: you never wrote back, and Ray said you'd called asking for Yosef as an attorney, and after your almost daily letters, your sudden silence plus that news was, to say the least, concerning."

"And so, you hopped a train with your infant son?"

"Yes." Caleb laughed. "Oh, Xan wasn't happy, let me tell you."

"Is he here?"

"No, Yosef is my escort on this trip. Xan and Urho wanted to come, but I insisted they stay and take care of the other two children. Honestly, I need a break from my alpha and my doctor. They are so overbearing when I'm pregnant or chestfeeding. Smothering with their love. It's awful." He glinted a grin. "But I'm happy. And also, happy to be away from them for a few days." He looped an arm around Janus's shoulders, and the baby slept away on his chest, oblivious to the wetness Janus had left behind. "So, tell me. What's going on? How can we help?"

"You can help by not touching him." Kerry's voice was deep

and threatening, and Caleb stepped away from Janus hastily.

Turning to the path, Janus found Kerry there with an open towel. "You forgot this again," he said, his eyes never leaving Caleb. The breeze from the lake ruffled his long hair and made the towel flap about. "Like usual."

Janus reached gratefully for the towel and covered himself. Nudity was something he'd become so accustomed to, especially when swimming in the lake, that he hadn't even thought twice about Caleb's impression. Besides, given Caleb's particular personality, he wouldn't have been much moved by Janus's body anyway. Well, beyond the desire to make jokes about it later when they'd both had a drink or two.

But Kerry didn't seem pleased to find Janus naked with his old friend, and when Janus put his arm out to pull Kerry close and introduce them, Kerry sidestepped him and waddled back up the path, going slower than he obviously would have liked.

"Oh, dear," Caleb murmured. "That wasn't the impression I'd hoped to make on him. Surely, he knows that I don't...well, that we aren't...? He knows I have no interest in any of that, correct?"

Janus shrugged. "It's not as though I spread your business around, Caleb. I kept that part to myself. I'm not sure what he thinks of you, but he knows I loved you once."

"Oh, good," Caleb said, laughing softly. "It's in the past now? What a relief."

Janus almost laughed, too. Caleb had a way of doing that to him. But he held it in for fear Kerry would hear and think that they were laughing at him. "Yes. It's in the past. I hope that's not a blow."

"It's the best thing I've heard in weeks. Well," he amended looking down at the infant in his arms, "the best thing I've heard today, at least. I do enjoy this little one's coos and my other two's laughter. But truly, Janus, if you need to go after him to smooth things over, please do."

"I'll make it right with him. But first, tell me what you're doing here again. I'm not sure I follow."

While he toweled off and dressed, Caleb explained his decision to come to Hud's Basin for a sojourn and to help however he could, and it was with sharp relief that Janus understood that Caleb's escort, Yosef, was *the* Yosef—the very attorney Ray believed could help Kerry.

Wolf-god did Kerry need help. And given how in love with him Janus found himself to be, he needed help, too.

"Thank you," he said gruffly, pulling Caleb and the baby close for another hug. "I don't know how to ever thank you enough."

Caleb squeezed him lightly and then tugged away. "Seeing you here, so changed from who you've been, and back to who you were when I met you? That's all the thanks I need." He smiled. "Now, let's go see if I can make nice with your omega."

KERRY DIDN'T KNOW who this Caleb Riggs thought he was, swooping into their home with his white clothes and his bright smile, looking all beautiful and glowy after having just given birth, but Kerry hated him. He especially hated the way Janus's eyes lit up when he looked at Caleb.

*Hated* it.

Which was ridiculous and unkind and, according to Janus, completely unwarranted. But it didn't matter because Kerry's heart was bitter and seeing Caleb's radiant happiness only made it more so. Here was a man who could have anything he wanted, including, apparently, a life where he gave birth to children he wanted, created with a man he loved. Wasn't that just lovely for him?

Kerry wanted to spit.

Dinner was annoyingly cheerful, with Janus and Caleb swapping stories of their shared past, and Caleb filling Janus in on the current doings of their shared family and friends. Kerry picked at his food, hoping that everyone would just shut up.

Pater, of course, was loving it, and laughing along with the others. Traitor. Kerry sent him a narrow glare, but Pater just rolled his eyes at him.

"And what do you do, Mr. Deckel?" Pater asked the lithe man with neatly trimmed white hair and beard. He looked to be in his late forties, or perhaps his fifties, and he dressed with such style that Kerry shivered with instant dislike.

He'd known men who dressed like this Yosef Deckel in the city, and they were all wealthy, foppish assholes across the board. Of course, they'd all been Wilbet's friends, and this man was far too old for that set, but the neatness of his beard and mustache, the exact fall of his suit pants? It was damning evidence against his personality no matter his age.

"I'm an attorney specializing in legal contracts of all sorts, but recently I've begun pursuing omega rights work," Mr. Deckel answered with a small smile. "That's part of why I escorted Caleb here. I understand that you could use my help."

Pater's eyes grew wide, and he reached out to grip Kerry's arm in excitement. "Oh, blessed wolf, indeed we could."

"We couldn't actually," Kerry said, setting his mouth firmly and darting an angry glance at Janus.

"Don't be—"

Kerry pushed back from the table. "We don't need his help."

"Sit down," Janus said with a deep, alpha order in his tone that Kerry wanted to obey, but he thrust his chin out and refused, sweeping out of the room instead. Well, waddled out of the room. He hadn't "swept" anywhere in over a month.

Janus was on his heels, though, and he gripped Kerry's elbow, stopping him in the hall before he reached the staircase. "What's this about? This is the man I intended to hire. Now he's here and determined to help, and you're refusing. Why?"

Kerry jerked his arm free of Janus's touch. "I don't like him."

Bewildered, Janus threw his hands up. "Why?"

"Because…" He darted a glance back toward the kitchen. It was quiet in there. Most likely, they were all listening.

"Because Caleb brought him?" Janus scoffed. "How many times do I need to tell you that Caleb is no threat to you. But this…this stubbornness and jealousy? It *is* a threat to you—to *us*."

"There is no 'us,' Janus," Kerry snapped. "How many times do *I* have to tell *you* that?"

Janus laughed then. Truly laughed, wiping a hand over his face and rocking back on his heels, almost hiccupping with it.

"What?" Kerry hissed.

Janus wiped at his eyes, and let out a long whooo sound, and finally grit out, "You keep on telling yourself that. It won't change anything, Kerry. There's definitely an 'us,' and you know it. But if you want to throw a jealous fit before agreeing to accept their help, go ahead."

The roots of Kerry's hair grew hot, and he snarled at Janus.

Janus didn't stand down, though. "That's fine. Be scared and angry. You're allowed. But they're here to help me as much as to help you, and they're not going to walk away from things this easily."

"I have to consent to be helped."

"Sweetheart, you're the most frustrating person I've ever met, and I'm in love with you. If you think I'm going to let you throw away this chance…" Janus threw his hands up. "Go on then. Upstairs. Pout and do whatever you need to do. But when you come to my room tonight, I'll know that you're ready to fight for us."

Kerry did as Janus said then, rushing up to his room, and flinging open the window so that he could stare down at the lake. Kiwi chirruped upon seeing him, and Kerry went to him, took him from the cage, and kissed his beak.

"He thinks he can bully me into doing what he wants?" Kerry firmed back his shoulders and let his hurt swirl around in his gut. Tears filled his eyes, but he fought them back. "I'm not his omega," he whispered to Kiwi. "I can't be."

He didn't go to Janus's room that night.

Or the next.

But on the third day of Caleb and Mr. Deckel's annoying visit, he ran into Janus alone by the lake and without words they crashed into each other's arms, hungry and eager to reassert their bond.

And as he panted in the aftermath, satisfied and happy for the first time since he saw Caleb in Janus's embrace, Kerry had to admit Janus was right. There was an "us" and, despite his fear and jealousy, he was ready to fight for it.

Now, if only his handsome alpha would learn to leave well enough alone.

# CHAPTER TWENTY-THREE

"I KNOW I agreed to give you time," Janus said, pushing Kerry's hair back behind his ear gently. "But sweetheart, there's not a lot of time left. What happens after he's born?"

Kerry rolled onto his back, gazing up at the puffy white clouds drifting happily across the sky. "Do we have to talk about this now? We just made love."

Janus grinned. "Say that again."

Kerry rolled his eyes and gently slapped Janus's hand away from where he was rubbing his bulging stomach. The baby somersaulted inside, and Kerry sighed. "You heard me the first time."

"I did. I never thought you'd admit that was what we were doing, what with your insistence that it was all pheromone delirium and alpha protection instinct."

Kerry, glad to distract Janus from the topic at hand, smiled and turned back onto his side, slipping his hand up Janus's chest. "We could do it again. The day is still young, and you feel so good inside me."

Janus groaned and leaned in for a kiss, his tongue hot and strong in Kerry's mouth. But then he ripped his mouth away with a bark of laughter and a touch to Kerry's nose. "Now, now. You're trying to get away with not telling me anything, aren't you? That won't do. What's your plan, Kerry? What happens when the baby comes?"

Kerry groaned, frustrated to have failed in his distraction. He sat up and pulled a towel over his lap, covering his half-hard cock.

"You won't like it."

"I'm sure I won't," Janus agreed. "But tell me anyway."

"I'll have him here. Then I have to take him to the city, where I'll chestfeed him for two years. Then I'll come back, wait for my next heat, and…" He shrugged. "Do it all again."

Janus's teeth made an ominous grinding noise. "I'm tempted to be distracted by your insistence that you'll have to spend another heat with him. But I won't let that happen. Yosef says that—"

"Yes. I know. But I don't want to believe you or him. It will hurt too much if you're both wrong."

Janus touched his cheek and left the subject behind. "But the baby, Kerry. What happens to the baby after those two years in the city?"

Kerry swallowed hard. "I leave him there. Monte and Lukas will raise him. That's what they want. And it's what I want, too."

Janus stared at him, his cheeks pale like the sun had never tanned them at all. "You can't do that."

"I can, and I will.'"

Janus swallowed thickly. "Kerry, they raised a monster."

"They're not entirely bad people," Kerry whispered, putting his hand on his belly, feeling the baby move beneath his palm. "And they aren't going to let me keep him. Even if I wanted to."

"And you don't want to?"

"I can't love him, Janus. I've tried."

"Sweetheart, you haven't let yourself love him, because you don't intend to keep him."

Kerry groaned. "Where's the problem with that? I'm a means to an end for that family. He'll be the heir if he's an alpha, and the first-born son if he's not, and…" Kerry shrugged. "He'll be better off with men who won't blame him for where he came from."

"Kerry…"

"I told you that you wouldn't like it, but I was honest," Kerry said bitterly, rolling to his back again and breaking eye contact. "Can't we just leave it at that? I'm sorry you're disappointed in me. I'm sorry that I'm not a man who can love unconditionally. I've tried, but Janus, you weren't there when he...when Wilbet..." Kerry's throat tightened, almost cutting off his breath.

"Shh," Janus said, pulling him close, kissing his hair and cheek. "I know. I know."

"You *don't* know. He chokes me. He punches me. He pinches and bites, not out of passion, but because he wants to hear me scream. He *can't come* unless I'm screaming, do you see? And if this child has so much as a single feature of his, then I will loathe him. Utterly. How could I not?"

Janus soothed Kerry, holding him close. "I'm sorry. I understand. It's your choice, Kerry. It should have always been your choice."

Kerry let Janus rock him, confused by his irritation at Janus's easy capitulation. Why he wanted Janus to argue for his son, he didn't know, but he wanted to know that if he did decide to ask Mr. Deckel to help him fight for the babe, Janus would want him, too. Had he ruined it all with his candidness? "Don't think about it," Kerry said, his throat tight still. "What I just said? Please, forget I told you. I don't want you to think about me that way."

"I love you," Janus said, his voice rough. "I won't ever let that happen to you again. I will kill him first."

"Good luck with that," Kerry said with a short, miserable laugh. "He's well-guarded."

"Accidents happen," Janus said darkly.

"No," Kerry said. "The last thing I want is for you to be in prison, too. Please. Just let this go."

"No, I won't let this go. And neither will you. That's why Yosef is here, and Caleb—to help you out of this. We'll do whatever it takes to keep you safe."

"I can keep myself safe."

Janus nodded, but they both knew it wasn't true. "Caleb wants to help, too, you know. With money. With my cousin Xan's social power. However he can."

Kerry stiffened slightly in Janus's arms. "Why should I accept help from your cousin's gorgeous omega who you were once in love with?"

Janus nuzzled Kerry's hair. "You are my heart now. You, and you alone."

Kerry let Janus kiss his neck, and they fell into lovemaking again.

But Kerry couldn't entirely banish his jealousy of the ethereal man who'd shown up like a dream and permeated the house with his scent and easy laughter. How could Kerry ever compete with a cultured, beautiful omega like that?

He supposed if Janus had to accept Kerry belonging to another alpha, then he'd have to accept that part of Janus belonged to Caleb. He just wanted to scratch the man's eyes out for having had Janus's heart first.

THE NEXT MORNING over breakfast, served in the dining room instead of the kitchen to accommodate the two new guests, Kerry agreed to meet with Mr. Deckel alone in the living room for a thorough interview regarding his situation as he understood it.

"At this point, we're still at the discovery stage," Mr. Deckel said, buttering his toast lightly. "I need to understand the situation inside and out, which means I'll need to talk with your pater, and most likely, Janus, too, if they agree to it, and if you will approve of it."

"If it'll help," Pater said, "I'd sell my soul to wolf-god's fallen kin and happily."

"I'm willing to be interviewed," Janus said. "If Kerry's all right with me disclosing what I know, amongst other, uh, *particulars* of our life."

Eyes downcast, Kerry nodded, understanding not for the first time his in-law's reluctance to discuss weighty matters while eating. He had to admit it did ruin his appetite. Still, he picked at his eggs and managed a few sips of the hearty morning stew Pater had served up. Then he put his spoon aside and waited for everyone else to finish up before shoving back from the table and asking Mr. Deckel, "How do we begin?"

"I'd like to start with Janus. I understand that his schedule requires him to travel up-mountain a bit to work with the doctor and that he won't be home again until afternoon or evening. The interview should be short, as he has the least experience with your contracted alpha's family. Then I'll likely spend the bulk of the day talking with you, Kerry. And, Zeke, if you don't mind, this afternoon I'd like an hour or two with you?"

"That all sounds fine with me," Pater said.

"Kerry?" Mr. Deckel asked, his kind eyes boring into Kerry for permission to dig up the worst part of his life.

"Yes. In the meantime, I'll…" He trailed off, glancing toward Caleb who fairly glowed in the morning sun coming in the windows and lighting on his hair. The man was ridiculously beautiful. No matter what Janus had said, how was it possible to stop loving someone who looked like that? He cleared his throat. "I'll wait in my room if that's all right."

"I have some work to do, but Mr. Riggs, you can feel free to explore the house or the grounds," Pater said.

"Of course," Caleb said softly. "I wanted to go back down to the lake and dip my feet in. Rumor has it that it's got healing waters."

"It does indeed," Pater agreed heartily.

Kerry couldn't stop himself from adding, "Be careful with the baby on the trails. There are wildcats out there. I'd hate for him to be eaten up."

There was a ring of shocked silence around the room, and Caleb's eyes went almost comically wide before he bent his head to kiss his son's soft, light brown hair. Kerry wished he didn't feel a dart of satisfaction at having rattled the imperious and impervious man.

"Don't mind Kerry," Janus said with an awkward laugh. "He likes to tease about the wildcats, but I've been here for months and haven't even really seen one yet."

Kerry shot Janus a glare. "I'm not teasing." He rose and nearly tripped over the edge of the large carpet beneath the table as he hastened to leave the room. "There are wildcats, and the baby shouldn't be left alone."

"I'm sure Mr. Riggs isn't going to leave—" Pater said, but Kerry shot him a silencing look, too.

"Excuse me. I'm not fit for company," Kerry said. "I should go to my room and get my head together for Mr. Deckel's interview."

"Call me Yosef."

Kerry nodded. "Certainly. Until then…"

He tried to sweep out of the room, but his belly made that impossible. So, he waddled with as much dignity as he could muster—which probably wasn't very much—leaving awkward silence in his wake.

Let them feel uncomfortable. He had felt that way for months physically, and now, with this well-intended invasion of his home by his lover's ex…well, ex *something*, he was even more uncomfortable. Why not share that joy around?

As he gained the second floor and turned to head down the hall to his room, he heard the scraping of chairs moving back from the table and his pater's apologies for Kerry's behavior. It was followed quickly by his insistence that there were indeed wildcats, and while they were usually harmless, it didn't hurt to stay aware of one's surroundings in the wilderness around the lake.

Kiwi tapped against his mirror and, seeing Kerry enter the room, turned to dance for him while bursting with demanding chirrups and screeches. Kerry released him from the cage, taking him in hand and letting him trot back and forth between his palms. Then Kiwi shook out his wings and flew across the room, landing on the windowsill to gaze outside.

"Do you want a bath?" Kerry asked, thinking that in his distraction of late, he hadn't allowed Kiwi much time to play in the sink.

Kiwi bobbed and clicked, and then flew to rest on Kerry's shoulder. Taking him into the bathroom, he stoppered the drain and turned on the tap. The water came out a bit fast, startling Kiwi into another scream. But Kerry adjusted it to a trickle and sat Kiwi in the basin, watching as he pushed his head under the stream, tilted his head from side to side, and then shook the water out over his wings.

Kiwi's joy in the water reminded Kerry of Janus in the lake. While he'd made it clear that he didn't believe in Hud's Basin's healing qualities, there was no doubt that Janus was in love with swimming in the lake. When the cooler months came, Kerry knew Janus would miss his long swims unless he was mad, like some of the older mountain alphas, and went swimming in the water even in the ice and snow of winter. Kerry supposed he wouldn't be here this winter to find out. He'd be in the city with the baby, chestfeeding, and hoping he could survive two years in Monte and Lukas's clutches.

He hoped he'd have two years, anyway. Once the chestfeeding came to an end, he'd likely go into heat within a month, and, well, that was an eventuality he wanted to stall for as long as possible.

A knock came at the door to his bedroom. Surprised that the interview with Janus had concluded so quickly, he shut off the tap and left Kiwi in the basin to investigate. Perhaps it was Pater coming to tell him off for scaring a boarder, and one doing him an incredibly undeserved favor at that. He'd deserved that lecture and would accept it shamefacedly.

But when he opened the door, he found Caleb—not his pater—standing there sans infant with a quiet expression and a ripe peach balanced in his palm. "May I come in?"

Kerry nodded and gestured with one hand for Caleb to sit in the only chair the room boasted. Situated by the window, it was where Kerry had left it several days before.

As Caleb took a seat in the chair, Kerry awkwardly realized that he'd have to sit in the sill. Or he could sit on the bed, but then Caleb would have to turn the chair, and wolf-god, this was already so awkward. But so was climbing into the windowsill when hugely pregnant. He hefted himself up, though, in the least graceful manner possible, and settled himself.

"You should have had the chair," Caleb said when it was all said and done. "I would have offered, but I assumed you'd refuse, and well, you're there now."

Kerry huffed a soft laugh and shoved his long, unruly hair behind his ears. He wished he had straight, perfect, chin-length hair like Caleb, instead of flyaway snakes curling every which way.

"Well, first off, this peach is for you," Caleb said, lifting it up. "A gift from a man who is quite obviously besotted with you."

"Besotted. Is that a word used outsides of romance novels?" Kerry murmured, not taking the peach.

"I like romance novels," Caleb said with a shrug. "And having never experienced the sensation of being besotted myself, I rather enjoy reading about others who do. The heart-racing violence of it all. It's charming."

"Charming."

Caleb laughed and shrugged. "Oh, I don't know. It's certainly *something*. Messy for sure, and I don't just mean the often-resulting sex that comes from it all. But emotionally. I'm glad to be clear of it all. Or I am now. There was a time I thought there was something wrong with me." He frowned and pushed the peach forward again. "I'm getting ahead of myself. Janus wanted me to see that you eat this peach. He said it was full of nutrients for the child and sweetness for you."

Kerry snorted again. "He thought I needed sweetening this morning?"

"Didn't you?"

Rather than be offended by Caleb's straightforward way, Kerry relaxed in the face of it. He reached out and took the peach. "Thank you. For delivering this and his message."

"Let me clear a few things up for you. Whatever you think of Janus and me, now or in the past, you're wrong," Caleb said in a quiet voice. "Mainly because you're jealous. And you shouldn't be. Not at all."

Kerry squirmed like a little boy, humiliation hot and thick pulsing in him like a living thing. "Because you didn't love him back."

Caleb startled Kerry with a laugh that was nearly as pretty as he was. Kerry wished he could be annoyed instead of charmed, but he wasn't. Well, not entirely. "Oh, I loved him, but not the way he wanted me to. Or thought he wanted me to." Caleb frowned, and his cheeks grew pink. "There are different ways to love, and I loved him dearly as a friend, as someone I would, quite frankly, have trusted with my future, with some stipulations and an understanding between us about my own needs."

Kerry tilted his head.

Caleb shrugged. "I don't usually discuss it. It's no one's business but my own. But given how much intimacy has been thrust upon us with this situation," here he gestured at Kerry's stomach, "I will be entirely open with you. Perhaps to the point of humiliation for us both."

"You don't have to…"

"I know. But I will. Because you must see that even though I loved him and he betrayed my love, it was for the best. For both of us. I'm an anomaly. I'm an omega who is, generally, repulsed by sex. I don't feel the same stirrings for an alpha. Even during heats, I struggle against the sensations and loathe the act."

Kerry stared at him, speechless.

"It's only with the help of my very patient alpha and our devoted doctor that I've come to a place where I can almost enjoy heats. If nothing else, I'm with an alpha I trust implicitly to help me with them, and to never violate me in any way, to always seek my consent and pleasure, and to not be hurt when I want nothing to do with him in *that way* otherwise."

Caleb's cheeks were still red, but he spoke with the same self-aware confidence that he spoke about anything else. He was not the least bit lessened by his confession, and Kerry was intrigued by that. But still…

"Your lack of desire for Janus didn't prevent him from wanting you, though," Kerry said.

Caleb shrugged. "Perhaps. But you've wanted other men, haven't you, Kerry?"

Kerry stared at him. "Yes."

"You've even been in love with another man."

Kerry shook his head. "No," he whispered. "Never."

"Never? Not even with your alpha before he…"

Kerry shook his head. "There were other reasons I contracted with him. But I didn't know what he truly was, either. I hoped to love him. One day."

Caleb nodded. "I see. Janus had feelings for me. Loved me.

Wanted me. Admired me."

Kerry's jealousy twisted like a hundred snakes in his gut. What was the point of this?

"But he never once treated me the way he's treating you."

"Meaning?"

"He walked away from me. He left me vulnerable to wolf-god only knows, rather than sacrifice his desires, or negotiate, or even just talk it over. The hurdle of loving me was too high for him."

Kerry stared at Caleb, trying to comprehend. Was he warning Kerry off from Janus? Trying to expose him as a player and untrustworthy?

"Now, look at this situation here with you," Caleb said with a kindness in his tone that would have melted any other man's reserves, but Kerry couldn't let them go just yet. "You're pregnant with another alpha's child, contracted to a criminal, dealing with in-laws who treat you without the respect you deserve, and legally hamstrung in ways that will make a future for you both difficult. And yet he's fighting for you, isn't he? He had Ray contact Yosef. He went with you to Blumzound to protect you from the Monhundy family, to fight for you if need be. That's what true love looks like, Kerry. The kind of love men share who are meant to build a life together, and be more than, well, just dear friends."

Kerry blinked. "What if I don't deserve that kind of love?"

"What if none of us do?" Caleb shrugged. "Have faith in him, and us as his friends—now your friends—that we won't give you up easily."

"We won't give him up at all," Janus growled from the door-way.

Kerry jerked, surprised to have been so captivated by Caleb's words, and so desirous of their truth, that he hadn't heard or scented Janus's approach. Now that he saw him there, there was no denying his delicious scent filling the air.

"Cheep chirrup reeep!"

Kerry laughed and slid carefully from the sill, again much less elegantly than he would have liked given Caleb's graceful presence, and hurried into the bathroom to retrieve Kiwi from the basin. Soaked and happy, he fluttered his wings and cheeped at Kerry before flying up to his shoulder to prance.

Janus crossed the room, saying, "I have to go, but Yosef is ready for you now."

Kiwi fluttered on Kerry's shoulder and then launched himself over to Janus where he promptly shat on Janus's clean white shirt. Janus blinked. Kerry froze. And Caleb's pretty laugh bounced around the room again.

"He's jealous of how Kerry cares for you," Caleb said, rising.

"It's good luck," Kerry said quietly, moving forward to remove a shameless Kiwi, and putting him back into his cage. "Or so Pater says, but Kiwi shits on me all the time and my luck is far from good."

"I…" Janus stared at the white mark on his shirt. Then he shrugged and focused on Kerry again. "I came to tell you that Yosef is ready for you and that I have to leave. Please, Kerry, it's safe to…" he glanced toward Caleb, "to trust Yosef with the truth. Even if it's hard."

Kerry swallowed thickly and said nothing at first, double-checking that he had locked the cage. "You should change and get going. Dr. Crescent will be crabby that you're late."

Janus nodded and then, with another fast glance at Caleb, tugged Kerry close and kissed his forehead. "I won't let anything bad happen to you again. I promise."

"Go," Kerry said, smirking at the attention. "You have shit on your shirt."

Janus rolled his eyes, kissed his chin and then his cheek, seemingly not caring at all that Caleb was observing, and then left the room.

"Where's Bekhem?" Kerry asked as he and Caleb headed back downstairs.

"Your pater has him out in the garden. He's asleep in a small basket in the shade. Your pater likes babies. He'll make a good grandpater for this one."

Kerry smiled tightly, and while it was clear Caleb knew he'd said something wrong, he didn't have time to explain what. Yosef met him at the bottom of the staircase and guided him into the living room to start the interrogation.

As Yosef shut the door behind them and Kerry settled on the couch, he rubbed his sweaty palms over his stomach and waited.

"I can't promise this will be painless," Yosef said, sitting down across from him in a chair, holding a notebook that already held many scribbles. "But I need you to be honest with me in every way. I need the details. Even the ugly ones."

"Where should I start?" Kerry asked, his throat dry and aching.

"Start with the first time you met Wilbet Monhundy. We'll go from there."

JANUS HADN'T QUITE understood the line of questioning Yosef had guided him through earlier that day. He'd assumed that he'd spend a lot more time clarifying and recapping the conversations he'd overheard between Kerry and the Monhundys in Blumzound the week before.

Instead, Yosef had grilled him on his intentions toward Kerry, the extent of his commitment, and what, exactly, he'd be willing to swear to in a court of law and before the Holy Church of Wolf with regard to his continued care for Kerry and his soon-to-be-born son, now and into the future.

Janus had replied honestly, but a niggle had started in the back of his mind that Yosef wasn't the person who should be hearing these things first. Kerry deserved the full truth, and he deserved it sooner rather than later. Not that Kerry would want to listen. He seemed most content when they lived fully in the present as if there was no baby on the way, and no future to plan for. And Janus, intoxicated by Kerry's person, had given in all too easily on that front.

That would need to change.

Yosef had made that clear, too, saying that part of their petition to the courts would include a plan presented with passion and commitment. One that both Janus and Kerry agreed to—something to appeal to the conservative judges, and the prudish hearts of the church leaders. Something preferable to sticking to the rule of law.

Entering the clearing from the path, Janus saw that one of the horses was gone and that two patients waited for a doctor outside the stables. Dr. Crescent was nowhere around. Fan, however, was hanging up the wash, his dark hair shining in the sunlight.

Waving at the two betas waiting for his attention, Janus approached Fan with a greeting on his lips. "And where's doc gone off to?" he asked once Fan had turned around to offer him a pretty smile.

"He left before dawn. Whitehoul showed up this morning. One of his omegas is giving birth. I'm afraid I can't remember which one. Hopefully, it's going well." Fan glanced up at the sun. "It's getting late in the morning. Those men have been waiting."

"Sorry about that. I was meeting with a lawyer. About Kerry."

Fan put down the shirt he was pinning up and then returned it to the basket of laundry, shading his eyes from the sun for a long moment. "He wants to fight them for the baby?"

Janus frowned. "He's going to fight them for *himself*."

"Ah." Fan stroked his chin, his eyes going to the middle distance. "I was under the impression he planned to give up the babe to the alpha's family to raise, once his obligation to chestfeed was over."

"He won't have any obligations to them at all if the lawyer can convince the court and the Holy Church of Wolf to dissolve the contract."

Fan's brows lifted. "That takes some big balls right there. What grounds is he going to put forward?"

Janus realized his mistake in mentioning this to Fan at all. It wasn't his place to share the details of the abuse Kerry had withstood. "The lawyer is gathering that information now. He feels there is a decent chance."

"Lawyers always say that, don't they?" Fan asked. "They want their money." But then he shrugged and said, "I wish him the best of luck. Kerry's not had an easy way of it. He's not a bad lad. He deserves better."

Janus agreed. "I better get to those patients."

Fan nodded. "Best to get them out of the way." As Janus walked away, Fan added, "I'm glad for him. I am. If I can help in any way, let me know. Though perhaps, given what else I know, it's best if I don't testify under oath as a character witness. I have a feeling that my idea of a good man and the court's idea might be very different."

Janus nodded and returned to the stable to help the betas. They were both suffering from stomach pains, most likely from a bad fish they'd shared, and Janus sent them away with a tin of tablets and orders to be more careful. Food poisoning was nothing to take lightly.

Neither was going before the court and church. But Janus was willing to do it.

For Kerry.

# CHAPTER TWENTY-FOUR

"H E'S ADMITTED TO trying to abort the child," Yosef said, stabbing the sand by the lake with a long stick. "I don't mean to scare you, Janus, but that doesn't bode well. We have to do anything we can to prevent that from being exposed in the court."

"No one knows except for me, Zeke, and the man who gave him the tin of pills. He won't be speaking, obviously, or he'd implicate himself."

"Kerry is easily shaken," Yosef said. "They'll want to question him about his feelings about the child and your feelings about the child. He might say something without meaning to that will lead them to ask. We need to be ready for that contingency. He must lie fluently. No hesitation."

"I'll work on it with him," Janus offered.

"Yes," Yosef agreed, the white of his beard shining in the sun. "I'm confident you'll do your duty by him, prepare him well. It's just that he's been through so much. I hate to put him through this, too. You know how these judges are, and the church leaders are even worse. The good news is that they'll respond well to the idea of you making a family together, of bringing more children into the world and raising them together. But the Monhundys have money. They'll fight it. Judges and church leaders are supposed to dedicate themselves to the law *and* the faith, but they can be bought."

"Then they *will* be bought," Caleb said from where he sat on the log, chestfeeding Bekhem. The child sucked hungrily, causing a red flush to rise up his pater's chest and into his neck, but Caleb, as always, seemed unperturbed by his situation. "I'll buy them. Or, rather, Xan will."

Yosef frowned but didn't argue, his bushy brows wrinkling up with the thought.

"Kerry wouldn't want—"

"Xan will be happy to do it," Caleb said with a ferocious firmness that Janus rarely saw or heard from him, except to reject his suit when he'd begged Caleb to defy his contract with Xan and leave with him. "He has his own score to settle with Wilbet Monhundy."

There was a darkness there that Janus wished he dared to confront, but Caleb just shook his head and turned his attention back to his son, cooing at him sweetly, as if he hadn't just looked ready to murder a man with Yosef's sharp stick.

"Kerry can't know," Yosef said, his brows unfurling. "Not just because I suspect he'd reject the help, but because, if questioned or it comes to light, he can't afford a bribery charge."

Caleb nodded. "Fair enough."

Janus hated the idea of keeping anything from Kerry, especially when it had to do with his life. He'd already been so violated, his wishes disregarded, and yet... There was no way he'd stand a chance against judges bought and paid for by the Monhundys. If Xan had some reason to want to screw that family over and free Kerry at the same time, then so be it. He'd let his cousin use his infinite amount of wealth for something undeniably good.

Like Kerry. He sighed longingly. Oh, his omega was *so very good.*

"Getting him to agree to testify to a future with you is going to be hard enough," Yosef said. "He was resistant to the idea in our interview." He pierced Janus with a hard look. "Haven't you told him how you feel? He seemed to think you wouldn't agree to such commitments, even when I told him that you'd already agreed to them in your interview with me. He seemed to think I pressured you."

Janus rubbed his hand over his face, a groan escaping. "I have told him I love him, but it's possible he doesn't believe me."

"Wolf-god knows he loves you. He's mad with jealousy about me." Caleb rolled his eyes. "Make all of this right, Janus. Fix this problem."

"He won't let me talk about the future!" Janus burst out. "I've tried. He shuts it down. I would dearly love to impart to him how deeply and ardently—"

"You admire him?" Caleb laughed. "Oh, Janus. Get down to the reality of it. I think your omega is going to need to have your intentions drilled into him." He smirked. "Make of that what you will."

Yosef sighed. "At the very least, you have to get him on the same page. The court and church might need bought off, and thank wolf-god Xan has the funds to see to that. But they will enjoy looking good for the press as well. The newspapers will be all over this, and having a compelling story about two lovers, an alpha and omega who are meant to be, will make the medicine go down a bit easier. No alphas enjoy seeing contracts broken. It leaves them feeling vulnerable."

"Though most aren't in the kind of contract that Kerry faces," Caleb pointed out. "My parents weren't very helpful when I contracted with Xan, but he made sure I had a top-notch attorney of my own, and well, of course, *you* would never have set me up with a contract that didn't give me certain rights."

"Exactly. And, of course, once he's free, I can walk him through a contract like that with you, Janus. Kerry will be allowed to leave you at any time, for any reason. He could leave you if you smile wrong."

Caleb laughed again.

Janus frowned.

"Oh, stop, darling. He will never leave you. Why should he? You adore him. And giving him the freedom of a weak contract will only tighten his bond with you." The babe popped off Caleb's chest, and he hastened to cover himself up again, before turning the babe over his shoulder and patting him until he let out a series of deep burps.

"Charming," Yosef said with a laugh that wrinkled his eyes.

"Of course, I have no problem with a weak contract," Janus said. "I just want him to be sure. People have forced him into far too much."

"Yes," Yosef said grimly. "It sickened me to hear the details."

Caleb grew solemn. "Does he need…other help? There are new doctors in the city. Men who help people with troubled minds."

"Kerry has his wits about him," Janus protested. "He only needs his wings back. It might take him some time, but he will fly on his own again."

"Like his bird," Caleb said with a smile.

The evening began to fall harder, and Caleb confessed to being hungry again. Nursing always left a man hungrier than usual. They started back up to the house together, their conversation reverting to more casual things, like Yosef's partner Rosen, and his art show in the city. Which led to Caleb bringing up the plan for a charity art auction and Yosef's assurance that, yes, Rosen would want to participate in that as well.

Janus enjoyed the sensation of beginning a friendship with Yosef, and the continuation of his friendship with Caleb, which for the first time felt unburdened by history or desires. He stopped, letting the others walk on ahead a bit, while he nudged a rock out of the path. It could be a tripping hazard if Kerry weren't paying attention, and with his newly shifted center of gravity, it could result in a dangerous fall.

"Janus!" Zeke called from somewhere up the path, his next

words coming in a panicked rush. "Come quick! It's Kerry!"

Janus's heart skipped a beat, and his mind filled with all sorts of horrible possibilities. "What's happened?" he asked, running up the trail, leaving Yosef and Caleb behind. "What's going on?"

"He's hurting. I think it's the baby." Zeke's accent thickened. "I think he's a'comin' early."

Janus blinked. It wasn't a good sign at all if the baby was on its way now. He'd be too small to live, and... He didn't have time to think about that now. He needed to get to Kerry, confirm Zeke's suspicions, and if they proved correct, then he'd need to get several items from Dr. Crescent's supplies. There'd be no time to waste on worry.

He didn't even realize that he'd left the rest of the group, including Zeke, behind until he was taking the stairs two at a time to get to Kerry, who was groaning loudly enough for Janus to hear as soon as he'd burst through the front door.

Throwing Kerry's already ajar door wide, he rushed to where he sat sweating on the bed, his feet on the ground, his shirt off, and his hands protectively over his stomach. He met Janus's eyes with a panicked expression of his own, but he said nothing, gritting his teeth and groaning as his stomach muscles tightened up hard.

Janus didn't need to see much more to ascertain that he would need to stop the contractions, but he did have to check the mouth of Kerry's womb. If it remained closed, it was likely these were preparatory contractions, often seen a week or so before the child's due date. So, still a bit early, but not as horribly so. If the mouth of his womb were open, however, then they'd need to prepare for a gruesome and sad outcome at this stage.

With a gentleness that didn't betray his anxiety, he smiled up at Kerry and soothed him. "It's all right. I'm here now. I've got you." He eased Kerry onto his side, putting the pillow beneath his head, and running his fingers over Kerry's brow. "I need to check inside.

All right, sweetheart?"

Kerry whispered, "Yes."

"Let me get something to ease in, in case your omega glands are inflamed." He turned his head as he heard the thunder of many footsteps coming up from below.

"Zeke, I need you to get to Dr. Crescent's house as soon as possible. If he's not home, then talk with Fan. He'll help you. I need Cramp Bark in both pill and cream, same with Black Haw. And might as well grab some Partridgeberry and Oat Flowers too. Tea form and pills."

Zeke's eyes had flown wide, but Yosef was there with a note pad and a pen, writing down what Janus said. "I'll go with you," he said, taking Zeke by the shoulder. "Let's hurry."

Zeke looked wary about leaving Kerry, but when Janus shot him an urgent glare, he didn't dally any longer.

Caleb lingered in the doorway with the babe strapped to his chest, being blessedly silent for now. Janus didn't know what else to ask of him other than the most basic of help. "Please boil water for the teas they'll come back with. And…bring me the tube of slippery grease I keep by my bed." His face flushed a little, knowing that Caleb would understand what that tube meant. But his friend said nothing, hurrying off for the tube and then disappearing downstairs as soon as he'd handed it over.

This left Janus alone with Kerry, who was still clutching at the bottom of his stomach and groaning. "Let me have a look. I'll need to take your pants off."

Kerry nodded, breathing in between gritted-teeth groans.

Janus made haste with the drawstring waist and dragged the pants down over Kerry's thighs and down to his ankles. Then he removed them altogether, knowing that he would need to check multiple times before this was all over. He left the room quickly to wash his hands and returned drying them on a clean towel. He knelt again.

"Bring this top knee forward. That's good. You all right?"

Kerry shook his head and groaned again.

Janus smoothed a good amount of grease over his right hand, and then, kneeling by the bed with one hand clutched in Kerry's, he slipped the other down past Kerry's cock and balls to his hole. He felt the rim—a bit puffy, but that could be from the use he'd made of it the night before—and then pushed just inside. A rush of slick pulsed out, and then another burst of it, almost a river. That wasn't as promising as he'd like. Yes, it'd make his way in easier, but it also meant Kerry's body was preparing for something big to enter or exit. And in this case, it seemed likely that it was readying his body for the baby to be born.

"Shhh," Janus said, gripping Kerry's hand more tightly as he moved into him with his fingers, and then his thumb, and finally the thickest part of his hand at the base of his knuckles. "Don't push out like usual," Janus said softly. He didn't want to risk expelling any part of the child from the womb at all, though the contractions themselves were strong enough to do that, regardless. "Just relax and let me in."

Kerry glared at him a moment, tears standing in his eyes, but he took a shaky breath, let it out. His thighs released their tension, then his lower back, and finally his ass seemed to release around Janus's knuckles, allowing his whole hand to slip inside.

"That's my sweet boy," Janus said, kissing Kerry's hip and squeezing his hand again. "You're doing great." He released Kerry's hand to kneel up and get some leverage. "Now, a bit deeper. Not too much. Your womb is low…and, ah!" He blinked hastily, hoping his dismay didn't show on his face.

The mouth of Kerry's womb was not entirely open, but it was starting to blossom like a flower. The tight, closed bud had softened.

"What?" Kerry gasped. "What do you feel?"

"It's a bit soft," he murmured. "A good paste of Cramp Bark and Black Haw will tighten it back up. It's all right. You're going to be fine." He prodded again to make sure he understood what he felt, and then he slowly withdrew his hand. Kerry turned his face into the pillow and breathed as his asshole clenched and spasmed before closing tight again. Janus pulled blankets over his lower half for modesty when Zeke and Yosef returned.

"What happens if we don't stop it?" Kerry asked when another cramp had washed over him and passed again.

"He'll be born, most likely, and…he won't make it."

Kerry's expression twisted up, and he chewed on his bottom lip, his dark eyes going tortured and bleak. "I don't know what I want to happen," he said softly. "Wolf-god, help me, but I don't know what's right."

Janus kissed his forehead and wished he'd also asked for Kava root, too. It'd help calm Kerry's nerves now. He didn't know what to say in the face of Kerry's brutal honesty. He thought Fan's suggestion that he say nothing—that he let Kerry feel whatever he felt and not place any demands on him about what he should want, or how he should see things—was probably good advice for this moment, too.

After all, Kerry could still refuse treatment. He had that right. And while a court of law and the Holy Church of Wolf might, if prompted, give a second look for his refusal to medicate, they probably wouldn't. Religion often went hand-in-hand with a belief in wolf-god's will, and that sometimes meant rejecting science. The establishment's hypocrisy around science was well known, but in all likelihood, no one would ever look into Kerry's situation beyond the superficial.

Zeke and Yosef returned with tins and teas, and bottles with tinctures, and a hastily scribbled note from Fan about how to employ some of the lesser-known medicines sent. Including one that would "hasten the miscarriage along should it reach an irrevocable point, reducing the trauma and pain during the expulsion."

Janus swallowed hard and set that bottle aside carefully, putting it far from the others he planned to employ to stop the miscarriage, assuming Kerry gave permission. He didn't explain each medication to Kerry, but he saw how Kerry watched him place the tins and bottles in a row.

"Tea will be up soon, too," Janus said. "And the paste I'll need to apply internally."

Kerry stared at him with dark, wide eyes. Then he nodded.

Unable to stay away, Zeke entered the room, and fussed around Kerry's bed, until he came to where Janus sat, reading over the note from Fan again. Then, with an urgency, and no apology for leaving Kerry alone, Zeke pulled Janus out into the hallway. "What's the plan?" he whispered, looking around Janus into the room where Kerry seemed calmer between his cramping.

"The plan is what it has to be: I'll do my best by him. But the opening to his womb has softened. I'm not sure if we can turn the tide back. But I'll try."

Zeke stared up into Janus's eyes. "And if he doesn't want to try?"

Janus swallowed hard, the pit in his gut tightening. "Then we don't try."

"You're willing to do that?"

"I'm not going to violate him," Janus said. "He's had far too much of that already."

Zeke nodded, then whispered with accent in full force, "Please keep 'im safe. The babe is...I could love that there babe even if he can't. But, if it comes between 'em, Kerry's my heart."

"He's mine, too."

Zeke pressed his lips together and nodded hard, water standing in his eyes.

Janus went into the room again and found Kerry by the bird-cage, Kiwi in his hand. He stood with the bedsheet wrapped around his swollen waist, his naked torso gleaming in the afternoon sun through the window as he watched the bird prance in his palm. To Janus's astonishment, Kerry sang to him in low, vibrating tones. Janus recognized the lullaby he sang to Kerry at night.

Watching as the breeze from the open window caught in Kerry's hair and lifted it, a clamping sensation over his heart overcame Janus. He'd do anything for this man. Anything at all.

He'd even administer the other medication that Fan sent if Kerry wanted it. He only wanted to see him delivered from the agony of pain and a twisted uncomfortable future full of fear. He wanted him to sing, and smile, and open to Janus like a bloom in the sun of love.

A cramp grabbed Kerry by the middle, and he hunched over hard, interrupting Janus's romantic mental lark. Kiwi flew up into the air and flitted around the room, screeching in worried fear. Janus hurried over to put Kerry back down on the bed.

"There's no time to waste," he said, though he'd been doing just that moments before. "We need to decide now, Kerry. Do you take these medicines to try to save him? Or do we see what wolf-god has in store without them?"

Kerry's lips trembled, and he shot a sharp look over his shoulder. His arm came up and then dropped again. "Kiwi," he said softly.

"You can hold him again later," Janus said. "Let's focus now. What do you want to do, Kerry? This is your choice. I'm just here to help you through it."

Kerry's long throat bobbed with a swallow. His eyes went to the window, and he stared out for a long time. Janus didn't look away.

He simply sat and breathed with him. In and out. Another breath. And another.

"It's like with the lake," Kerry said finally, his voice sounding crushed.

"What is, sweetheart?"

"Wolf-god gave us the lake to heal us. He expects us to use it. Science is like that. And so are you."

Janus shook his head, confused.

"Wolf-god sent you here to me. You found me in the woods. You're here beside me now." He looked up at Janus. "He sent you, and I suppose I should use you like I would the lake."

"You don't have to do this because you think it's what wolf-god wants," Janus said. "He's forgiving." Not really, according to the Holy Church of Wolf, but Janus wasn't so good at believing in all of that anyway. He didn't want Kerry making his choice because of fear.

Kerry nodded, his gaze going to the window again. "If I could have lost him when I took the pills, that would have been for the best. But I didn't. If I lose him now, it'll be…" He brought his gaze back to Janus. "It won't be pretty, will it?"

Janus shook his head. "He won't survive more than a minute or two. But it will be a hard couple of minutes."

"I don't want that."

"It's up to you."

"I said I don't want that," Kerry spit out, sudden rage rising in his eyes. "I wanted to be rid of him before, and if I could have done it then, fine. But not like this. So, give me the pills. Put the paste inside me. I'll carry him as long as I can. I might not love him, but I don't want to see him die like that either."

Janus took a slow breath to keep from letting out his own cry of frustration. There was no good answer today—nothing to feel relief over or pride in. He took up the first tin and began to explain the medication, handing it over to Kerry one tablet at a time, along with a glass of water to swallow the bitter pills down.

KERRY WAS GRATEFUL that Dr. Crescent hadn't been home when his pater and Yosef had made their way up to the cabin. It wasn't that he didn't trust Dr. Crescent with his best interests, but now that he'd been with Janus, he didn't want any other alpha putting his fingers and hand inside him to apply the paste and check the opening of his womb.

Caleb's baby cried off and on as the hours passed, and the cramps came and went, they grew more aggressive and then waned again. And when they finally faded away entirely, they left him feeling wrung out and sad. The cries of Beckhem were a distant hymn. Almost like a song of grief. He didn't know how to feel when Janus told him that his womb was still sufficiently closed, the paste had done the trick. So, he stared at the open window, laying with his back to the door and to the concerned group of men who stalked outside it.

A hammering knock at the front door jolted Kerry out of his near slumber, and the sound of Dr. Crescent's voice asking for entry rolled up the stairs. "I don't want him," Kerry said, rolling his sweaty head back and forth on the pillow. "Don't make me see him. Just you. I only want to see you."

Janus pressed a kiss to his temple and made no promises as he left the room to fill Dr. Crescent in on the situation, and hopefully pass on Kerry's request to be left alone for the night.

As Janus reached the lower floor, and they moved into the living room, shutting the door, their voices became hushed and muffled. Kerry couldn't make out everything he wanted to hear. But he listened all the same, taking relief in Janus's steady tone, and the responding assurance in Dr. Crescent's voice, too. He was in good hands with his alpha.

He sighed, too tired to correct his errant thought. For today, for this moment, he would let himself have it. Right here and now, he'd be Janus's omega, and he'd let himself feel safe in that protection and love.

He let his eyes drift to the cage across the room and the strange choice he'd made earlier. A trade of sorts. A bargain.

He didn't know if wolf-god worked that way—tit for tat, a sacrifice for a favor—but he'd felt it down deep all the same. So, he'd said nothing as he'd made the deal. Or almost nothing. He'd only called out Kiwi's name. Otherwise letting his silence seal the bargain. He hoped Kiwi could learn to be free after so long in his cage.

He didn't know if he'd ever get the chance himself.

JANUS SPENT OVER an hour reassuring Dr. Crescent that all was well, explaining the choices he'd made, and letting Dr. Crescent assure him that he'd made the right ones. Dr. Crescent would have liked to have a look, but when Janus told him that Kerry had explicitly asked for Janus alone to treat him, he'd just laughed. Then he'd proceeded to ask all kinds of questions about how long they'd been fucking. Which Janus hadn't wanted to discuss in detail, but Dr. Crescent was keen to know what plans were in place for the future since they'd obviously bonded beyond the "servicing" aspect of things.

Janus had divulged what seemed prudent, which wasn't very much.

He'd gone into the kitchen where Zeke had been making a late-night snack for all of them after their trying evening. He owed Zeke an update, and so told him over a sandwich all that he'd told Dr. Crescent. Well, most of it. He left out the information about how long he and Kerry had been fucking.

"Was this because of his deformity?" Zeke asked.

Janus blinked at him. Despite stroking his hands over Kerry's body almost every night, he'd nearly forgotten about the deformity. It'd simply become part of the omega he loved, and the thought that it was the deformity leading to this early labor struck him as obvious now. The baby had grown quite large. He could feel that much with his hands. And given how big an alpha Wilbet was, from what he understood, the babe's size couldn't be much of a surprise. Monhundy was, from all reports, a massive man.

Another omega's ribs would shift slightly to make space, but Kerry's couldn't shift enough, and the baby needed more room— so, of course, Kerry's uncomprehending body had deemed the babe better out than in, rather than allowing him to take space needed by Kerry's vital organs.

Dr. Crescent hadn't brought up the deformity, but he might have forgotten about it. Who knew how long it had been since he'd seen Kerry with his shirt off or examined him? Kerry was a private man. Not to mention the Monhundys' city doctor provided most of his health care.

After ending his conversation with Zeke with reassurances that he would do all he could to keep Kerry safe while helping him carry the baby for as long as possible, he'd stopped by Caleb's room to check on him. He accepted a hug and reassurance from his friend, who was still awake and reading in a chair by the window. After answering Caleb's somber questions, Janus then took a long minute to gaze down at the living, breathing baby resting in the rigged-up crib, soaking in the hope and sweetness around him.

Lastly, he'd ignored the sound of Zeke and Yosef's voices still coming from downstairs as they discussed politics and mountain ways. Instead, he was keen to return to Kerry's room alone.

He found Kerry on his side, wrung out and mostly sleeping. He brushed the long silky hair from Kerry's cheek, bent low and kissed his sharp cheekbone. "How are you feeling?" he asked.

"Kiwi's gone," Kerry murmured, his exhaustion taking him down into sleep. "S'all right. I let him go."

Janus jerked his head toward the birdcage with a sharp pebble of worry in his gut. It quickly turned into a sinking stone. The birdcage was wide open, and so was the window. How had he not noticed before?

A quick search of the bathroom, the bedroom itself, and the upstairs in general produced no evidence of Kiwi. He stared out the window as the dark, moonless night swallowed the outside world. Janus turned back to stare at Kerry as he slept in the bed, a wedge of fear in his heart. Kerry slept peacefully, though. His eyelashes sweeping down over his cheek, and his lips opened with each puff of slow breath.

Janus went to the cage and swung the door as wide as it would go. He left the window open and put another blanket over Kerry on the bed. He didn't know what else to do.

Kiwi had flown.

# CHAPTER TWENTY-FIVE

ANOTHER WEEK HAD passed, and summer had come into full fruition with heavy green leaves and hot, humid air under a scorching sun by the time Kerry was allowed to leave his room and come down to sit on the back porch in his favorite rocker. He had finally finished Janus's scarf, but had final touches to put on a few more baby clothes.

In another week, it would be safe for him to stop taking the tablets and teas. If the baby came, he'd be big enough to survive, Janus said, and the medicines, if taken in too high of a dose for too long might do more harm than good.

The day before, Caleb and Yosef had packed up to return home, and they planned to leave shortly. Yosef would return to his artist partner in the city and begin the work of starting a court case to free Kerry from his contract or, at the very least, from his obligation to endure his heats with Wilbet.

For his part, Caleb would return to Virona, where he had two alphas anxiously waiting for him and Bekhem. Kerry wasn't dense, and the way Caleb talked about Xan and "our Urho" made it all quite clear that there was something akin to the polyamorous relationships happening up-mountain going on in fair Virona as well. But he didn't ask questions. Who was he to judge?

Caleb came to sit with him on the porch, his all-white ensemble strangely pristine despite the baby's tendency to spit up. He crossed his feet at the ankle and Kerry realized that he was barefoot, as was his wont when he was in the house. The baby must have been

330

sleeping inside because he was alone. "Are you going to be all right?" Caleb asked after he got settled and began to rock.

"Your guess is as good as mine," Kerry said with a smirk as he threaded the needle. "What do you think?"

"You're strong and young. Plus, you love him. That's a bonus."

Kerry glanced Caleb's way. "Even if the babe's not his?"

"Of course." Caleb rocked in the chair. A creak lifted from the boards on the porch. "Will you keep him?"

"The baby or Janus?"

Caleb laughed. "I meant the baby, but I'm happy to talk about the keeping of Janus if you prefer."

"I don't know. About the baby. I don't think I'll love it." He frowned. "My alpha is a bad person. I don't know if I can stand to see his face in this baby's features."

Caleb rocked back and forth with an open expression. Kerry saw no judgment there, so he went on, "My in-laws will love him. They'll spoil him. Give him everything he needs. And if he's an alpha, he'll be the heir."

"I see."

"But I think it'll still be hard," Kerry said. "I suspect that when I see him, hold him, nurse him…I might feel something. I don't think I *want* to feel it, whatever it is."

Caleb nodded but said nothing.

"Do you feel something? When you hold Bekhem?"

"I do. Yes. But I wanted him. And I love his father very much. Well, in my way of loving, which is perhaps different than yours. But he's the best man I know. So…it isn't quite the same." He gave Kerry a sympathetic smile. Not pitying, which would have been so easy and even deserved, but sympathy was so much less condescending. It was at that moment that Kerry decided to like the man despite it all.

"I always wanted to be a pater," Kerry confessed. "Growing up,

I would hold dolls and imagine they were mine. I didn't understand back then that I'd need an alpha to help me make one. But once I got old enough, and Pater explained the facts to me, I was keen on that, too. I wanted to be someone's omega. The lover of someone good and strong."

"Janus is good and strong."

"Is he? He said he wasn't good to you."

Caleb smiled. "No, he was awful to me. And worse to Xan. But he's good deep down, and he's shown that, hasn't he? I believe you'll make him even better."

"He should find an omega who can be—"

"Shh. We don't talk about shoulds when it comes to love. You love him. He loves you. There's no 'should' about it."

"I don't know—"

"I do. We have to work to make our best life out of the broken pieces of ourselves and the world around us, and that's all we can ever do."

"And if that life we make is against the rules?"

"Even better." Caleb grinned sharply.

Kerry's heart rose in his chest with something like hope for the first time in a terribly long time. "Do you believe that?"

"I live it." Then he rose from the rocker, bent low to kiss Kerry on the cheek, and said, "The birth will be easy and the babe healthy. You'll be strong. Wolf-god make it so."

Kerry accepted the blessing as Caleb intended it, grateful to have made a friend.

KERRY'S MISTAKE WASN'T that he forgot to send the Monhundys letters, because he had sent them faithfully every other day, even during the Oat-Flowers-laced confusion following the near miscarriage.

No. This time his mistake was in sending too much information. Oat Flowers and a touch of liquor at night to aid sleep might also have aided in his pen being too free with his in-laws. And the result this time was not a note. But rather the Monhundys themselves, and Dr. Rose, standing on the Monk's House front porch with enough bags to make their plan to stay evident.

Pater alerted Kerry to this fact by stomping up the stairs, speaking loudly, with the Monhundys in tow. "He's right up here in bed where he belongs. Yes, yes. Of course, he can get up and down. No, he's fine enough. Just takin' it easy, and—hey! No need to push past me!"

Kerry sat up in the bed, having returned for a nap after breakfast, and blinked wildly. He wore a white nightshirt and soft, drawstring pajama bottoms, and his hair had to look a mess. His room felt empty without Kiwi, but it was in otherwise good condition. Which was good since the door to his room burst open, and Monte and Lukas, followed by Pater, and then, more politely, Dr. Rose, all rushed in.

Kerry stared at them with wide eyes and an open mouth. He didn't even bother hiding his shock or dismay. This was so unprecedented an action on the Monhundys' part that he didn't know what to do or think. At least Janus had already left for his work with Dr. Crescent, but he'd be back, and then everything would fall apart. Unless he could convince the Monhundys to leave, and he suspected that wasn't likely. Not with the determined expression on Monte's face, and the sharp way Lukas took in the room as a whole.

"What are you doing here?" he finally managed to get out, failing to ward off Monte's kisses all about his face and head. Lukas, for his part, hung back and looked at him with narrow, suspicious eyes. "You never come up here."

"Thought it was about time we did," Lukas said gruffly.

"Oh, your letters worried us so, darling," Monte rushed on. "All this about a near miscarriage and pre-term labor, and Dr. Heelies treating you with pastes and whatnot. It seemed positively barbaric. Dr. Rose was free and willing to make the trip. We wanted him here to attend you for the rest of your pregnancy. And we want to stay to help, too."

"I don't need—I mean, we're fine here. We don't need help. There's a good doctor in residence and—"

"Yes, this 'Dr. Heelies'," Lukas said with a stern expression that cut Kerry to the quick. "I've been looking into him after your letters mentioned your distress. And, well, I think you know what I discovered."

Kerry swallowed hard but shook his head in denial.

"Yes, I think you do," Lukas said coolly.

Kerry shook his head fervently again. Not that he knew why. He should cop to everything now. But…what would happen then?

"Janus Heelies is no doctor. He's barely a nurse. Worse, he's an alpha. It was quite awkward indeed to call up Doxan Heelies to ask after his prestigious beta doctor nephew, only to find that the only nephew he has in Hud's Basin is not only *not* a beta, but not a doctor either. He's a nurse and an alpha. An embarrassment, really. With absolutely no medical experience in your particular deformity."

Monte's eyes had grown wider and wider as Lukas talked. Clearly, the man hadn't shared this information with his omega yet. He turned back to Kerry with a look of astonished rage rising beneath his usual polite mask. "You *lied* to us? To stay here in this shithole with *him?*"

Kerry thought it was probably best to say nothing at all. He couldn't defend himself, so he simply stared up at them defiantly. He hoped. He might have been too sick and scared to appear defiant, though.

"Come now," Dr. Rose said with a firm quietness that Kerry appreciated. "Let's not lose sight of our priorities. The child must come first, and in this state, any upset to Kerry is a risk to the child. We must attempt to postpone the labor for as long as possible. Every hour counts at this stage. In some cases, every minute. The babe's body is undergoing the finalization process and interrupting that now could be deadly."

Lukas's jaw flexed and released, but he bowed his head and stepped into the hallway. Monte stared at Kerry a bit longer with a glow of hatred in his eyes, and he whispered, "I will find out why you did this. And you will be held accountable for any harm that comes to this baby."

"Fuck you," Kerry whispered back.

Monte's face trembled with fury, and he came at Kerry, but Dr. Rose swiftly stepped between them and Pater grabbed hold of his arm. "I'm not leaving this house until this baby is born," Monte said. "And then it will go with me. You? I haven't decided yet about you."

Kerry didn't flinch at the threat. The worst wasn't over yet. They'd soon know the full truth about Janus, and that was bound to be ugly in more ways than one. Gathering his strength and calm, Kerry turned to Dr. Rose and said, "I suppose you want to examine me?"

"I do."

"My alpha won't like that."

"Your alpha is in prison and has no recourse," he said, confused. "You've never protested before."

"My alpha lives here in this house. And he won't like you touching me," Kerry said calmly.

"Wilbet Monhundy is in this house?" the doctor said with concern. He turned to his bag and began to fish around inside. He pulled out a thermometer for the mouth. "Have you been feverish?" He looked toward Zeke who lingered by the doorway, refusing to leave Kerry alone, and keeping an eye on the Monhundys who stood whispering furiously in the hallway. "Has he been quite right in the head?"

"Yes, perfectly," Pater said. "And no, his alpha won't like you touching him without permission. I advise that you don't. He's already been examined today, and he's fine."

Dr. Rose stared between them like they'd lost their minds.

And then, as if he'd sensed something was amiss from all the way up-mountain, the downstairs door banged open, and Janus's heavy footsteps fell.

"Whose car is that parked out front?" he called out, his voice cheerful and in good humor. So, he hadn't sensed their peril then. "More surprise guests?"

His footsteps sounded on the stairs. Pater stared at Kerry in horror, his mouth open and fear frozen all over his face. Kerry figured he probably looked the same way. Especially since he knew certain things Pater didn't. Like...

"You!" Monte's voice shook the entire upper story. "You were at the hotel."

"*You're* the alpha nurse?" Lukas roared.

"Kerry!" Janus called, and there was the sound of a scuffle in the hallway. Dr. Rose moved toward the door, and between his body and Pater's, Kerry could only make out the white of Janus's shirt and the black of his pants. He seemed to be grappling with someone, but Kerry couldn't see who.

With a pounding heart and no grace whatsoever, he forced himself out of bed and toward the doorway. Dr. Rose and Pater had moved into the hall, and the shouts rising from the scuffle showed that Monte was pounding on Janus, shouting at him, and Lukas was trying to tear him away. "Darling, please, you'll hurt yourself.

Monte! Stop!"

And Janus was holding back with all he had to keep from punching the man. Kerry could tell by the red of his face, the balls of his fists, and the growl coming from deep in his chest. Dr. Rose had taken up position st Janus's back, trying to keep the tussle from moving toward the stairs where a tumble would be a disaster. And Pater was shouting, "Lukas, get your man in order! I will go for the police!"

As if the police could do anything. By the time Pater left and came back with them, they'd have murdered each other.

Kerry stepped farther into the hallway, his stomach pushing up against the fray. "Stop!" he cried out. His deep voice cracked hard. "Stop it now!"

Everyone stopped moving, except Monte, who took the opportunity to punch Janus square in the jaw before Lukas pulled him back and away. "You filthy mongrel. Fucking our son's omega. Getting involved in his life," Monte hissed, squirming against Lukas's hold, his hands out, eager to get his claws back into Janus's flesh.

"Kerry," Janus said, his eyes darting from the danger he perceived in the Monhundys to his omega. Because that's how Kerry knew he saw him. As *his* omega. "Get back in your room and lock the door. Don't let anyone inside until I say it's okay."

Kerry shook his head. "And what do you plan to do? Beat them to death?"

"I wouldn't mind."

"Everyone must calm down," Dr. Rose shouted, his formerly fresh and pomaded hair flopping around madly. "You need to calm down before this man loses this baby."

Monte and Lukas stopped their grappling, and Janus carefully took Kerry's hand, looking into his eyes. "You're all right?" he asked.

"Yes."

"I need to check."

"All right."

"He didn't touch you, did he?" He turned to glare at Dr. Rose, who blinked in affronted confusion at this accusation.

"No." Kerry smiled at Dr. Rose. "I told him you wouldn't like that."

"And who, pray tell, is *he* to get any say in what happens to your body? You are contracted to my son, and in his absence, I have control over you, and—"

"No." Janus lifted his hand as if stoppering up Monte's words. "He's a human being. Not a slave."

"The court and the Holy Church of Wolf will have something to say about that."

"Let them," Janus said with a snarl. "Go on then. Go get a court order, or a priest, or someone up here right now to make this man do anything at all." He stepped forward menacingly. "I will tear each one of them apart if they touch him. He's mine. And no one else's."

"That child in that whore's womb is my son's!" Monte exclaimed.

"Good luck taking him if Kerry wants him," Janus said darkly. "Once he's born, he'll be under my protection, too."

"Your protection," Monte scoffed. "Did you hear that Lukas?"

"I did." Lukas was pale, but his expression was more shocked understanding than rage. "I think we should go to our rooms and calm down, Monte. Before you say or do something we can't take back."

Monte gasped. "What? Are you…Lukas, this baby is our chance at a do-over!"

Lukas bent close and said sharply. "Yes. This is likely our only chance, Monte. Now shut your mouth. This very second."

He gripped Monte's arm tightly and then seemed to flounder a moment in confusion of where to go.

"This way," Pater said quietly. He motioned them down the hall away from Kerry's room and to one of the open rooms on the opposite side. He didn't give his usual spiel about the lights, or the candles, or mention the bags, which they had abandoned at the foot of the stairs from what Kerry could see. He closed the door on the two of them and then turned to Janus as if awaiting instructions.

"If you'd like, Dr. Rose," Janus said with a bit of an edge to his voice that showed his struggle for calm, "you can come into Kerry's room and watch my examination of him from the distance of the doorway."

Dr. Rose nodded his agreement to that offer, and Kerry let Janus guide him back into his room, where Janus promptly pulled him into his arms and scented him from neck to chest and back again. Then as soon as Janus was satisfied that he was, in fact, untouched and healthy, he guided Kerry onto the bed.

"There, sweetheart," he whispered. "Now, slide under the covers and take your pants off. I'll be gentle. And he won't see a thing."

Kerry didn't take his eyes away from Janus as he did as Janus asked, submitted to the internal exam, and then the external, too. He rejected the opportunity to listen to the baby's heartbeat through the stethoscope. An option that Dr. Rose had never allowed him, always pressing the device to his ears without asking. And then Janus turned to Dr. Rose with a stern expression on his face. "So? Are you satisfied?"

"I am." Dr. Rose stared between them. "How did you…I mean, when did you know?"

"Know what?" Janus asked.

Kerry stared at him blankly.

"You mean, you don't know? I mean to say, it's not the case? How can it be that you act so much like *Érosgápe*, and yet…" He shrugged. "You don't sense a pull?"

Kerry and Janus turned startled glances on each other. Janus crossed his arms over his chest and turned narrowed eyes on Dr. Rose. "He's mine. That's all I know or care about. But that's come to us slowly. We're not *Érosgápe*."

Dr. Rose frowned, confusion descending on his features. "If you say so," he said uncertainly. "I'm sure you'd know."

"Yes," Kerry said, staring up at Janus wonderingly. "We'd know."

JANUS COULD ONLY assume that the stress of the Monhundys' arrival was to blame.

Kerry's pains started up again in the middle of the night. Strong this time, with a rush of water and blood, too, that told the full tale. There would be no stopping the birth now. They had to hope the child was strong enough and ready to breathe on his own.

Zeke—unwilling to trust Dr. Rose and worried that Janus, as Kerry's lover, would lose his wits if something went wrong—sent for Dr. Crescent, and, so, as Kerry labored, there were far too many cooks in the kitchen, so to speak. There was Dr. Rose with his steady, unemotional suggestions, Janus with his panicked focus on Kerry's every pain, and Dr. Crescent with his robust, down-home, all-will-be-well attitude that, on most days, left Janus feeling secure and happy, but on this day drove him to want to murder the man.

"I want to go to the lake," Kerry cried out as another pain gripped him. It'd been an hour and a half since Dr. Crescent had arrived, and the babe seemed no closer to being born. "Please. Let me go to the lake. I *want* the lake."

"Sweetheart, you're all right. I'm here with you."

"I said I want the lake," Kerry bit out with a hint of frenzy in his eyes. "Now. I want it now."

Dr. Crescent looked away from where he was keeping an eye down below for any evidence of the baby's head crowning. "You want to birth in the lake?"

"Yes. Please. In the lake. Now."

"Kerry, it's the middle of the night, and you're too close to—" Dr. Crescent interrupted Janus before he could say more.

"Then into the lake we'll go, lad," Dr. Crescent said with a silencing clap on Janus's shoulder. "Whatever makes our omega feel strong and ready." He caught Janus's eyes. "Understand? What do I always tell you about births?"

"Attitude is half the battle of it." But that seemed so much easier to believe when it was someone else's omega giving birth. When it was his own, and that omega wanted to go down the dark path of the forest, with wildcats and their young, and who knew what else, to a lake in the middle of the night, while his pater and his in-laws hovered outside the door judging every decision and finding it lacking, well...

Janus blushed as though anyone could have heard his thoughts. Kerry wasn't his omega, and this child wasn't his either. Just because they'd grown intimate over the last few months, and his sense of ownership of Kerry's body had grown exponentially with each touch, kiss, and caress, didn't mean that this man was his in any way, shape, or form. Never mind that *he* belonged solely to Kerry now, whether the man wanted him or not. Legally, he had no rights no matter what either of them wanted, or what anyone had said in the hall earlier in the night.

"The lake," Kerry said again, rolling onto his side and making to get out of the bed. "Now. I want to go now. It's important. I need to be there."

Dr. Crescent gave Janus a meaningful look, and even though it went against his better judgment, Janus helped a sweaty, naked

Kerry out of bed. Dr. Crescent led the way, and between Dr. Rose on one side, and Janus on the other, they ventured out of the room.

"Where are you taking him? What's happening?" Monte asked, his eyes red and tissues balled up in his hand like he'd been crying.

Zeke swerved a glance at Janus and then said, "To the lake, then?"

And how the old man knew, Janus didn't know. Perhaps he'd overheard, or maybe Kerry had shared these plans with him long ago. Whatever the case, Zeke held the Monhundys back from following or crowding, explaining the situation, long enough for them to get Kerry down the stairs and out the back door.

They made it down to the lake under the light of the half-moon. Janus noticed, not for the first time, how bright the moon was in the sky up in the mountains. So much clearer and whiter than in the city where the electric lights dimmed it.

"Wolf-god, please smile on this birth," he asked, taking in the white half-moon, the wolf's teeth bared in either joy or anger. He prayed for joy.

It took longer than he'd like to get Kerry down to the water. They had to pause several times for increasingly painful contractions. But once they were there, Dr. Crescent shucked his shoes, and his pants, leaving on just his underwear and shirt, and forged into the shallows like it was the most normal thing on earth.

Kerry, for his part, lunged as best as he could toward the water, too. Janus let him go, so long as Dr. Crescent had a grip on his arm, and as soon as he'd shucked his own shirt and shoes, he went in, too. His pants clung to him, but he didn't have time to wait. Kerry was determined to wade in, and Dr. Rose seemed uninterested in following at all, much less in all his clothes.

Janus got his arms around Kerry's waist and guided him out until the shallows dropped off to a deeper area up to their waists. Kerry groaned and sank down, letting his sweaty body dip into the night-cooled water. He whimpered as another pain took him, and Janus held on to him, running soothing fingers through his hair, as he squirmed, trying to get away from the pain.

"This is worse than the day on the beach, the day when—"

"Shh," Janus cut him off with a furtive glance at Dr. Rose by the shoreline. He noticed the bobbing light of flashlights on the trail. So, Zeke had made them wait long enough to get better light to guide them down. That was good. It had given them time to get into the water without the Monhundys' protests. "I know it hurts, sweetheart. We're almost done. I hope."

Kerry took hold of Janus's hand and gripped it hard. A shout ripped from him as another contraction took hold. They were coming faster now. Faster and faster.

"You promised you wouldn't let anything hurt me ever again," Kerry panted as this one released him. His eyes were dark and wide, and exhausted pain was written all over his face.

"Oh, sweetheart, if I could take this from you, I would. I'd do this ten times over if it would spare you the pain, and I'd—"

Kerry's cry echoed over the lake, bouncing off the mountains. It reminded Janus viscerally of the day he'd found Kerry crawling out from the wilderness naked and bleeding in an attempt to prevent this very moment from ever happening.

"I can't!" Kerry screamed.

"You can."

"No. I won't."

"You can," Janus said calmly. "I have you in my arms. The lake has you. Let go. Let him out. Push."

Kerry huffed and breathed and finally pushed with all his strength. Dr. Crescent had moved to squat down in the water with just his head above, his hands out between Kerry's legs, feeling, seeking...

His face lit up. "That's the head now. I feel it. Just another big push, Kerry, and it'll be over, and you can hold this wee one."

Kerry started to sob. "I don't want to," he whispered, turning fearful eyes on Janus. "I don't want to—ahhhhh!" He screamed again and pushed hard.

Dr. Crescent scrambled forward and almost went over, but he rose up fast, holding the baby triumphantly in front of him. Water ran off the child as the cord between him and Kerry pulsed and bulged, and then slowed. The child was silent, its head flopped down, and Janus's heart sank like a stone.

Kerry whimpered. "Is he...why isn't he...oh, wolf-god, he's dead?"

"No," Janus said, taking the baby from Dr. Crescent. "No, he's not dead. He can't be. No."

The baby didn't move.

"Turn him upside down, right fast," Dr. Crescent said. "Press him to your chest, belly to your sternum. Let him hear your heart. That's good." Then he slapped the baby's bottom, and the baby jolted against Janus's chest, his tiny scream splitting the night air.

Kerry started to cry, lifting his hands for him. "Please, please," he whispered, tears running down his face. "Please."

Janus passed the baby, who was wailing in earnest now, into Kerry's waiting hands, shocked when Kerry started wailing, too. He held him stiffly, away from his body, sobbing with his eyes screwed up tight and shaking like a leaf.

Dr. Crescent seemed to know what to do, though, and guided the baby to Kerry's chest and held him there until Kerry was doing it for himself. Holding the baby and rocking in the water, crying and whimpering. Exhaustion and relief flooded through them all.

Kerry scented his son, leaning in close, and then he startled, his eyes turning to Janus. He took a deep breath and groaned.

"What?" Janus asked, crouching down to get close to them both. "What's happening?"

And that's when he scented it, too. The difference between a combination of berries and musk and sheer perfection. Heaven. *Home.* The world tipped on its axis, and the sky was beneath his feet. When he could breathe again, he found himself wrapped around Kerry and the baby, his nose buried in Kerry's neck, his tongue tasting the perfection of his mate.

"Well, I'll be wolf-goddamned," Dr. Crescent whispered from somewhere nearby. "Fuck me and the horse I rode in on."

Janus pulled back and gazed at Kerry first in shock, and then in recognition. "You," he said, reaching for him, kissing his mouth hard. "It's you."

"Yes," Kerry whispered. "It's me."

When the sound of splashing came from behind them, Janus was in no mood to deal with Monte Monhundy's arrogance, and he turned to roar at the man who would aggravate his *Érosgápe* so soon after birthing a child.

"What?"

"They're bonded," Dr. Crescent said. "*Érosgápe.* Unbelievable."

Janus turned his back on the now cowering man and then turned his attention solely on Kerry. "Let's get you out of the water. I need to check you, and he needs to feed."

Kerry stared at Janus in wonder, the air around them thick with new knowing. He nodded slowly, and Janus guided his beloved toward the shore, keeping one hand on his back and the other on the babe in his arms. He glowered menacingly at everyone but Zeke, though it took all he had to let Zeke approach to see his grandson.

Monte and Lukas, he kept away, and Dr. Crescent didn't even try to approach, laughing under his breath in shocked amazement. "I'll be wolf-god damned," he kept whispering. "Just wait until I tell my Fan about this."

The baby didn't cry anymore once Janus helped settle him on

Kerry's milky nipple. He sucked half-heartedly and then more aggressively, and Kerry took turns staring down at him, and then up at Janus, with a wild mix of emotions swimming in his beautiful dark eyes.

"It's going to be all right," Janus said firmly. "Now that I've found you. It's all going to be made right."

# CHAPTER TWENTY-SIX

"**B**UT THE CHILD is ours," Monte said, banging his fist on the dining room table, his cheeks going as red as his hair. "He belongs, by rights, to Wilbet."

Law was clear about a few things: babes belonged to alphas, despite omegas being the ones to grow and birth them, and then feed them with their bodies. The laws around a babe born to an imprisoned alpha were less clear, and Kerry wished that Yosef were here with them to give his opinion about things.

"He's not leaving this house," Janus said ominously, his hand firmly on Kerry's lower back and his fist clenched on the tabletop.

Kerry held the child closer, bending low to scent his head. He didn't smell like Wilbet. He didn't smell like anything bad at all. Not as wonderful as Janus, but still appealing and sweet. Better even than Caleb's baby had smelled, or Charlie's little Ellis, though all infants were delicious for a reason. This reason.

"You wanted me to chestfeed him for two years," Kerry said quietly, still tired from his ordeal and tender below from the expulsion of a child of such a great size. That was one obvious way the baby *was* like his father: he was big. Kerry tried not to think about that.

"In the city. With us. You *agreed.*" Monte was the one doing all the talking. Lukas sat at the table in silence, a force to be sure, but a silent one. He didn't offer his thoughts or opinions, but let Monte make the arguments. Kerry didn't know what to make of Wilbet's father's silence. He was afraid to think it might be good.

"That was before he knew about me," Janus said.

"He'd already met you!"

The timeline around Janus's arrival and the two of them becoming involved had been documented now, laid out like some kind of map on the table. A single line, marking dates and activities—the sexual bonding written out in only the loosest euphemisms or technical of terms—showing the start to finish of their stumble into understanding.

"The babe obscured his scent," Dr. Crescent said, leaning back and putting his hands over his round stomach. His grizzled smile was easy like they weren't all seething with barely restrained tension around the table.

Those in attendance were Kerry, Janus, Zeke, Dr. Crescent, Monte, and Lukas, and Dr. Rose, of course. He nodded at Dr. Crescent's statement, adding, "It's happened, but rarely. An omega impregnated with his *Érosgápe*'s child will obviously take on a different scent, but it isn't obscuring in nature since the child is his *Érosgápe*'s son. An omega impregnated with another alpha's child, though…well, it can obscure the scent enough to prevent the full imprint from taking place until after the babe's birth. I read about another such occurrence in medical school. It's rare, though. Quite uncommon."

There were also about six dozen people out on the front lawn—all of them patients of Janus's and Dr. Crescent's. Charlie, Dax, and Ellis were among them, along with Whitehoul and his omegas, and others. Someone had sounded the alarm that city folk were trying to take a mountain omega's baby, and that mountain omega was the *Érosgápe* of the man known to them as Dr. Janus Heelies.

The last time Kerry had looked out the front windows at them, they'd had shovels, axes, and a general air of "don't fuck with us." He found himself reassured by that almost as much as he was by Janus's strong presence at his side. He suspected Fan had sent out a call when Dr. Crescent's note had arrived declaring Kerry safe, the babe healthy, and the surprising *Érosgápe* news. No doubt Crow had also explained about the citified in-laws here to make trouble. And Fan would know what to do from there, and had, no doubt, done it.

"So, what does this mean?" Zeke asked.

"It means Monte and I will leave for the city, where we'll draw up the documents to nullify the contract between Kerry and our son," Lukas said, finally breaking his silence.

"What?" Monte swiveled his head, eyes wide. "No!"

"You know the laws as well as I do. The *Érosgápe* bond takes precedence over all other commitments or promises."

"Fine, but that child is ours," Monte hissed.

"No, he's not," Lukas said. "He's better off with Kerry. We had our chance and look what came of it. I don't like what this pregnancy is doing to you, Monte, what it's done to us. I don't like what we did to obtain this child, and if Kerry can find it in his heart to love the boy, then *he* deserves to raise him. He'll do a better job of it than we did."

"We can't be blamed for Wilbet's behavior. We couldn't have known. And Kerry won't love him! He *doesn't* love him. Look at his face. It says everything."

Kerry tried to keep his expression flat, but he knew it was true. Guilt seeped out of him like a leaky balloon. He didn't love the baby. He hadn't even named it yet. But some part of him wasn't willing to hand him over to Lukas and Monte either. Maybe they weren't responsible for Wilbet being a monster, but then again maybe they were. It didn't matter, though, because…

"*I* love him," Janus said with no room to brook an argument. "No matter how Kerry feels, I'll love this babe enough for the both of us."

Dr. Crescent let out a soft sigh as if he was holding back strong emotions. Then he took out a handkerchief and blew his nose.

Zeke piped up, "And I love him, too. He'll be safe here. Loved. Taken care of. We'll raise 'im up right."

Monte's jaw clenched and unclenched, a volcanic explosion on the horizon, when he suddenly crumpled, sobbing on the table. Lukas rubbed his back, saying nothing and looking up at the ceiling, blinking rapidly as if holding back his own tears.

"I think that's the end of it," Dr. Rose said, standing up. "I'd have your lawyer draw up an agreement before they change their mind, but we all know this is the right decision."

"Excuse me?" Lukas said, annoyance with Dr. Rose's audacity snapping him from his despair.

"I said what I said," Dr. Rose murmured. "If you'll excuse me, I'll pack my things. I assume we'll be going right away?"

Lukas nodded. Then with some pains, he managed to gather Monte into his arms and carried him from the dining room. His back was straight and his head up, attempting to maintain dignity, but Monte had lost all of it. He clung like a child and sobbed, broken-hearted and lost. Kerry almost felt sorry for him. He knew what it was like to see one's future hopes dashed into shards on the floor.

But just then the baby started to whine, and Kerry's attention diverted from sympathy to the burden of paterhood. He undid his shirt, pressed the baby to his chest, and closed his eyes as the sharp suction took hold. The milk releasing felt like sharp, stinging needles in his armpits and chest that gradually faded away. Dr. Crescent said this was normal.

Kerry's eyes popped open when Janus nosed at his neck, scenting him again, the way he had for hours after the birth. The dining room was empty now—just the two of them and the baby. Janus nosed at his hair, his jaw, and then down to his chest, scenting the milk as it went into the baby's mouth.

"What will we call him?" Janus asked when he finished, a blissfully peaceful expression on his face.

Kerry swallowed hard and shrugged. "I haven't thought about it."

"All these months and not a single idea?"

Kerry smiled gently, surprised to find the answer there in the back of his mind. "I suppose I thought Monte and Lukas would name him, but…"

"But?"

"But when I was sewing clothes for him, in my mind, I'd think of him as…" He broke off, feeling oddly shy now that he had to speak the name aloud.

"As?"

"Tristan."

"Tristan Heelies," Janus said. "I like it. Do you want a middle name?"

Kerry's throat went tight, and he squeezed Tristan tighter than he should, making the baby pop off in protest. Kerry relaxed his hands quickly and fought a shock of tears as he asked, "You want him to have your name?"

Janus looked up from where he was guiding Tristan back to Kerry's nipple. "Of course. Yes. Whose name should he have? Yours? I suppose if that's what you want. Tristan Monkburn is a fine name, too."

Kerry's chin began to wobble. His eyes were wet, and he knew tears would slip down at any moment.

"Oh, for wolf-god's sake," Janus murmured, leaning close to wipe the tears away. "As if I'd ever let our child have *his* name. He's ours now. They walked away from the bargaining table. Lukas knew they'd lost the moment he saw me, and Monte knows it now, too. It's over, sweetheart. You, me, and Tristan are a family. And Zeke. Can't forget him."

"Tristan Ezekial Heelies?"

Janus nodded and kissed Kerry's forehead. "Perfect. Let's go upstairs. We both could use a nap. It's been a long day and a half."

Kerry didn't protest, letting Janus help him up the stairs and into his room. They both tried to ignore the sobs coming from the room down the hall, and instead curled up in Kerry's narrow bed together, the baby, still suckling, in between.

The golden cage stood empty in the middle of the room. The window was still open as if Kiwi might fly back into the house, and make his way back inside. But Kerry knew he wouldn't.

A caged thing, once freed, never wanted to go back again.

He curled into the arms of *his* freedom, his lover, his *Érosgápe*, and breathed in deep. For the first time in a very long time, peace settled over him, and he knew, deep down, he was truly safe.

And loved.

# EPILOGUE

## Three weeks after Tristan's birth

*Dear Janus,*

*Congratulations! That is the first order of things, isn't it? A hearty blessing on you and Kerry on the felicitous event of discovering you are Érosgápe. I am on the one hand astounded by the news, but upon the other not at all shocked. Reflection has made a few key things evident, and I recognize that, yes, there were signs even to me.*

*As for our business, I'm glad to write up the custody arrangement and ensure that it is signed. I will also cancel my dealings with the omega freedom groups on Kerry's behalf. I admit, my sole regret at finding you are Érosgápe is the loss to the freedom groups who were ready to champion his cause. The precedent set, should they have obtained a humane ruling, would have put other omegas in a much better position going forward.*

*As it is, Érosgápe you are, and the laws around that are clear. Other omegas will have to wait until another desperate man is in a position to fight the brutal laws. As science progresses and birth rates improve, as well as survival rates for omegas, I pray that the draconian measures will be put aside permanently.*

*Rosen and I are including a small gift for your new son. It's adoption paperwork. I had to look through many historical documents to find a good source for a clear-cut adoption with no loopholes. As you know, unlike the pre-Great Death days, there is rarely a need for adoption procedures, but understandably we want to keep this all binding, lest Wilbet himself, or his parents, change their minds.*

*Please sign the papers, have Kerry do the same, and I will handle the signatures from the Monhundy end of things. Have no fear. I will ensure this gets handled.*

*Give my best to Kerry and his pater. Kiss the babe for me.*

*Yosef Deckel*

Janus set aside the letter and broke open the package that had been delivered at the same time. This was from Caleb, Xan, and Urho, according to the tag, and inside were several soft toys, blankets, and more for the baby. There was also a letter:

*Dearest Janus and Kerry,*

*My heart sings with the news! I wish I could say that I saw it all in advance, but I was as blind to your Érosgápe link as you. I'm so pleased that it takes both Kerry and the sweet child out of jeopardy in one fell swoop. Please accept these gifts for the wee Tristan, and the camera as well as a contracting/bonding gift. Xan insists that you'll love it and has included film, too. Send it back to us to be developed, and we'll return the pictures to you. It will be great fun!*

*Bekhem grows daily, as do my other delicious babes. Riki has started spelling now. He's a bright little thing. Like his pater, if I do say so myself. And Levi has learned to run, but it's full speed or nothing. I'm afraid he's going to run off a cliff, but Urho says the exercise is good for him. Exercise, yes, but he should pay more attention to where he puts his tiny body!*

*I wish I had more time to write, but I am already going to be late to the organizational meeting for the First Annual*

*Mountain Medical Charity Auction. Expect an influx of help-ful cash soon.*

*Sending my love to you, Kerry, and Tristan,*
*Caleb*

Janus showed the notes to Kerry as they read by the fire that evening. Zeke had already gone to bed, and the baby lay curled up in Kerry's lap, nursing—as he always seemed to be doing. Janus held Kerry's feet in his lap, massaging the arches and heels, and wearing the scarf Kerry had made for him. It was soft and a little lumpy in a few places, but Janus loved it.

Kerry looked toward the stack of things Caleb had sent and said, "We'll never be able to pay him back for all of that."

"They're family, sweetheart. It was a gift."

Kerry nodded, scented Tristan's head, and then gave Janus a smile. "This is nice, isn't it?"

"Perfect."

Kerry tilted his head. "What are we going to do for money, though? With the official dissolution of my contract coming soon, I don't assume they'll be sending anything more our way. Not now that you're adopting him."

"My uncle sent a letter as well," Janus revealed. "Mine is the only *Érosgápe* bond in the family since his own to his omega George. It seems he's rather thrilled by it and has offered me a large sum as a bonding gift. It will hold us for several years. Hopefully, until I'm earning something more substantial as the doctor around these parts. Rumor has it, Dr. Crescent would like to retire before long."

"But living off another man's charity is…"

"There's always the boarding house income. Now that Tristan's arrived, safe and sound, your pater can open the rooms back up again."

Kerry nodded thoughtfully. "I've become rather spoiled living here so quietly with just you and pater." He rubbed his nose against the top of Tristan's head. He hadn't kissed him yet, as far as Janus knew, but he was growing closer and closer to that action. "And now this one."

"He's a good baby," Janus said. "An observant, quiet boy."

"A hungry one, too," Kerry said, sighing, and switching Tristan from one nipple to the other. Kerry's wet, abandoned nipple remained exposed, and it called to Janus. He loved to sample the sweet milk Kerry produced, and the scent tempted him to lean forward now to taste it.

Kerry closed his shirt a bit, hiding the nipple from view. Janus smiled at himself. As much as he longed to bury himself deep inside Kerry again, to relish their *Érosgápe* connection now that they'd discovered it, he needed to wait until his beloved finished healing. And though suckling from Kerry was sweet, he also knew, given the tentative affection that was growing between Kerry and his previously unwanted child, Janus shouldn't do anything to color the caregiving experience for Kerry in any way.

"He's going to be a good boy," Janus said reassuringly, knowing how often Kerry needed to hear it. "He's going to be a good man, too."

Kerry nodded, a wrinkle appearing in his brow. After expelling a heavy sigh, and as if it took effort, Kerry released his frown until his forehead was smooth again. "Another month of quiet would be good, and then we can open the place up for fall boarders. We'll have the usual rush of folks escaping the flu season in winter. We'll be fine."

"Yes, we'll be all right," Janus agreed. He rubbed Kerry's feet a bit more vigorously and then bent low to kiss one toe. "I love you."

Kerry smiled, his dark eyes softening with trust and joy. "I love you, too."

The baby farted, and they both laughed.

### *Thirteen months after Tristan's birth*

"FEED! FEED. PLEASE, feed. Please," Kerry whispered urgently to Tristan. His nipple looked puffy with unspent milk, and Janus knew that when a baby began to wean from chestfeeding it could be unpleasant for the pater.

"It'll pass," Janus said reassuringly, stepping into the room. "I know it's uncomfortable now, but in a few days your body will learn to make less…or if he's given it up, none at all."

Kerry stared at him with bleak eyes, holes of pain.

Janus's gut tangled into a pile of writhing snakes. "What's wrong?"

"He needs to feed."

"He's well old enough to eat on his own. Your pater was giving him mashed peas the other day. You can't expect to nurse him forever."

"If he stops feeding from me…" Kerry trailed off, closed his eyes, and gritted his teeth. "If he quits, my heat will come back."

Janus's stomach went from lightly roiling to full-on nausea. He hadn't considered that.

Kerry tried to push his nipple into Tristan's mouth again, but the little one was having none of it. He turned his face away and flailed out with his hand, his stubborn little jaw set.

"You can't make him feed, Kerry. And you can't stop him from growing," Janus finally said, taking Tristan from Kerry and pushing the baby's sweaty curls off his forehead. He put him down on the ground, watching as he rolled and crawled with great determination toward his blanket and the pile of soft toys Caleb had sent. "There has to be another solution."

"I'm scared," Kerry said miserably, wiping a hand over his face.

"I know you wouldn't hurt me, but heats have always been…" Kerry shivered. "And I'm afraid it will change what we have if…if it hurts and…I can't go through that again. Losing everything I thought I had. The whole…wolf-god damned thing." He blinked, and his voice went deeper, darker. "Forgive me. Please. I'm so sorry for being scared of this."

"You don't have to apologize to me, sweetheart. Of course, you're scared. But we can't stop it from coming, and so we'll have to promise each other to do our best. I never want to hurt you."

Kerry nodded, still miserable, his eyes downcast and sad.

Janus chucked his chin up. "I love you. Heat is supposed to be a blessed union between *Érosgápe*. We'll be fine."

Kerry swung his arms around Janus's neck and held on. Janus held tight, too, praying to wolf-god that his sweet, traumatized omega would find ecstasy in his arms. The heat would come regardless, and so would orgasm—which, without love, could be a hollow, relentless pleasure. It would be up to Janus to bring the joy.

It was clear that Kerry was too nervous about it by far.

### Fifteen months after Tristan's birth

KERRY SAT WITH Fan having tea and letting the man play with Tristan when the sharp pinpricks of oncoming heat first began. It was a relentless stinging under his skin that he knew wouldn't fade no matter how many cold showers he took. This was the sign that had let him know it was time to alert the Monhundys that he'd need transport to the prison very soon.

Now everything was different. He didn't look forward to the heat, exactly. He wouldn't go *that* far. But the stone of horror that had rolled around in his gut for far too long had dissolved over the last several months of Janus's reassurances. His devoted alpha had sworn that a heat between them would be like nothing Kerry had ever experienced before.

He trusted Janus implicitly, and so he had to trust him in this, too.

"Fan," he said cautiously, as if talking too loudly or quickly might trigger the heat to come on faster. He had time. He still had plenty of time. "Fan, I need to go home. I think I need to prepare for a few days' respite. The heat is starting under my skin."

Fan got up from where he rolled on the floor with chubby Tristan, and promptly went to the front door, opened it, and yelled down to the stables. "Janus! Come quickly!"

"Don't scare him like that," Kerry said, laughing. He rose carefully, pushing his hair behind his ears, and then bent to gather Tristan and his baby things. "He'll think that—"

The door burst open, and Janus came racing in, almost skidding to a comical stop in the middle of the room. "What's wrong?" he said, eyes casting around for the trouble. Fear left his face as he saw Kerry and Tristan, alive and well, on the floor picking up toys to go home. Tristan, for his part, was chewing a toy, but that was his way of helping.

"My heat's coming," Kerry said. "Not immediately," he amended, raising his hand to ward off Janus lifting him up and carrying him away to fuck him silly. "But soon. We have time to prepare."

Janus grabbed up the baby, all the things, and then helped Kerry up, too. "Let's go."

Kerry laughed. "We have time."

"I know, but…let's go." He shifted awkwardly, and Kerry shook his head, still laughing.

"It's not like we need to practice."

"Yes, we do," Janus said. "And your pater is going to have to watch this little one for a few days at least."

"I can help, too," Fan said. "Have Zeke bring him up to me when he needs a break." Then he ushered the little family to the door. "Have fun, you two. I always loved heats so much when I was your age. All that potential. So much fun."

Kerry didn't bother telling Fan that they'd agreed in advance to use alpha condoms for the foreseeable future. Kerry wasn't ready to undergo pregnancy or birth again, and Janus was in no rush either.

He hugged Fan as he left, accepting his best wishes, and then took Tristan on his hip, and Janus's hand to walk home together.

Already a family.

"DO YOU THINK they'll hear us?" Kerry asked, tossing a glance back toward the dining room where the cluster of two betas, one *Érosgápe* couple, and a solitary, elderly omega were still eating their supper.

"Don't worry about that," Janus said, his heart aching at Kerry's vulnerable tone.

Over the few days, they'd spread the word in the house that Kerry's heat was coming, and two alpha boarders had chosen to leave before their vacation was up, not wanting to submit themselves to the frustration of scenting what they couldn't have. But those who remained below were only supposed to stay one or two more nights, and had decided to brave the commotion that the heat would no doubt cause.

The *Érosgápe* couple seemed excited about it, no doubt planning to let the heat scents arouse them to their own heights of passion. The betas, for the most part, were immune to the scents, but would definitely not be deaf to the sounds. Janus pitied them the most. Their sleep would undoubtedly be disturbed. Zeke had offered to give them their final nights at half-price to make up for it.

"At the prison, they watched," Kerry said as the bedroom door shut behind them both. He rubbed at his arms and shuddered, the heat coming on faster and faster as the minutes passed. Soon he'd be delirious, and Janus would have to act.

He needed to help Kerry calm down before it came to that.

"No one is going to watch us here. You're safe."

Kerry squeezed himself tightly, and Janus stood across from him with his arms open wide. Kerry stared at him and then dared a small smile. "I'm safe with *you*," he countered. "Always safe with you."

As Kerry moved into his arms, Janus whispered, "I can still tell them to go. Pack their bags. Get out of here. They'd leave."

"I know," Kerry whispered back, a huff of laughter following his words. "I can imagine how you'd be. They'd run out without getting their things."

Janus nodded. "If you need that…"

Kerry shook his head. "I'm all right. Just hold me. I'll forget about them soon enough."

Janus held Kerry tighter. "We don't need the money if that's what's stopping you from letting me turn them out."

"I know. It's that I want to prove to myself that I can do this. I'm safe here in our home. With you." Kerry trembled in his arms. "It's coming now. I can feel it."

"Don't be frightened, sweetheart. I've got you."

Janus helped divest Kerry of his clothes. He wouldn't need them for a few days. His stomach held stretch marks from the rapid growth of Tristan within, and Janus loved those smooth, silvery lines. He ran his fingers over them and left kisses as he knelt to tug Kerry's shoes and pants off, tossing them over his shoulder. The shoes landed with clunks, and Kerry laughed.

Janus grinned up at him, pleased that his sweet omega could find humor now.

"Now you," Kerry said, helping with Janus's clothes, but hindering more than anything. He was shaking so hard now that Janus knew he was resisting the heat. It was pointless, though. The heat would come.

361

Janus guided Kerry to their big bed across from the fireplace and helped him onto the mattress. He slipped in next to him, pulled his body close and whispered. "Just let yourself go, sweetheart. I have you. You're safe with me."

Kerry nodded and then turned to Janus, his eyes wide. "It's coming. It's here. Oh!" He clutched Janus's shoulders, sweat breaking over his skin and his pheromones rising strong and hard. The scent of slick filled the air, and Janus held back every instinct telling him to flip Kerry onto his stomach, watch him lift into an instinctive lordosis position, and plow into him hard.

Instead, he quickly put on an alpha condom, slipped between Kerry's thighs, spread him open, and slid inside, murmuring love and comfort the whole time. Kerry shook around him, coming immediately. His cock—which had been hard off and on for days as the heat ramped up—erupted with fluid, and his sun-kissed skin flushed all over. The bond between them grabbed hold and tears sprang to Janus's eyes. When had he ever felt closeness, such protective adoration? He kissed Kerry's throat, pushed back his long hair, and nuzzled behind his ear, scenting and tasting, loving him.

"I've got you," he whispered again, increasing the tempo of his thrusts and shaking all over as Kerry came apart on his cock, slick and omega come and words spilling out of him wildly.

"Harder, please—I need—help me, Janus—oh, help me! It's so good. It's so good. Please, please."

Janus wasn't ever able to deny his *Érosgápe* anything, least of all pleasure. But in the midst of this heat he gave everything he could. Kerry moaned and convulsed, trembled and came, and never fought his pleasure for an instant. Janus crooned his praise, his soul melting and reforming, his heart breaking and healing, his pleasure cresting and then growing to crest yet again.

Beautiful. Perfect.

"Oh, give me your knot," Kerry growled, squirming and gripping Janus's ass in both hands. "Give it to me. Now."

Janus howled, tossing his head back, pleasure wracking him. He pushed hard, feeling the head of his cock breach Kerry's womb. The unbelievable pleasure of the strokes in and out tore him to the quick. Pushing in as far as he could go, he froze and locked in place, ecstasy like a pump inside, rocking him blind and insensible to anything else. Only Kerry's happy sounds made it past the wall of bliss.

As his heart calmed from its thunderous pace, Janus groaned. Kerry's sweet pulse thudded on his knot, and the mouth of Kerry's womb milked him of every spurt of come. Janus nuzzled Kerry's neck and asked breathlessly, "All right?"

Kerry shivered beneath him, his trembling body still shuddering with pleasure. "Yes."

Janus kissed his ear, his nose, his chin. "I love you."

"I know. Stop talking."

"Why?"

Kerry cried out and shivered again, his hole gripping around Janus's shaft and his womb shivering around the head of his cock. Janus laughed, and the rush of wild pleasure built and crashed around them again. His condom was full of semen, and he was knotted in tightly.

The heat of Kerry's body was perfect, and the scent of his pleasure was absolute heaven. "I love you," Janus said again, pushing some of Kerry's hair away so that he could get at his earlobe. "I love you."

Kerry gently slapped his arm. "I *know*."

"Say it back."

"I love you, too."

"And was this…" Janus trailed off, kissing the shell of Kerry's ear. "Was this all right?"

"You know it was," Kerry said breathlessly. "Stop talking. It keeps making me come."

"But you like to come."

"Janus."

"Kerry."

Kerry stared up at him, but he was too astounded for his eyes to truly express a scolding. He whispered, "I love you, too."

"I know you do."

They started to laugh together, which set off another explosion of pleasure in them both. Once they'd calmed down, Kerry whispered, "This isn't anything like I feared. It's like Fan said. Good." He kissed Janus's shoulder and then took hold of his face, gazing up at him seriously. "Beautiful."

"Will you say the words?"

Kerry swallowed thickly. "Yes."

"They're holy words."

"I said them to him, but he didn't deserve them."

Janus worked hard to keep from gritting his teeth at the thought that Wilbet had spoken the holy vow to Kerry. But Kerry was with him now, safe and loved. *Érosgápe.* No other vow could ever matter. "I'll deserve them. I promise."

Kerry nodded. "Yes. You already do." He nuzzled Janus's neck and then met his eyes. "Alpha, with wolf-god's blessing, knot your omega."

Janus thrust forward slightly, pressing his knot harder into Kerry's body. The exquisite convulsion of pleasure that gripped Kerry took Janus's breath away and brought tears to his eyes. When his orgasm had passed, Kerry gasped, "We are alpha and omega, the beginning and the end."

"We are alpha and omega. The everything," Janus spoke his part solemnly.

"Yes," Kerry agreed. "My everything."

*Four years after Tristan's birth*

KERRY'S HEART HUNG in his throat. There on the path stood little Tristan, tall for his age, with a rock in his hand, his chubby arm raised to throw it at an innocent bunny near the edge of the forest. Before Kerry could call out to stop him, the rabbit hopped toward Tristan, and from the woods leapt a huge wildcat, hissing and angry. It skidded to a halt in front of Tristan's small form.

"No!" Tristan ordered in a firm voice, moving to put himself between the cat and the rabbit. "Bad kitty! That bunny isn't for you!"

Kerry's heart jolted. Instantly, the world re-ordered itself with a fresh understanding of the situation—a much more horrific understanding. A wildcat, bigger than Tristan by far, stood with its fangs bared and one paw raised as if to bat the stuffing out of Kerry's small son.

"Tristan," Kerry whispered, but his voice was only breath. He stood paralyzed in fear. The cat stood too close to his son, who was, Kerry realized with breathtaking force, too precious to lose.

Time hung in a glossy, green-tinged silence, the forest holding its breath, too.

Without warning, a small green and orange bird dove from the upper branches of the tree behind Tristan and flew directly into the face of the cat. The cat reared back, batted at the air, and turned to race into the forest with a snarl. The bird fell to the ground at Tristan's feet.

"No!" Tristan cried. "Oh, birdie! No!" He fell to his chubby knees, tears starting down his cheeks, and he sobbed. His tiny shoulders shook over the body of the bird.

Kerry raced forward and scooped Tristan up, holding him close to his chest and burying his face in his neck. "Shh, baby," he murmured. "Shh, Pater has you now. It's all right. I've got you."

Kerry shook like a leaf, eyes wide and shocked, staring down at Kiwi's lifeless body. He hadn't seen his bird or heard his calls since the night he flew out of the house. And yet here he was...

Tristan's wailing, horrified sobs drew attention up at the house. Janus and Pater came racing down the path, their eyes wide, and Pater limping slightly from an injury to his foot a few months before.

Janus reached them first. He pulled both Kerry and Tristan into his arms, looking around wildly for the source of danger. "What's happened?" His eyes fell to the bird on the forest floor. He blinked and then said, "Is that...?"

"Yes. It's Kiwi," Kerry said, his voice gruff and deeper than usual.

"Did *he*..." Janus stared down—fear and horror in his eyes—at the top of Tristan's sweaty head where the boy pressed it against Kerry's chest. "Did he kill him?"

"No," Kerry said, holding his son even tighter. "Kiwi saved Tristan. From a wildcat. Tristan was trying to protect a rabbit from being eaten, and the cat came at him... I froze. Afraid if I moved, the cat would strike. And if I didn't, then he'd *definitely* strike because Tristan didn't understand to hold still." His voice broke. "And then..." He gestured at the dead bird. "He swooped in out of nowhere. Attacked the cat. Drove him off."

"Wolf-god," Janus breathed. "Holy wolf-god."

"Yes," Kerry murmured, and then pressed a fervent kiss to his son's head. His heart still hadn't stopped pounding, and his throat was tight with panicked tears that wanted to force their way up and out.

"Come inside," Janus said, turning to where Zeke stood staring in bafflement at the bird on the ground. He took Tristan from

Kerry's arms, kissed his cheeks, and wiped them dry. "We need a box to have a proper burial for our friend, don't we?"

Tristan shook his head. "Please, Father," he said in his little voice. "Birds don't go in the ground. They go into the sky."

Kerry met Janus's eye and swallowed hard, his heart aching at the earnestness of his son's voice.

"You're right. They do." Janus looked thoughtful. "Perhaps what this friend needs then is a funeral pyre. The fire will turn him to ashes, and the heat will take him up into the air. How does that sound?"

Tristan's eyes welled with tears that spilled over again as he looked down at the bird on the ground. "He won't fly, Father?"

"No, baby. I'm afraid not."

He nodded, his chin wobbling, as he said as stoically as possible, "Aw'right. The fire and ash can help him then. But not in the earth, Father." He put his fat fingers on Janus's cheeks. "Not in the earth, aw'right?"

"I promise."

Then Zeke reached out for his turn with Tristan and took him by the hand, starting up the path toward the house slowly, cooing soothing sounds at the boy. Kerry collapsed into Janus's arms. Tears and fear rolled out of him in waves.

"Shh, it's done now. He's safe."

"We have to do something to keep him away from the paths on his own. I was so scared, Janus. I thought...I thought..." Kerry shook in Janus's arms, his heart hammering. "I love him so much."

"I know you do."

"I love him," Kerry said again. "*So much.*"

"Mm, I know," Janus said, hugging him tightly. "Now you know, too, even if it took terrifying you to death to comprehend it. Thank wolf-god for Kiwi. I wonder where he's been all these years."

Kerry clung to his alpha, his heart hammering hard, and lost in wonder at the immense amount of love he'd discovered flowing through his bloodstream. It'd been there a long time, he saw now. Long enough that he believed Tristan didn't know it had ever been absent.

"Let's go, sweetheart. We have a small funeral pyre to build."

Kerry allowed Janus to lead him up the path, one arm around his waist. "He's a good boy."

Janus smiled at Kerry. "Yes. A sweet boy. He's like his pater."

"Me? I'm bitter."

"No, you're sweet as a peach."

When they had finished building the small pyre by the lake, the remains of the beautiful bird Kerry had taken with him from a tropical island years before were placed on top. Janus stepped forward and, after a prayer, carefully lit the kerosene underneath. As the flames burned gold, Kerry thought of the gilded cage now residing in the attic. It'd been empty for so long now. He'd never imagined seeing Kiwi again. They'd both been freed.

"Sing him to wolf-god," Tristan said. "Please, Pater? Sing for him."

Clearing his throat, Kerry started to sing. He chose the song that he'd learned from Janus, and he sang it with all his heart, lifting his sweet bird with the ash into the sky. Janus stood close, and Tristan wrapped his arms around Kerry's leg, holding tight. Together, they watched the heat from the fire lift the burning feathers into the air. Pater stood solemnly by, and their little family was complete in their respectful mourning.

Suddenly, Tristan began to sing too, his small voice quavering with emotion. Images from Tristan's short life flashed in front of Kerry's eyes: his birth in the lake, his small crib in their bedroom, his toddling first steps, and his squeal of joy playing in the puddles one recent rainy afternoon. Overwhelmed by love, and with tears rising to his eyes, Kerry stopped singing as his voice broke on a note.

Tristan hugged Kerry's leg tighter. "Sing, Pater," he said. "It's all right if you cry. I'll comfort you. But sing."

"Yes, sing, sweetheart," Janus urged.

Heart full, Kerry opened his mouth and let his love come soaring out.

## THE END

# Letter from Leta

Dear Reader,

Thank you so much for reading *Bitter Heat*, the third in the *Heat of Love* series! If you enjoyed this book, I hope that you have read the first two books in the series, *Slow Heat* and *Alpha Heat*. Also, if you loved Jason and Vale from *Slow Heat*, you can catch up with them in their own side story: *Slow Birth*.

Extra stories for this and other book universes can be found at my Patreon.

Be sure to follow me on BookBub or Amazon to be notified of new releases in this series and others. And look for me on Facebook for snippets of the day-to-day writing life. To see some sources of my inspiration, follow my Pinterest boards. I'm also on Instagram, so add me there, too!

If you enjoyed the book, please take a moment to leave a review! Reviews not only help readers determine if a book is for them, but also help a book show up in searches.

Also, for the audiobook connoisseur, the first two books in the series, *Slow Heat* and *Alpha Heat*, are available at most retailers that sell audio, narrated by the talented Michael Ferraiuolo.

Thank you for being a reader!
Leta

*Book 1 in the Heat of Love series*

# SLOW HEAT

by Leta Blake

**A lustful young alpha meets his match in an older omega with a past.**

Professor Vale Aman has crafted a good life for himself. An unbonded omega in his mid-thirties, he's long since given up hope that he'll meet a compatible alpha, let alone his destined mate. He's fulfilled by his career, his poetry, his cat, and his friends.

When Jason Sabel, a much younger alpha, imprints on Vale in a shocking and public way, longings are ignited that can't be ignored. Fighting their strong sexual urges, Jason and Vale must agree to contract with each other before they can consummate their passion.

But for Vale, being with Jason means giving up his independence and placing his future in the hands of an untested alpha—as well as facing the scars of his own tumultuous past. He isn't sure it's worth it. But Jason isn't giving up his destined mate without a fight.

*Book 2 in the Heat of Love series*

# ALPHA HEAT
by Leta Blake

**A desperate young alpha. An older alpha with a hero complex. A forbidden love that can't be denied.**

Young Xan Heelies knows he can never have what he truly wants: a passionate romance and happy-ever-after with another alpha. It's not only forbidden by the prevailing faith of the land, but such acts are illegal.

Urho Chase is a middle-aged alpha with a heartbreaking past. Careful, controlled, and steadfast, his friends dub him old-fashioned and staid. When Urho discovers a dangerous side to Xan's life that he never imagined, his world is rocked and he's consumed by desire. The carefully sewn seams that held him together after the loss of his omega and son come apart—and so does he.

But to love each other and make a life together, Xan and Urho risk utter ruin. With the acceptance and support of Caleb, Xan's asexual and aromantic omega and dear friend, they must find the strength to embrace danger and build the family they deserve.

*Book 2.5 in the Heat of Love series*

## SLOW BIRTH

by Leta Blake

**Jason and Vale are back in this side story set in the *Heat of Love* universe!**

A romantic getaway turns dramatic when an unexpected heat descends on Vale, leaving Jason with no choice but to act. The resulting pregnancy is dangerous for Vale and terrifying for Jason, but with the help of friends and family, they choose to embrace their uncertain future. Together they find all the love, joy, and heat they need to guide them through!

**While this story follows the characters from *Slow Heat*, it would be most enjoyable if read directly after *Alpha Heat*, as it takes place contemporaneously with that book.**

*An Omegaverse by Leta Blake writing as Blake Moreno*

# HEAT FOR SALE
## Heat can be sold but love is earned.

In a world where omegas sell their heats for profit, Adrien is a university student in need of funding. With no family to fall back on, he reluctantly allows the university's matcher to offer his virgin heat for auction online. Anxious, but aware this is the reality of life for all omegas, Adrien hopes whoever wins his heat will be kind.

Heath—a wealthy, older alpha—is rocked by the young man's resemblance to his dead lover, Nathan. When Heath discovers Adrien is Nathan's lost son from his first heat years before they met, he becomes obsessed with the idea of reclaiming a piece of Nathan.

Heath buys Adrien's heat with only one motivation: to impregnate Adrien, claim the child, and move on. But their undeniable passion shocks him. Adrien doesn't know what to make of the handsome, mysterious stranger he's pledged his body to, but he's soon swept away in the heat of the moment and surrenders to Heath entirely.

Once Adrien is pregnant, Heath secrets him away to his immense and secluded home. As the birth draws near, Heath grows to love Adrien for the man he is, not just for his connection to Nathan. Unaware of Heath's past with his omega parent and coming to depend on him heart and soul, Adrien begins to fall as well.

But as their love blossoms, Nathan's shadow looms. Can Heath keep his new love and the child they've made together once Adrien discovers his secrets?

*Heat for Sale* is a stand-alone m/m erotic romance by Leta Blake, writing as Blake Moreno. Infused with a du Maurier *Rebecca*-style secret, it features a well-realized omegaverse, an age-gap, dominance and submission, heats, knotting, and scorching hot scenes.

# Winter's Heart

### Winter-fox always brings Tristan the best gifts

Tristan wakes every winter holiday to find a present that delights him or teaches him an important lesson.

Learn more about the character of Tristan, *Bitter Heat*'s Kerry and Janus's son, in this short winter holiday-themed story. This small bonus book doesn't contain the heat level of the full-length novels in this series, but it has all the cozy, hopeful warmth for a sweet holiday read. While it ends on a romantic note, the story does **not** contain a romance arc.

This story is **not a standalone** and is best read as an addition to the *Heat of Love* series, preferably after reading *Bitter Heat*. But if you should happen to read it out of order, you can find the rest of the books on Amazon and in Kindle Unlimited. *Another Heat of Love bonus novella by Leta Blake.*

# Winter's Truth

### Winter-fox brings Viro some surprising truths for the holiday

Viro Sabel is eleven years old and still entirely innocent about life. This year winter-fox brings him some surprising truths that alter the way he sees the world and his place in it.

Learn more about the character of Viro, *Slow Heat*'s Vale and Jason's son, in this **winter holiday-themed novella**. This medium-sized bonus book **features spicy scenes** between Vale and Jason, family scenes, and emotional moments. While the novella's epilogue teases a relationship for an adult Viro, it ends with a mystery regarding this person's identity.

This story is ***not* a standalone** and is best read as an addition to the *Heat of Love* series, preferably after reading *Slow Heat, Alpha Heat,* and *Slow Birth*. But if you should happen to read it out of order, you can find the rest of the books in the series on Amazon and in Kindle Unlimited.

# Gay Romance Newsletter

Leta's newsletter will keep you up to date on her latest releases and news from the world of M/M romance. Join the mailing list today and you're automatically entered into future giveaways.
letablake.com

# Leta Blake on Patreon

Become part of Leta Blake's Patreon community in order to access exclusive content, deleted scenes, extras, bonus stories, rewards, prizes, interviews, and more.
www.patreon.com/letablake

# Other Books by Leta Blake

Any Given Lifetime

Mr. Frosty Pants

The River Leith

Smoky Mountain Dreams

Angel Undone

Raise Up Heart

The Difference Between

Heat for Sale

Omega Mine: Search for a Soulmate

Bring on Forever

**The Training Season Series**

Training Season

Training Complex

**Heat of Love Series**

Slow Heat

Slow Birth

Alpha Heat

Bitter Heat

Winter's Heart

Winter's Truth

**Stay Lucky Universe**

Stay Lucky

Stay Sexy

**'90s Coming of Age Series**
Pictures of You
You Are Not Me

**Co-Authored with Indra Vaughn**
Vespertine
Cowboy Seeks Husband

**Co-Authored with Alice Griffiths**
The Wake Up Married serial
Will & Patrick's Endless Honeymoon

**Gay Fairy Tales**
**Co-Authored with Keira Andrews**
Flight
Levity
Rise

**Audiobooks**
Leta Blake at Audible

**Free Read**
Stalking Dreams

**Discover more about the author online:**
Leta Blake
letablake.com

# About the Author

Author of the bestselling book Smoky Mountain Dreams and the fan favorite Training Season, Leta Blake's educational and professional background is in psychology and finance, respectively. However, her passion has always been for writing. She enjoys crafting romance stories and exploring the psyches of made up people. At home in the Southern U.S., Leta works hard at achieving balance between her day job, her writing, and her family.

Printed in Great Britain
by Amazon

31071727R00223